The Three Pleasures

(Kuroshio)

ALSO BY TERRY WATADA

FICTION
The Blood of Foxes (novel)
Daruma Days (stories)

POETRY
The Game of 100 Ghosts
Obon: the Festival of the Dead
10,000 Views of Rain
A Thousand Homes

NON-FICTION
The TBC: the Toronto Buddhist Church 1995 – 2010
Bukkyo Tozen: A History of Jodo Shinshu
Buddhism in Canada 1905 – 1995

CHILDREN'S BOOKS
The Nishga Girl
Seeing the Invisible: the Story of Irene Uchida – Canadian Scientist

THE THREE PLEASURES

KUROSHIO

A NOVEL BY

TERRY WATADA

anvil
PRESS
VANCOUVER

Anvil Press Publishers Inc.
P.O. Box 3008, Main Post Office
Vancouver, B.C. V6B 3X5 CANADA
www.anvilpress.com

Library and Archives Canada Cataloguing in Publication

Watada, Terry, author
    The three pleasures / Terry Watada.— 1st edition.

ISBN 978-1-77214-095-8 (softcover)

    I. Title.

PS8595.A79T47 2018   C813'.54   C2017-903382-4

Printed and bound in Canada
Cover design by Rayola Graphic
Cover painting by Tom Carter
Interior by HeimatHouse
Represented in Canada by Publishers Group Canada
Distributed in Canada by Raincoast Books and in the US by Small Press Distribution.

The publisher gratefully acknowledges the financial assistance of the Canada Council for the Arts, the Canada Book Fund, and the Province of British Columbia through the B.C. Arts Council and the Book Publishing Tax Credit.

The Three Pleasures is dedicated to Dr. Michiko "Midge" Ayukawa, Dr. Wes Fujiwara, Frank Moritsugu, Jesse Nishihata, Thomas K. Shoyama, Dr. Irene Uchida, and Harry Yonekura — seven extraordinary *Nisei* who inspired and encouraged me. It was such a pleasure to have known them.

Special thanks to my son Matthew "Bunji" Watada for his love, support, and reminding me of what it's all about.

At no other time in the life of the second generation, when hostile voices rise in sharp crescendo, has there been a greater need for some medium through which the Nisei might speak his thoughts and his hopes to the Canadian public at large ... To the future greatness of Canada and the part of the Canadian born Japanese in this future we pledge our sincere effort and our endeavor.

— *The New Canadian*, February 1, 1939

PROLOGUE

Fall 1946

As we rode the westward-bound prison train deeper into the void of the Prairies, I wondered about the place where we were going. Some small town called Moose Jaw. There was nothing but miles and miles surrounding us. The landscape was so different from Ontario and BC, of course, with their rough terrain, mountains, and thick forests. Moose Jaw was probably some backwater town in the middle of nowhere. I wondered what I had done to end up here. During the war, I and my compatriots had come back east this way, but we weren't going to stop and get off.

Some of the *ganbariya* panicked at first but soon calmed themselves with the steady boredom of the trip. The prickly heat inside the train was also a distraction. No one was inspired to act. My mind started to wander with all the time and wide-open space at hand.

I had heard through the grapevine that Tommy Shoyama was coming, or had come, out this way. Where exactly in Saskatchewan I didn't know. Someone had taken over the reins of *The New Canadian*, maybe Irene, and he decided there was no future in BC. Couldn't blame him, but why Saskatchewan? I mean, I was forced to come here, but he made a conscious decision. I doubted that I would ever see him again, but it would be nice. I'd like to tell him how sorry I was.

But it was more than our tormentors' whim that brought us to the middle of nowhere. Yes, it was World War II, of course, a war that defined me. And I knew the arbiters of that definition: the Three Pleasures.

They were three men well known around Powell Street in Vancouver, two *Issei* and one *Kika Nisei*, Watanabe Etsuo, Morii Etsuji, and Etsu Kaga. *Etsu* in Japanese means "pleasure" — a term well-suited to these three. They represented three different types of pleasure. Morii Etsuji and his criminal gang, the Black Dragon Society, controlled the type men paid for: gambling, drink, and prostitution, the pleasures of the flesh. Watanabe Etsuo, secretary of the Steveston Fishermen's Association, made a deal with the devil to save his loved ones; in the end, he suffered for it and never regained the pleasures of family. And there was Etsu Kaga, a ganbariya of the Yamatodamashii Group, a real Emperor worshipper. His obsession destroyed him and all involved with him; he enjoyed the pleasure of patriotism until it became a curse.

I kept as far away as possible from these men, but eventually found myself drawn into their circles, attracted by, and afraid of, what each had to offer. Each had his moment; each had a profound effect on me and all Japanese Canadians.

In each of these three I saw hope. I wondered which would be the hero who would return to us what we used to have.

Even on this train to nowhere, I still had hope. It was all that was left me.

"Added proof that the Japanese population in British Columbia now regards itself as a permanent and fixed part of the Canadian nation is seen this week in the announcement that no evacuation of Japanese nationals is being considered, although a program for such evacuation is now underway in three other sections of the British Empire."

— *The New Canadian*, September 21, 1941

1.

At the start of it all, I was just a kid in my second year at the University of British Columbia in Vancouver. To most, such an accomplishment signalled an assured future. But it wasn't all hearts and flowers for me. I heard the insults of my fellow students wondering what I was doing there studying English Literature of all things. *Shouldn't he be out working somewhere? Like in a lumber camp, in the mines, or on a fishing boat. What's he want? Doesn't he know he's not welcome, he doesn't belong? No fraternities for that monkey-boy.*

The name-calling, the moronic slanting of the eyes to mock me, and the exclusion from social groups, formal and informal, hurt. At least I could fight back: not by dirtying my clothes in a schoolyard brawl, but by quietly going about my business, earning top marks in every class. "Turn the other cheek" as the Christians advised — that was something I could do.

You'd think I was used to it. I never saw a movie from anywhere but the balcony. I couldn't join a club made up of *hakujin*. Couldn't eat in a downtown café with any sense of comfort. Then in 1936 Japan allied with Germany. I was walking along Davie Street one weekend, just wandering, dreaming, when I turned a corner and three *keto* boys about my age, high school for sure, blocked my way. They had brown, unkempt hair and pimples.

"Can I do something for you fellahs?" I asked.

"Well, what do you know, the Jap can speak English," remarked the freckled one.

What? I could've been Chinese for all they knew, I thought. I said nothing in return. Didn't have to since they began pummelling me right there where I stood. The kick to the groin was the worst pain I ever felt. I fell to the ground and the kicks kept coming for an eternity. I curled to defend myself. Then everything stopped. As I lay barely conscious, I heard "Goddamn Nazi lover" and laughter as the anonymous bullies ran away.

I then sensed two older Canadian ladies hovering over me. I only saw grey hair, kind eyes, and concern. They comforted me. I think they drew a police officer's attention.

I don't remember much more after that, don't even know how I got home. I didn't want to remember, but I did realize long afterward I should've known better. I was outside of Powell Street after all. On walls and lamp posts and buildings along the downtown streets, the patriotic posters screamed out against the enemy: "Loose lips sink ships!"; "Stand firm!" (my favourite, with the lion sitting strong and vigilant); "He's watching you" (with the German soldier menacing with glowing eyes); and "Winston Churchill says we deserve victory" (Winnie's finger seemed to point straight at me, though I couldn't help feeling I was the enemy). Canada was at war with Germany, but the Japs were committing murder in China, making noise about expanding their war into the South Pacific and beyond. Then the Axis formed.

Powell Street — only hakujin called it Little Tokyo — was our part of town. It was where I knew everyone, where the shops and institutions were familiar, where my family's dry goods store was. From roughly Main Street in the west to Princess Avenue in the east, Alexander Street in the north, and East Hastings Street in the south, most Japanese Canadians lived within the confines. Powell Ground or Grounds (as some called it), the clay park in the middle, was the home of the mighty Asahi baseball team, our very own heroes. Homey surroundings with Union Fish, the fishmonger so important at *Oshougatsu*; Uchida Bookstore with English and Japanese books, comic books, and magazines; and Doc Fujiwara, our dentist. I enjoyed talking to the Reverend Tsuji, the first Nisei *bousan* in Canada; dancing to the Asahi Swingers Big Band, made up of several high-school friends; and hanging out at Ernie's Café. I had close friends in Dicky Mitsubayashi and "Hammerhead" Nishizaki. I loved the painted houses along Jackson and Cordova, each with its own colour. Then there were the notorious places — the Three Sisters at Jackson and Alexander, a restaurant of ill-repute; Goto-*san's*, a flat out cathouse — and scandal-ridden people — Seko-*no oba*, whose husband hanged himself; and Miyamoto Yoshiko, a Morii underling and murderess. Morii's Nippon Club, at 362 Alexander Street, across from the language school, was the centre of it all; everyone knew of its secrets, yet no one knew every secret.

My parents owned Sugiura's Dry Goods, a storefront on Powell Street just kitty-corner to Powell Grounds. The building was flat-faced; two broad windows looking out onto the street, flanking a perfunctory middle door with a silver bell to announce customers. A small but steady stream came by to shop. Never knew why they sold dry goods. I knew Dad had money from his father back in the day. I guess he saw a need in the community for textiles, flour, and the like. In any case, the business made enough money to keep us in rice.

Typical of the area, we lived upstairs in a three-bedroom apartment with kitchen and bath. So going to work for my parents was a matter of walking down the stairs.

My dad, Sugiura Haruo, kept the shelves well stocked while my mother, Hanako, took care of the upstairs and helped with sales when she could. *Otousan* was a man of few words and little emotion. Muscular and tall for a Japanese at five-foot-eight, his grim, hard face told everyone his outlook on life. *Okaasan*, small even for a Japanese, under five-foot-nothing and petite in stature, was a cloudburst of a woman, crying at the drop of a hat. Her face was withered by worry. They made for an odd-looking couple, but they got along.

Mom never wanted to come to Canada, I suspected, but she obeyed her father when he was asked for a daughter of marrying age. Even if she was the fifth child and a girl of sixteen, she never imagined she'd have to leave her home in Hiroshima-*ken* to be the wife of a *gaijin*. She always looked sad whenever she talked about Japan and that was seldom. For all her teary complaints, she never betrayed her innermost thoughts and opinions.

My older brother, Herb, took after my father. When he could, he left to work in the Cumberland mines. Maybe he was looking to find a wife, start a family. In any case, we seldom saw him. He wasn't the sentimental type.

Yes, I was safe on Powell Street, or so I thought. In March 1941, the government put out an edict that made me feel less so.

"Did you hear?" Dicky, my childhood buddy, asked between university classes. "We gotta register with the RCMP. That's right, they take our picture and we gotta give 'em our names and addresses."

"What?"

"It's not right! We're citizens, born and bred, damnit!" he yelled in the hallowed halls. He was furious with tears, his feelings getting the better of him.

By August we had to carry ID cards with photos and thumbprints attached. Typical of Dicky, he did not cooperate, running the risk of immediate arrest. He also took to stealing the "I AM CHINESE" buttons from Chinese Canadians right on Pender Street to go about freely. He wasn't the only one.

"Why don't you register?" I asked Dicky.

"*Shikataganai.*"

"What do you mean it can't be helped?"

"I got no choice. I have to fight back."

It was a small act of defiance. Those of my generation all felt the same way. We had to fight, but how?

IN EARLY SEPTEMBER, 1941, Tommy Shoyama of *The New Canadian* started combing the ranks of UBC's student body, especially in the English Department, for potential Nisei writers for the paper. He suspected, as managing editor, that the paper would need more staff to cover all the unfolding events: the March registration, the August ID cards, and the Japanese incursion into China and other parts of the South Pacific. There were a few of us in the English Department, and I was the last he approached.

Tommy was from Kamloops. He may have looked Japanese, but as he told me, "My father had no wish for me to be Japanese." Shoyama Ginaburo immigrated and settled in the small town on purpose to keep himself away from the Vancouver community. In one of the early editions of the *Tairiku Nippo*, one of the first Japanese language newspapers in BC, Tommy's grandfather put in a notice from Japan looking for his son's whereabouts. Some Japanese resident in Kamloops knew the man and so responded. The Shoyama family then decided to send a bride from home so she could keep them informed. His father accepted the wife but still wanted to live apart from the Japanese in BC, especially those in Vancouver. "Too many dirty mouths there," he insisted. He hated the gossip and backbiting nature of the community. So the couple settled down in Kamloops and had a son.

Tommy grew up seeing Rita Hayworth movies, tapping his toes to the Dorsey brothers, and slurping sodas and milkshakes, just like any Nisei, but alone. Even when he was ready for UBC, he stayed with a hakujin benefactor near the campus, far from Powell Street. Tommy paid for his room and board by being the houseboy. To save more money, he rode his bike to school every day. As a result, he never picked up much of the Japanese language or customs, except maybe the profanities and slang. He eventually graduated with a combined Bachelor of Commerce and English degree, hoping for a better future as a Canadian.

Despite that, Tommy did make a life for himself in Vancouver after graduation. He couldn't use his degree, given the prejudice of the times, so the only job he could manage was running *The New Canadian*.

The weekly paper was fairly new, established in 1939. The

readership was small (mainly because it was only in English) — barely enough subscriptions to pay staff a meagre sum and to print up copies — but growing with Tommy at the helm. All the stores and community institutions stocked it and a few volunteers delivered it or sold it in the street and at community gatherings. I liked its motto: "The Voice of the Second Generation" and the stories were about Nisei sports, dances, and newsworthy items like the first Nisei Buddhist minister. Opinion pieces, like what it meant to be Canadian, and short stories and poems by the young people also filled the pages. It made me and my friends feel it was a paper just for us.

So there I was in my second year at the university, when Tommy met me at Ernie's on a Saturday in mid-September, 1941. I liked him right off. He had wise eyes and a humility about him. He acted more like an *oniisan*, an older brother more than my real brother.

"The job doesn't pay much," he explained, "but the experience is invaluable." He sounded like one of my profs; looked like one too. All the frail-looking newspaper man needed was a pipe and tweed jacket with patches on the elbows to go with his round specs. In his eyes I saw the man's concern for the Japanese-Canadian community. I was all but convinced when Tommy added, "You'll get to know the people."

"Okay, it's a deal. Where do I sign?" With a cavalier attitude and a handshake, I became an *NC* reporter; I even had my own byline: *By Daniel S. Sugiura.* I was the only one from UBC to say yes.

ON THE SECOND FLOOR of the New World Hotel (a boarding house right on the corner of Dunlevy and Powell), *The New Canadian* office was small, packed with everything needed to put out a regular newspaper. Several uniform windows, half-blinded by Venetians, looked out onto Powell Ground, the heart of the Japanese section of town. The one room was divided into a work area and one office for Tommy. The place was furnished with more than a few odd sized and mismatched desks. Frank Morimoto, a fresh-faced high schooler who joined the paper just before I did, and I strained our backs dragging one from the Franciscan Sisters, the building a few doors south of the boarding house on Dunlevy Avenue. That's the kind of operation it was.

It was a good place to be, populated by talented and intelligent Nisei, possibly the smartest of the community. Everyone accepted me right away as one of their own. Tommy's say-so was good enough.

I soon realized *The New Canadian* gang liked each other and had a good time putting out the paper, especially when our purpose became clear. In time, I knew it was a far closer-knit family than my real one. No need to be blood relatives.

As a journalist, I was a rank amateur. I majored in Milton and Shakespeare, not *The New York Times*. I had no appreciation of the utilitarian uses of writing; I instead revelled in the magic of words, as in poetry. Symbols, scansion and prosody, imagery and word-play excited me.

That changed with the job, but it took more than a little time. First of all, I had no idea how to put a news story together. My initial pieces about simple things like the *Bussei* teen dances sounded like essays for class. Finally Tommy took me aside, giving me a few pointers. The headline should always read like a sentence (grammatically correct or not), not a pithy short-story title. "Union Fish getting tuna early for the New Year." "Police nab teenager for shoplifting at Soga's Department Store." "Reverend Tsuji to come home after ordination."

He also told me to justify every story. "Why is it in the paper? What's its relevance to the Japanese community?" So I couldn't write about the prime minister talking to ghosts. Maybe if the ghosts were Japanese, I suppose.

I gradually learned how to frame a story, but I didn't know how to dredge up the facts. Tommy could point me in the right direction, but he couldn't teach me what to do next. Fortunately, I could talk to people. Perhaps it was my plain looks that appealed, made me "safe" to talk to as the girls used to say. No matter the reason, most people I eventually interviewed opened up, and not in the guarded way they did for Tommy and others. Instead they told me things they wouldn't even tell their own relatives. In this way, I managed to get the dirt, and there was plenty of it.

ON A TYPICAL late-summer afternoon at the *NC*, Frank Morimoto was leaning back in his chair with his hands behind his head, his legs lazily suspended in mid-air, when he suddenly sprang forward. He must've felt himself falling. He was quite a sight, all arms and legs flailing about, his face as pale as a ghost's.

Irene Kondo, the paper's spitfire columnist, laughed. *"Baka!"* she sneered in a good-natured way, like an *oneesan*. Tommy, standing as he always did, his arms easily folded in front of him to balance his slender body, just chuckled.

At first I had my back to them looking through the windows watching the Asahi baseball team practising their acrobatics in Powell Ground. Roy Yamamura was my favourite. For anyone's money, he was the greatest shortstop who ever played the game. Somebody had rightly nicknamed him the "King of Baseball." I couldn't think of a sobriquet more appropriate.

After Frank sprang to his feet and grabbed my attention, Tommy, with an impish grin, started talking about Morii Etsuji, his favourite topic. For some reason, maybe because he wanted to bait Irene, he turned the conversation to the *Oyabun's* love life. "I heard he never touches, you know, the women who work for him. Morii, I mean."

"Tommy!" Irene said as she swung an arm around to hit him. "I'm surprised at you." Her pixie eyes sparkled as she flashed a frown at his indiscretion. "Besides, how would you know? You been to the Showa Club or the Sisters'?"

"I said I heard. I don't know for sure," he said blushing as he rubbed his arm. Irene gave as good as she got.

"Hey, maybe that's what makes his wife so happy!" chimed in Frank. "You know, maybe he's good, you know, in bed."

Irene drew in a deep breath, turned on her heels, and headed straight for the door. "That does it. You boys can talk dirty all you want but without me as an audience!"

The three of us burst out laughing as the fireplug reporter complained noisily all the way down the stairs.

Tommy soon assigned me to keep tabs on the gangster, maybe discover something incriminating about his organization, the Black Dragons. And maybe write it up if it was compelling enough. It was a great opportunity.

For a long time, I had been fascinated with Morii like everyone else in Powell Street; he was our Al Capone, after all. The Canadian newspapers said so. So I grabbed the assignment willingly. Tommy told me to go listen to the man as he spoke at the Japanese language school and the Buddhist church in early October. The Oyabun was making speeches in support of the Japanese invasion of China. Problem was I didn't have enough of the language to understand the complexities of his ideas. Like all the other kids, I went to Japanese school six days a week after regular English school. It was a real pain, but what could I do? My parents wanted to be able to talk to their children and to maintain ties to the homeland. My mother insisted on it.

Though I could speak, somewhat, and understand the language on a rudimentary level, I stopped going altogether once I graduated high school. I couldn't see the use of it. Like most Nisei, I wanted to be Canadian. Yet with the job at the NC, I regretted paying so much attention to recess rather than the grammar and vocabulary lessons.

Fortunately, Kunio Shimizu, Tommy's good friend, volunteer at the paper and Japanese Canadian Citizens League [JCCL] secretary, accompanied me. He was fluent in Japanese because of his Kika-Nisei background.

Kunio was a Victoria boy. He wore the clothes of a big man, but on closer examination, his body was thin and every jacket he owned draped over him like robes. His family owned and operated the Shimizu Rice Mill, located on the outskirts of Chinatown. The eldest son of nine children, Kunio was the only one at the age of ten to move to Japan with his grandmother. With a Japanese education, it was commonly hoped he could have a career with a Japanese company anywhere in the world and escape the employment limitations imposed by racist Canadian governments. He returned in 1927 and enrolled at UBC. After graduating and settling in Vancouver, he started seeing a Kitsilano girl and they had bright plans for the future even though he couldn't find a job in his field of physics and math. Everyone was in the same boat, so he didn't feel so bad. In any case, he and Marion Akamatsu planned to get married and have kids in the future.

When we walked into the Japanese Hall, the language school's auditorium, I stopped in my tracks. My brain kindled with memories — the long, boring classes spoken in an unintelligible tongue, the stern looks of Kozai *Sensei*, the quick thwap of a ruler to the hand to instill cooperation, the easy friendships I formed, recess and the exquisite release of home-time. Then I heard Morii's words dancing in the cavernous room. A sudden coldness entered my stomach. My feet would not move until Kunio gently nudged me forward.

We sat in the back row as my forehead broke with sweat. I couldn't explain my reaction, except that Morii was a larger-than-life character. True, the Black Dragon boss was no more than five-feet tall, and his stubby moustache gave him a comic look, more at home in a Chaplin movie than under an Al Capone headline. Still, watching Morii burning with all the passion of an evangelist, I grew nervous with, and fearful of, some of the ideas emanating from the stage.

> *Japan is the roof over the house of the Orient! All countries must stay under that roof — China especially! Do not listen to those who would call us thugs and murderers. The Emperor and the Emperor alone is the protector of all of Asia. Look at any map of the Orient. You will see Japan is shaped as the leading wedge against the invading forces of America and Europe! Realize then that the Emperor is fulfilling His manifest destiny in places like Nanking. Hear His words and be His instruments of His divine will. Imperial Japan is today fighting a holy war in China.*

I felt an electrical thrill go up my spine at his words, even if I had to wait a bit for Kunio's translation. The sight of him too affected me. Morii's skin glowed from the sun; his eyes were crazed with his absolute truth, his body shook with every word. I squirmed in the menacing presence. He appeared ten-feet-tall.

Money given by the Buddhist Japanese women of British Columbia
for comforts to soldiers overseas is serving a double purpose.

Besides providing $100 worth of cigarettes for ten months, the $2043
fund will enable the British Columbia Services Canteen to be operated
solely by B.C. women in London.

— The New Canadian, October 10, 1941

2.

I never talked to Morii Etsuji face-to-face. I mean, the Oyabun was a gangster and everyone knew about his Showa Club, the Powell Street gambling joint; his bootleg booze (my otousan bought a bottle of *sake* every month); and his prostitution operation out of the Raku Raku, later known as the Nippon Club (members only). But no one knew the particulars of the operations or personal details about the man: his age, his birthplace, how he got to Vancouver in the first place. At least no one was telling.

I knew that Morii could usually be found sitting behind his large oak desk in his bare-walled office on the second floor just down the hall from the main part of the Nippon Club, situated in an anonymous building right across from the Japanese language school. He had established the club in the early 1920s. It sat in the old Red Light District of Vancouver from the Klondike Gold Rush days. The Yoshino-tei, a restaurant, was on the bottom floor, and the men's club was upstairs.

Most of what I knew about the man came from a surprising source: my father. In a rare moment of openness, my otousan, with a silly grin, let forth a few secrets. He was drunk of course; imbibing sake from his monthly bottle made his tongue loose. I had seen him drunk before, but I was a little scared this time.

"Listen to me, you little *ketsunoana*," he rasped in Japanese. He often called me "asshole" when he had been drinking. "That wife of his... that wife!" Cloudy recollections filled his eyes. "It was back in 1910, when the Oyabun left for Japan on the Yokohama Maru. Oh, it was big news down on Powell Street where we had just opened the store. All my customers had something to say. When Morii returned three months later, he showed up at the Buddhist church with his bride, Matsuoka Misao. I tell you, tongues started wagging even more."

"Why, who was she?" I asked.

"*Damare*, you *kusotare!*" he demanded. I hated it when liquor got the better of him. "People guessed that Morii-no *okusan* was connected to *the* Matsuoka family."

My father said that around the turn of the century, the Oyabun first came over with Matsuoka Yosuke, a diplomat's son, to attend school. If that were true, then Morii's wife just might be the sister. What everyone knew for sure was that Matsuoka Misao was no ordinary woman. She carried herself with much grace and dignity.

"Oh, she was something, I tell you." Otousan beamed with the memory.

I had to agree after seeing her at the church's recent fall bazaar, with her lips thickened and sharply defined by bright red lipstick, her face smoothed by rare and exotic powders, unguents and creams, like a fine sculpture carved out of soapstone. Her clothes, the finest Western dress. Her perfume exuded an aroma like a field of dogwood flowers. "She bought downtown, never at Soga's, that tightwad bastard," Dad claimed. The merchant Soga only stocked his store with inferior goods because he wouldn't spend the money for better quality garments.

Her deportment spoke of a privileged upbringing. What Morii Misao thought of her husband's criminal activities only she knew. Otousan observed she never even let on she had an inkling. The word was as long as she remained in her exalted position with no outward accusation of scandal, she didn't care.

I didn't believe that, but I wasn't going to question my otousan. He then recalled Morii Misao at the Buddhist church in the early days. She really played her role with relish. From the outset, the *fujinkai* women of the church came to know their place.

"Fukunaga-san said to that high-*kara* woman, in a comical falsetto voice, 'Morii-san, you'll want to help cook for Hanamatsuri next week.' What nerve!" he remarked almost guffawing.

Fukunaga Toshii was an earnest and diminutive member of the women's group and spoke in her crude Wakayama dialect. She always presented herself with a stupid grin, though her eyes gleamed with enthusiasm.

Dad simmered down to a chuckle. "Morii-no okusan looked down at her, waving her gloved hand as if bothered by an insect. 'Ah-hem,'" he said returning to his falsetto. "'Morii-san, don't these women know how to address their betters? They should learn to use proper Japanese.' Fukunaga-san's face was as red as the *Hinomaru*. The fool. She skulked away as Morii-no okusan decided to take charge and teach these women proper manners."

And we laughed, my otousan and me. To my surprise, I hugged him and helped him get to bed. There were precious few times afterward or before for that matter, when we acted like father and son.

SO WHEN I GOT the assignment to dig into Morii, I started listening in earnest to all the rumours around Powell Street. I actually was surprised how much there was about the man. In the churches; around community bazaars, concerts, and festivals; in the language schools and in the bars and restaurants, people talked like there was no tomorrow. Verifying facts was impossible, but my notebook started to bulge with writing.

Besides running the gambling and drinking clubs, he was a judo master in control of a thriving *dojo*; hence his alleged connection to Kojima Sensei, the self-proclaimed "Father of Judo." The Sensei's students were always around Morii, ready to protect him. As a result, the Oyabun's words were to be obeyed without question. Pity the poor soul who didn't. If he said there wasn't enough of the Emperor in the Japanese language school curriculum, then more lessons on the *Tenno* were installed. If any Buddhist church needed a new minister, one was sent, but only after his approval. All charity or fundraising events were conducted with his say-so. He obtained and maintained his power through money, connections, and especially brute force. Morii saw violence as a tool, a means to bring the Japanese in line.

Some believed Morii was born into a well-connected family in Hiroshima. An uneventful childhood led to an adolescence full of trouble. Kojima Sensei let it slip once that the man's father had lost everything in a shady land deal, but no more details came from the stone-faced Sensei. He realized he had stepped beyond the bounds of his alleged relationship with the Oyabun.

On one remarkable occasion, Rikimatsu Kintaro, Morii's *yojimbo*, all muscle and bones, came into the Tengu on Powell Street wobbly and loose-tongued. Restaurant customers, my parents and I included, guessed that he must have been punished for something he had done and, as revenge, decided to spew forth with stories about his boss. His courage was fuelled by alcohol, of course.

Otousan told me to ignore him; my mother urged us to leave, and they did. I was too fascinated, so I stayed behind.

"Adolescence is for dreaming," Rik-san began profoundly. His face drooped with the heaviness of the booze inside him. "When the Oyabun was a kid, he had big thoughts. Stupid thoughts, mind you, but big ones. Dreams. I'm sure he'd be embarrassed by them today."

"Well, do tell, Rikimatsu-san!" encouraged a smirking café patron.

"I don't know," said the yojimbo, rubbing the back of his neck as if anticipating something he was about to regret.

"You might as well. You're halfway there already!"

"He was a goddamn Red!" he blurted out all at once.

Fortunately, Rik-san spoke an easy-to-understand Japanese. Customers around me translated any unfamiliar terms. So the yojimbo said that in high school Morii became interested in socialism of all things. As a young student in Japan, he must've read Kotoku Shusui, a well-known socialist, in the *Heimin Shimbun*, a Tokyo newspaper. I was surprised to hear that Morii led student protests against the coming war with Russia. Apparently the police reacted badly with nightsticks and the gathering turned into a riot. Morii narrowly escaped capture and arrest. Knowing he was in danger of imprisonment, he turned to his father, who called in a few favours and enrolled his son in the government's *shousei* student program. He was soon on his way to America. I later learned from other sources that he was under the care of Matsuoka Yosuke, the son of a career diplomat, and brother of Morii's future wife. Interestingly enough, Yosuke would later negotiate the Axis alliance on Japan's behalf — the agreement that got me beat up more times than I care to remember.

In America, Morii wasn't much of a scholar and soon fell in with a Japanese student *seinenkai*. "That little bastard," roared Rikimatsu at his astonished audience, "blackmailed the consul general..." With craning necks, everyone pushed forward to hear. Even Matsumoto, the bloated cook, came out of his kitchen, wiping his hands on his grease-stained apron, to listen.

"Consul Gomyo?"

Rik-san whipped around on his chair and growled, "Not now! In San Francisco, you *ahotare!*" Rikimatsu took another drink from from his pocket flask and lit a hand-rolled cigarette. "Where was I?" He slumped with the weight of his dulled head. "Ah right, he blackmailed the consul into helping some bastard out of jail! Said he liked little boys! Imagine that? The consul general liked little boys! Ha!

"And the hell of it was the Oyabun did it for no money! Can you believe that? He did it for nothing. He could of gotten something outta the consul or that kusotare's family. But no, he wanted ...he wanted...oh shit, I don't know..."

"What did he say?" someone in the back asked.

Rikimatsu shook his head and muttered the word "obligation."

It was after that gambit Morii Etsuji became a prime candidate for the Black Dragon Society, a right-wing criminal organization in Japan and offspring of the infamous *yakuza*.

AROUND THE VANCOUVER Buddhist church, Morii was said all along to have been a promising candidate of the Black Dragons. The details were sketchy, but some of the Issei believed that the future Oyabun had been caught in a San Francisco gambling house raid.

"Ya, that Morii was the lookout for the place," spit Fusuma-san, a church elder in conversation with me at the Sunday after-service lunch. His sagging face was testament to the fact that he no longer cared to hide the truth from us "young people." He let forth with a story that mesmerized me. "Morii was on duty when the police crashed through the door, whistles blowing, truncheons raised."

I imagined there were screams, yelling, and confusion; chairs flew, tables were overturned, bottles smashed against walls, splashing the crowd haphazardly with rot-gut sake. Found-ins swore and fought back. Bodies fell unconscious and bleeding to the floor.

I took notes and later elaborated the points in my notebook: "When it was all over, Morii stood over a policeman with a bloody knife in hand. The cop had grabbed him and ordered him to cooperate. Morii grabbed for his knife and wounded the cop. The man instantly fell to his knees. Morii ran out as fast as he could.

"Morii turned to his local boss. The Black Dragon Oyabun knew the boy was in trouble and offered to send him to Vancouver. He was to be under Shiga Mitsuzo's wing. I guess he figured Morii would never be found in a foreign country."

A little lurid on my part perhaps, but I needed the practice. In any case, Morii ended up in Vancouver under the care of the local Oyabun, Shiga Mitsuzo.

IF MORII'S TRUE origins were a mystery, then Shiga's rivalled the pyramids of Giza. He was a short, squat man who didn't wear his excesses well, and a professional gambler. His age, what prefecture of Japan he came from, or the events of his past, were anyone's guess. There weren't even any good rumours. Perhaps there were reasons for that. Certainly he was hands-off for me and *The New Canadian*.

I did make note of whenever Shiga-san appeared in public. Usually he attended the Buddhist church bazaar or the language school's assemblies or meetings. Shiga Oyabun knew his community obligations as the Black Dragon leader, but he preferred the racetrack or the card games played after dark at the old Raku Raku club on Gore Avenue. Attending community meetings, funerals, store openings, significant birthday or anniversary celebrations of honoured Issei bored him. Most assuredly he had welcomed the young protégé with open arms because Morii gradually took over the mundane public demands while Shiga pursued his vices in the newly opened Nippon Club.

As a result, Morii Oyabun's illegal activities in Vancouver became common knowledge but, as he was very careful to cover his tracks, nothing could ever be proven. Some people claimed that he even did away with his enemies — how, no one knew for sure, but there were more than a few unexplained disappearances connected to him. There was the suggestion that he and Rikimatsu buried the bodies in the lime pits up the coast. Back in the 1920s, the police had arrested Morii once and even brought him to trial for murder, but they had to let him off with a lesser charge since the sole eyewitness was nowhere to be found. To my mind, they should've searched the lime pits.

For Tommy, my father's stories and my interviews were just the ticket to give me the opportunity to cover Morii.

"You're doing a good job," my editor said encouragingly by my third week of covering the Oyabun's speeches at the language school.

"Couldn't do it without Kunio."

"Yes, yes."

"When should I start writing up a story? What angle should I take?"

"Oh no, you can't write it up." Tommy grimaced.

"Why not?"

"Too dangerous," Tommy said. "You report on last night's Purple Seven Gang game against Abbotsford."

"But Tommy ..."

"Listen, your beat, our beat, is the community doings. Leave Morii to me. Just keep providing me with information."

And that was that. I sulked in the corner in front of my typewriter thinking about the Oyabun. My hands were tied, but I took solace in the fact that my observations and opinions were preserved in my notebook.

Kunio and I continued to attend Morii's speeches, but no stories appeared in the paper. Instead Tommy wrote editorials protesting the Japanese incursion into China:

> As a Nisei, I rise to support my Chinese-Canadian brothers and sisters who see the wrong being done by the Japanese in their ancestral homeland. The Japanese people themselves do not want war; this is shown by the fact that the majority of parliament voted against the military leaders. The workers, peasants, and business people do not want war. It has been argued that war will benefit Japan. It will bring prosperity only to the financial elite and military cliques; to the common people, it will bring only poverty and further enslavement.
>
> — The New Canadian

The loudmouths around Powell Street observed that the paper's editorials were in English only (a stupid complaint, since the whole paper was in English) and the writer never mentioned Morii by name. But they knew, everyone knew (even me eventually), to criticize outright would have been foolish. A false step would bring a couple of Black Dragon goons rushing up the stairs of the New World Hotel to break through the flimsy wooden door of the Nisei newspaper office. A mere mention in the paper was all the reason Morii needed.

Tommy's worst nightmare involved Rikimatsu, Morii's yojimbo, rising before him like one of the four horsemen of the apocalypse, baring brown, jagged teeth in his skeletal head, pounding with his fists, kicking with his legs as he tore at the type, the layout sheets, and the vulnerable parts of everyone who worked there.

Still Kunio, Irene, I, and even young Frank knew something had to be done about this "tiny despot," and so Tommy's voice rapidly became the one voice representing the Nisei, the younger generation, all around Powell Street and then BC.

3.

1940–1941

My only real encounter with the Oyabun's activities was indirect and came about through my childhood friend, Kazuo "Hammerhead" Nishizaki. "Hammer" and I met at Strathcona High School. He got his nickname when our schoolmates said his head was shaped like the predator shark. There was no telling if he liked it. He was all rough and tumble, downright crude, with a fireplug build; yet, with kind eyes, he always had time for a pal.

I saw him off and on through the years until I made it to university. Once I was in, he called me "Professor." I didn't mind since I worked so hard to get there. I enjoyed hanging out with him because he looked out for me.

Take women for example. My parents were no help. Silence, not counting my mother's constant worry, dominated the household. (I suppose I thought it was normal not to talk about things, especially about women, but I knew enough to yearn for the warmth I saw in other families.)

Just once, I summoned the courage to ask my mother: "I've never... um... kissed, you know, a girl. How ...?" She said nothing; she rose from her knitting and walked away, leaving me confused, alone, and ashamed. I retreated under the staircase, my coal-red eyes burning.

My naive question reminded me I wasn't handsome. My "lantern jaw" was just too hideous, and I could not build confidence when it came to girls. The few dates I had in high school and university always ended with "You're a good boy, Daniel," and, "Let's be friends." I didn't need more friends.

I had "Hammerhead" to thank for my "worldly knowledge."

One day early in my first year at UBC, I asked him, "So how do I get in good with Mitzi? Flowers?"

"Who's Mitzi?"

"Classmate."

"Danny, my boy, there's nothing to it," Hammerhead bragged. "Step into my office," he said as he pulled me aside. "Flowers is good, but not so soon. You can't go around blowing money on some honey with no guarantee of getting somewhere."

"How then?" I said.

"You got to be smooth."

"Smooth?"

"Yeah, sweet-talk her. Sweet-talk her like your life depended on it. After a cheap date or two, a walk in Stanley Park or a soda at Ernie's for instance, get her alone. And then make your move."

"You mean...? No, she'll slap my face."

"No she won't. She'll think she owes you. Play it right and you'll be knocking on heaven's gate."

"Huh?"

"Yeah, a little *alky-hol* wouldn't hurt."

"Give me a break. Where am I gonna get booze?"

"You wanna get past first base or what?"

"I don't do such things. I couldn't..."

"What d'ya mean, you don't do such things?"

"It's not right. I don't...I mean I never."

"You mean, you...?"

"Never."

"Never?" he chortled.

"No, never," I said, more than a little annoyed and embarrassed.

"Well, my friend, we got to get you to the Sisters."

"Where?"

"Three Sisters'. You wanna lose your cherry, give it to the sisters."

The Three Sisters' Coffee Shop was a greasy chopstick on the east side of Jackson near Alexander, the border of the old-time "Red Light District," that offered Canadian breakfast and lunch; and fried salmon *ochazuke* with pickled vegetables on the side. Upstairs, the real business took place.

Upon entering, I sat at one of the window tables, so nervous I couldn't eat the blueberry tart Hammerhead advised I order so as not to look like some kind of "pervert." So I did, innocently looking at the language school across the way while keeping one eye on my pal.

Hammerhead stood at the counter negotiating on my behalf with Yamada Hatsuko, the oldest sister and owner of the establishment, and pointed at me several times. That made my left leg shake uncontrollably. So much so I couldn't stop it, especially when I caught snatches of their conversation.

"Don't insult me and my sisters!"

Hammerhead asked for a moment and rushed back to me. "You got a fin?"

"Five dollars! Are you kidding me? It costs that much? All I got is three, maybe some change. No wait, I owe for the blueberry tart."

"Okay, okay. Hold on." He whispered my dilemma to Yamada-san. "That's an awfully steep price. The most should be two —"

"*Bakatare!*" she erupted. "Go to Goto-san's for that price. That's what her keto girls cost."

As far as I knew, Morii had no part of the Sisters' unlike Goto-san's. Maybe they paid him tribute to leave them alone. I mean, the place was right around the corner from his Nippon Club. At that moment, however, Rikimatsu came down the stairs. On his arm was the youngest and prettiest sister, Yamada Kifumi, dressed in a thin kimono and clutching a clear alcoholic drink in her hand as if she needed it.

"What's all the rumpus down here?" he asked in his gravel voice.

Hatsuko-san barked out immediately, "This ketsunoana is trying to cheat me. Wants a go for only two dollars."

"What?" Rik-san said, turning to Hammerhead. "Who do you think you are? This here's a class joint."

The obviously intimidated Hammerhead quickly and quietly explained the situation to him. My face burned red.

"Really?" Rik-san said. "Yamada-san, here's the money for the kid." He peeled out five one-dollar bills from a roll that would've made a dead man stand up and pay attention. "Got to give the boy an education." He then turned to me. "What's your name?"

"Sugi...Sugiura Shinobu," I stammered.

He shook his hand. "Remember me, boy. Rikimatsu Kintaro, your sensei in matters of love."

I heard the room explode with laughter; I think I chuckled nervously.

EVERYONE WAS AFRAID of the yojimbo. Who wouldn't be? With half of his nose sliced off by a Chinatown Tong, a head like a dried out skull, and quick temper, he'd cut you dead in a heartbeat if you crossed him. Not that day, though. He baffled Hammerhead and me with his generosity, but I was eternally grateful.

I walked nervously to the assigned upstairs room. I, at first, didn't want to be alone, but, no, I thought better of it. My face was red with shame enough. The creaking floor was my only companion. I knocked on the door and heard, "Come in." The room was small, and too hot to be comfortable. Not much furniture: a dresser with a mirror and the bed. The sheets looked dirty, used at least. The walls were paper-thin. I could hear everything in the other rooms down the hall. Sounded like someone was slapping a woman around somewhere. No one did anything, so I didn't. Too nervous anyway. The lack of privacy was too much. I would've cut out if not for the fact that I gazed upon the landscape of heaven before me.

Satoye lay glowing on the bed. It was her room, apparently, but it seemed like she had been waiting for me all along. The afternoon sun shone through the sole window and onto her naked body. Her skin was pale and inviting; her hair, splayed out thick and black, smothered the pillow. Her flawless legs lay architecturally crossed on top of the sheets like some mysterious archway to paradise. Her breasts were like spongy mounds of Castella cake, perfectly shaped with raspberry peaks, a ready dessert if ever I saw one. She had the most beautiful face I had ever seen: round, pure white with bright lipsticked lips staining the topography. She reminded me of one of those princesses I read about in Japanese storybooks when I was a kid.

I remembered hearing that Kifumi-san was Rik-san's favourite. She was everyone's really, since she was such a stunning beauty, but not to me.

Satoye-san was very kind by nature. And she was more than tolerant of me who was so scared that I made *shiishii* several times. Despite the embarrassment, she matter-of-factly washed me clean every time with a wet face cloth while talking to relax me. All this even while we sat together on the bed in our all-together.

"You a Nisei?" she asked with a quick, thick accent.

"Yeah...I mean, *hai.*"

"No be scared," she said before switching to Japanese. "It's like falling off a log."

She wouldn't let me kiss her, though I wanted to. I thought I had to. "Occupational hazard," she explained with a smile after she stopped my advance. I didn't understand, but I didn't care because she started kissing my body. Everywhere but my lips... everywhere. My head then went into a spin as she suddenly pushed me down on the bed and straddled me. My body was in a vice grip between her legs. I felt myself pop into her warm and moist womanhood and then we let nature run its course.

Everything happened so fast; the next thing I was aware of was sitting back at that window table, fully clothed, with Hammerhead slapping me on the back.

"So you did it, Danny boy! Today you are a man!" he laughed, mocking and congratulating at the same time.

"Yeah, I guess so." I didn't say much after that; didn't need to since my friend did all the celebrating for me. "Oh Danny boy, the pipes, the pipes are a-callin' you!" he bellowed.

I sat in vain embarrassment, but I was happy in the realization that I wasn't a "good boy" anymore.

4.

December 7, 1941

The sun gave the late morning a clarity seldom seen on an early December day in Vancouver. Church bells — the sound bouncing off the snowcapped coast mountains ordinarily masked by mist and cloud, but sharply exposed that day in the lazy heat shimmer of an unexpected, but welcomed, return of warm weather. Trees swelled and swayed in the warm wind, the green undersides of their leaves flashing in the sunlight. The streets remained empty of their weekday hustle and bustle; the wood-frame houses around town seemed to relax after the sustained weight and drab rain of late autumn. The domestic peace of a Sunday descended upon the town as if all were right with the world.

Down in the Powell Street part of town, the churches buzzed with the Word of God or the Teaching of the Buddha. Hymns and chanting, coated with incense, rose to the rafters and seeped through to the clear air made heavenly by the tempura being prepared for lunch. The luxurious smells of miso soup, sizzling fish, and fresh-baked pies wafted out of open windows. The streets were empty except for the odd game of shinny hockey being played by the more secular of us Nisei.

The hot jazz that Jelly-Roll'd out of the Patricia Hotel and migrated to other nearby dives the night before had disappeared with dawn. The midnight fights outside the Showa and Nippon Clubs were long forgotten with the combatants incarcerated in the

Cordova Street police station and jailhouse. The latest basketball victory by the Purple Seven Gang over the Abbotsford Knights, celebrated with deafening cheers, was tucked away in the league's record book and put away. All was as it should have been inside and outside the Japanese part of town.

Dicky Mitsubayashi and I sat, each with one leg casually draped over the arm of a booth in Ernie's Café, not thinking about much, girls probably, certainly not about our futures. We were best pals, both in second year at UBC. Dicky, thin and a little anemic, was studying commerce; not his first choice, but it was better than the ministry, his father's vocation. Anything but that, he often growled.

Despite Dicky's enmity towards religion, he was close to his otousan. My pal would've laid down his life for him. I'm not sure I could say the same — the regret and eternal shame of my life.

Between us strawberry milkshakes erupted with creamy, sweet bubbles. The diner's radio, tuned to the Canadian Broadcasting Corporation, played Glenn Miller's "Pennsylvania 6-5000." Our toes tapped to the infectious rhythm in the free air.

"Hey, you guys! Get your feet off of dem chairs!" ordered Ernie Tabata, the grey-haired owner with a recessed jaw and a slow look to his eyes.

"Yeah, sure," Dicky replied as he lazily dropped his leg to the floor with a thud. A snarl came to his lips, signalling me to comply. As if on cue, we flipped out black combs and swept back our identical pomaded hair just as the old upright RCA in the corner suddenly crackled and the smooth swing music cut out, a well-spoken, even-toned CBC announcer's voice taking its place.

>   We interrupt this program to bring you a special news bulletin. The Japanese have attacked Pearl Harbor, Hawaii, by air, President Roosevelt has just announced . . .

I LOOKED AT my pal wide-eyed and open-mouthed. An electrical shock rammed up and down both our spines. "Holy shit," Dicky cursed, "we're in for it now!" In a panic, I jerked myself out of the booth and left the café with my buddy right behind. We scrambled down the pavement, Ernie shouting after us. We hadn't paid the bill.

All over Powell Street, everyone heard the news. Most had been listening to the CBC retransmission from Pearl Harbour. The Buddhist church members heard about it after the service during the lunch of *soba*, rice, and fried baloney prepared by the Fujinkai ladies. Others heard it from their children, like me, who had run home to tell their parents.

"Mom! Mom!" I called, red-faced and puffy, while stumbling noisily into the house. The interior was dark with the brilliant sunshine outside.

"*Naniyo*, Dani *chan?*" she answered. Just forty-three with the expanding hips and tired shoulders of middle age, she stood in the kitchen irritated.

"The Japs . . . the Japs just bombed Pearl Harbor!"

"*Nihongo hanase!*" she insisted with a scowl.

"No, Mom, we can't speak Japanese anymore!"

Okaa shook her head, not understanding anything her *nonki* son was saying.

OTHERS AROUND POWELL STREET understood immediately and quickly dug out anything incriminating. Just in case. They desperately clawed through their houses, gathering up postcards, letters, large ornamental *oningyo*, Japanese grocery store calendars, magazines, old newspaper editions of the *Tairiku Nippo*, rice bags, wooden Oriental carvings, *butsudan*, photographs of holiday visits — anything Japanese — and built bonfires in their backyards. Black clouds rose above, spread and billowed over the streets that day.

Soon, in every Japanese household in BC it seemed, parents wrestled away wooden *kokeshi* from their daughters, confiscated *kisha* sets from their sons, and smashed popular records into pieces and buried them. They hid sacks of Japanese money in places no one — not even they — would ever find again. No one spoke Nihongo except in whispers. Japanese food was kept to a minimum — only rice and the indispensable condiment *shoyu*.

No longer did the Issei stand and cheer in solidarity for the defeat of China. No longer did, the "Kimigayo" play over the loudspeakers at community events. With the attack on the West, we had to sing a different tune: "God Save the King".

Our house was no different. Once my mom understood what was going on (a neighbour told her; she didn't believe her own son), she excavated a cache of papers from the attic and stumbled down to the basement to stuff it into the furnace. She burned photographs, official papers, letters, and anything with Japanese writing on it. As the house grew hot with the cremation, she cried a rainstorm of tears. She never did stop pawing through our belongings. Even when there was nothing left.

THE POWERS THAT BE, the "Government," took swift action. Like rising floodwaters, the determined RCMP flowed into Powell Street looking for the "dangerous" and the "potential troublemakers" — teachers, ministers, union bosses — anyone with an opinion.

Dicky and I then took to sneaking out at night against our parents' wishes and our better judgment. It was risky since we had heard rumours of lynchings in Seattle, Portland, and up Fort St. John way. Still, we had to find out what was happening. The streets were eerily empty, the night establishing its dominance. No official word of a blackout or curfew had come down, but most lights were choked off. Sugiura's Dry Goods saw a surge in sales of black cloth to people who needed to cover their windows to block out the light from within. At night, only the moon carved dark lumps out of buildings, debris, and street furniture.

Keeping to the back alleys, we scanned the area while hiding behind piles of garbage, stacks of wooden crates, keeping a sharp eye for any patrols. Dicky only stumbled once; I knocked over a few trash cans.

"Keep it down!" he chastised.

"See anybody?" I asked as I rubbed my shin.

Dicky shook his head. "I can't see nothing in this dark, but I can smell 'em."

"Cut it out, will ya?"

"What?"

"The wise cracks, okay?" I said. "Keep your ears open."

It was true, we heard them before we saw them in the moonlight. Burning like the propaganda posters warning the public against a hidden enemy, the grim Mounties marched along Cordova in chevron formation. I feared their cold, determined look, their grey and ashen complexions, their clenched teeth, their hard hands rolled into fists.

The patrol came swiftly before suddenly stopping when someone emerged from a vestibule.

"Who is that?" I asked.

"Don't know, but I'm gonna find out." And with that Dicky crawled away quietly, carefully making his way while keeping out of sight. "Wait here."

I started breathing heavier. What was I going to tell his otousan if he got caught? From my vantage point, I saw the Mounties talking to...no, interrogating a man. One even grabbed his coat and shook him. The man gave a short yelp and the harassment stopped.

In what seemed like an eternity, Dicky came back, but didn't say anything, he just kept looking back and around.

"So? Spill," I demanded.

"Some guy named Sam or Sammu. I couldn't catch any more."

"A Japanese?"

"Nah, he's one of us, a Nisei."

"How do you know?"

"Spoke good English," he said simply.

"C'mon, give. Whadda he say?"

"I told ya, I didn't hear much. A couple of 'How's by you?,' I'm guessing, and that's about all," he said. "Now quit your yapping and let's scram on outta here."

We left, being careful not to make any noise. We went out once or twice more; lucky we weren't caught like that Sam or Sammu guy.

The Mounties were on the hunt, and maybe they caught one, maybe more. But in the end, it was far easier for them to come into our houses.

Once, while I was spending the night at Dicky's as I often did, the yellow door of their house shook with a violent pounding.

Two Mounties in trench coats stood in the entrance, their faces indistinct with fedoras crunched down low and the shadows created by the porch light, but they were big, beefy men ready for any violence that might come their way.

"You Masu...Masu-basu...?" growled one. Finally in frustration he asked, "You the minister?"

"Yes, I am Mitsubayashi," Otousan corrected in a clear, accented English. He was amazingly calm but he motioned to his family to keep back; I was glad his baby daughter was asleep. I instinctively backed into a corner of the kitchen, but Dicky tried to push himself forward. His eyes, bleeding red, were intense enough to cause his mother to move to block him for fear of what could happen. Dicky obeyed her for the moment.

"You were a captain in the Japanese Army?"

"Yes, but that was long ago."

The two Mounties turned to each other and nodded a confirmation.

"Doesn't matter, come with us," the voice said as arms pulled the minister into the night like tar does trapped animals.

"Can I get a coat and hat?"

"No," the officer stated resoundingly. "No phone calls, no lawyers, no visitors."

"Who the hell do you think you are?" Dicky yelled, never realizing how vulnerable he was without an ID card.

"Listen, Bucko, you keep out of this," advised one Mountie, "C'mon, Captain, let's go."

Dicky screamed a resounding, *"No!"* and rushed forward. He was met with a violence I had not seen before. Piston arms threw him against the wall. I grabbed him before he fell. His okaasan moved to her stunned son in a panic and, with glistening eyes, wordlessly begged the officers to stop.

Outraged and fearful, the Reverend Mitsubayashi stepped between the stormtrooper and us. Both men stood their ground waiting for the next move. The Mountie's partner then acted with a cooler head. "All right. All right. There's no need to let this get out of hand. Stand down, Constable McGregor."

"Okay, we go," the Reverend said conclusively. "But where we go?"

Silence was his answer.

THIRTY-EIGHT OTHERS were caught in the net of the manhunt that night, their fates unknown to their families. My father was a shopkeeper and not considered a threat; he was someone without an opinion, so we were left alone. I believed the Mounties saw some use in keeping a dry goods store open.

I had a harder time explaining why to my mother. "It okay Okaasan, they don't want Otousan." I spoke in my barely competent Japanese, hoping that she understood.

"But *bocchan*, they're coming after everyone. What will we do if Otousan is taken? What will we do?"

She always frustrated me with her paranoid ways, but maybe she had a right to be this time. She perspired with concern. My first impulse was to hug her to reassure her, but no, I couldn't. She wouldn't have allowed it, and I would've been embarrassed. Japanese Canadians don't do that. Though she was weak and vulnerable, I could only dredge up a drop of comfort for her; I knew my father even less.

The next day Canada declared war on Japan. The Government shut down all community newspapers except *The New Canadian*, the only one in English. It was allowed to publish, but was carefully scrutinized and open to censorship. On the plus side, the Government paid to print and distribute the paper; they even subsidized staff pay. We still needed our subscribers, but the burden was not as bad.

The Government closed the churches (except for funerals), the various judo dojo, and the fifty-nine Japanese language schools in the province; they forbid most public gatherings.

While standing outside the Buddhist church during a funeral, I overheard a group of Issei talking.

"Matsumiya was lucky to die now."

"Why?"

"He won't have to go through what's coming."

THE GOVERNMENT QUICKLY sent notices to Japanese-Canadian fishermen living in villages up and down the BC coast — their 1,200 Japanese fishing boats would soon be impounded, gathered, and lashed together all along the various harbour fronts like massive log jams. The problem was they did not say when, and the men and their families lived in fearful anticipation. Within two weeks all Japanese Canadians lost their jobs. Only shopkeepers like my parents managed to stay open.

Powell Street bent toward the breaking point. The Government acted so quickly, so efficiently, so thoroughly, that I wondered how long the centre could hold. There seemed to be no end to what was happening.

I wrote various stories trying to keep up with the rapid changes.

"Tommy, here's a piece about Amitani's boarding house," I said. "I expanded it to include the back stories of some of the boarders."

My editor read it carefully and then concluded, "You're getting better, but we can't run it."

"Why not?" I asked with a note of irritation.

"The Government won't allow it. We've got to be careful."

"Then what do I write about?"

"Nothing, for the moment. We'll paste up the announcements. We'll keep the community informed."

"We're not a mouthpiece for the Government!" My frustration must've coated my face.

"Take it easy, Danny. Our time will come."

I sat at my desk that evening frustrated and angry. I took a handy notebook and copied my stories into it. From then on, I filled notebooks with copy, stories, and interviews. Tommy may not print any of it, but I would not lose any of them. I would not forget what happened to us.

MY MOTHER MELTED with worry. She could no longer speak to anyone in Japanese out of a fear of arrest; my father remained silent as he always had. I wished he'd said something to ease her groundless paranoia (no one was arrested for speaking Japanese), or at least tried. But nothing.

Most Japanese could no longer support their families; most could no longer worship as they chose; most could no longer give spiritual and moral guidance. They couldn't even understand their only community newspaper; they now had to depend on their children to understand what was happening to them. I wanted my father to fight back, but I knew he couldn't. He neither had the resources, nor the resolve, to mount that kind of resistance.

My older brother Herb had moved out long ago. He was much like my dad, stubborn, silent, and quietly angry, about what I never knew. He even looked like him. He got into it with Dad one day over an invoice from a supplier. No fisticuffs but a lot of yelling. A trivial thing but it was the straw that broke it for Herb. He startled everyone by packing up and moving out. I later heard that he'd married. So out of necessity and my mother's nagging, it fell to me to translate everything that came into the house. *The New Canadian* was not easy, since it was filled with Tommy's editorials and the Government's announcements. I squinted as if to make the translation easier. At times, I concentrated so hard I imagined the smell of burning wood, but I think I got the major points across.

Measures to provide employment for all Japanese Canadians deprived of their livelihood by restrictions imposed following the outbreak of the war on the Pacific have been submitted to Ottawa, according to a press statement issued today by the Federal Standing Committee on the Oriental question in BC.

— The New Canadian, January 3, 1942

These orders apply now and are to be maintained until further notice.
Between sunset and sunrise:
   1) Porch lights on homes must be kept off.
   2) Stores and other business premises must not display outside lights, neon or otherwise.
   3) Outdoor advertising signs must not be illuminated.

— The New Canadian, January 9, 1942

Kishizo Kimura
Secretary of the Canadian Salt Herring Exporters has been appointed by Ottawa as a member of the three-man committee known as the "Japanese Fishing Vessels Disposal Commission" which will supervise the transfer of Japanese-owned fishing vessels to buyers. Mr. Kimura will represent the owners.

— The New Canadian, January 26, 1942

MY MOTHER WAS always on the verge of tears, visibly shaking where she stood, and was constantly at me to make the words come out right. "Bocchan, please tell me we won't lose the store. They won't come for Otousan at night, will they? Will they?"

I had no idea what would happen to the store or Dad. What could I say to her? I just wanted to yell at her for her old lady's ways, but I knew I couldn't. There was no use in that.

Otousan would keep the dry goods store open as long as he could — that I knew. His customers were all Japanese and so he felt himself a target for the Mounties. But he remained as stoic as ever. Besides, the need for black coverings for windows was great for business.

AT NIGHT, I sat in the darkness of my room upstairs from the shop, brooding about recent events. I cupped my face in the palms of my hands. What was happening here? Were we like some helpless girl attacked...interfered with? We hadn't done anything; we were not the enemy. The real villain behind it all was the Government, the anonymous personification of evil in the east.

More importantly, I kept trying to tell everyone our immediate and obvious enemy were the BC politicians. They didn't care about the Germans and Italians living in this country; they only wanted us out of their industries, like logging, fishing, and mining. It was racism pure and simple. That should've been in the paper. I stared out of my night-black window, sensing a seismic shift in my world.

The prominent Issei had been imprisoned. So we looked to guys like Tommy Shoyama. For his part, he was confident his Canadian education and patriotism would see everyone through, eventually giving the Nisei the means to provide for their families. The "British sense of fair play" would surface as sure as rain, he insisted. Many Nisei would pick up the gauntlet, but the major questions remained: were we ready for it? Were we fully aware of the stakes?

I looked in one of my notebooks and found a story I had heard in conversation with a Skeena River fisherman visiting the Buddhist church. I never identified the speaker for fear of reprisal if I was ever found out, but I found hope in the story:

> *A Japanese man stood on the banks of the Fraser River. He carried with him two swords, ancient* katana *given to him by his grandparents before he rode the Kuroshio to Canada. The wind was up and he felt water drops on his face as if it were a blessing from the Shinto gods. Another, at a different part of the river, held on high a full suit of Japanese armour, hesitating but always mindful of his duty. Still another piled a stack of Canadian bills in a freshly dug hole and then readied his shovel to hide his treasure. He knew he would never be able to retrieve it in the future, but then again nobody would. At some precise moment, the two men threw the swords and armour into the water and the one shovelled clumps of dirt. Small acts of defiance to prevent the hakujin from stealing their possessions. Shikataganai.*

February 7, 1942, has been set as the official deadline for aliens of Japanese race and citizens naturalized since September 1, 1922, to report to the registrar of enemy aliens to sign the required undertaking.

—The New Canadian, December 12, 1941

5.

During December, 1941, there was no Christmas for Japanese Canadians. New Year's was our holiday anyway — the most important one on the calendar. Celebrate it with an abundance of food and traditions and the rest of the year was guaranteed to be prosperous. It truly was the only time of year I fooled myself into thinking I had a close-knit family. Patrons and friends came by the house to pay their respects. Extended family was supposed to visit as well, but my brother was a no-show, as usual. My mother relaxed and my father chortled with friends over sake and stories.

But January 1st, 1942, stood in stark contrast to other years. No one visited as I communed with my parents in front of some Chinese takeout containers and a bowl of kuromame to insure good health at least. Mom brooded in mournful contemplation. Japanese food stuff in Chinatown had shot up in price, forcing her to open a saved can or two. Grocery stores on Powell Street simply closed their doors for fear of reprisal and Mountie persecution. Good thing we had bought a can of shoyu and a one-hundred pound bag of kome just before Pearl Harbor.

My okaa quietly cried off and on all day long that New Year's. With the slow shuttering of her community, her bit of home, I saw that she began to feel lost. I wanted to shake some sense into her, but that would've been too cruel.

"Mama" was all my father said as he reached out to touch her arm, the first time I ever saw him offer any kind of comfort or affection — done without drink. Dad was in his mid-twenties when he married Mom. He had already been in Canada a good decade before writing home to find a bride. He saw life as a struggle, and faced it with grim determination. The closing of Powell Street was just another torment to endure.

Certainly my mother was upset that we couldn't celebrate with the whole family, the one time during the year we all came together, my brother included, she hoped. But what really brought her down was a letter I had received. It was from UBC.

TOMMY HAD STOOD over me with a comforting hand on my shoulder as I read the letter at *The New Canadian*. "All the Nisei are in the same boat," he informed me. "The high-schoolers, too." We were all locked out. No reason was given, but we knew why. "I guess we had to expect it."

Nodding at Tommy's words, I didn't gripe about my dismissal or even shed a tear. A university degree meant very little when it came to a career. Look at Tommy: he didn't need much of an education to be the editor of a community newspaper.

I just felt badly for my mom.

"Don't worry, Okaa, I'll make out," I said with as much sincerity as I could muster. "Good thing I'm working at the paper. There's some money coming in."

"Baka!" she slammed in an outburst surprising even for her. "That will lead to nowhere. You need education..."

"Okay, Ma, okay, maybe I can pick up where I left off when things settle down."

Who was I kidding? I thought. No one really knew how far the government was willing to go. Our faces marked us. Tommy still believed in the country's sense of fair play, but not me. I wasn't worried about my education; I was just plain scared about what would happen next. I may have eased my mother's mind momentarily, but I saw everything falling apart right before my eyes.

AS THE DAYS crept deeper into January, Powell Street, mostly empty during the day, was completely dead at night. No one talked to another out in the open. The laughter, random chatter, and business quibbling had disappeared. The loving sounds of comfort and family were inside houses and dampened to a murmur. Middle-aged women no longer visited friends to chat in front gardens; instead, they scrambled home from their errands as quickly as they could.

Despite the ominous feeling in the air, I breathed a little easier. Everything had been taken care of by this point: the troublesome Japanese language had effectively been choked off, and the potential troublemakers had been taken into custody. I worried about my parents who were Japanese immigrants, but the Government seemed uninterested in small fry. I naively hoped businesses would open again, as would the churches and other institutions once the crisis passed. Everything would get back to being normal in short order. A "phony war" had settled in Powell Street.

Younger guys like Frank Morimoto thought it was all good. "We don't need to speak the language now or ever," he enthused in the *NC* office, though he knew some had no choice but to communicate in their native tongue, the only language they had. "We should start thinking about moving out. Move to Kitsilano, Surrey, or maybe even North Van. Break us up; we don't need to be together. It'll be better that way, less . . . you know, out in the open, obvious, and eventually . . . we'll be accepted."

I listened without making eye contact. Irene buried herself in her work, her typewriter clacking along to Frank's diatribe. Kunio stood against a wall with his eyes glazed over. Tommy suddenly appeared at the door to his office. His face was pinched, grey, pale, and thinner than usual, his eyes dulled with the lack of sleep, his body slightly slumped with the stress.

Frank stopped talking, Irene paused her hands over the keys, and Kunio and I looked his way. Tommy pointed at me and beckoned me into his office. I felt a tingling in my stomach as I tried to remember what I had fouled up. I followed him inside the other room as Frank continued his argument. Kunio turned away while Irene returned to the typewriter. "Yup, we gotta move...Powell Street is the ghetto and..." Frank's opinions became muffled once Tommy closed the door.

"That Frank, give him a soapbox and he'd jump right up on top of it," I chuckled, trying to lighten the mood, but Tommy didn't bite. He had something serious to say.

"You know about the boat roundup," he began. "The fishing boats have been impounded and are being taken to various dry docks."

I froze, not knowing what to expect next. "Yeah, they issued the order last month."

Tommy pivoted away for a moment. "You ever been to Steveston?"

"Uh...no, but I know some guys down there."

"Okay, you're going for a couple of days," he said with a smile. "I want you to observe and report back to me. You can expand your horizons."

"Steveston?" I asked incredulously. "C'mon, Tommy, that's a hick town."

"I'm not asking you to move there."

Steveston was a backwater despite being so close to Vancouver. I knew it was a town stocked with fishermen, a place to work in the muck of fish guts and throat-grabbing stink all week. Saturday night was the time to get drunk and spill onto the dirt street rolling and scrapping until the police dragged the flotsam and jetsam away to jail. Sunday morning, they'd be repenting with family at the church of their choice. Then Monday would come along and the cycle would begin again.

I swallowed my new assignment like a kid does cod liver oil. "What could possibly be of interest there?"

"I told you the boats are being rounded up. I want you to observe and report back to me."

"Can I write it up?"

"We'll see."

"What about Morii?"

It was true, the fishing boat story was more important. Tommy wasn't printing any of the Oyabun reports anyway. As much as my editor's instincts about the crime boss were coming true, he knew he had to shift his focus. I grumbled a lot, but in the end I agreed to go down to "Hicksville."

The truth was I only knew one guy in Steveston, and I didn't know him well. Jimmy Isojima was a young fisherman who worked hard in his prized craft every day from February to November. He supported his father, his mother, and his sister, Gladys, "a gal with personality," and he kept up the payments for the $50,000 fishing boat.

As a principal organizer, I always saw him and his pals at the Bussei fall and Christmas dances held at the Odd Fellows Hall in Vancouver. There would be soft holiday lights strung along the walls; the Asahi Swingers playing brassy big band music that all the "hep cats" loved, with bandleader Bob Shimotakahara the "dreamiest"; and an array of cupcakes, *manju* and pie made lovingly by the Fujinkai women on long tables covered with brilliant white cloth. It was easy to talk to Jimmy, easy to get to know him.

Jimmy would be dressed in his best suit, which hung off his too-thin body, with his hair done up in the latest Brylcreem style, and his person reeking of Old Spice like a hovering ghost. He seemed a little like an outsider as a result, but his best girl, Hedy, didn't seem to mind. I always smirked at him but kept comments to myself.

And so it was I ran into Jimmy Isojima at the Steveston pier. Given the urgency of the situation, we didn't talk much, only a nodding acknowledgement. We stood in silence along with several other men from the village as the fleet of thirty boats was herded by us. The crisis linked us in a comfortable union.

The saltwater-saturated air filled my senses. The Kuroshio, the Black Current, ran deep below the surface of the Pacific Ocean. Legend had it the Issei, my parents included, rode the back of the warm water current to come to Canada. The depths used to be comforting and inviting, the horizon bright with hope.

I drew in that acrid aroma. It permeated every part of us whether it was in Steveston, up the coast, or in the streets of East Vancouver. It was familiar, it was welcoming, it was home.

Jimmy became restless when he saw the vessels lashed together and bumping into each other while all the Japanese owners had been corralled onto one of the larger ones.

"Don't do that! Omigod, they're wrecking them," he said in a querulous voice.

Word from up the pike soon spread through the crowd about the cruel herding of the fishing fleet. Far up the Skeena River, the navy had tied thirty or so of the boats to Canadian Navy vessels and then ordered the owners onto the deck of the largest one without adequate food and water. When all was ready, they pulled out headed for a distant dry-dock.

By all accounts, a chilly, naked wind was a constant during the voyage — invisible frosty fingers digging deep, tormenting the floating cattle. Whitecaps licked at the boats as the naval crew tried to ignore the hollow and shivering men teetering on the deck just twenty feet off the bow.

The flotilla arrived in Steveston after four days when we saw them, the military personnel intentionally indifferent to the fact that the Japanese could barely stand, some hunched over with fever and abdominal pain, their senses dull, their eyes sea-cold and hard.

Once off the boat, a few of the still able-bodied men told us that something bad had happened onboard one of the boats. A day and a half into the voyage, the naval and army guards heard a commotion coming from the stern of the prison flotilla. Guards found Onizuka Kazuo, one of the owners, lying wounded against the engine block, his shirt blackened with fresh blood. He had a couple of oozing stab wounds in his abdomen. Onizuka's fellow

fishermen yelled for help and then started a ruckus, accusing the
military of the assault. They were held back by two soldiers with
bayoneted rifles at the ready. One of the fishermen swore he saw
blood on a soldier's blade.

The captain of the detail questioned the wounded man, but
Onizuka was incoherent, the loss of blood, the shock, too great.
He then ordered a stop for medical help. Onizuka was seen to by
the local doctor of a small settlement up the coast. Fortunately the
doctor was able to stabilize Onizuka and ordered him transported
to Vancouver by truck.

The incident made the rest of the men forget about their hunger
until they realized there was a grocery store in the coastal village. Unfortunately the fishermen, without much money, bought very little.

Is this what war is like? I pondered once I heard of the casualty:
the random stabbing of a defenceless fisherman by some guard.
But why? Was the soldier provoked? Was he ordered to stab the
fisherman? If so why, again? I suspected there would never be any
answers to my questions. I felt sick to my stomach just thinking
about the victim. As a kid, I romanticized the warrior-soldier van-
quishing the enemy with raw courage and patriotic resolve. The
British flag flew overhead and "Rule Britannia" thundered all about
the battlefield. The reality was bleaker and more horrific than I
had ever imagined.

I bent over and threw up where I stood, though I turned away
to avoid total embarrassment. The puddle of vomit lay like some
protozoa oozing and undulating away. Jimmy sprang to my aid,
his soothing hand on my back while he shouted for cold water.

The young fisherman then had the presence of mind to call for
volunteers to billet the men. "It's the right thing to do," he argued.
The entire Steveston community seemed to rally, and took the
victims in to give them a hot bath and a meal.

The Isojima family invited the grizzled fisherman Kego, a character from up Tofino way, into their home. Jimmy asked me as
well to come along so I could recover. Tommy had given me hotel
money, but I couldn't think of a more generous offer.

Their house was a *kyabin* on Third Avenue just off Moncton Street near the Fraser River docks. The structure was built of roughly hewn wooden slats with a window or two; the inside was small, but cozy, with a potbelly stove, bedrooms and a kitchen. I was a bit shocked when I saw Jimmy's father for the first time. He sat still in what looked like his favourite chair. The blank expression on his face and his limp, useless hand on his lap made me wonder what had happened, but I was too Japanese to ask, causing embarrassment.

"*Ohaiyo gozaimasu!*" I greeted once I recovered, but got no response.

Jimmy just smiled and introduced me to his mom.

Isojima-no okusan was a portly woman with a kind face and disposition. She welcomed me like an aunt does a long-lost nephew.

And then I met Gladys.

She served us hot *misoshiru*, while Isojima-no okusan fried up fresh fish. For Kego, leftover rice, despite being cold, must've been a treasure. "Oh, *oishii desu*," he exclaimed.

I was instantly attracted to Gladys, though she wasn't the beauty of Hollywood picture shows. Then again I was no magazine cover myself. A tomboy perhaps with a small, stocky body, but her warm personality came out in her smile and sparkling eyes. An Isojima smile. Her long hair was beautiful.

It wasn't love at first sight by any means, but in the weeks and months to come, I often thought about her. Only one problem: she was far too young for me. She had to be in her mid-teens and I was twenty-one going on twenty-two after all. Now I was keenly aware my father married a sixteen-year-old and he was well into his twenties, older than I was. But he was a different generation, in different circumstances. They were Japanese, not Canadian like Gladys and me. The Nisei didn't do things like that.

"Give Kego-san some *biiru*," Isojima-no okusan ordered Gladys in Japanese.

"No, no, Okusan, that's okay," he assured. "I don't want to cause no trouble."

"No trouble at all. Gladys, serve," she again entreated.

When the evening turned quiet, Jimmy and I sat with Kego who pulled out a pipe to enjoy himself. We spoke to each other in Japanese; or rather they conversed, I mostly listened.

"Oh, I'm full," Kego complained as he stretched, rubbed his stomach in large circles and sat back deep into the chesterfield. "That was so gooood. Haven't felt this good in many a day." He drew on his pipe and then blew out a cloud through his wrinkled and collapsed lips. "What's wrong with your otousan, if you don't mind me asking?"

I was surprised by Kego's candour, but I was glad he asked.

"No, no, that's fine," Jimmy answered. "He had a stroke."

"Stroke-ka? That's a tough break. He looks too young for anything like that."

"Yeah, his right side is frozen. Can't talk but he can walk with a bad limp."

"I'm sorry. How is your family doing?"

"We get by, or at least we were. Don't know now with all this business going on."

Kego went silent.

It was Jimmy's turn to ask. "What happened on board to Onizuka-san?"

"Don't rightly know. We just found him lying there, bleeding bad."

I felt queasy again, but was able to gain control over it. Though I had been weakened by the emotion of the day and cold air, the food had revived me somewhat.

"If you ask me," Kego continued, "them's the ones that done it. The navy boys. Everyone knows Onizuka was hopping mad about this roundup. Probably shot off his mouth to the wrong guard. Yeah, probably the big keto did it. A corporal, he was a bloody mean guy, a real S.O.B. Or it was revenge."

"What do you mean?" I asked.

"Some say Onizuka scuttled his boat on purpose so's them sailor boys wouldn't have an easy time of it!" He laughed over that one. "Don't blame him. He wasn't the only one. I'd do the same if I had a boat."

"But they'll give them back after the war," Jimmy stated.

"You go on believing that. As for me and the others, we have no other choice."

Shikataganai.

AS THE EVENING progressed into the small hours and Kego snored in a deep sleep, Jimmy and I sat by candlelight enjoying each other's company with beer. The women had gone to bed shortly after putting Otousan to bed.

"Poor fellah, must be all done in," Jimmy observed, gazing at Kego sawing logs.

I gave a half smile in the muted light. "Can't say I blame him. That was a rough ride."

"What d'you think gonna happen next?"

"Don't really know. They got the malcontents," I offered, finding no real comfort in that statement. "What about you? They coming after your boat?"

"Probably. We got the notice right after Pearl, but I don't know when they'll take her away."

"Sorry to hear that. She must be a nice boat."

"That she is, but I can't regret losing her."

"No? Why?" I asked, a little surprised by Jimmy's attitude.

"It's just a boat. I'll get another or maybe I'll get her back... you know, after. If they don't bust her up. Anyhow, I ain't gonna sink her, just in case."

"Yeah, I suppose so," I said, not knowing what else to say.

"You lose anything?"

"Yeah, my education. I'm pretty sure I can get that back though."

"That's good. It's not like you lost something like a loved one or something."

"True," I agreed, a little sad, and perhaps a little fearful of a premonition. I didn't go into the breakup of Powell Street. It was happening here too, but what could I say? We spent the next few hours nodding in agreement and in a growing friendship.

WHEN THE NAVY came to retrieve the men the next day for the rest of the trip, they encountered much resistance. The fishermen, backed by Jimmy and the Steveston community, had decided to stand their ground and refused to return. "They ain't gonna stab me and leave me for dead!" Kego declared in Japanese.

Word of the protest spread so fast that Morii Etsuji sent his thug Moriyama with money to support the men. With such an act of charity, Jimmy mustered much more respect for the Oyabun. He knew of Morii of course; the gangland boss was the one who tried to take over the Steveston Fishermen's Association a few years back. But the Oyabun's generosity put him into a new light for the young fisherman.

"Kuso *Mountain* Police!" Kego yelled in Japanese. "They can take my boat, but they ain't taking me to kill in the middle of nowhere!"

Unable to spend that much time in rounding up their quarry, the navy abandoned the task and continued to take the boats in but without their owners. The Mounties interviewed Ensign Frank Macleod about the "incident" with Onizuka much later, but dismissed him in short order. The military and Government soon forgot all about it.

I reported most of the story to Tommy upon returning to Vancouver, but kept quiet about Morii's role. Miracle of miracles, he let me report it.

"Why'd you edit out the Onizuka part?" I asked, confused at all the red marks on the page.

"Never get past the censors," he said succinctly. "Too dangerous to us."

"But it's the heart of the story!"

"Be that as it may . . ."

That night at home, I added the incident to my notebook, then I kicked my garbage can across the room yelling, "Dangerous my eye!"

Like Jimmy, I was particularly impressed with the Oyabun despite his loyalty to the Japanese Emperor. Maybe underneath it all, he really wanted to protect all of us Japanese Canadians, though I still harboured a suspicion that he did it for some personal gain. Just what, I couldn't fathom.

*Measures to provide employment for all Japanese Canadians deprived
of their livelihood by restrictions imposed following the outbreak of
the war on the Pacific have been submitted to Ottawa...*

*A second recommendation submitted is a plan to make use of the immo-
bilized fishing fleet. This plan has been "agreed to by all concerned" and
representatives of the fishing industry have given assurances that "there
would be sufficient crews available to man the boats and maintain the
necessary production of fish for both Great Britain and the domestic
market..."*

*First action of the committee... was to get in touch with a commit-
tee of Japanese citizens to ask them for support and cooperation so
that registration of all Japanese could be undertaken... The Japanese cooperated in every way and eventually 23,423 Japanese were
registered.*

— The New Canadian, January 3, 1942

6.

A couple of weeks later, I found myself back in Steveston.
This time I volunteered to go and Tommy stood arms
folded and legs apart, sporting a wide grin. I felt like a kid
sour at knowing my dad was right. Jimmy, now the
Steveston District representative, contacted me about another
flotilla headed for New Westminster.

When I stood with Jimmy and his fellow Japanese-Canadian
fishermen on the banks to watch the boats being towed by navy
ships, I saw in the distance the huddled owners as before grimac-
ing and standing against the spray of wind and sea. Once again,
they had no control; they were just passengers, or prisoners.

The crowd shouted in dismay when they saw the vessels, each loosely tied to a navy boat, in close formation, banging up against each other, with random buoys, piers, and stationary markers damaging the hulls — like toy boats floundering in wave-angry seas. Jimmy lowered his head and told me his was next. It was to be rounded up next week, more than likely to be tossed and cracked open somewhere in the entanglement of everyone's livelihood. Would he puncture his own boat to make a slow leak? No one as far as we knew was planning to scuttle his own craft.

The apparent leader, Watanabe Etsuo, uncomfortable in his oversized three-piece suit, bowed before the impotent fleet, his face streaked with defeat, his back slightly stooped like a man burdened by events. "It's like a death in the family," he observed, his feet planted firmly on the shore. With his face turned to the tragic wind, he stretched to his full height and looked ten-feet tall.

Watanabe Etsuo, the secretary of the Steveston Fishermen's Association, was a well-respected man. He stood five-feet-four-inches at most, with thick hair and a keen, intelligent look about him. His small hands and large feet worked against him. The thick glasses perched on his prominent nose dominated his features. I'm sure there were plenty of jokes being said behind his back.

Most in Steveston knew his story. Watanabe was educated by Buddhist monks back in his village in Japan. Reading the old texts by candlelight must have made him go blind. Wearing such heavy, thick glasses, the joke went, made his nose grow large to hold it up.

His father arranged a good marriage for Watanabe and sent his son and wife to Canada. As the second son, I guessed, he would inherit nothing as was the custom.

His bride, Akiko, was part of the Hayashi family. Startling, since in Vancouver one of the bride's cousins was known to have murdered her daughter and husband for her lover, a gigolo. The scandal must've dogged the couple.

Watanabe Etsuo and Akiko came to Vancouver in 1920 during the *Yobiyosejidai*. Not built for hard labour, Watanabe immediately used his innate intelligence and education to land a position with the *Minshu*, a Japanese union newspaper. As a reporter, he covered the important and sometimes chaotic events of the city and surrounding area. Sato Ryuichi, the president of the Steveston Fishermen's Association, impressed him in particular. Here was a man of integrity with a keen sense of justice. A bit too hot-headed for his own good, but a leader among men. Many believed Watanabe patterned himself after him.

Watanabe eventually relocated his family to Steveston and joined the association; he progressed through the ranks quickly, primarily through his suggestions to combat the racism against the Japanese fishermen by Canadians and the cancerous influence of the Black Dragon Society, until he became secretary. Everyone in the fishing village and up the coast came to know and admire him. Jimmy was thoroughly inspired by the man. He came to address him as "Mr.," but then again Jimmy called anyone older and in authority "Mr."

With his square, clean-shaven jaw Watanabe looked like a man determined to make life in this new land as easy as possible for his wife and children. He always enjoyed watching his two *yancha* daughters constantly getting underfoot in the large rooms of their low-rent cannery house on First Avenue north of Moncton Street, Steveston's main drag.

As the flotilla moved past, Watanabe said, "There's no time to grieve. We have to make the arrangements and receive the mourners. Go to the docks, billet the men. They'll need friendly faces and a hot meal! This is hard to bear again, I know, but we must forget our personal feelings for the sake of our families and our place in this country."

JIMMY CONVINCED ME after another pleasant night's stay with the Isojima family that we should talk to Watanabe. The next morning the sweat of my pal's labour and fish oil quickly infused the musty darkness of Watanabe's office above Curly's Billiard Hall. It served as an announcement of our arrival.

"Mr. Watanabe," Jimmy said as we both bowed out of respect.

Watanabe Etsuo greeted us warmly in Japanese. "Ah, Isojima, I'm glad you're here. Who's your friend?"

"I'm from Vancouver," I jumped in with English.

"He's an honest-to-goodness newspaper reporter!" Jimmy enthused.

A little embarrassed, I countered, "Cut it out, Jimmy. It's no big deal."

"It is around here."

"Be that as it may, welcome to Steveston," Watanabe-san said.

"They're taking away all the boats up and down the coast," Jimmy interrupted. "Steveston's next!"

"Yes, a bad business," Watanabe-san said as he adjusted his thick eyeglasses. "The wives and children are afraid — so confused and in a panic. I've tried to reassure my own family, but it would sound better if I could back it up. They can't see how we'll survive, *ne*," he said reaching over and resting his hands on Jimmy's shoulders.

Jimmy's face turned red, embarrassed by the intimacy. I smiled a little and warmed toward the man.

Watanabe-san's conviction was obvious, his sincerity true. "We've got to do something," Watanabe emphasized. "You're good at figuring things out. You were responsible for getting the towns-folk to billet the fishermen. You convinced everyone to do it."

"That was nothing," Jimmy said.

"We're going to need more of that kind of 'nothing' in the dark days ahead." Then he turned to say with conviction, "Let's pay a visit to the ketsunoana."

So it was that the secretary of the Steveston Fishermen's Asso-ciation, the Steveston District representative and I, a *New Canadian* reporter, walked respectfully into Commandant Edwin Fitzgerald's office at Garry Point Naval Base, our heads bowed. The comman-dant stood waiting, tall in full uniform, with nary a wrinkle or speck of lint in sight. He was wound so tight he couldn't laugh if a joke bit his *oshiri*, as Jimmy observed. The light-green room had a high ceiling that echoed every sound we made. It smelled "official."

"*Gomen nasai, Komanda* Fitzgerald," Watanabe started as he looked the commandant straight in the eyes, showing no fear. "Excuse me for bother."

"Hmm, you speak English?" Fitzgerald said, relieved at hearing a version of the Queen's English.

"Hai. I am secretary of..."

"I know who you are," he stated abruptly, and turned to Jimmy and me. "And I know you, but who's this then?"

"I'm from *The New Canadian* —"

"Hey, no reporters here," he said, pointing to the door.

"I'm here off the record...for moral support," I assured. Tommy wouldn't let me write about this anyway; maybe in a perfunctory fashion at best.

"All right, then. Now be quick about it. I'm a busy man." He lowered himself into his chair smoothly.

Jimmy nervously said, "It...it is about the..."

"Our boats," Watanabe interrupted. "You-no men breaking our boats. Our future..."

"I suppose so," replied Fitzgerald. He actually sounded like he felt sorry for the Japanese. "But we really need to round them up slicky-dicky. I'm under orders."

"We know that. We wondering could we sail by ourself?"

He paused before he next spoke. "What do you mean?"

"We could sail boat for you," Watanabe said.

The tall hakujin man turned away as if to take in the full meaning of the idea. "You mean, you'd bring them into dry-dock yourselves?"

"Hai. That way, you get job done and we save our boat." Watanabe frowned as he tried to find the right words. "How can we hurt Canada? You know, sabotage? These boat are our future. I want to give to my son."

"Good!" Fitzgerald shouted, startling us. He was supposed to round up over five hundred boats within the month. "Impossible," he admitted at the time. Most of his men were inexperienced; the real sailors had left for the St. Lawrence, reassigned to look for U-boats. The three standing in front of him were the answer to his problem.

My respect for Watanabe-san was truly born that day, and for Jimmy it grew enormously that day. Watanabe didn't own a boat and had two daughters. He really wasn't a fisherman, either. Morii paled in comparison.

The fishing boat round-up in Steveston progressed last week. It however progressed smoothly thanks to the leadership of Jimmy (I won't identify him to spare his family embarrassment from seeing their name in the paper), who negotiated the sailing of their own boats.

By Daniel Sugiura
The New Canadian, January 21, 1942

7.

Just a week ago in January, an order-in-council under the War Measures Act created a protected area up and down the BC coast to one-hundred miles inland. Another order came on February 24th that gave the minister of justice the power to control the movements of all Japanese Canadians in the protected area. Irene wrote about both in the pages of *The New Canadian* along with the announcement that all male Japanese-Canadian citizens were to be removed from the area. My neutered stories about the fishing boat round-ups were buried deep in the paper. It was clear the exile had begun.

SUBSEQUENT TO THE edicts, the Government ordered all Issei men and their sons — not only foreign nationals but Canadian-born children — between the ages of eighteen to forty-five, to "volunteer" for work gangs in road camps.

The office took on a sombre tone as the shadows stretched long into the early evening. Kunio sighed deeply as he perched on the edge of a flimsy wooden chair. His suit settled its material like a blanket over his undersized torso. I sat hunched over a piece submitted by a teenage girl worried about the loss of Bussei dances. Tommy ruminated at his own desk, stress etched prominently into his face.

They had started the breakup of families, the next phase of the methodical disintegration of the community. The crying of many wives and younger family members echoed in the dark recesses of Powell Street.

"Canada has a tradition of fair play," Kunio said in an exasperated tone. "Our government can't be doing this to us, its own citizens."

"Now don't get your knickers in a knot, Kunio," Tommy advised. "I believe in the British sense of fair play, too, and I know Canada will come through for us."

I was about to add my two cents when the dark walls shook as Frank Morimoto burst into the office.

"Jesus! Where's the fire?" I exclaimed.

Gasping for air, his thin cheeks glowing, the teenager leaned over a convenient desk to recover. "Tommy! At the...at the..."

"Take it easy, Frank. You're gonna blow a gasket!" assured Kunio with a smile. "Catch your breath."

"At the language school," he finally got out, "they're holed up.. .about eighty of 'em!"

"Who are?"

"The gang for the road camp."

"Good God!"

"They were a no-show at the CPR depot...went to the language school instead."Tommy, Kunio, and I grabbed our hats and coats as Frank, still huffing, led the way down the steep set of stairs and out into the cold and uncertain night.

The language school on Alexander Street, a grey block of concrete and stucco with a weather-worn wooden edifice attached, the only remnant of the original structure, was as black and solemn as a tomb except for a soft glow deep within its belly. Someone didn't care about the threat of aerial attack. A tiled plaque above the entrance of the main building identified the place as the "Japanese Hall — 1928." Inside the solid front doors, a linoleum foyer featured twin staircases, wide with a dogleg to the right and left, leading to the classrooms upstairs. The institutional odour of fresh floor wax filled the air. At the far end of the foyer, two more doors with frosted glass were sandwiched between the staircases. Through them, the auditorium opened up to a cement floor that ran to a raised stage.

I did not want to be there again. I could hear Morii's speeches echoing in the halls. I could also hear my mother's voice berating me for skipping more than a few lessons.

It was Frank's idea to sneak in through the back since there were more than a few suspicious-looking cars sitting in front, their passengers in shadows so thick even the act of lighting a cigarette couldn't reveal its owner's identity.

Inside and huddled on the auditorium's grey painted floor were the eighty Issei men with an agitated, uncertain look to them. They were the first to be sent to the work gangs. Still wearing their over-coats, their fedoras scrunched down low, they drew into themselves fearful and suspicious.

Standing over them was a sour-faced Morii Etsuji addressing them in an earnest, if chiding, voice. The corners of his mouth drooped toward his chin, his eyes moist and enflamed. He spoke in a clear, crisp Japanese, ably translated for us by Kunio.

"This is a stupid thing to do. You think the *Mountain Police* will let you get away with this?"

"But we gotta do something!" shouted one of the Issei men. "For our families..."

"Baka!" Morii cursed loudly as he adjusted his bow tie and jerked down his vest. He continued with his jaw clenched tightly: "I can do more for your families than you ever could! If you volunteer now, I guarantee that you'll be back with your families."

"Yeah, when?" someone insisted angrily.

"Sooner than you think," was Morii's response.

A grumble rippled through the crowd signalling their dissatis-faction.

"What do you think you'll accomplish?" Morii said with emphasis. "You can carry on and on, prolonging this sit-down as long as you like. But in the end, you'll be dragged off to the immigration building as prisoners. Is that what you want? To be taken away like criminals? You'll only bring trouble to me. I have to answer to many people back in the homeland. *Meiwaku kakeru.* You will cause embarrassment for many, right up to the Emperor. Is that what you want?

Mark my words, everyone in Japan will know how you brought trouble to your families. And they'll be blamed for allowing you to come to this country. I can hear the dirty mouths saying how spoiled you all are. Think for a moment! How will your families be able to live with the shame? If you cooperate, your families can live in dignity. And as a result, they will have an easier time of it. I can promise you that.

Now what do you want? To be dragged off to the immigration building as prisoners, leaving your families to an unknown fate? Or will you go as heroic Japanese men with your heads held up high, as an example for all of Japan to look up to?"

"How do you know they'll do as you say?" cried out another.

"I give you my word. If I fail in this, I will commit *harakiri.*"

"But..."

No one surely believed he would commit suicide, but some were impressed. I certainly was, though I could feel myself being pulled in several directions at the same time. We needed a leader, but Morii? I still suspected an ulterior motive.

"I've talked to the authorities and they've assured me that this is a temporary measure," Morii explained calmly. "If you cooperate, your families here will be safe in their homes and you will rejoin them soon."

Another grumble erupted in the crowd, louder this time, and more insistent.

It sounded as if this whole "volunteer" thing was Morii's idea. "Trust me!" he commanded. "We must think of Japan and the Emperor! Don't bring down the glorious efforts of our troops on the battlefield. Don't surround the Emperor with suspicion and

TERRY WATADA • 69

doubt. I have always had Japan and the Japanese community's best interests at heart! You all know that!"

A temporary measure. I shuddered at the implications. I wanted them to cooperate, but for their own good, not for the Oyabun, and certainly not for the Emperor. I tasted bitterness at the back of my throat.

Before the Issei could react, the auditorium's double doors opened and in marched a contingent of Mounties, police, and military personnel.

I had the feeling there would no longer be any small acts of defiance.

Coordination of public expression of fear of the Japanese-Canadian community on the Pacific Coast is the aim of a "Citizens' Defence Committee" comprising twenty prominent Vancouver citizens, which opened a Marine Building office today.

The committee is circulating a petition urging that military authorities be authorized "to remove immediately enemy aliens and all persons of Japanese origin from key points designated as vital to defence and public safety," and that the government proceed immediately with and announce plans for "humane evacuation of all Japanese from the coast areas."

— *The New Canadian, February 25, 1942*

8.

I started taking aspirin. At first a couple once a day, but eventually I found myself taking multiple pills all day long. I was not one to take pills, but I needed to mask the body pain, caused by stress, I guessed. But then my stomach started to hurt — that and my thoughts were enough to keep me awake at night. No more pills, I decided. I looked for relief somewhere else.

"Otousan," I began, "maybe we can go have dinner at Fuji's Chop Suey? Maybe we can invite Herb and his new wife? We haven't met her yet. I could go look for them," I offered, not knowing Cumberland at all (if he was still there). "It would be nice to be together again."

"Aho," he said abruptly, "you think I'm made of money? And who wants to see that kuso brother of yours?"

"But he's your son."

He dismissed me with a growl and a wave of the hand.

The callousness evaporated off him like cold steam on a frozen pond. I could see a family dinner wasn't going to happen. I then decided to go to Steveston without anyone's knowledge, especially Tommy's.

I knocked on the rough-hewn wooden door of the small kyabin. I felt a pang of guilt for just dropping in on them, but Iso-jima-no okusan did say to me, "Come anytime. You'll always have a place to stay." She was such a great-hearted woman. With her I didn't fear the sting of gossip about my outlandish audacity.

Gladys appeared at the front door, much to my joy and slight embarrassment. She may have seen my consternation, but she ignored it completely. I, in turn, noticed the worried look on her face.

"Oh, Danny, I'm so glad you're here," she said as she reached out to touch my forearm.

"What's happened?" I asked, trying to control my reaction.

"They've come to take our boat. Jimmy went out to bring her in."

SOON GLADYS AND I stood on the muddy banks of the Fraser River waiting for the procession of boats to arrive. The stinging wind slashed around me, reminding me of the Issei journey to this inhospitable, yet promising, land. The Kuroshio, running below the Pacific's pleated surface, was driven by the salt air; the men drew strength from the seascape.

I leaned slightly into the wind, my coat muffled about me to ward off the cold. I thought about putting my arm around Gladys — she might've been shivering, I didn't look — but I didn't. Couldn't do it. Beside us, Watanabe-san, distinguished in his three-piece-black suit, and several of the other now boatless victims bowed their heads in a show of respect and solidarity, for this time, the orderly procession was manned by the individual owners. None of the boats were lashed together.

"There he is!" Gladys shouted as she pointed.

Jimmy stood proud and determined at the helm of one of the boats closest to the shore, closest to us. His back was straight, his hands tight, hard against the cold, making sure his vessel and the others for that matter sailed smoothly and without collision or damage. No sabotage here. I swelled with pride at seeing my friend heroic, defiant. The wind combed his hair smooth as he stared straight ahead, his eyes gleaming, yet tinged with resignation.

Perhaps I romanticized the situation a bit, but on that day there would be no loss of dignity, no sign of weakness in the face of such injustice. Though the hakujin may have been the executioners, these Japanese fishermen sailed to their fates unhumbled.

THAT EVENING AFTER a dinner of delicious fried mackerel and garlic, one of Okusan's specialties, Gladys and I had our first real conversation sitting by the open-faced potbelly stove. The flares of the flames softened her features, shaping her face into a vision of beauty. I was completely enraptured by her.

"Jimmy was late coming back for the holidays, you know," she said with a smile. "He just had to haul in a little extra for us."

The holiday season was from the end of November to the beginning of February, but Jimmy had stayed out into December and so he had not heard about Pearl Harbor until after his return. He had come home to a quietly sobbing mother, and an ever silent, frozen, and damaged father, and worried sister.

"He wouldn't believe me. About Pearl Harbor, I mean."

"I guess I wouldn't either if I hadn't heard it on the radio," I responded.

"Then I told him they're coming for our boat. He didn't believe that either."

I didn't hear her so much, as I was distracted by the firelight playing around her face and hair and the attractive curve of her legs covered by her longish brown dress.

"To think he believed it was a 'temporary measure,'" she smirked.

I knew he didn't. He had known for a long time through his

work with the Fishermen's Association that the hakujin wanted the Japanese, especially in Steveston, out. This was their chance.

"We shouldn't worry so much, if not for papa." She turned to look at her father, who sat expressionless, his mouth slack and drooling, his right hand limp, curled and impotent in his lap, and his one damaged leg, nearly useless, at rest. A skein of fine lines and gouged skin were a testament to a lifetime of skin-shredding wind, flaying salt-water spray, and soul-cracking work.

Our thoughts drifted after that, as if everything paused waiting for us perhaps to fall in love.

MY TIME WITH the Isojima family stood in stark contrast to my own. They reminded me of the Mitsubayshi family: warm, welcoming, and appreciative. When I left Steveston the next morning, knowing full well I'd miss Jimmy — who was probably on his way back from the Annicville Dykes where the boats were impounded — I thought about Dicky, his father and mother, my own mother and father, and then Powell Street. I travelled back into the darkness with only the memory of Gladys to light my way.

Curfew!! — Gosh, and I was all set to write about spring fever and walking in the moonlight with Arabella and so on... now the only way we can enjoy the moon is to poke our heads out of the window and look at it and hope that the love of your life is doing the same thing and thinking the same nice thoughts... what a life.

— The New Canadian, March 3, 1942

9.

March 1942

Dearest Gladys,
  I know I just saw you a short time ago, but I miss your beautiful face and...

Dear Gladys,
  I really enjoyed my visit to your home. Your mom is so generous and such a good cook. Of course, the best part was being with you. You really are a lovely girl...

Dear Gladys,
  I really enjoyed our time together. I trust Jimmy returned okay. The round-up went so smoothly mainly because of your brother. All of Steveston should be grateful...

I never completed the letter. All Japanese-Canadian mail was being censored now. They would've torn it to pieces, and I wasn't comfortable having a stranger read my personal thoughts about Gladys. I put down my pen after a few more attempts when I realized that I may not have the right to court her.

IT WAS MARCH and spring approached as warmer winds descended from the mountains. As a bad omen of things to come, the weather remained cold and bitter when the Government established the British Columbia Security Commission to oversee the "Evacuation" from "strategic" areas of the coast. The commission's first order was a curfew. The second was directed toward able-bodied Nisei between the ages of eighteen and forty-five. They weren't satisfied with Morii's tactic of asking for volunteers. Too slow. We were to join the Issei in the road camps. Our banishment had come.

A few days afterwards a hundred Nisei men were ordered from Vancouver Island and other regions up the coast to leave their homes. They were to have forty-eight hours in which to settle things with their loved ones before reporting for exile to Vancouver and then to parts unknown in the Interior — forty-eight hours to calm the shattered nerves of parents; just forty-eight hours to settle and reassure nervous wives and to comfort frightened children; forty-eight hours to stew in the outrage of the injustice done to Canadian citizens.

I thought about my parents and wondered if I could ever reconcile my feelings about them in so short a time. I could see us saying goodbye (though Mom would be standing in a puddle of defeat) and never seeing each other again. That tragic prospect weighed heavily on me.

And in those forty-eight hours, they came to realize Morii was not to be trusted. They should've known: the man's name was now on every evacuation order, ostensibly as a community representative, but it was obviously a nod and a wink to both the Japanese and the Security Commission — the sign of the devil's "assurances."

The panic took hold as the Nisei scurried around the Powell Street area upon arrival in Vancouver. These men were downright angry as they made their way through the streets from all parts of Powell Street to the Japanese Hall, through the foyer with the freshly waxed floor to the auditorium where they staged a sit-down. They had sweat on their brows and a nothing-to-lose attitude that would make them stand up to any authority that dared get in their way.

Word spread quickly. The police from the Cordova Street Station came in force. I was pasting up the latest issue of *The New Canadian* with Frank when somebody phoned to get reporters down to the scene. I called Tommy in the back room.

It was all too reminiscent of the Issei act of protest last January, only this time the police came loaded for bear. Crowds of onlookers stood in clumps across the street from the Japanese Hall. The drizzle of rain was unrelenting, but no one moved. The grey, ominous clouds seemed to thicken, tightening their grip on the Coast Mountains.

The police formed a semicircle in front of the entrance with truncheons and rifles at the ready as they waited for the order. No anger seethed within them; no visible hatred coursed in their veins. Just a rock-hard sense of duty painted their otherwise blank faces.

Everybody wondered what was going to happen. Would the Oyabun emerge from his Nippon Club lair just as he had done for the Issei? Surely he was watching from his club across the street. And what good would that do anyway? These were Nisei who had little to no respect for Morii. Everybody feared the worst.

As soon as we got there, Tommy went straight for the police captain who stood with a stout man with an umbrella wearing an overcoat and fedora. Captain Delano Maxwell was keeping close counsel with BC Security Commissioner Major Austin Taylor when Tommy broke in on their conversation.

"I'm sorry but you can't do anything rash here!" Tommy said.

"Who the hell are you?" a soggy Taylor asked. He removed his glasses to take a good gander at him.

"I'm Thomas Shoyama, managing editor of *The New Canadian*," he said as authoritatively as he could. "Listen, I know those folks in there. I'm one of them. I can make them cooperate."

"He's all right, Commissioner," the captain said wiping his forehead clear of rain.

Taylor thought a moment before snorting a short puff of

steam. "All right. I'll give you ten minutes. But that's all. You tell 'em I mean business."

The building was musty and humid from the weather. Our clothes took on its heavy odour. Frank stayed outside, like a hostage. The ammonia smell would usually remind me of stern faces, corporal punishment, and echoes of a foreign language that marked us as the enemy.

As Tommy and I walked through the front door this time, I oddly appreciated my parents' insistence on Japanese school. I sensed all that was disappearing. My past was being dismantled, and I ached for its restoration, its salvation, for the sake of those younger than I, if not for myself.

Some families had already moved out of the "ghetto" long before Pearl Harbor; many of my Nisei friends did too as soon as they had graduated high school to look for greener pastures. Kunio and his fiancée were considering Kits and beyond, maybe back east. Perhaps Frank was right; it was a good thing to get away from the pack — just not like this.

The auditorium, with its high ceiling and concrete floor, rumbled with discontent and apprehension. The one-hundred men milled about; some were sitting, others standing to smoke. Huddled together, they shivered, soaked through to the skin, their clothes crushed, but their resolve was unshakeable. They were all Nisei; they were my kind, and we were all of one mind.

The hollow, exhausted look to them gave Tommy and me pause as the crowd shifted to see who had entered. A hundred faces, familiar yet strange, jerked up all at once with curiosity.

Tommy stood before them silent and still. Taking in the enormity of the situation, I suddenly realized he didn't know what to say. Even though he hadn't grown up in the community, he knew them; not individually, of course, but the generation as a whole. He didn't have their nerve, though he felt their frustration. He just couldn't express it.

A lanky man thankfully spoke first. His Nisei accent was at once distinct and friendly. He introduced himself as being from Nanaimo on Vancouver Island. "Say, you're Tommy Shoyama. You write for

The New Canadian. I read you every chance I get!" He smiled broadly as he extended his hand.

Tommy returned the smile and grabbed the hand in a hardy shake. "Glad to meet you…um…"

"Sab. Saburo Hashimoto."

"Sab," Tommy said loudly so everyone else in the room could hear. "I'm here to see if we can't clear this up."

"It isn't that easy. I was on my way to the University of Alberta when they nabbed me. University, Tommy, university," he said with great emphasis. "I was halfway up the Okanagan for Christ's sake! I had a future. Now what happens? I gotta have guarantees," he said, almost in tears. "The rest of the fellahs are in the same boat."

I stood frozen on the spot wondering what Tommy was going to do or say.

"They expect us to fight back," Tommy began. "They're itching for us to act like the enemy. But we're not going to give them the satisfaction. We've got to show them we're as Canadian as any of them.

"Don't think about yourselves in your present situation. Think about the future when we'll be fully accepted. Think about your parents and their safety. And think about your future children, the *Sansei*," he said, looking at me to make sure the term and pronunciation were right. "Make them proud of your actions today and tomorrow."

After some deliberation and a long, excruciating pause, the men decided to cooperate and give up their sit-down. My admiration for Tommy grew ten-fold that day. Perhaps he was the leader we really needed.

The men's only conditions were to be allowed a day's extension to write letters to their families, settle banking matters in the city, and be guaranteed that they would be safe from retaliation.

"You give your word they'll be at the train station tomorrow afternoon?" Major Taylor asked Tommy, his glare probing for deception.

"They promised," he sighed, as a heavier fatigue weighed upon him.

"I want your word."

"You've got it."

AT THE RAILROAD terminal the next day, Frank Morimoto stood looking straight up, watching the birds flitting about the high, iron-trellised ceiling. Tommy and I stood next to him. I puffed on a cigarette to keep warm. It was a habit inspired by Frank; I was sorry I started but it kept me company in the bleakest moments of a bleak time. Tommy paced a bit. He looked tired, fatigued. I don't think he'd had a full night's sleep since Pearl Harbor. The stress was gnawing at his too-thin body. He was not a man who could afford to lose weight; anyone could see that.

I looked sideways at him, evaluating the wear and tear. He worried most of all about his staff — Frank especially, shivering with his thin jacket open because the zipper was broken. Tommy must've felt responsible, and perhaps guilty, since he had asked him and the rest of us to join the *NC* in the first place.

"Don't you have any sweaters?" asked Tommy, pulling at his own beige overcoat to ward off the cold and rain.

"Left them for my *bachaan*," Frank answered.

"Think she'll wear 'em?"

"Probably not. Just like her to mothball them for me, I suppose."

With several Mounties and a couple of Security Commission officials in grey suits and Mackintosh coats to match, the Vancouver press and many well-wishers waited for the next group of men to be shipped out. Every so often, the train exhaled steam in its dock, its grimy cars ready and open for the "evacuees." But no one was there to board. No one to hear the goodbyes of relatives and friends. None of the Nisei "evacuees" had shown up.

"Not again," Frank groaned like a youngster.

The Mounties immediately cordoned off the platform and began examining everyone's permits, ID cards, and other papers.

Nawata Toshiichi, an elderly Issei gentleman who was a regular customer of Sugiura's, stooped over a crooked cane, began speaking in a panic to the officer who had asked for his. "Don't send me to jail!" he begged in Japanese, reaching out at the same time. "Please, I'm an old man. My identity papers are in my Bible at home. I'm a good Christian. I'm here for my son. He's a good boy. Please, you've got to believe me."

"What are you talking about?" said the Mountie, pulling the grasping hands away from his person. "Don't touch me! I don't speak your lingo."

My first impulse was to intercede, but Frank stopped me by saying, "It ain't worth it. Keep a lid on it. You'll just end up in the Cordova Street jail." I froze at the idea of a cold wet cell, and so I retreated — a shame-faced bystander.

"Nawata-san, what's wrong?" a community representative asked in Japanese, trying to relieve the tension. After some discussion, the rep told the RCMP officer, "Mr. Nawata is a retired tailor here to see his son off. He thinks you'll arrest him because of his son's absence."

The Mountie nodded, understanding.

UNFORTUNATELY TOMMY, FRANK, and I weren't so lucky. In the blink of an eye, we found ourselves in an office in the gleaming white Marine Building at the foot of Burrard Street. The room was perfumed with the heavy smell of floor wax, and bedecked with the Union Jack, the Canadian Red Ensign, and a painting of the King. A portly man in a woolen three-piece suit came in through the door, all piss and vinegar. "What the hell happened at the railway station?" Commissioner Major Austin Taylor bellowed.

"No one showed up," Frank offered in his cocky way.

"Oh, a wiseacre, eh?" Taylor yelled. "You wanna be behind bars?"

"The last time we saw them, Commissioner," Tommy interjected, while glaring at Frank, "was yesterday afternoon at the sit-down."

"Yes, the sit-down. I thought you boys cleared that up," he said as he settled into his chair behind his desk.

"We thought we had as well."

"You gave me your word!" accused the commissioner, his mouth suddenly spitting with bile. His mood had turned on a dime. "What do you three know about that sit-down? You didn't organize it, did you?"

"No, of course not!" Tommy said as he turned to me. "It surprised us as much as it did you."

"Where are the men now? What happened to them?"

"I don't know. The last time I saw them was at the Japanese Hall. Just like you."

"So what was that protest all about? Who was responsible?" His face shiny with sweat and blood, the commissioner grew angrier by the second while trying to keep a tight rein on himself. The pressure from his superiors must have been heavy and unrelenting.

"No one was responsible. They were all willing to cooperate. They just needed some guarantee as to the future safety and well-being of their families."

"And they had that!" Taylor said emphatically as he wiped clean the beads of nervous sweat from his receding forehead with a handkerchief. "Brother, you try to show some Christian charity, and what do you get?"

We took a step back as Commissioner Taylor stood and continued his rant to the portrait of the beloved King George VI. "When I catch those sons-of-bitches, straight they go into concentration camps! No cushy roadside camps, no guarantees for their families, no more anything. They've spoiled everything for themselves."

We stood before the elegant desk mulling the irony of his words in nervous contemplation.

JUST BEFORE CURFEW that night, I ventured up the stairs to *The New Canadian* office ahead of Tommy. I noticed an odd light faintly emanating from the top of the stairs. After I brought it to Tommy's attention, we slowed our pace. We heard the murmur of voices. Burglars? There was nothing to steal. We continued to move forward, despite a tingling sense of danger.

Reaching the top landing, we came across a remarkable sight: most of the mob of missing Nisei men, their skin soft in the dull light, were pooled in the small newspaper office as best as they could. The rest flooded the hallway and some of the empty back rooms. They called Tommy and me inside. The crowd shifted and cleared a path for us.

"Tommy!" called Sab Hashimoto. "Come on in." He reached out and pulled Tommy inside. I observed from outside. "Hope you don't mind, but the door wasn't locked, so we made ourselves at home so we could talk to you. We know we put you in a tough spot."

Sitting on his desk with an ease that belied the tension of the situation, Tommy nodded as he listened as calmly as he could to the agitated and disaffected group of Nisei, his compatriots. He was not angry, with no words of accusation forming on his lips. He had forgotten his own situation with the Security Commission.

It was then I noticed a strange aura around his head. His spirit insinuated itself throughout the cramped and crowded room.

"It's just plain wrong, Tommy," Sab said almost plaintively, his oversized nose and thick, round glasses shaking. "They can't take us away like this. If you could've seen my okaasan and my sisters. It was bad enough they took Papa . . . how can they survive?"

"I know, Sab, but you were willing to leave them to go to university . . . your mother and sisters must be strong," he assured. "You know that."

"That's not the point."

"I know," he said in anticipation.

I moved past the door jamb and stretched on tiptoes to see over the crowd.

Tommy cleared his throat before he spoke in a voice that he hoped would be unequivocal in its message, and strong in its conviction. "I know," he repeated to the entire room, "what all of you are going through, but you must cooperate. There's no alternative. If you don't, you'll be taken and thrown in jail. What's going to happen to your families then?"

A disquieted grumble ran along the floorboards as I marked the echo of Morii's words. Was Tommy sure he wanted to go down that road? "Hear me out now," Tommy said with hands raised above his head. "We're not the passive, good little Japanese that Etsuji Morii has painted to the authorities. We don't care about the Mikado, or how much shame we'll bring Him by what we do. He's safe and guarded by a million soldiers! We are Canadians. I told you that yesterday! You must remember that in your hearts!"

Cries of "That kuso Morii!" rang out in agreement.

"It's just that no one in this country believes that," Tommy continued. "Oh, there are those who sympathize with our situation and have taken action to get through to the government, but they're too few and far between. Those against us are nameless, unidentifiable, and numerous, with overwhelming power.

"So the onus is on us. We must prove ourselves to be good, loyal Canadians. And by cooperating with these clearly unfair measures, we will be doing just that! Cooperate and we will earn our place in Canada! Cooperate and be Canadians!"

The men grumbled their displeasure again as a sudden gust of air came through the windows, blowing the black curtains open and swirling around each man like a current of water around rocks. I tasted the salt carried on the breeze. Kuroshio.

A few complaints of "What did he say?" came from the hall, but most heard the message. Soon Sab responded with, "We'll take a flyer on that, Tommy, but, forgive me, not for the reasons you say."

"Then why?"

"It's a damn shame what the government's doing to us. We'll cooperate, yes; we'll cooperate to show them how shameful an act it is."

And with that the men rose to their feet and shuffled out, leaving for the train depot, their mass eventually meandering down the moonlit street like a sluggish river to the sea. They showed no concern for the curfew patrols.

"Property delivered to the Custodian will be administered in the interests of the Japanese evacuated," according to a statement of the Security Commission. "This is not confiscation," declares the statement, which points out that "there seems to be a lack of understanding of the Custodian's duties."

Confusion thus far has arisen over the fact that the administravtive policy of the Custodian had not yet been defined. He is thus unable to answer many details which arise in the disposing of various kinds of property.

— *The New Canadian*, April 6, 1942

10.

March–April 1942

One afternoon, the whole *New Canadian* gang sat in the Fuji Chop Suey House, a Japanese-owned Chinese restaurant on Powell Street near Gore. We had just finished our late lunch of chow mein, sweet and sour pork ribs, tofu and *char shiu*, fried rice, and chop suey. I sat smiling in the middle of what was rapidly becoming familiar; we chewed the fat as if we had done so thousands of times before.

Maybe it was our full stomachs, or the Oriental fantasyland around us with hanging red and gold *chouchin*, Japanese waitresses in *cheongsams*, and a world-weary Chinese cook in back, angry that he had to work in the Japanese part of town when Chinatown was just a few blocks away, but Tommy relaxed his guard. I would never see him as relaxed, in fact, ever again. We certainly needed the break.

I don't know who brought up Ruby Kojima but Tommy waxed poetic about her. "I was knocked out the first time I laid eyes on her. I never believed in love at first sight, but she made me a believer."

"You are too goofy about her," Irene scoffed.

"We do act like teenagers sometimes. We used to meet on the QT in the alley next to the Franciscan Sisters. It smelled of garbage and cat and dog leavings, populated by mice no doubt, but it was paradise to us. During the evening, the light there grew dim, human traffic disappeared, and the noise of the day lessened to a dull, distant roar."

I imagined them standing in their embrace, the curve of their bodies conforming to one another's, her perfume filling his senses.

"I'll admit it, I definitely am in love. I can imagine spending the rest of my life with her," he ended just as the bill came.

I once declared them the Romeo and Juliet of Powell Street, though I didn't want the fate of the star-crossed lovers to be theirs. Maybe I overly romanticized their relationship, but it must've been exciting to sneak around.

"When will it my turn?" I wondered aloud.

"I'm sure it'll be soon," assured Tommy.

"Ach, you're too young," Irene commented. "You're too young to be an idiot in love."

"Irene!" Tommy admonished.

"Oh, right, he's already an idiot." She smiled at her double insult.

The table laughed while Gladys drifted into my mind.

A few days later the war came back to us in full force. Two orders-in-council called for *all* Japanese Canadians to be "evacuated," and for Japanese Canadians to turn over all property and belongings to the "Office of the Custodian of Enemy Alien Property," a bunch of nameless bureaucrats in Ottawa. The Government called them "protective measures" and "temporary measures." The commission began its task by announcing that all Japanese within a hundred-mile security zone along the coast were to be "evacuated."

It wasn't enough that most of the able-bodied Japanese-Canadian men had been kidnapped in the night, torn away from their families. They wanted all of us now. Each of us was like some tumour to be cut out of the precious body of the BC coastline. Our "mass exile" had begun in earnest.

I was grateful I would be spared because of my job, and my parents because of the urgent need of Japanese Canadians for black cloth to guard against airraids (a blackout had now been imposed), but all I could do was stare into the palms of my hands as if some answer were hidden within the lines and creases. Maybe I was fooling myself, but I craved my former life, my childhood full of light and warmth. I lived in a shadow world now, a place where I couldn't escape the very real forces facing Powell Street and BC.

THE SECURITY COMMISSION, Mounties and military acted like some gigantic whirlpool, sucking in all the "Enemy Aliens" along the coast from Vancouver Island to as far north as Stewart, BC, next to the Alaskan border, and sweeping them into the Hastings Park Manning Pool of the Pacific National Exhibition grounds in Vancouver. Only the Vancouver Japanese were spared at this point.

The "Pool" was the staging area; it consisted of about twelve buildings, some former livestock buildings, enclosed by a chain-link fence and guarded twenty-four hours a day by armed sentries. The edges were well-defined, the inside expansive. The men's and women's dormitories were cavernous, each reeking of quicklime and animal excrement. For most, the trauma of the journey ending with the sight of their new homes — row upon row of open cots, or empty horse stalls with their contents barely swept out — was too much. The first arrived on March 16, 1942.

Mrs. Tamaki from up Woodfibre way was there. Mrs. Tanimoto with the club foot was there. The Washimoto family with the daughter who was a little touched in the head was there. Exhausted and depressed, women fell to their mean beds often with their children or babies wailing on top of their silent, still bodies.

Irene Kondo, our five-foot-tall firecracker at *The New Canadian*, tended to the sick and desperate women and children in the Pool. Her shoulder-length curly hair set off her smiling, mischievous eyes, high cheekbones, and toothy smile to marvelous effect as she moved among the desperate women worn out by uncertainty and confusion.

She actually was ideal for the job. In the mid-1930s, her parents pulled her out of UBC and took her to Japan to care for an aunt. Family first, after all, and she was a "girl." As a result she understood the culture, and she could speak and read the language — not as well as Kunio, but "good enough" as she used to say. She was certainly better than I was.

With the build-up to war with the United States, Irene's family thought it best she went home. She shipped out for Vancouver, and then Pearl Harbor hit. Her parents were stranded in Japan. She brooded about them, of course, and turned bitter. To get out of her mood, Irene decided to volunteer at Hastings Park. She had investigated and wrote a column describing conditions. To everyone's astonishment, the commission allowed it to be printed in the *NC*.

> *What circle of Dante's Hades does the "Pool" belong? It's filled with horse stalls! That's where the women and children are expected to live. No matter what's done to the "sleeping quarters" (and the Security Commission has only done the bare minimum) the smell dominates! There's no privacy. The women put up blankets but really there's no privacy. Forgive my language, dear readers, but the toilets stink; wide open and unsanitary, and there are not enough of them for the numbers in the place. Babies cry loudly everywhere as if pitch-forked by demons, their mothers too weak to offer any comfort. Disease is bound to follow in this Dante's inferno.*
>
> *Kay Takahashi, a friend I used to visit in Abbotsford with my family, stood up to one of the security guards when she fished out maggots from the lime sprinkled along the wall of her corral with a stick. The officer just said, "Good enough for you Japs!" She screamed at him, "You ***! You think we're pigs? This place isn't fit place for human beings! For pity's sake, why are you doing this to us?" — By Irene Kondo*

Her words fell on deaf ears.

11.

Because of Kunio Shimizu, I started hanging out with elements of the JCCL. I guess I was seen as his sidekick, like a "little brother." Mostly, though, I was happy to be following him to the meetings; I liked the younger Nisei members of the organization.

Roy Shintani was a man born with a lot of nerve, a man with "bloody intestinal fortitude" as he would've crudely put it. After graduating from UBC, he worked in Port Moody in the lumber mills, but was often seen in Vancouver hanging around the offices of the defunct *Tairiku Nippo* or at BC Hardware with his soon-to-be brother-in-law Tamio Tanemitsu (Roy's sister was engaged to Tamio's brother).

I first knew Roy by reputation only at UBC. With the war, I came to admire him since Kunio Shimizu vouched for him. They were both Victoria boys.

Roy started off as the youngest member of the Japanese Canadian Citizens League, the political body of all the Nisei organizations. At twenty-three years old, Roy had the energy of his youth and was blessed with innate intelligence, even though, with his characteristic bow tie, slight body, crew-cut hair and high forehead, he looked rather conventional.

ONE DAY KUNIO took Roy down to the Steveston docks. Roy observed an RCMP officer and several soldiers standing with their rifles at the ready around a bunch of fishermen on Pier 68. There were mounds of suitcases, boxes, and trunks tied with rope or wire scattered everywhere on the platform. The Mountie, a head or two taller than the crowd around him, was a real sourpuss. He obviously had no sympathy for any so-called "Enemy Alien." The wife of one of the men grabbed at him. "Please," she begged in Japanese, "let me go with my husband. I can't survive by myself!"

"Jesus Christ, lady, get away from me!" he said, pushing her away. "I can't understand a word you're saying and, if I did, I couldn't do anything anyway." Even with a translator, the Mountie stood emotionless, unsympathetic. "I got my orders."

She collapsed right then and there. Her dress quickly absorbed the pool of saltwater on the dock, the distinctive blood of Steveston. Kunio helped her up and escorted her away.

"Come on, give her a break," Roy begged.

The Mountie stood resolutely silent.

This scene was being played out not only on the docks up and down the coast, but on train platforms in Vancouver. So it was right then and there that Roy resolved that cooperation was not the answer. He had to step up his fight for justice — to the last ounce of his strength if it came to that.

"GODDAMNIT, I CAN'T believe what's going on out there!" Roy said to disgruntled JCCL members gathered in mid-March, 1942, after the sawdust of the Powell Street hardware store had settled for the day. The small gathering stayed in the back because of the newly imposed curfew and blackout. I was there as a courtesy, a representative of the newspaper, though mum was the word. "I don't like the league's stand on cooperation!" Roy continued. "I feel like we're letting them sons-of-bitches put a gun to our heads and asking them to pull the trigger."

"Now, take it easy, Roy," Tamio, the storekeeper, advised in his comforting voice in the pall of moonlight shadows. Tamio was a smart guy, only a couple of years older than the others in the JCCL, but much wiser than his age. His round face went in and out of the shadows as he patiently rested his hands on his lap. "You know they just want us to set a good example. Look what happened after the two sit-downs, all the threats and carry-throughs. We've got a lot of bad blood to mop up."

I simply nodded, having played witness to those sit-downs. I kept quiet about the insidious nature of the Government and the ulterior motives of the BC politicians.

"Ha!" Roy foolishly said, dismissing him out-of-hand.

By the next JCCL meeting, the Security Commission ordered Roy to move to Vancouver. It was no sweat off his brow since he was spending most of his time there. He was lucky to stay with his brother-in-law, instead of Hastings Park, a place said to be overrun with rats, maggots, and dysentery. His move was also unfortunate for the JCCL, because both he and Tamio could campaign for their position of evacuation of families a lot easier.

"No one leaves Vancouver without his family!" Roy demanded to yet another secret and perilous after-hours gathering of the league at the *Tairiku Nippo*, this time including anti-JCCL parties. The office was a place of chaos with its high windows and black curtains and cluttered furnishings. Dust from inactivity covered everything. Piles of past editions advertised community dances, bazaars, and baseball games: glimpses of the not-so-long-ago days.

"Are you against us?" Kunio asked.

"Look," Roy said, "We're all friends here, but we can't just lie down and give in to government demands. We just want what's best for our people."

"So you are against us," concluded Kunio.

"We all have parents and young brothers and sisters to look after," Tamio added. "How are we going to do that if we're sent to some lonely camp in some godforsaken location?"

Everyone agreed, but still the "damned thick-headed league," as Roy characterized them, preached cooperation. Tommy Shoyama adjusted his glasses as he rose to speak. "I understand your anger, Roy, but the commission can't change its position. They're under pressure to complete the evacuation, and don't have the manpower to carry it out in family groups."

"What?" Roy exploded. "Stop being some kind of *inu!*"

"Now listen here! That's not fair," Kunio Shimizu shouted as he grabbed him by the collar. He was ready to strike, like when they were kids. But he didn't, much to everyone's relief. Instead, Kunio addressed everyone in the room, though he was looking straight at Roy and Tamio. "We've been in negotiations with the commission for weeks, and it's very clear a temporary separation is inevitable. You've got to understand, there's no way to avoid it. Tommy and I believe they'll make every effort to reunite the families in due course. But let me be clear: we know it's not in our best interests that we be interned." Crimson in the face, Kunio turned away from Roy with a dismissive grunt.

By this point, I was only in the JCCL out of loyalty to Tommy and Kunio. In my heart of hearts, I disagreed with cooperation. I yearned to stand and fight. Present a united front and hit back hard, violently if necessary, though I doubted I would. My parents were always present in my mind. I couldn't put them in jeopardy of reprisal or bring shame to them. They were still holding on to the store, but only by their fingertips. I saw my parents' relationship fraying at the edges. With a disgraced son, there was no telling what would happen to them.

"We also know we can use that pressure to our advantage," Tamio continued calmly. "Every day the newspapers are full of complaints that there's more Japanese in Vancouver now than there ever was before Pearl Harbor. If we stick to our guns, we can force them to evacuate us in families."

SUCH AN IMPASSE could not be allowed to stand. "United we stand, divided we fall." Tommy and Kunio knew their position would be compromised if the Government saw division in the ranks. Sure enough, Kunio soon asked to have a word with Roy. It was a Sunday afternoon, and the three of us sat in the New Pier Café, the usual hangout for young couples or single people looking for a decent meal for a good price. Kunio and Marion always liked the red chouchin that hung in the windows, obviously bought in Chinatown, but fancy enough to bring a little romance, maybe glamour, to Powell Street.

Everyone had a crush on the proprietress, Hiraishi. She was married, but flirting wasn't off-limits. Her husband Naotoshi was a milquetoast. "Bullet" Gotanda, the eighteen-year-old left fielder for the Asahis and local bully, would make faces at Hiraishi through the café's window every morning as he waited for the streetcar. She would do the same back.

Unadvisedly I used to make fun of him. "Hey, Bullet, you chewing cud or what?" He always chased me, but never caught me. Thank the Buddha. I knew I was playing with dynamite, but deep down I never really thought the big galoot would do me any great harm.

Roy sat patiently in the café waiting for Kunio to say something. They had ordered pie, but I nursed a glass of water — something that irritated Hiraishi.

Even though Kunio was older than Roy by a few years, they had played together growing up in Victoria until Kunio left with his grandmother for Japan. The two boyhood adversaries got into many fist fights. Even Roy didn't know why, since he never won. He couldn't help himself, he claimed, but he did have a temper that went off like spit on a hot griddle.

Roy didn't see his childhood friend again until Kunio returned at age sixteen. By his twenties, university-educated and about to be hitched to Marion Akamatsu, a Kitsilano gal from a good family, Kunio had certainly changed, but to Roy he was the same: generous, opinionated, and the kind of guy he liked to fight.

"Roy, I'm here as a friend," Kunio finally said after he dug into his cherry pie.

"Now that doesn't sound like good news is around the corner."

"I'm being serious."

Roy dropped the pose and let his face settle. "Okay, what's up?"

"I'm here about this 'mass evacuation' business."

"Kuni, I'm not changing..."

"I know. That's just it. The league wants you, Tamio, and Tak Kawai to resign."

"What? Why, goddamnit?" A few customers looked his way. Hiraishi frowned.

"Quiet, lower your voice," Kunio admonished as he looked around the café. "For once in your life, control your temper." As an afterthought, he added, "You swear too much."

After a strategic pause, Kunio continued: "Your 'viewpoint' . . . your stand is only causing dissention within the ranks and that can't be good for our negotiations. You'll be getting a formal letter soon, but I wanted you to hear it from me first."

Roy shouldn't have been shocked or angry, but he just had to react. "Is this Tommy's idea? He's been against us from the start!"

"It wasn't just Tommy's idea. You've ruffled more than a few feathers."

"I appreciate it, Kuni," he said, resigned to his fate. "Not your fault."

"Look, I tried to stick up for you, but the times are so uncertain for this kind of divisiveness —"

"I said it's not your fault," Roy assured. "Don't worry about it, old friend. It'll all work out in the end."

"But I do worry about you, Roy. I've known you too long not to. Your anger's gonna get you in more trouble than you can handle one day."

Kunio's dismissal of the *namaiki* was his last JCCL act.

ONE DAY SHORTLY thereafter, Frank made his usual crashing entrance into the *NC*.

"Geez-us!" Irene exclaimed. "Do you have to do that every time?"

"Tommy! Tommy!" Frank yelled in a panic.

"What?" Tommy answered as he came out of his office.

"Tommy, Kunio's gone. They got him."

None of us could do or say anything. We stared at each other for a few moments, until Tommy retreated into his office and picked up the phone. I don't know who he called, but it was a heated discussion. After he hung up, he came out to the rest of us. "It's true, they got him right in front of his house. Morii must be behind this."

"Morii? Why him?" Frank asked.

Irene barked, "Oh, wake up!"

Frank's naiveté was endearing, but he could be thick once in a while.

Tommy opined, "We all know the Oyabun is jealous of our perceived influence with the Security Commission. He wants to be the only game in town, and that means neutralizing us. With or without Kunio, we won't let him."

Something in the way Tommy spoke made my eyes water. I felt a swelling in my chest; I suppose we all did.

Tommy later talked with his fiancée Marion to see if she knew where they had taken Kunio, but she didn't know.

"Probably back east," I concluded.

Without Kunio, Tommy had no "in" with the younger Issei, older Nisei and Kika Nisei, the Oyabun's constituency. Irene and I could understand Japanese, but she wasn't as good as Kunio, and I only had simple conversational ability. Also, being a woman, she hadn't much credibility with Morii's crowd. Her university background was not an asset, either. And I was too young to be taken seriously. This was going to be a problem.

A COUPLE OF days later, the league sent Roy, Tamio, and Takashi Kawai, another member who wanted mass evacuation, a letter requesting their resignations.

"...engaged in activities contrary to the best interest of the League," Casey Nakanishi read aloud. The meek grocery clerk with two others had carried the message to BC Hardware.

Roy confessed to being tickled at the thought that the league considered them such threats. Nonetheless, he simmered in a slow burn. "Contrary to the interests? You dumb bastards!"

"Hey you..." said the brawny, but dim, Bullet Gotanda. I suppose Bullet was there as the "muscle," just in case. Bullet predictably grabbed a convenient hammer, and Roy countered by picking up an axe handle.

"Go make faces at your girlfriend!" Roy retorted.

Like a fool I stood between them. What was I thinking?

Tamio, as quick as ever, said, "Use them, bloody them, do anything to 'em, and you pay for them!" They relaxed and backed down.

*Major Austin Taylor and Assistant Commissioner FJ Mead at noon
today told The New Canadian and the Citizens' Council that the
statement published last night by the "Nisei Mass Evacuation Group"
(to the effect that the Commission had ruled that the Nisei are "by law
Japanese nationals") was "absolutely untrue"...*

*"As far as the evacuation is concerned, the regulations must apply to
all persons of the Japanese race," he continued, "but it would be stupid of us to make a statement as untrue as that."*

— *The New Canadian*, April 18, 1942

12.
March–April, 1942

Someone at Powell Grounds pointed Jimmy Isojima out to
me. I was there to cover the JCCL rally to convey information to the remaining inhabitants of the area. Turns
out my fisherman pal came looking for me.
"Danny, you gotta come back to Steveston!"

I shushed him because Hisaoka Bunjiro, the well-to-do Vancouver businessman, had begun speaking. He announced the
formation of the Naturalized Japanese Canadian Association or
Kikajinkai. He and his people were about to negotiate with the
Security Commission for self-supporting camps. A grumble rolled
through the crowd. Jimmy was particularly agitated.

At the end of the rally, the two of us sought him out to talk to
him. We hardly had any credibility with him, but Tak and Roy soon
joined us to escort Hisaoka to the offices of the defunct *Tairiku
Nippo* newspaper. We tagged along.

The place was an ancient ruin with Roman columns of disorganized newsprint and dusty and spent bottles of ink. Uneven piles of files on lonely, unused desks. The waste baskets were full. Seemed like a sad, perfect mausoleum for our dying community. The musty smell made my nose run, and I was forever pulling out my handkerchief.

Tak, Roy, and Jimmy surrounded the businessman who sat calmly at an empty desk. I leaned against another desk out of the way, occasionally blowing my nose and apologizing. I resisted pulling out a cigarette to smoke.

"I'm with you fellows all the way, and I want to talk to you about your actions in the future," Hisaoka said in Japanese.

"So you won't talk to the commission?" asked Jimmy in response.

"I haven't yet."

"They're about to give in and talk to us."

"You mentioned a meeting in Steveston?" Hisaoka said, as if to distract the conversation.

"Yes, yes, a big one next week." Tak raised his voice as he cupped his ear. Being middle-aged, he appeared to be losing his hearing. "It's being organized by the Steveston Fishermen's Association. Jimmy here's in charge."

"Mr. Watanabe's in charge," Jimmy corrected. "He said that he'd like to see you there."

"All right, I be there," Hisaoka said in broken English.

"Right and you won't mention your new association? Just give us some time." Hisaoka nodded in a non-committal way.

Afterward I pulled Jimmy aside on the street. "What is this meeting in Steveston?"

"That's what I was trying to tell ya. You gotta come," he urged. "We're having a meeting, an important meeting. We're gonna see what we can do about this here 'Evacuation' that they're calling for. Mr. Kawai, Mr. Uchiboro, and Mr. Shintani are gonna be there. Mr. Watanabe —"

"Okay, Jimmy, okay," I assured.

He then added with a grin, "My okaa'll make you her famous misoshiru again."

"Sure thing Jimmy, count me in," I said.

"And Gladys will be helping," he added.

Was I that obvious? Guess he thought I needed extra incentive. It worked; the deal was sealed in my books. Maybe Jimmy was giving me the green light, his blessing.

Tommy readily gave me permission to go as a newspaper rep. "I know about the meeting," he said, giving me a knowing look.

I had to ask, "How? I just found out about it."

"I just know," was all he said.

ON A DREARY, rainy night in late March, the public meeting at the Steveston Buddhist church began at seven o'clock to discuss the possibility of "Mass Evacuation" as opposed to mere "Evacuation." The guest speakers, Takashi Kawai, Roy Shintani, and Uchiboro Shigeichi had been kicked out of the JCCL for wanting to fight the Government about breaking up families. They were considered namaiki. Nevertheless, the Steveston fishermen wanted to hear what they had to say.

The modest building — a converted Methodist church with picket fence in front and peaked roof on top — had been painted a gleaming white to maintain its anonymity from the prying and pious Christians. The inside, too, was white, stubbornly clean, and bright when the sun came out. The members kept up the place, even though the weather and sea air really tore the paint right off the walls. The inside felt dull and clammy despite the packed house. It was a large one-room building with a makeshift altar at one end that had a scroll said to have been owned by the Lord Abbot Rennyo. How it got there, no one ever knew. The word on the street was that a Mr. Sato had brought it as a gift from Reverend Shigeno in Japan, but no one knew for sure. Volunteers had cleared out the folding chairs of the *hondo* making the event standing-room only. The one lectern stood in front of the butsudan. The church's large incense burner stood silently off to the side, cold and unlit.

Jimmy had lined up five chairs behind the lectern for the special guests. The middle-aged Takashi Kawai, a Nisei, sat closest to the podium. His closely shaved head nodded every so often, looking as if he was enjoying the attention. Next to him was Roy Shintani, the good-looking fellah with a slim body and youthful face. He was reputed to be the smartest of the bunch. I'd have to agree. Uchiboro Shigeichi, an Issei and the oldest of the speakers, moved around next to him, nervous for everything to commence.

I sat with Jimmy in the front row, twitching in anticipation, though I really couldn't understand why. I wasn't going to speak. Maybe it was the energy of the crowd. There were a lot of men there that night.

The situation in Steveston was worse than in Vancouver, despite the recent sit-down by the Issei road gang members at the Japanese Hall. There seemed to be an urgent need to band together in the fishing village.

Watanabe Etsuo, the meeting Chair, stood to address the crowd just as the noise level reached its loudest. He set his notes down, put on his small, round glasses, and looked at the crowd of working men, wearing boots, coveralls, plaid shirts, and broken-peaked caps. They stood with grim resolve with their five-o'clock shadows making their faces darker.

"Gentlemen," he said as he opened his suit jacket, "you know why we're here tonight. I thank you for braving such bad weather to attend." His Japanese was clear and angry enough for the back of the room where the Fujinkai ladies waited to serve the refreshments — green tea, manju, and *senbei* — after the meeting. "The matter of mass evacuation as opposed to individual evacuation is obvious. We cannot settle for the latter. It's not democratic. This is not Fascist Italy! We are loyal Canadians!" A burst of applause as Watanabe-san finished in a loud voice, impressing the crowd, before giving way to the next speaker, Uchiboro Shigeichi.

Of the three leaders, Uchiboro's booming voice was by far the most emotional. "I will not stand for this anymore!" he shouted in commanding Japanese, his eyes spiking with anger. "Our people are literally disappearing right off the streets! The BC Security Commission's offer to send families together to Alberta is a devil's bargain. I've been getting reports of bitter weather, brackish water, and of men using pickaxes to break through the dirt. It's no favour they're doing us!"

"But it's a sign they'll negotiate!" someone cried out desperately.

"Think that if you want!" he snapped back. "Remember that when it's forty below and the wolves are howling at your door."

"Then we should cooperate like Morii-san said!" someone else shouted.

"Baka!" Uchiboro thundered. "Morii's in it for himself, and nothing else! Don't be fooled by false gods! Morii acts like our saviour, but whatever he gives with one hand, he and the government take with the other!"

Everyone mumbled agreement on that point. I continued taking notes as Jimmy translated for me. I just couldn't catch it all given my limited Japanese.

"This is stupid!" called an unexpected voice from somewhere in the middle of the room. A young Nisei with a crazed look pushed his way through the crowd, finally breaking through to stand next to the speaker. He stood obviously nervous in a white undershirt, dungarees, and work boots, the uniform of the troublemaker. "I'm Kaga Etsu and don't you forget that!" he shouted in flawless Japanese. "Don't listen to him or his stooges," he added, as he waved in the general direction of Uchiboro and the other two.

I stared at the intruder, tingling at Kaga's audacity; how such a "teenager" could stick his nose into something so obviously beyond him was outrageous. I self-consciously looked away, hoping no one connected us because of our shared youth.

Several men rushed forward, but stopped short when Kaga raised his hands demanding to be heard. Watanabe Etsuo signalled to let him speak. "Don't you people know?" Kaga asked in desperation. "You call yourselves Canadians because you immigrated here or you were born here, but think about how the Canadian government's treating you. They only make promises if it works for them! Think about it, and you'll see how you've betrayed the Japanese blood that's flowing in you!"

Everyone laughed hard at him. "Put some clothes on!" someone yelled from the crowd.

"Yeah, come back when you're decent and grown up!"

Self-consciously tugging his undershirt down over his dungarees, Kaga soldiered on, even though his pimples, his slicked-back long hair, and his muscular, but skinny, body made him look like a kid who just lost his ball. No one was taking him seriously. "You must act like true Japanese and fight with everything you've got against this damn country!" he insisted. "Be true to our Japanese principles and you'll be rewarded for your loyalty! It's our duty to cause as much trouble as we can for the enemy Canadians!"

"Ketsunoana!" someone shouted. "Go back to where you came from, you goddamn Emperor worshipper!"

"No, listen! Listen to me! It's not like that!" Kaga insisted.

"Order! Order!" Watanabe called. "We must have order here!"

The men in the crowd pushed and elbowed, ready to do some harm to the young guy.

"Get that boy out of here!" Watanabe finally called.

Jimmy moved at the command and he and two others removed the troublemaker from the premises.

DURING THE LONG, four-hour meeting in that cramped room filled with loud talk, humidity, and lung clogging cigarette smoke, many yelled out their personal situations. All the leaders could do was sympathize and present only two alternatives: further cooperation through either the JCCL or Morii, or negotiation to allow families to stay together when they left Vancouver. My ears pricked up when someone suggested that maybe Tommy Shoyama was right: cooperation was the key. But that was soon dismissed in a fog of muttering and complaint.

Throughout the proceedings, I couldn't help but think of Etsu Kaga again and again. I began to give him credit and the benefit of the doubt. *His voice was just as relevant as anyone else's*, I reasoned. Something about his passion, his *bushidou* ideals, stayed with me. Still, I didn't want to talk about him or anything else, not even to Jimmy. I could see that if these rubes could toss the young man out, then Tommy's views about cooperation didn't have a chance.

At long last, Watanabe-san called on Hisaoka Bunjiro, the wealthy Vancouver boat builder. There was some confusion since he wasn't scheduled to speak. Then again, he was no Etsu Kaga interrupting the proceedings with so-called namaiki nonsense.

Just by standing with his hands on his wide hips, his jaw set, his eyes filled with blood, Hisaoka willed the crowd to settle down to a standstill. He drew in his breath to speak in plain Japanese: "Our primary concern here should be to keep our families together. The separation of fathers from their wives and children is what's causing all the hardship, especially when the dogs come preying on the weak. These men, these good men, advocate mass evacuation in families," he said, pointing to the three seated guests. "And I respect these good men for their intentions, but they have no idea what they're up against. There's no guarantee the BC Security Commission will negotiate. There's no guarantee they will even consider the idea of mass evacuation of families!" He paused before delivering the final blow: "I've been in personal contact with Commissioner Austin Taylor and he has agreed, in principle, to allowing families to be evacuated together if they can afford to go it alone. We figured about $1,800 per family should just about do it. Everyone will be relocated together in what will be known as self-supporting camps."

The crowd got ugly with that. They began weighing the significance of what was revealed and shuffled their feet. The whispers became loud arguments as a few started to shout their disapproval. "We can't afford that!" A few clenched their fists while looking for things to throw.

As a heavier rain pounded against the windows, punctuated by thunder, Hisaoka raised his arms to call the meeting back to order.

TERRY WATADA · 103

Neither nature, nor the crowd, could be quelled. "He's right!" called out one Issei fisherman who held up a small book. "I'm not going to one of their goddamned jails or work gangs or whatever," he declared, "and if this here bank passbook can allow me and my family to evacuate together, then so be it!" The mob's roar rolled like a gale-force wind tossing a hapless boat.

"Gentlemen, gentlemen," Hisaoka called, "I know that for most of you this is an impossible solution, but these are difficult times."

"How can you do that?" Jimmy suddenly shouted from beside me. "We're under the gun, and you've pulled the trigger! You were right there with Mr. Takashi Kawai, Mr. Roy Shintani, and Danny when I told you the Commission was ready to give into our demands!"

I scanned the crowd anticipating a riot. My belly tingled like soda water. I felt exposed, right out in the open.

"The Commission's getting a lot of pressure from the public," Jimmy reasoned, twisting away from Hisaoka to face his fellow fishermen. "Don't you know? People are mad that Vancouver has more Japanese in it now than before Pearl Harbor! The Commission has...had no choice but to negotiate with us." He then wheeled around and pointed at Hisaoka. "You promised not to go to the Commission with your plan. Now why should they listen to us? They'll just claim a plan is in place to evacuate families together!"

"I'm sorry Jimmy but...I didn't promise anything."

"Damare!" he shouted with a force that surprised everyone. "We must be united! Divided we fall! We must negotiate for mass evacuation, not better treatment for the wealthy!"

A tidal wave of protest rose up. I was just as taken in by Hisaoka's duplicity, and was caught up in the crowd's emotion. "As I said," Hisaoka resumed, his booming voice once again quieting things down to a dull murmur, "these are difficult times. If I have the money to save my family, as one sane man said tonight, then I'm damn well going to use it!" His words rang out, stunning everyone into silence.

At the end of the evening, the majority voted to continue to negotiate for evacuation with families leaving intact. The decision became known as the Steveston Resolution. It was a profound move. Being poor fishermen, they couldn't afford the self-supporting solution.

Despite the establishment of the formal proposal, Jimmy was rattled by Hisaoka's double-cross. *How could anyone go back on their word?* Jimmy was probably thinking in his innocence. He remained dumbstruck as participants milled about exchanging opinions and niceties.

After the meeting, the principals began the task of forming a new organization. Jimmy Isojima agreed to take on a key leadership role in the newly formed Nisei Mass Evacuation Group [NMEG].

13.

I gave up the chance to see Gladys that night. Jimmy was too upset for me to ask to sleep over. I took Tommy's money and stayed overnight in a local hotel — a bit of a dive, but I just wanted to sleep. I hoped at least to dream about Gladys. I felt a sadness come over me as I sat on the bed. I soon fell over and got under the sheet for an uneasy and dreamless sleep.

The next day, I found myself in Vancouver again. I first went to the store to change my clothes and to check on my parents; I hadn't seen them in a while.

"Oh, you-ka?" said my father. "Did you go somewhere?"

I didn't answer.

It was business as usual: my father sweeping the floor; my mother nervously cleaning the kitchen upstairs. When she came downstairs, she immediately rushed to me to say something. She stood constantly rubbing her hands in front of me.

Apparently the Mounties felt the business was still hands-off. Sugiura's Dry Goods provided a service, but who knew how much longer that would last. Despite the uptick in prosperity, I found my mother still crackling with worry, my father steadfastly stoic.

"Okaa, everything all right?" I asked.

"Dani-chan, no one's coming in anymore," she blurted.

"I guess that's to be expected. Everyone's got what they need," I explained as my father turned his back and walked into the back.

"What's going to happen to us? Are we leaving like everyone? I don't want to go to Hastings Park."

I knew she wouldn't have to go, but I didn't correct her. She wouldn't have believed me.

After a bath and a bite to eat, I headed over to the *NC* office. Everyone was there to greet me. It all seemed normal. I knocked on Tommy's door. He sat as usual behind his desk, mulling over the editorial, I guessed. He didn't even look up.

"I'm back," I said.

"So you are. How was it?" He lifted his gaze to me as he adjusted his glasses.

"Good. I got a great story about the meeting. The ousted leaders of the JCCL were there to —"

"All right, we'll mention it in the paper."

"Mention? Tommy, this is the start of a new organization: the Nisei Mass Evacuation Group. They're gonna renegotiate the breakup of families."

"Okay, and how far do you think the Security Commission will allow that in the paper?"

"Who cares?" I surprised myself. I couldn't believe I raised my voice to my editor, but my writing was becoming useless. I didn't even have my byline anymore.

"I care," he said in an equally loud voice. "Listen, you write what I tell you to write! Do as I tell you."

"But Tommy, that's censorship. We can't tolerate..." I was immediately sorry and my eyes pleaded with him.

"That's enough," he said abruptly. "I'm sick of your whining. Get to your desk and write it up anyway you want, but I will cut it any way I want."

I couldn't say anything after that.

AS I WAS leaving the office, Frank pulled me aside and said, "Let's get some air."

Outside the street was pretty well empty, which suited me fine. The sun shone overhead; Powell Street was at peace, giving the day a cheery feeling, but it was anything but.

"What's with Tommy?" I asked. "I've never seen him so angry."

"You don't know?" Frank began. "He broke up with Ruby."

"What?"

"Her father, Kojima Sensei, ordered her to breakup with him."

"Ordered? This isn't feudal Japan."

"I know that, but Ruby told him she, or rather her father, didn't like what he was printing in the paper."

"Like what? There's nothing in there that —"

"The editorials against Morii."

"Oh, come on, his name's never mentioned."

"Yeah, I know, but the Oyabun probably didn't like what wasn't said, if you know what I mean."

"Man, oh man," I fretted while hand-combing my hair. "No wonder Tommy's so mad."

"You know Kojima-san is under the Oyabun's thumb."

"I know, I know."

"His students give Morii protection."

"I said I know," I said rather abruptly. We were all on edge.

As shocked as I was at Tommy's outburst, I understood. Still, I had a feeling my time at the *NC* was rapidly drawing to a close.

SOON THEREAFTER HAMMERHEAD introduced me to Etsu Kaga, but really I was aware of the namaiki leader long before that from judo, and some of his community activities.

By the time Kaga was twenty years of age, he had already had a hard life. As a young fisherman's son up Skeena way, he always did what he wanted, no matter what his father said or warned against.

As the story went, the family moved to Vancouver while his father remained in the wilderness earning a living in the logging camps. Kaga and his mother took a room at the New World Hotel on Powell Street so that he could attend school. He was short, plump, with a face full of pimples, so kids teased him constantly. He was often the target of the bully boys and silly girls because of his *inaka* manners. "It's Windy Kaga!" the boys and girls yelled or squealed from a safe distance. "Don't stand too close to him. He farts in school, in church, all the time! Windy, windy, windy! *Onara Face!*" And bully boys like Bullet Gotanda beat him on a daily basis. Kaga was seen so many times dragging himself home, head hung low, body cramped up, and quietly cursing. I felt sorry for him, but what could I do?

In the 1920s, he and his mother went to Japan. His father remained in the Interior, until a donkey machine's wire snapped and cut him in two. The local Buddhist minister sent a letter to Japan, but no response came back. Nobody saw Kaga again until 1930 when he returned to Vancouver as a full-fledged Kika Nisei. He appeared different: confident and trim with a muscled body and woodblock head, walking tall, his loyalty to the Emperor and Japan unending. They must've accepted him warts and all over there.

With confidence comes brashness. Within the first month, Kaga searched the streets until he found Bullet Gotanda, his old tormentor. I stood on a nearby corner and witnessed the whole episode.

Bullet was a huge boy, raised on meat and not much else. He played baseball and engaged in most sports. He wasn't much for school and let his fists do the talking. He stood with his girlfriend, Sachi Tokunaga, a not-so-very-pretty girl with an underbite, before Kaga, just like Goliath before David. "Well, if it ain't Onara Face!" Gotanda guffawed. His girl chuckled into her hands.

"Damare, you ketsunoana," Kaga exploded in Japanese.

Though Bullet didn't understand the language fully, he knew he had been insulted. Without thinking, he threw a punch, which Kaga easily avoided. He then jumped into the air and viciously jack-knifed a kick, catching Sachi by the side of the head. She fell in a lump on the sidewalk, stunned.

"You touch me again," Kaga warned, "I'll beat her worse."

Bullet looked at him in shock. "You nuts or something? You don't hit a girl."

"I did and will again. Mark my words."

Bullet quickly helped the hapless girl to her feet and led her away. The look on their faces told me Kaga wouldn't have any more trouble from the bully boys or silly girls.

Everyone heard about the incident and, though people were horrified at what Kaga did to poor Sachiko, no one bothered him as they watched him and his mother move into a boarding house on Alexander Street. They made no comment when he joined the Vancouver Honbu, Kojima Sensei's judo dojo. He had excelled in the fundamentals of the sport in Japan. As it so happened I was taking lessons. Being a yellow belt at that point, I never got to know him, other than hearing about his achievements. More importantly, when word of his prowess got around Powell Street, no one called him "Windy Kaga" ever again.

PERHAPS BECAUSE OF his Kika Nisei background, Kaga began attending Morii's lectures about the war in China. I, of course, saw him there but I paid him no mind.

"It is His Imperial Majesty's manifest destiny to rule not only China but all of Asia! This holy war with China will bring about the Emperor's true exalted place in history and the world!" Morii spewed his propaganda every Saturday evening in the Japanese Hall to a stamping and shouting audience of Issei labourers and businessmen, whose sense of loyalty to the homeland made them open to every word he said. They cheered at the end with a standing ovation. "Japan is superior in culture and military might. I know that. You know that. Now everyone must come to know that! We have no choice!"

Etsu Kaga sat with the crowd with his mouth wide open and eyes nearly in tears. Morii was a kind of patriotic god. Kaga fell under the spell of Morii, all fire and lightning at the podium, confident in the certainty of his views.

IN THE DAYS leading up to World War II, Kaga became known for his Imperial nationalism and recruited like-minded Nisei. Behind his back, people started calling him namaiki for the way he ran around town distributing pamphlets, carrying Morii's weekly anti-China message. He scrambled in and out of businesses, up and down boarding-house steps, proudly wearing the *hachimaki* with the hinomaru of Imperial Japan around his head.

After Pearl Harbor, when the Mounties came after the leaders, Kaga got worse. He kept complaining to his growing group of Japanese loyalists and possible recruits about living in the "enemy's country." Many "Canadian" Nisei had pointed suggestions for him as a result: "Don't like it here? Go back to Nippon, you Mikado-loving bastard!"

The first time Kaga formally spoke out in public was at that Steveston meeting. It was the perfect occasion with the Government rounding up the boats. Though the namaiki was shouted down that evening, I saw the spark of greatness in him. I couldn't understand why no one listened to Kaga, calling him a trouble-maker. That got my dander up, but I was powerless to do anything. His kind of talk was considered dangerous, even though many had seen their friends and fathers picked up by the RCMP for being Japanese nationals. No charges were ever laid. No lawyers. No communication of any kind was allowed. Just boats confiscated while many faced incarceration and exile.

I wanted nothing to do with Kaga or his followers. His kind of talk meant trouble.

ONE DAY I was cornered in Ernie's Café by Hammerhead.

"He needs our help," Hammerhead insisted.

"Who?" I asked.

"Tenno Heika."

"The Emperor?" I was taken aback that my childhood friend had fallen in with the namaiki.

"Hey, keep your voice down! And speak Japanese," Hammer-head advised. "You know just as good as I do what's happening in the South Pacific and China. You know about all the young Japanese joining up."

"What're you saying?" I asked in English. Who was listening anyway?

"I'm just saying the war's gonna come right to Canada, maybe right to Powell Street. Don't you see?"

"What're we gonna do?" I complained.

"We want to start a resistance movement!" he said suddenly in English. Speaking the "mother tongue" was just too difficult for what he had to say. "We got to do something here to support the Emperor's army."

"Who are *we*?"

I was pretty sure Hammer didn't know what the word "resistance" meant. My guess was his pal and mentor Kaga got the idea from some old Japanese magazine. It's the kind of thing that was being printed all the time.

"You should meet Etsu Kaga. He'll set you straight."

I thought about an exclusive story for the *NC*, so I went along for the ride. He introduced me to Kaga a couple of weeks after Steveston. Shikataganai.

RIGHT OFF THE bat I could see that Kaga was a natural-born leader, if a little fanatical. Even as a young man he was a runt, standing only four-foot-ten-inches, shorter than most. But there was a fire in him, a pride that might've attracted death. His eyes were bright like twin rising suns. His body was always tense, always coated with a slight film of sweat, as if he was ready for action. His talks, more like rants, always centred on Japan and its glorious position in the world. He really had the gift of the gab.

I wasn't an Emperor worshipper by any stretch of the imagination, and I didn't think Hammerhead was either; I didn't think he'd fall for a guy like Etsu Kaga. But I listened to the two namaiki intently. They figured since Japan was going to win the war soon, maybe in a month or two, they had to form this resistance movement to ensure their families and people were safe. There was no telling how much further an angry Canadian government would go if faced with defeat.

I couldn't argue against the logic. Japan seemed so omnipotent, so unstoppable. I wasn't completely sold, but I leaned in their direction. So I started hanging out with them, out of an increasing journalistic interest, I told myself. And it was fun for awhile.

IT WAS OBVIOUS to me that Kaga and Hammerhead were beyond comrades, they were brothers. I somehow managed to be part of them; we became like the Marx Brothers or maybe more like the Ritz Brothers; we spent more than a few nights in a Vancouver bar or two; sometimes we hung out on Pender Street. Kaga said he really liked the girls in a Chinatown establishment or two, their cheongsams were plenty sexy, especially with those slits halfway up the girls' thighs. The waitresses at the Silver Dragon were something else, though none of us could get to first base with them, because of the language and all. That's why we felt most comfortable on Powell Street. We got drunk there a few times together, met the ladies together, got beat up together, while getting in our licks. I never did go back to the Sisters'; it was too expensive. Rik-san wasn't likely to play teacher again. But the story was retold over and over again.

"Hey, you ketsunoana!" Hammerhead slurred at the Imperial Arms Hotel and Pub in Gastown one night when we drifted out of district.

"Who you calling an asshole?" I slurred back.

"You, you dumb bastard! You're a good guy."

"Hey, you Japs wanna keep it down. It's bad enough I let youse drink in here." The barkeep had a limit to his charity.

Kaga lunged at him for that remark and started a fracas. The three of us ended up in Kaga's parlour with his mother attending to our cuts and bruises.

"My, oh my," Okusan said in her worried disgust.

We smiled at each other. It was the solidification of a real friendship; unfortunately the fun ended all too soon, and everything became much too serious.

"OUR HOMELAND HAS struck an enormous blow. Not only Pearl Harbor, but Manila, Singapore, and Hong Kong, too," Kaga began in a loud whisper during a clandestine meeting. He then insisted we speak only Japanese. "The *shouji* have ears," he kept saying.

Hammerhead replied enthusiastically, "They're on their way to Vancouver!"

The sawdust floor absorbed the sound, but we kept our voices low. The late afternoon shadows of the Matsumiya Grocery hid us from prying eyes. The barrels heavy and silent, the piles of vegetables still blushed with the warmth of the day's business, the dry goods settled for the night. The dull light of the radio was a comfort as we listened. The RCA squealed and then crackled alive before revealing the Imperial Armed Forces' exploits in the South Pacific.

"What I wouldn't give to be there!" Hammerhead said, smacking his hands together.

"You can't leave your family, your okaa especially," I advised.

"A small sacrifice compared to what the homeland is going through," Kaga answered in the Hammer's stead.

"Are you kidding me? If you could've seen all the faces at the CPR station," I added.

"Yes, yes, it's a painful blow, no doubt about it, but we've got to remain strong. Maybe we can join the Imperial army or navy," Kaga offered, forgetting his prohibition of English.

"I'm not sure I want to give up my citizenship. We're Canadians, you know. That should stand for something. Maybe they're willing to negotiate."

"You're Canadian by birth and still they treat you like kuso. You said so yourself. Look how they treat families. Broke them to pieces. You saw. Who knows how far they'll go?"

He used my own words against me. "At least my parents are okay." Powell Street was disintegrating. It was like the Government was attacking a defenseless woman. It left me in shock with a heart gone cold.

"Let's talk to the consul," Kaga suggested as he slapped his hands together.

"You mean it?" Hammerhead said, trying to make sense of what he was saying.

"Sure, why not?"

"He's still here?" Hammerhead asked.

"I heard. It takes a while to move a consulate out of the country, you know."

"You think we can get in?"

"We'll just tell him how loyal we are and that we want to volunteer to serve in His army, the Emperor's army."

I gasped. I didn't like where this was going.

"And that'll do the trick?" Hammerhead further asked.

"Why not? It's the truth ain't it?"

We soon found ourselves in an office that smelled of rich leather and expensive cigars. We sat on a green couch in an outer office nervously staring at the closed inner door. We were as silent as corpses in a tomb. All had been said the night before, anyway, when Kaga had come up with his plan of action.

We were dressed in our best wool slacks held up by suspenders, white collarless shirts, and mismatched jackets, too nervous even to fidget. I scratched my inner thigh every so often to pass the time. I never got used to those pants.

Eventually the door opened a crack and the consul general's voice boomed, expressing something complex to someone inside. It was a very formal Japanese, which none of us could understand. Finished with his conversation, the consul general opened the door wide and stood before us, a lot taller than rumoured.

"I was told I had some distinguished guests," he said in a flattering manner, and beamed a broad smile.

We jumped to our feet. Kaga was the first to step forward, bowing and speaking the best Japanese at his command. "Consul General Gomyo, thank you for seeing us today. I know you are extremely busy, but it is a matter of urgency," he said, selecting his words carefully.

"Is that so? Well then, you had better come inside."

The office was large, with a high tin ceiling and several luxurious leather chairs, a wide coffee-table and rich oak desk. Everywhere, wooden packing boxes stood in stacks. It was the consulate's last days, though it seemed the skeleton staff wasn't in that much of a hurry to leave. The Hinomaru with sunrays was draped behind the consul general's desk, regal and proud. A second door led to the outside hall, I assumed, since the last visitor was nowhere in sight, leaving behind only his telltale cigar butt in an ashtray and smoke hanging in the air. Like a disembodied spirit.

"Excuse the mess. You've caught me at a bad time, ne?" he said leaning against his desk. His Japanese was clean — far less starched than we heard before.

While standing at attention, we nodded as Kaga continued. "Your Excellency," he began bowing again. "*Taihen shitsurei itashimashita. Yoroshiku.* Thank you for this audience."

Gomyo in turn waved away the formality. "To whom am I addressing?"

Kaga clicked his heels before he spoke. "Kaga Etsu, *desu.*" He then turned to introduce us. We each bowed deeply.

"My friends and I, and in fact many more of us, feel offended that we have to participate in this country's war effort against our homeland. We're also upset that the enemy has stolen our cars, fishing boats, and is illegally breaking up our families and taking them to who-knows-where. The enemy has put us all to shame."

"Wait a minute," the consul general said raising his hand. "When you say 'participating in the war effort,' what do you mean? Are you in the munitions factories, in the army?"

"No. No. Just by mindlessly cooperating we are supporting the government."

"Oh, I see." He nodded knowingly. "I didn't think you were deliberately working against the Emperor. You look to be good, loyal Japanese boys."

I didn't like being called "a boy," but Kaga was filled with pride by being praised for our "loyalty." "We would never betray our sovereign. We were hoping you could help us get back to Japan and join the Imperial army."

I cringed.

The consul general lowered his eyes to think. With a deep breath, he rose to his feet. "I must admit there's an enormous amount of confusion. It's beyond imagination. I blame all this on the lack of racial integrity amongst the Japanese here. To act so cooperatively with the *Canadian* government is in effect assisting the enemy. *Canada* is a weak nation. I doubt it'll have the strength and will, when the time comes, to deal effectively with a mere twenty-three thousand people. Not without their full cooperation! And they will cooperate. They have forgotten how to be Japanese!"

Kaga and Hammerhead grumbled and shook their heads in disgust. I took a step backward.

"Don't you see? You must remain in this enemy country. Do all you can to upset the war effort. Encourage all who have already gone, and those who are about to go, to oppose the government in every way possible. Inspire them to rise up against the tyranny.

"You'll probably be arrested for it, but you'll be prisoners with honour. You have chosen to stand by your homeland, and you must choose how to deal a mighty blow against the enemy."

"Maybe we should help Morii-san?" Kaga offered.

"No. Don't go to him," the consul general said rather abruptly. "Do not seek his counsel. He's on their side now. A pure traitor."

Kaga and Hammer again shook their heads in disbelief.

"Morii preaches cooperation. Even called himself the 'Emperor of his people'! He told the men at the Japanese Hall to be '*Canadian*.' Treason, I tell you, treason and blasphemy. He shall be dealt with in time."

Even as emotional as the consul general appeared to be, we had no idea what he was talking about. The contradiction was confusing.

The consul general finally stopped and sought calm by rolling a fresh, fat cigar in his fingers and then lit it. With a great puff of smoke, he waited for a reaction. My friends sat stunned. Kaga was particularly affected; he never believed his hero, Morii, was sincere in advocating cooperation. It was some kind of tactic, he thought.

The consul general continued, "The best thing you can do to serve the Emperor is, as I said before, to stay here and find as many ways as you can to cause trouble for the enemy.

I will report your spirit to the Imperial government back home," he said with emphasis. "You are Japanese and, after we've won the war, in say two or three months, you'll be released and treated as heroes. Japan will force the defeated *Canadians* to compensate you."

As if on cue, my comrades cheered. Kaga was nearly in tears basking in the prospect of serving the homeland. I retreated, somewhat fearful of such misbegotten patriotism.

"No matter how much you suffer," continued the consul general, "you will not be forgotten. If you have to, eat the very grass beneath your feet to survive, but keep hope in your hearts. Eventually the strong hand of help and compassion will reach out to you from your homeland."

OUTSIDE THE BUILDING on Cordova, the chilly April winds raced along the street. Above, threatening clouds cast a wicked spell over the Powell Street area. The three of us huddled together to take stock.

"Did you believe what he said about Morii-san?"

"Ah, that was just a story," Kaga insisted. "The Oyabun wouldn't betray us like that."

"So why'd Gomyo tell us he did?"

"Listen, wiseguy, you think a mucky-muck like him's gonna tell three nobodies like us the truth about Morii? It's a secret plan between the two of them."

"Forget him and Morii," advised Hammerhead. "If the Oyabun really did anything, the Emperor will punish him. Just remember, we've got a duty to perform."

"I don't know guys..." My voice faded into the ether of heated patriotism.

"We should demand the rights owed to us as Nisei, and then

smear mud in the face of the government!" Kaga said. "Their actions are sucking the very blood out of our people."

"We are Japanese in our heart of hearts!" Kaga and Hammerhead shouted for all the world to hear. "We will be prisoners with honour!"

*Hear Ye! Hear Ye! Hear Ye! A concert is coming to the "Pool" this
Saturday night. Swoon to the velvet voice of Sam Furuya, accompanied
by the inimitable Vernon Hakkaku on piano. Swing to the sounds of
the popular Akebono Orchestra, led by the heppest of all hep cats,
Freddy Watada. Laugh at the comedy of our very own Red Skelton,
Mats Matsuba. Come one, come all.*

— The New Canadian, April 21, 1942

14.

On a brilliantly sunny day, a Hastings Park security officer
tapped Irene on the shoulder and pointed her in the
direction of Building C, the administration office near
the centre of the complex. She had grabbed me from
where I had been helping out at the Pool for the day, and the security
officer didn't mind. It was hard to say "no" to Irene, so I went along.

Inside the office amid cheap furniture and piles of government
paper sat a well-groomed man with smooth features, regulation
haircut, and a suit only the "swellest of swells" wore, like in a Hollywood movie. He didn't even look up from behind the desk when
Irene and I entered the room. My impression was we weren't important enough, or he was just being rude. "You are Irene Kondo?"
he asked without looking up. His voice was low in timbre and
echoed from several directions.

"Yeah. Who's asking?" she answered in her way.

"I'm sorry." He smiled, lifting his cool gaze, cracking the ice of
her suspicion a bit. "I'm with the Vancouver RCMP constabulary."

Inspector Benjamin Gill, a Mountie mucky-muck assigned to
Vancouver from Ottawa, was grey at the temples, tall like a typical
hakujin and sported a full dark moustache. I had seen him a few

times before, mostly at commemorative events like Armistice Day or Dominion Day. Gill was always dressed in expensive grey leather gloves and fine suits that shone in any light, he presented an affable manner to community leaders. With ordinary civilians, and especially reporters like me, he was officious and at times cold and implacable.

What was disturbing was his friendship with Morii Etsuji. I had seen Gill and the Oyabun in each other's company in and about the judo club on Dunlevy. No one knew the connection between them, but everyone guessed it wasn't good.

"A Mountie," Irene said.

"You surprised?"

"Not really, but I was expecting a BC Security man."

"Ah well, you're too special a case for just anybody," Gill said to Irene.

I didn't like the sound of that. As Irene sat down in a nearby chair, she crossed her legs, the pants tightening over her short calves. "What's so special about me?" she asked, squinting with suspicion.

"Who's your friend?"

"I'm Danny. Danny Sugiura."

He waved his hand to sit.

"Are we finished with the niceties?" she asked angrily. "Why am I here?"

"Well, Miss Kondo. Everyone has told me how wonderful a person you are. How you're really concerned about the people here."

He was smooth — I gave him that — but I could see Irene was determined not to fall for it. "Yeah, well, wouldn't you be, given the conditions here?"

"Yes, I suppose I would be," he said laying it on a bit too thick. "And that's why I've asked you here. We want to find a way to boost the morale of all our guests."

Guests, who was he kidding? Irene seemed intrigued enough not to let her dander get up and get the better of her.

"We thought you could organize a show."

"A show?" Irene said, taken aback. "Here? Now?"

"Sure. I'm serious. My men could fix up a stage and provide a record player or..."

"A piano?"

"Sure."

Against her better judgment, she warmed to the idea. The community concerts before Pearl Harbor had brought everyone together for a good and happy time.

"You get the entertainers, and we'll provide everything else."

"Are you on the level?" I asked. My skepticism got the better of me and I tugged on Irene's sleeve. She pulled away, glaring at me.

"I certainly am," he said with all sincerity.

"Can everyone from Powell Street... Little Tokyo attend?"

"Of course," he said affirmatively. "Look, Miss Kondo, the situation is bad enough without us representatives of the government appearing so heartless. I've seen how your people are suffering. We're not all without sympathy."

She shook his hand, but neither she nor I could detect any deception; that's how smooth an operator the man was.

IMMEDIATELY AFTER THE meeting, I tried to warn Irene of Gill's connections to the Oyabun.

"I'm well aware of them," Irene said.

"Then why get in bed with him?"

"What are you implying?" she said angrily, just about ready to sock me.

"Nothing! You know what I mean," I insisted. "You're so sensitive! Shouldn't we be talking to Tommy?"

"I may be cooperating with the devil himself, but first of all, that's all rumour about that Mountie and Morii being partners in crime, and second, you know what a show can do for morale. We're falling apart for pity's sake. And as for Tommy, he'd understand."

I could say nothing, but I wondered about Gill and Morii.

In the weeks that followed, Irene became very busy. She started by getting as many Nisei involved in this "show" as she could. Frank and I were her first recruits.

"Are you nuts or something?" Frank blurted to Irene. "A show in the middle of all what's going on?"

"Look, Irene, I was there and I don't trust Gill," I added.

She flashed such a dirty look that we had to cooperate.

We were close friends and colleagues, family really, but Irene was older, at times brusque and too outspoken for me. I did respect her for all her qualities, but she just wasn't my type. Not that I was thinking about it, but she was more like an oneesan than anything else. Like Tommy, I liked smart but demure girls, attractive in that Ginger Rogers kind of way with savvy, fashion-magazine looks and smart comebacks, yet feminine. I was attracted to Gladys, but it was more than her developing beauty; her personality could make a shy man confident, make a miser generous, or a criminal honest. It helped that, if given the right opportunities, I knew she would grow into an elegant, beautiful woman. On the other hand, I'd do just about anything for Irene. She was right about the community: it was falling apart. A show might just be the ticket to lift everyone up. If nothing else, it would be our last hurrah.

Irene liked tall men. She was short, so she believed that a tall man would give her tall children. Her man had to be smart, and resourceful, confident, and ambitious. Tommy was almost there, except for his height — just an inch or two short she judged; besides, though he was free now, he was more like a big brother to her, and all of us for that matter. Above all else, she didn't take any guff from anybody. If crossed, she would work and work until she got even. It took somebody really big, like the Government, to get the best of her. It took the entire country to make her cry.

The ad hoc committee for the show, made up of NC staff, Buddhist church youth, and other interested parties, shifted on the couch, kitchen chairs, and pillows on the floor of her absent parents' place. They had similar misgivings.

"Remember the last Red Cross show at the Ukrainan Hall back

in...when was it, Fall 1941?" she began. "Wasn't little Eddie Doi great, dancing and singing? We had such a time!" Irene said, her face and voice animated with excitement. "I'm sure we can get Vernon, maybe even Sam Furuya! I hear he's still around," she said, mustering as much enthusiasm as she could. "Can't you just see it?"

Frank Morimoto spoke up. "Come on, Irene, will the people in the Pool want this?"

"Never mind. This is exactly what they need. What's more uplifting than listening to Sam singing 'Someone to Watch over Me'?"

The clinching argument came from the main newspapers. *The Province* had complained that there were "more Japs in Vancouver than the rest of BC, with Hastings Park burgeoning with them!" The concert became Powell Street's project. Irene's spirit was infectious. I certainly could feel it build amongst us. The community was alive again, for a just a little bit longer anyway.

The Bussei asked Reverend Tsuji if they could use his living room for rehearsal space. He had a piano and often used the room for small memorial services.

During the day, while the young, newly ordained Sensei with the tightly slit eyes and underfed build was out making calls on families in distress, Vernon Hakkaku, a long, cool drink of a guy with the slicked up hairstyle of the day, tickled the ivories in the lilting style required for Japanese music. Hisaye Furuya and her brother Sam, the Nisei's own matinee idol, sang Japanese hits like "Shina no Yoru" and American songs like "Besame Mucho," much to the delight of everyone present.

The gang at *The New Canadian* printed up posters in English and Japanese announcing the concert. Frank and I ran around the Pool tacking them up. Small groups milled about the announcements making positive comments. Others posted the English ones up on lampposts and bulletin boards around Powell Street. The organizing committee wanted all the Japanese Canadians to know that every one of them was welcome. The Sagara brothers beat up some Chinese boys to steal their large, round "I AM CHINESE" badges in order to get things done like purchasing material for costumes, sheet music, and whatever else was needed. That way they avoided suspicion until they were arrested, but they caught a break with a lazy desk sergeant. Irene didn't like their delinquent tactics, but it was faster than going through the RCMP.

Inspector Gill was as good as his word. Irene reported to everyone that the Mounties were hard at work. "It's funny watching those men gussying up the stage so that we Japanese can have some fun," she informed us earnestly. "They're the jailers, after all."

The work and rehearsals were filled with joy and purpose. That was the thing that I enjoyed the most. We may not have been able to stop the dismantling, but we were keeping the forces at bay. Maybe I was fooling myself.

Tommy realized this, and promised Irene full coverage in the paper. She was family, after all. Since I was helping anyway, Tommy assigned me to the story. He had forgiven me my outburst, though I wasn't sure how much he would let me cover.

The stage, a wide, raised platform with no curtains, sat glumly against the back wall of the basketball court in Building L where the children went to school. The workmen had given it a fresh coat of paint, but the "house" lights overhead diminished any sparkle it might have produced. To compensate, Ayako Tsuji, a gifted Nisei artist, created a large blue and black mural of the Steveston fishing docks as a backdrop, men with nets in shadows labouring around nameless boats; the irony was not lost on anyone.

An upright piano brought in from a church stood erect at one end of the stage. With hands at the ready, Vernon sat poised behind it in a tuxedo, a strange image given the circumstances. But it was Vernon all the way, with his romantic and lofty ambition to play a grand piano at Carnegie Hall one day after all this "craziness."

The audience, made up of a good mix of "locals" and "evacuees" from the Lower Mainland and coastal Japanese communities, rumbled into the hall until the place buzzed. It was impossible, but it seemed everyone in the Pool and Powell Street was there. I told my parents, but Dad was uninterested, grumbling about a waste of time. He stood glaring at me with dismissive eyes. Mom worried about the rumoured rats and maggots. I tried to assuage her fears, but then there was a small outbreak of dysentery. That did it; she would stay home.

I spied Jimmy in the audience. Could never miss that head of hair, all poofed up and sculpted with pomade. I was happy to see him, but surprised he was even there. Had his family been moved into the Pool? I had heard not a word from them.

Gladys, with her gleaming and smooth complexion, sat beside him. My heart quickened and my legs grew weak seeing her with her deep, darkly shadowed ocean eyes. I thought about approaching them to ask what was going on (where were their parents, for example), but since they were in the middle of the pack, I busied myself elsewhere, deciding to bide my time. Maybe I could catch her after, and so I kept an eye out for her. I took solace in seeing they were enjoying themselves. This was a good idea, after all. Everyone else sat in squeaking wooden folding chairs, scratching the floor in quiet anticipation of the first act.

Onto the stage stepped the regal Hisaye Furuya, her face radiant with ruby-red lipstick, rouged cheeks, and long, full eyelashes. Her floor-length chiffon gown swept across the stage as she made for the centre-stage microphone. Her broad smile brought applause from her eager admirers. When Vernon arpeggio'd into a minor key, the smile migrated to her eyes. She gave forth with full-bodied voice, and the crowd settled into its rapture.

From the side steps of the stage, Irene and I watched; Irene beamed at the performance and the size of the audience. It was wonderful. We were all together, and I held the moment for as long as I could.

Sam Furuya in his white evening jacket, black tuxedo pants, and patent leather shoes bounded up the steps and, as everyone saw, gave Irene a hug. She swooned and the crowd laughed before going wild as he stepped onto the stage. With his Hollywood sneer and thick, black hair, Sam Furuya turned heads wherever he went. His muscular, V-shaped build made the girls shriek if he paid them any attention. Everyone knew his voice was like velvet, wrapping around a song like a humid breeze on a hot summer's day. Audience members swore his eyes and teeth sparkled when caught in the light.

When the suave crooner stepped toward the microphone, everyone in the place fell silent in anticipation. He nodded to Vernon, who trilled the piano keys as an introduction to "Someone to Watch Over Me." Sam's honey-coated baritone then rose and fell with the emotion of the music, the climb and slide of the melody massaging his listeners until he finally descended toward the ending coda. Many girls sighed, enraptured. With his trademark grin, he bowed and the audience rose to a standing ovation. In the next instant, the stage was empty.

After I gently nudged her out of her spell, Irene seized the opportunity to enter the stage to make introductions for the next act, a troupe of baton twirlers from Britannia High School, but was pushed aside by a sudden and ominous presence. I swung around to see an agitated Inspector Gill and two constables rushing to the microphone.

"Ladies and gentlemen," Gill began, "there will be a slight delay in the show. Just sit tight." Confusion reigned as several more RCMP constables appeared and fanned throughout the room. Inspector Gill then jumped to the floor in front and called forward someone in a three-piece suit and pinched shoes.

Isamu Otagaki, a Nisei man with narrow shoulders and weak jaw, came forward and walked through the audience, inspecting each face with a keen eye. Every so often he pointed at certain individuals, whereupon constables pounced on the hapless victims and took them to a holding area outside the main doors. Otagaki was an inu, a dog, a traitor, selling out his own for favours and future considerations, for thirty pieces of silver.

Jimmy sprang to his feet and rushed the man. "You ketsunoana!" he shouted in Japanese. He was still the young buck I knew him to be, but there was now a fierce fire in his soul; it was clear he had a cause to live for and he was deeply angry.

Two soldiers immediately grabbed him, but Otagaki stopped them from dragging him away to jail. "He's not one of them," he casually declared. "But get him outta here."

This was Inspector Gill's plan to flush out Japanese nationals still hiding in Hastings Park. Someone later told me that he'd heard Gill saying, "A friend of mine once said that there's only one man who can tell one Jap from another. And that's another Jap." Otagaki was that man.

Otagaki had always been an outsider. He was by generation a Nisei, but the same age as the Issei, who wouldn't accept him because he didn't observe any of the Japanese traditions and tried to be "Canadian" instead. More importantly, he couldn't speak any Japanese.

With tears welling up in her eyes, Irene's mouth fell open wordlessly. She reached forward in a useless gesture to try to stop the travesty, but soon squeezed her hands into fists. I tried to comfort her with an arm around her shoulders, but she pushed it away. She had been duped; she was a patsy, a fool, a real "ultra maroon." She shook uncontrollably, seething with the betrayal.

In a moment of clarity, she rushed to Gill's side and grabbed his arm. "What do you think you're doing?"

Gill turned with the yank on his elbow and glared. "Stand back, Miss Kondo, this is a case of national security. My job — no duty — is to use whomever and whatever means necessary to protect Canadians and Canada."

Irene shrank from the harshness of his voice and the coldness of his eyes. This was Gill's plan all along. It was the time of dogs and villains.

IN THE MIDST of the chaos, I managed to catch up to Gladys just outside the front doors of the Pool. She smiled instantly when she saw me. My heart melted with that smile.

"What are you guys doing here?" I asked clumsily.

"What do you mean?"

"When did you move into the Pool? Where are you staying in here? Are your parents here?" I said rapidly.

"Slow down, Danny!" She laughed and touched my forearm. My skin tingled. "We received notice a few days ago, but we were exempt from Hastings Park because of Otousan's disability. We left Steveston to stay in Vancouver. We're staying with friends. Mom and Dad are with them now."

"Why didn't you tell me?"

"No time. Besides, I figured I'd see you sometime before we left."

"You're leaving?"

"Mom, Dad and I are being 'evacuated' to some place called Tashme." The look on her face told me she wasn't fooled by the euphemism.

"When?"

"Soon."

It felt like a death sentence, but Gladys grasped my arm tighter, letting me know everything would be all right.

"Jimmy moved here before us, moved with the NMEG. He'll be staying in town working with them. He won't be evacuated yet because of that. He said he's 'got a lot of work' to do," she said with a knowing smile. "He'll be at the Patricia Hotel on Hastings."

The NMEG's new headquarters. I had heard they established the operation there. That made sense, about Jimmy, I mean, but I worried for her and her parents wandering into the wilderness alone.

"We'll be okay," she said assuredly. In the next breath she asked, "Danny, will you do something for me?" Her voice was anxious yet comforting, almost intimate.

"Sure, anything."

"Take care of my brother."

To that end, I resolved to join the NMEG. I'd tell Tommy later.

As Gladys and I parted ways, I felt truly empty, like my heart had been torn out of me.

*Evacuation of women, children and aged men from the coast to interior
"ghost towns" will begin in earnest tonight, when a party of seventy
people will leave Steveston for Greenwood, via the CPR Kettle Valley
line.*

*Every consecutive day thereafter, a party of similar size will go forward
from Steveston, until some 700 have been accommodated in the first
location of the Interior Housing Project.*

— The New Canadian, April 25, 1942

15.

Things were crazy. I had to get away from Irene, Hastings
Park, Tommy, the *NC*, Kaga, and Hammerhead for the
time being; I turned to the safety and comfort of Jimmy
Isojima and the NMEG. After the Steveston Resolution,
which led to the formation of the NMEG, Jimmy had stayed with
a friend in Vancouver for about a week before moving into a dingy
one-room at the New World Hotel, unbeknownst to his family, I
assumed. It was close to the group's headquarters at the Patricia
Hotel. His duties started almost immediately, first as a go-between
for the Issei evacuees, and then as an assistant to the leadership.

His time spent in Vancouver consisted of meetings in a series of
rooms. He constantly moved from his hotel room to a backroom
to a closed church basement. He formed many friendships. Jimmy
appreciated me, but the man he admired most was Mr. Roy Shintani. His high regard for him in light of Morii's fall, and Hisaoka's
deceit, carried Jimmy through much adversity.

Still the NMEG's survival, never mind its expansion, didn't seem possible at first. We were labelled namaiki and mocked in public, but then Roy and Tak Kawai produced a pamphlet to outline our concerns and demands. I printed the English-only pamphlet at *The New Canadian* office late one evening by lantern light and Jimmy organized a bunch of us to distribute it by hand to Nisei only. Though he objected, Tommy allowed it as a favour, a kind of peace offering. Maybe he felt a might guilty.

To the Nisei:

Mr. Austin C. Taylor says we are Canadians. Yet we are subjected to the curfew; our boats, cars, radios, and cameras have been confiscated. Our jobs have been taken from us, and many of us have lost our homes and businesses. We have been boycotted, jailed, interned, forced to register, and thumbprinted. We are being denied every right and freedom of a so-called democracy, like any Enemy Alien.

After being made to suffer for the sake of a few crooked politicians seeking publicity, and those who hope to gain materially and financially by the wholesale evacuation of Nisei, how can we by any stretch of the imagination be Canadians? Why are not Canadian-born Germans and Italians treated likewise? Canada is making a war of race out of her so proudly upheld ideals.

How can Mr. Taylor and his commission expect us to be good Canadians, when he and his associates are teaching us that we cannot expect justice from Canada? This democracy is making a farce out of her own constitution.

If Mr. Taylor finds it against his judgment to treat us as Canadians, while calling us Canadians, then let him consider us as Aliens and intern us. If he and his associates can do neither, then let us all ask him to evacuate us in family groups, providing us with transportation, a decent place of abode (or materials to build a home), and a means of a fair living (employment or farming). Nisei, we have in our lifetime proved beyond question that we have been a credit to

*Canada. If Mr. Taylor should refuse this, then let us fight together
with our backs to the wall with one mind and one hope in our hearts
for a common cause and right of a free people.*

*Remember this, Nisei, when you report to the RCMP: say, "We will
gladly go if this thing we ask be granted." Till then, we must coordi-
nate and fight with whatever means we have on hand and with one
thought: "ONE FOR ALL, AND ALL FOR ONE."*

As the pamphlet made its way around the community, the
NMEG grew in number. As a result, meetings were held everywhere in Vancouver and Steveston where the highest concentration of Japanese lived, but there were detractors. The JCCL refused
to listen, even though their own negotiations with the commission
had failed altogether. Iisaoka Bunjiro with his Kikajinkai continued to negotiate self supporting camps with the Security Commission.

Following the NMEG's formation, Watanabe Etsuo had made
himself scarce. He was seen only at the late-night meetings held in
the Patricia Hotel. And only from time to time, which caused
much speculation amongst the members. Not that Jimmy noticed,
but there was a change in Mr. Watanabe. Gone was that strength
of conviction, that indignation at injustice. In its place was a cloud
of secrecy surrounding him. I may have been fooled by the Oyabun, but not again, and not by Watanabe.

The Steveston secretary, it seemed, only attended meetings to
be updated. It didn't help that most attendees took rooms to avoid
breaking curfew but, curiously, Watanabe did not. After the meetings, he would suspiciously leave to make his way to who-knows-
where, even with the authorities patrolling the dark streets.

I, as a newly minted member, didn't care much about Watanabe
— stronger men than he had turned inu after all — but I was
increasingly worried about Jimmy. I tried talking to him about his
one-time mentor, but he didn't want to hear about another betrayal.

"Why don't you come more regularly if you want to know so

much?" Roy Shintani said indignantly to Watanabe on a night when he finally had had enough. Everyone in the room was startled at the irritation in Roy's voice, but he did speak for everyone, it seemed.

Watanabe adjusted his glasses and kept his temper under control. "I've come all the way from Steveston," he began, every word coloured by irritation squeezing through his teeth like venom. "I've still got my responsibilities with the association and my family."

I knew he was lying. Getting past the patrols all the way back to Steveston was impossible. I looked at Jimmy and saw that he hadn't even considered that fact. I could've called the inu on it, but decided to stay silent. I watched with the curiosity of a reporter.

"It's for your family you should be more involved!" Roy said as a comeback. "What do you think we're doing here?"

"And I'm still committed to the cause, but I am still the secretary to the Fishermen's Association!" he said to everyone.

"What use is that? All the boats have been confiscated and the men are being rounded up!" There was no comeback to that. Steveston was a ghost town. Just the other day, the Buddhist church closed and its members boarded it up against possible looters. I imagined the Custodian, some secret and unseen civil servant, rubbing his hands together like Scrooge, a miserly devil.

Jimmy climbed to his feet from a nearby sofa chair and addressed the membership. "We can't treat Mr. Watanabe this way."

Roy broke in, his impatience getting the better of him. "I think you're spending too much time with Hisaoka," he said to Watanabe, ignoring Jimmy.

"What are you saying?" Watanabe asked, his body tensing up as if getting ready for a fist fight.

"Are you an inu?" Roy asked him bluntly. "Are you joining the Kikajinkai?"

"Now hold on," Jimmy said, stepping back into the fray. "I've heard enough of this! You got no right calling Mr. Watanabe names! He's been doing everything he can for the community in Steveston. Remember, he was the one who organized the meeting for us. If not for him, we wouldn't have the widespread support we have."

"For Christ's sake, stop defending him, Jimmy!" Roy roared. "You did all the work organizing that meeting. We all know it. He just took the credit!"

"Okay Jimmy," Watanabe interrupted. "You don't have to defend me." Taking a deep breath, Watanabe removed his glasses and spoke in a resigned voice. "It's true. I've talked to Hisaoka-san. He makes sense. If there's an out for me and my family, and if I've got the money, I'm taking it."

Jimmy fell back into his chair with his mouth open. A grumble of complaint ensued. "How can you do this?" he said after a time. "You stood right there with me in your office asking for my help. Encouraging me to do something, take responsibility for —"

"You're not listening to me," Watanabe continued. "I said I talked to him. But honestly I don't have the money he's talking about. I am advising anyone who can to take the deal."

The mercurial Uchiboro Shigeichi stepped forward and leaned into the dog. "You bastard! You know as well as any of us, we have to be a united front. Once we show division, the commission'll tear us apart."

Watanabe shot back: "Our purpose here is to get out of Vancouver in family groups. Am I right? Hisaoka-san has a solution, but I can't take advantage of it! I say again, I simply don't have the money."

"You not having the money is beside the point," Takashi Kawai asserted, squinting his bad eyes in the dull light. "You can't go around encouraging everyone to his way of thinking. It'll pit the rich against the poor. It'll be a case of the haves and the have-nots." His eyes sparked with emotion. "Everyone should be evacuated with their families. Everybody equal!"

Watanabe ended the conversation with a shrug and headed for the door. "Look, the deal's not set yet. Taylor only approved it in principle. Hisaoka-san'll talk to him later this week to hear the final decision. And if the plan gets approval, a lot of people are going."

With that, he carefully closed the door behind him, leaving a stunned group sitting in the dark.

Quickly the muttering began. Jimmy rushed to the door.

"No!" Uchiboro-san commanded. "Let him go."

Jimmy froze on the verge of tears. "How can he walk out like that?"

"Something is rotten in Denmark; the patrols should get him," Roy observed. "Uchiboro-san is right, we can do nothing except go on as we've been doing."

"Let him go," Uchiboro-san said bitterly. "And let that two-faced bastard Hisaoka make his deal with the devil."

Dear Sir: I see your paper still carries the caption "The Voice of the Second Generation." It may be the voice of a few second generation yet but certainly not all of us. Now it is merely the voice of the BC Security Commission under Mr. Austin Taylor.

I believe the article in the paper went through a severe censorship by Mr. Austin Taylor and the BC Security Commission. Therefore I suggest that you omit the caption entirely or get down to facts and change the wording to "The Voice of the BC Security Commission."

Disgusted Nisei

— The New Canadian, April 29, 1942

16.

Morii, Gill, and Otagaki: it was truly the time of dogs and villains. Along with Jimmy, we all internalized the duplicity of Hisaoka and Watanabe; there were very few we could trust.

After the concert at Hastings Park, Isamu Otagaki walked out and about the Eastside streets with a puffed-up chest while flashing a monkey's grin. The smug look on his face wrinkled the skin of his narrow, balding head into ridges. He lorded his new status over everyone, often threatening arrest to any who bothered him in the local hangouts.

"That's him, the inu," I murmured to Frank at Ernie's.

"Who's the ketsunoana?" Otagaki cursed as he whipped around. "Listen, you Mikado-loving Japs, you keep a civil tongue in your mouths, or you'll have to answer to my friends. That's right. You know who my friends are. Don't you? Don't you?"

Whether Otagaki was bluffing or not, no one wanted to call him on it. Though Frank said he wanted to give him a "fat lip and a half," I thought it wise to stay clear of the inu, but I did observe from afar. At first, I was stunned by the depths of evil percolating amongst our own. I expected it from Gill and Morii, but not from a Nisei.

I did try to understand Otagaki. What was in it for him? Surely he didn't think he would be exempt from the exile? Maybe just being Big Man on Campus for a while was enough. Then it hit me. "Isamu" was "Sam" amongst Canadians. Was he the one rousted by the Mounties on Powell Street that long-ago night just after Pearl? Dicky might know. He was the one that played spy, but I had no idea where my buddy was. It made sense. Maybe that was the night Otagaki became an inu. Or maybe he always was.

At the Hastings Park concert, I felt just like Frank. I wanted to punch the dog right where he stood, but sensing guards nearby I changed my mind and turned to more pressing matters. *Coward*, I chastised myself. Ever since I was little, my parents taught me not to question authority, and in fact fear it. I couldn't see the wisdom in that and came to despise my parents, especially my mother, for their cautious ways. But I followed their advice more times than I cared to admit.

"No make trouble with Canada," Okaasan insisted in her broken way. Otousan's silence was his tacit agreement. Whenever faced with insult or racist attack, and there were plenty, I went into a slow burn, but did nothing. It happened at university when faced with the bullying; it happened whenever I went beyond Powell Street to nearby downtown; and it happened at the Pool. I kept fooling myself into thinking I would stand up for myself if provoked enough, but I never had. Maybe it was time.

Irene Kondo was understandably the most affected by Gill's deceit and Otagaki's treachery. In the coming days, we watched her grow more and more despondent, moping around the office like someone had died. I was really worried about her as she fell deeper into her mood. Sometimes she let her innermost feelings out.

"First the Japs hold my parents in virtual country arrest. Then my own country uses me to arrest my neighbours. Why don't they just come get me and put me in front of a firing squad?" she said.

That was the hell of it: our own country, never mind the inu, was truly betraying us. The country to which we swore loyalty to the King we loved and respected; the country to which we sang proudly "The Maple Leaf Forever" and "God Save the King." I saw it and it sickened me. I yearned for everything to be normal again, to be everything we thought, dreamed, and wished it to be.

Most days Irene retreated to the comfort of *The New Canadian* office, sitting behind her desk meandering over the copy, proof-reading text in a half-hearted manner.

"Come on, Irene," Tommy often said in an encouraging tone, "snap out of it. No one's blaming you for what happened." His sincerity and compassion beamed from behind his round, silver-rimmed glasses, for he had genuine concerns for his spitfire reporter and friend. As sorry as I was for Irene, I could see the effects of the worry, never mind the stress and sleepless nights, on my editor, my mentor, my friend. I was still on the "outs" with him, but concern for him still lived in my heart.

Tommy didn't complain about inu as much as he questioned the Oyabun's role. What Inspector Gill had been saying around town stayed with me. "A friend of mine once said to me that there's only one person who can tell one Jap from another. And that's another Jap." Was his friend Morii? Gill had been seen with the Oyabun, but not even the gang boss would sell out his own, would he?

Tommy was just as bewildered at the idea as I was. "Look at the Steveston incident during the boat round-up," he reasoned. He knew about Morii's largess but didn't elaborate about how he knew. I hadn't told him. I didn't ask.

By this point, Tommy had concluded that he couldn't beat Morii, the Mounties, or the Security Commission. He just knew he had to keep on fighting, because he still held faith in Canada.

"I'm all right, Tommy," Irene assured him with a sigh. "It's just that I was...I was...all I wanted to do was to boost morale! I feel like such an idiot. If I ever meet that son-of-a-bitch Mountie again, I'll give him what for, that's for sure!" she declared.

As Tommy patted her shoulder, he said, "I know. I know."

We tried running the Hastings Park concert story as truthfully as we could. Irene wrote most of it, but we knew the censors would never let it pass. But she had to try; I could see her spirit lifting as she wrote.

Other overzealous Nisei inu got into the act in the days after, perhaps feeling they could prove their loyalty and get something in return by ratting out some poor Japanese national overlooked in the first sweep by Inspector Gill and his fellow Mounties. Duplicity became the norm. As Frank would say in his way, "No one could trust nobody."

17.

Perhaps the most significant and shocking outrage of the Evacuation or *Idou* period (as the Issei called it) was the appointment of Morii Etsuji as community representative by the BC Security Commission. He had been acting in an unofficial capacity as it was, but now he had Government backing. It was clear the Oyabun saw himself as a saviour of his people, but at the same time he was very close to the Canadian authorities. How was anyone's guess: he was the Black Dragon gang leader after all, so vocal in his support of Japan, and it was common knowledge that he had sent money to Steveston to stand against the naval forces. So many contradictions. How could he possibly have convinced the Government to trust him? He was such an Emperor worshipper.

One night, Tommy had a meeting with Roy Kinoshita, a Yama Taxi driver. I just so happened to be there. Roy described how, just before Pearl Harbor, he picked up Morii and his old benefactor, Shiga Mitsuzo, at the consul general's residence.

"I tell ya, Tommy, I picked them up in Shaughnessy. They was talking pretty good in the back of my cab," Roy continued. "Shiga said it was the last time."

"Last time for what?" Tommy asked.

"Hell if I know. Maybe it was because Shiga said he's leaving. Going back to Japan. I think the consul general can arrange that. In any case, they were in tight with him."

"Beelzebub and Mephistopheles."

"Beezel-who?"

I could see the cold sweat rise on the back of Tommy's neck as he listened to his informant. Morii's connection to the consul general was, to borrow from the great Sir Winston Churchill, a riddle wrapped in a mystery inside the enigma of the Oyabun's "assurances" from the Canadian officials.

As chair of the newly formed Japanese Liaison Committee, Morii's job was to oversee the smooth removal of the Japanese from the West Coast. Almost within a day, the Oyabun set up a structure to deal with those who refused to cooperate. Tales of the victims swirled around us like dust on a windy day.

Mits Fujioka told me of his Issei father, a frail sixty-nine-year-old, breaking down in front of his family as the Mounties came at midnight to take him away to the road camps. He kept blubbering out Morii's name as if, as Mits guessed, he had been betrayed.

Or as "Chick" Sugiyama, a chicken sexer from Richmond, revealed to me and Tommy from his jail cell that he had stood before Morii, frightened yet hopeful of a deferral. He had paid a hundred dollars for an audience with the "great man," only to see that he might as well have put a match to the money.

"Tommy," he said in tears, "I just wanted a deferment because my mother is crippled. She can't make it on her own."

"I know. I know."

"That kuso Morii — not one ounce of compassion. He just laughed in my face."

"How'd you wind up in here?" I asked.

"I couldn't take it, the laughing, so I threw a punch at the man," he said angrily. "But I missed and his thugs jumped me. Next thing I know I'm in the Cordova Street jail."

Tommy tried to get him out, but it was no use. Chick was soon on a train to an Ontario concentration camp named Angler — a prison for the worst troublemakers.

But there were exceptions. One case in point was Sadao "Sad" Maikawa. The young Nisei came to me with the story of his encounter with the Oyabun in the Nippon Club office, the Liaison Committee's headquarters.

"I had a lot of trouble getting in to see the Oyabun," Sad began.

"How so?"

"I had to pay his thug Moriyama fifty bucks to get past him," he revealed. "Fifty bucks! That's all I had."

My guess was there was no standard fee.

"I thought if that cost me that much, how much would Morii be asking for?"

"Sad, why'd you go?"

"I just had to try. I heard he could arrange it so we could evacuate as a family. My okaa is sick with worry, and my wife is pregnant. My family won't make it without me or my otousan," he said. "He's somewhere up in the mountains with a road gang, and I'm supposed to go too. Maybe he would feel sorry for me."

"So what did Morii say?"

"At first, he said I should volunteer and be a 'hero' to the Japanese Empire," he said bitterly. "Me, a hero to them Japs! That really stuck in my craw. Then he said I could 'contribute' to his 'emergency fund' and that would get me a free ticket."

"How much?"

"Don't know, but $4,000 was mentioned."

My face must've expressed surprise, because Sad stopped his story for the moment.

"Now you know, I ain't got that kind of money, but then the Oyabun says to me out of the blue, 'Maybe you could use my help. You go home and I'll take care of everything.' And just like that, it was done. I tell you, I got outta there as fast as I could before he changed his mind."

Before he left, I had to ask one more question. "Sad, why'd you come to me with this?"

"I wanted you to know Morii ain't all bad. Your readers should know."

I smiled at the irony of his words.

Morii kept his word: not only did Sad leave Vancouver with his family, but his father joined them in Slocan shortly after they arrived.

So what was Morii's game? This question kept me up for many

a night. Tommy, Irene, I, and even Frank in his way, spent endless hours chewing it over, offering opinions and speculation. Of course there were no answers, just more questions.

Here was an avowed Emperor worshipper turned quisling. What then was his payoff, or was he really trying to keep his "people" from embarrassing their families, the Emperor, and ultimately Japan? In light of Pearl Harbor, how could a country be any more disgraced in the eyes of the world?

Maybe the Government thought Morii useful in his efforts to protect the Japanese in BC. He might be easily manipulated into delivering the Enemy Aliens into their hands. The Issei at the language school was a case in point. Every one of us at *The New Canadian*, however, was more than a little skeptical. It was clear the Oyabun had something up his sleeve. Still, Morii's collusion and the Government's machinations meant we couldn't stop the destruction of the community. Everything ending in ruins seemed inevitable.

There came a tiny ray of light soon after Morii's appointment. Thirty-six representatives of Japanese and hakujin organizations outside of the Oyabun's sphere of influence were said to be preparing a brief on Morii's activities for Ottawa. No one knew what the effect of it would be, but it was our only hope.

18.

By the middle of April and into May, the "Evacuation" was in full swing with all Japanese Canadians moving off the Coast. The BC Security Commission first separated the community by religion: Buddhists to Sandon, Anglicans to Slocan, United Church members to New Denver, and Catholics to Greenwood.

The first internees arrived at the detention camp at Greenwood, BC, in early April; in the days and weeks to follow internees arrived in Kaslo, New Denver, Slocan, Sandon, and Tashme. The lines of communication were sporadic, ragged like a sputtering radio. There were no telephones or short wave available to the Japanese in the Interior. Letters were delivered defaced beyond legibility and comprehension. The censors' ink blacked out words, sentences, and paragraphs, like the pages had developed a debilitating dementia. We at *The New Canadian* began to depend on bits of inaccurate information: rumour, conjecture, and hearsay. Our sense of community became blurred, its consistency tenuous at best.

It was about that time I decided to tell Tommy about my joining the NMEG. He didn't take it well.

"Are you out of your mind? You must know the commission will be keeping a tight watch on them. On you! You could be headed for jail."

"Come on, Tommy. Something has to be done. All respect to you, but cooperation isn't gonna do it."

"You're not a teenager anymore. Stop acting like one."

The words stung. I didn't want to fall out with my editor, my oniisan, again, especially over this. We were just about over the last blow up, time healed that wound. "Okay ... how about I cover the NMEG? Great story there."

"It'll never get in the paper."

"Not now, but they won't be around forever, and neither will the war. It'll be for history ... for our children. They have a right to know."

"Well, Tommy's kids will want to know," Frank commented at the office door. "You'll be lucky if you find a girlfriend." He had been listening all along.

"Clam it, wise guy," I snarled.

I CAUGHT UP with Jimmy at the Patricia, the NMEG's headquarters. The lobby of the hotel was a study of past glory. A grimy and stained portrait of Queen Victoria hung limply over the cracked and equally grimy fireplace mantle. The hand-coloured and framed photograph pictured Her Majesty in a typical pose: full body in a quarter turn with her face in profile. Her regalia were evident, but not as resplendent as they must have been. The couches and lounge chairs were still serviceable, but the cushions were caved in and their frames decrepit. The carpet was scuffed and frayed at the edges, obviously last cleaned long ago. An odour of decay hovered in the air.

I did marvel at the adjacent bar-room. The long mahogany bar, dulled with age and misuse, still offered booze, the clientele content with cheap, hard-throated whisky and watered-down beer. The room still vibrated with the ghostly music of Jelly Roll Morton, who played the outpost long ago. Any port in a storm, I guessed.

Jimmy and I sat at a low-lying coffee table. I stared at my friend, searching for any clue to his state of mind. "You okay, pal?" I opened.

Jimmy tilted his gaze upward. "Yeah, fine."

"Well, that doesn't say much."

"What do you want me to say? Life is a bowl of cherries?"

"Well, no," I answered, taken aback by Jimmy's sarcasm.

"Well, it isn't. Times are bad, the situation is bad. My family's gone. Hedy and her family too. I'm fighting an uphill battle, and guys like Mr. Hisaoka and Mr. Watanabe are sabotaging everything."

"Take it easy, Jimmy. It ain't that bad," I assured. "Forget about them. They're nobodies, only looking out for themselves. Not like you."

"You know sometimes I feel pretty low ... like I'm in a deep dark cave."

Hedy Nakamoto lived with her family on Princess Avenue a few blocks from Powell Ground. Her father, a clerk at Soga's Department Store, had been picked up and sent to a road camp back in January; Jimmy knew Hedy and her mother were to be "evacuated" to a place called Sandon, a camp where most of the Buddhists were sent.

Jimmy had met her at a Bussei dance at the Odd Fellows Hall downtown. He must've been "hound-dogging on the sly" as I once observed. I never knew they were a couple until Jimmy told me of their last moments together. He sat with her on her veranda just before she left town.

"That day was warm, the sun shining on us," he whimsically told me. "Who would've thought anything was wrong? Hedy was sure pretty in her 'downtown hairdo.'"

"It was okay. I held her hand and we ... well, you know. But it really was a sad day. I didn't think I was ever going to see her again."

I placed my hand on his shoulder.

MAYBE IT WAS that bad. Ottawa was in cahoots with the BC politicians in assaulting us. All property was in the hands of the Office of the Custodian of Enemy Alien Property, an appendage of the Government I didn't trust would give it back. The *temporary measures* they initiated looked all too permanent.

Then there was Morii Etsuji and his Japanese Liaison Committee. Jimmy heard the same stories of deception and extortion I did, and Morii's sheen of heroism faded to nothing. The first time Jimmy saw the Oyabun's signature on an evacuation order something fractured inside him. And when the deluge of notices came and that signature swirled around him, that thing in Jimmy, his innocence, his soul perhaps, finally shattered.

Jimmy may have descended into cynicism and indifference, maybe even madness, if not for the NMEG. It actually helped that his family were quickly "evacuated" first to Vancouver and then quietly to Tashme, about one hundred miles from the city.

The internment camp was just outside a small town called Hope. The internees nicknamed it "No Hope, BC." Gladys once wrote to her brother and me to say everyone joked, "Don't worry, Hope is just down the road." Jimmy responded with, "Trust my sister to say something positive about a bad situation."

Despite feeling his family were safe, he missed them terribly, Gladys especially. His sister spoke perfect English without any accent so Jimmy thought she would be all right, but he was really worried about his otousan. Recovering from the stroke, the old man could walk in a way, but was in no shape to travel long distances. The Government and the Mounties didn't see an old man crippled by his own body; they saw an Enemy Alien.

19.

Etsu Kaga dubbed his new band of patriots the "Yamato-damashii Group," a name I didn't understand at first. It sounded too "Japanesy" to me. The Yamato Boys, as they were called, decided to join the NMEG to be less conspicuous. That way, they could work behind the scenes until it was time to come out in the open. Everyone knew their intentions, but the Nisei group as a whole was happy for the increased membership.

Tommy Shoyama's Japanese Canadian Citizen's League and other pro-cooperation factions derisively called the NMEG the ganbariya or "stupid diehards." Even though Kaga liked the idea of being a diehard supporter of the Emperor, he didn't like the implied disrespect, and thus adopted the Yamato name connecting them to the first Emperor and spirit of Japan.

I found myself in a rather difficult position: I was torn among three factions, each headed by friends. Being a part of the NMEG, however, was a good thing for me: I reunited with Jimmy Isojima; it was good to be with him on a consistent basis. I came to terms with Tommy, since I insisted my interest in the NMEG was purely journalistic. I'm not sure he bought it, but he backed off, not saying one word of objection. And then there was Hammerhead. Kaga and the Yamato Boys were just too obvious. Their rhetoric made them targets, and I couldn't tell if Hammer was genuine about the "Yamato thing," or he was going along with everything to please Kaga. At least, as part of a bunch of rebellious Nisei, we could all hide from unwanted individual scrutiny. But not for long.

Shortly after the meeting with the consul general, Kaga upped the ante with his pamphlet campaign. He stopped people in the streets to talk "sense into them." His goal of mass evacuation by family was in line with the NMEG's goals, but his words, shot through with references to the Emperor and Japan's "great destiny," separated him from most.

"Those against us are just a bunch of opportunists anyway," he warned. "That Hisaoka and his Kikajinkai! Watch Watanabe — he's the worst. He'll sell you out for the right price."

At the time, I couldn't see what he had against Hisaoka; he was just looking after his own. Who really cared about a few rich snobs getting their own camp? They could sit around together pooh-poohing the efforts of peasants like us for all I cared. They were still prisoners.

Jimmy tolerated Kaga and the others, but he did object to Kaga's character assassination of his mentor. My guess was he didn't want to believe "Mr. Watanabe" was anything but a well-intentioned, good man. He had conveniently forgotten Watanabe's recent support of Hisaoka.

"You stop that kind of talk!" Jimmy warned Kaga. "Mr. Watanabe has done more work for our people in the last few months than you'll ever do in your lifetime."

"You be careful of that man, Jimmy," Kaga advised. "Just be careful."

As unconvincing as Kaga was, I could see that his words stung Jimmy, and perhaps added to the doubt in his soul.

A few of the newer NMEG members noticed that Kaga never mentioned Morii Etsuji in his ranting. Some asked me, but I told them that was a sore spot for him. So no one ever brought it up, though there remained many questions.

Without any real opposition, Kaga just got more and more passionate as time went on. "We've been called *Canadians* by this government when it suits their purposes, but what rights have we been given for our *Canadian* cooperation in return? Jailed and exiled just like our parents. We must take advantage of the fact that we were born in Canada and fight as Japanese!"

When Kaga received the order to report for "evacuation" to a road camp, he defied it and became a wanted man, in his own mind at least. He encouraged everyone to do the same. He began to carry a small valise with him all the time. "I have my papers and provisions in the event of my arrest," he explained.

As time pressed on, I saw less and less of Kaga and Hammer-head. I missed the old days, which weren't that long ago, when we were close pals, fighting the good fight in the street or bars.

Sulking around in corners and lane ways to avoid detection, the two fugitives occasionally showed up at the Patricia Hotel. I was certainly glad to see Hammerhead during those rare moments.

Inevitably Kaga made a fatal mistake. The Yamato Boys became part of the well-wishers gathered along the CPR tracks north of Alexander Street near the docks seeing off the "evacuees." It was one of the few times Hammer, Kaga, and I were all together.

As the passenger train filled with internees passed by late one afternoon, everyone roared a series of stirring "Banzai!" that was heard above the steaming locomotive and the clacking Pullman cars. By this time, the commission had become even more para-noid, if that was possible, and was no longer segregating Japanese Canadians by religion. Anything, they suspected, could spark a pos-sible insurrection based on a common belief (like religion). Many waved white handkerchiefs out of the train windows in acknowl-edgement. The spirit of the gathering reminded Kaga of the time he last visited Japan and saw the soldiers leaving for Manchuria. Everyone back then waved white handkerchiefs to the departing warriors.

Unfortunately, many lingered until after curfew, and so had to scramble home to avoid arrest. Kaga, Hammerhead, and I, caught up in the spirit of the day's reunion and events, decided instead to head for the Hayashi Ryokan, a favourite restaurant, to celebrate the spirited departure of our compatriots. Kaga personally asked Hayashi-san to stay open and serve us. The timid owner's eyes kept darting to the front door, frightened of a possible raid, but he gave in to the celebratory mood. The money didn't hurt either; times were tight. In one of the special *tatami* rooms, we drank, smoked, ate, and sang deep into the moonlit night. It felt good to be free to enjoy the evening for old time's sake.

"Aikoku Koushinkyoku" played on the record player and we sang the unofficial Japanese anthem over the steady military beat. Hammerhead and I clapped our hands to the music while Kaga rolled up his shirt sleeves, tied a makeshift hachimaki around his head, and comically danced like it was a *bon* dance on Powell Grounds.

At approximately eleven o'clock that evening, we left the restaurant, staggering and supporting each other as it were, through the back door into the dim alleyway. Slapping each other, we huffed and puffed like the drunks we were. We suddenly stopped cold in our tracks when we realized we had walked into a trap. Three police cars with about ten policemen stood waiting. I instantly sobered up.

The jail cells of the Cordova Street Police Station were cramped, and they were . . . well, dark and dank. Solid concrete and iron bars made the place icy cold. Water dripped somewhere in the gloom.

Hammerhead and I huddled together on the cement floor of Cell 1 in silence. Kaga paced back and forth in the next cell waiting for something to happen. Our faces burned with the alcohol and disgrace. I certainly didn't feel the "greater glory of Japan" in that jail.

I didn't sleep a wink as the irritating itch of self-doubt drove me crazy all night. I thought about my parents; I thought about Tommy. I grieved in the muddy shame that surrounded me.

Fortunately the next morning, the sun lightened my load and the ocean breezes relieved my distress, if not my doubts. The smell of the sea filled me with hope. The Kuroshio beckoned and forgave. We were released on five-dollars bail each, and headed straight to the Patricia Hotel. Kaga led the way all pumped up, laughing and bragging to the gathered. "Those baka police! Are they the best the keto have? They had us, dead to rights . . . and . . ." he said guffawing to a stop.

Hammerhead picked up the story for him: "They didn't even know he was a wanted man! They just asked some dumb questions and let us go!"

"How'd they know you were there?" someone asked. "Someone tell on you?"

"Oh, we made so much noise, it's no wonder we was caught," Hammerhead explained, and laughed.

The story got out that we fought and beat the police to a pulp in the restaurant alley before voluntarily going to jail, even helping the injured. Kaga spoke so eloquently and convincingly before the desk sergeant that they had to let us go the next morning. No one believed it, but people couldn't explain why a fugitive like him had escaped the law. So they took Kaga at his word.

Tommy wasn't so charitable when it came to me. "What were you thinking?" he asked in his chiding way.

I couldn't look him straight in the eye. I felt the guilt of a six-year-old caught with his hand in the company senbei. "I…I guess I wasn't."

"That's right, you weren't. You didn't even consider the consequences. They could've been devastating. Do you want a criminal record staining your whole life? How were you going to work? How do you think your family could stand the humiliation?"

I bowed, embarrassed for my poor parents.

"I think you're getting too close to Kaga. No good can come from that association."

"It's not like that, Tommy. I want the story. It's always been like that."

"Listen, word's come down that we're moving the paper to Kaslo."

I choked on the sudden news. "Where?"

"Kaslo, about five hundred miles from Vancouver. You'd better come with us."

"When?"

"It'll take a while, but we're definitely moving, maybe at the end of summer when this 'Evacuation' is done. And you're coming." Tommy hung his head low, and in a confessional tone revealed, "In the meantime, the commission is taking over the paper."

I stood, suddenly shocked. I didn't believe him. "When? Now?"

"No, maybe in July. They want *The New Canadian* to be ... how did they put it? 'A medium for official announcements.' They want to present 'only the truth,'" he said with a bitter grin.

"They can't do that! We need a free press."

"Just how free do you think we've been?"

Our time was nearly up. I turned away from Tommy and thought of my parents; their luck couldn't hold out much longer. They would soon have to leave. I wondered how they were reacting to their fast-approaching fate.

20.

Sugiura's Dry Goods crouched on its corner perch near Powell and Dunlevy. It looked tired as I approached it from the NC office. The windows were smudged and dirty. The lights were on midday revealing an empty interior. The roof sagged. The building looked as if it had exhaled its last breath, as if it had given up.

The store had done well right after Pearl with everyone rushing to buy black cloth. My parents couldn't stock the shelves fast enough. The money was good. But by spring, business slowed to a near stand-still. Money became tight. Yet every day, my dad opened promptly at eight o'clock in the morning — easy since we lived in the upstairs apartment — but no one came into the store, not customers, not even visiting friends who were left in Vancouver; hours would go by without even one soul on the street; a desperate quiet settled in and outside the store. As I entered, I saw my parents arguing as usual: my mother haranguing my father who was silent.

"What are we doing this for?" Okaa angrily questioned.

Dad busied himself with sweeping. Sweep. Sweep. Sweep.

"There are no customers. The *Mountain Police* must've taken them all away. Can't you see? The shelves are empty. We're going away soon ourselves. Someone will be coming for us," Mom said, her voice fragile and brittle. She constantly rubbed her hands together.

Otousan suddenly raised the broom and swiped at the irritant near him. Mom gave out a little yelp before sidestepping the blow and ran up the stairs, crying in a scream. Dad went back to his sweeping.

154 • THE THREE PLEASURES

I stepped in front of Dad with arms raised. "What're you doing? Leave her alone!" Though I was confused by the abrupt violence, I had to approach the situation logically. Maybe he would see. "Otousan," I said in Japanese, "you do know what's going to happen here? Don't you?"

He turned his back on me.

"The Government's gonna send you and Okaa away."

Again, he bent over and concentrated harder on what he was doing.

"Otousan, did you hear me? You're going away soon, damn soon."

Otousan stood straight up and closed his eyes.

Switching to English, I continued, "Face it. Now I don't know which camp you're going to, but it seems maybe you'll at least be going together."

He twisted and glared at me with a determination that frightened me. But then his face collapsed in defeat. He pointed to a crumpled piece of paper on the floor.

I picked it up and unfolded and smoothed it. It was a Security Commission order to prepare to move. One hundred and fifty pounds of possessions per evacuee, including cooking utensils, bedding, and "personal effects." No radios, or record players. It advised food for three or four days, probably longer. Oddly enough, there was no deadline date. I imagine the Security Commission men and Mounties would just show up and, if the Sugiuras were ready or not, they would be taken.

"I'm sorry, Dad," was all I could say.

He glared at me and growled, "I no go."

"But..." I said and let it go.

21.

Jimmy made sure the NMEG's pamphlets got delivered. His English wasn't so "high-faluting" as he put it, so he didn't write any of the copy, but he did translate for the Issei. In effect, those remaining were told that the group kept asking for negotiations for evacuation in family groups to start right away. The Security Commission ignored the pleas while Major Austin Taylor said in public the requests didn't mean anything.

Amid the chaos, NMEG members began disappearing off the streets, picked up by the RCMP in sweeps. It was finally our time to go despite our political clout. Uchiboro-san was the first. Without a "by your leave," they kidnapped him while he was walking home from the Security Commission of all places. It was clear there was an inu inside the organization.

At first no one wanted to believe it, especially Jimmy, not so soon after Watanabe's desertion. At yet another night meeting at the Patricia, Roy thought Watanabe was behind the arrest.

"Stop saying that!" Jimmy said, nearly screaming. "You have no proof, and you won't ever find any, 'cause there isn't any."

"Take it easy, Jimmy," I said as I saw Roy's face turn red.

Roy did nothing to retaliate. I suppose he understood. Jimmy's mentor may have walked out, but he could never believe "Mr. Watanabe" was capable of such treachery.

TAKASHI KAWAI WAS soon extended a personal invitation to come to the Marine Building, the gleaming white skyscraper at the foot of Burrard Street. His sagging face was weighed down by fatigue.

"You aren't going, are you?" I asked Kawai with great concern.

"Sure I am," he said emphatically. "Kinda curious, actually."

And off he went, only to return to the Patricia in a couple of hours. He had a bemused look on his face.

"Tak! What happened?" I asked.

"Oh, there I was standing in front of Major Taylor's desk with my hat in my hand and my overcoat slung over my arm. I waited for him to say something. Then he makes a joke about my name."

"Your name?"

"Yeah," he said, changing his voice to imitate an overstuffed politician. "Kawai? Like Hawaii only different!

"I ignored him."

The major then offered him a deferment until June as long as he played ball: be a spy and tell him of our whereabouts and movements. Taylor gave him a week to say yea or nay.

ABOUT A WEEK later, we held a meeting. The headquarters was really one of the Patricia's lobby rooms — empty of furniture except for an old kitchen table with matching chairs someone rescued from the Buddhist church before it completely closed and fell into the Custodian's hands — but it worked out fine. With only a fraction of the membership left, we just sat cross-legged face-to-face in a small group on the floor. It was easy for me to be there since I had moved into the hotel.

"The inu are everywhere," Takashi Kawai said, raising his thick eyebrows as he stared straight ahead. "I'll be arrested soon."

"How do you know?" everyone asked. The repeated question twirled like a dust devil.

"I know the dog has gone to the *Mounties* and told them of my movements. There's nothing I can do to prevent capture," he said rubbing his bald head.

"Who is he?" Jimmy demanded. "Is he here now?"

"No, and I won't say who he is. You'll know soon enough," he said ominously. "We don't need that kind of trouble in the ranks. He'll be taken care of."

"Come off it!" Roy Shintani shouted out. "Tell us who the bastard is!"

"Uchiboro-san's gone already. What are we gonna do if we lose you?" Jimmy fretted.

We decided he must have been targeted because of his visit to the Security Commission the week before.

The day after Major Taylor's deadline, Kawai was sitting by himself at the Chidori Restaurant, having the *soup-du-jour* and reading the paper. I was with a group of friends at another table some ways off. Two hakujin in black overcoats entered and approached him. They identified themselves as RCMP before asking him to come with them. I saw him make no attempt to escape, but he did signal with a half salute to me and other members as if to say he was right.

THE LOSS OF Tak Kawai was a blow to us in the NMEG. Everyone took it hard but the worst was yet to come.

I was at the *NC* office when Tommy and Frank came in with several packing boxes. Tommy faced me and, acting like my oniisan, straightened my tie. He flashed a small smile before speaking. "Bad news, Danny. Jimmy's gone, picked up last night."

The words toppled like bricks in a construction site. I was devastated. I anticipated such news would come, but not that day, not so soon after Tak. I didn't know whether to cry or yell to the high heavens. In the end, I could do nothing, so Tommy turned away and walked into the next office.

"How'd it happen?" I asked Frank.

"Ernie Tabata said he ran into Jimmy on Cordova just after sundown. Right by Powell Ground. They exchanged greetings and parted. Then two squad cars pulled up and flanked Jimmy. It happened so fast Jimmy had no choice but to stand still. Two men got out and started questioning him. After about a minute, they put Jimmy in the car and drove away. And that was that."

"Do you know where they took him? Maybe I can visit."

"Probably long gone by now."

I nodded and pondered what I was going to tell Gladys.

"Ernie said one more thing. He saw someone watching nearby — couldn't tell who he was 'cause he ran after the capture, but it was definitely someone watching. Maybe the set-up dog of a man."

Was I next? I wondered about Roy and Tamio Tanemitsu. I expected it for Roy long before any of the NMEG members started to disappear. It was his audacity that made him a target. I said so to Tommy. Tommy agreed, and predicted the "upstart" would soon be gone.

With the stand for cooperation by the JCCL and the lobbying by Hisaoka for the Kikajinkai's "self-supporting solution," Roy Shintani pushed for direct negotiation with the BC Security Commission. On an overcast April morning, that son-of-a-gun actually marched down to the Marine Building to confront the commission face to face. "Baka!" the NMEG membership later said. Many, however, held him in high regard after hearing the story.

His first interview was with Thomas Finlay, a lower-echelon official. The man's office had the acrid smell of ammonia cleanser and dusty paper. Finlay's round glasses, small moustache, and small stature indicated a man who wanted to be taken seriously, but wasn't. As soon as Finlay started talking to him, Roy knew the "pencil-pusher" couldn't be easily swayed. Roy saw he was *nil intellectually* and so stubborn once he took a position. Once Roy presented him with the NMEG's plea, the milquetoast threatened immediate internment and forced evacuation under martial law. It took all of Roy's will not to sucker-punch the bakatare with a left hook, but he controlled his temper and somehow convinced the "clerk" to let him talk to the big boys upstairs.

At about 2:30 that afternoon, Roy walked into a decidedly different office: grander, well-kept, with heavy oak furniture, and a high ceiling. This was Austin Taylor's office. When the "great man" himself entered in his three-piece wool suit, his middle bulging out from underneath his vest, Roy saw right away the man was cold-hearted, a man doing his job, and not open to any workable plan. With him was Assistant Commissioner F.J. Mead, the second-in-command, another big stinking cheese. Roy was impressed that a little guy like him warranted such attention.

Roy tried to recite to us verbatim what he said: "You seem like men who will listen to reason. I'm desperate; my community is desperate. What you people are doing is a damnable thing. You must know that. We've no kick with leaving our homes if it proves we're good Canadians, but why can't we go together? Why split up families? You must have families of your own. How would you like it if you suddenly faced the possibility of never seeing your children and wives ever again? I'm asking you...no, begging you, to do the right thing: evacuate us in families. Send us to ghost towns if you have to, but together."

Mead seemed to sympathize; he seemed to think we were good, law-biding citizens, but Taylor coldly told him, "We've got a job to do. And I'm going to do it as economically as I can. I know my duty."

Roy tried to argue that it was economical to send us in family groups. With proper food and materials, we'd be happy to do the labour. And they'll be happier for it. But no dice. They were convinced they were doing it for our own "protection." Canadians might rise up in anger, and in fear attack us.

"Such bullshit!" Roy cursed at the after-hours meeting in the Patricia. Taylor was cold-hearted, a man doing his job with no intention of listening to any workable plan. He certainly had no love for his fellow man. "And Mead? He was somebody who can't be trusted. He's supportive on the surface, but underneath it all, he's a snake. You know what happens when you lie with a snake. They're doing us a favour! A temporary measure!"

I disagreed, but said nothing. Mead sounded as if he was a man of compassion thrown into an untenable situation. He didn't agree with the Evacuation, but couldn't do anything but follow orders.

At least Roy tried, even if the effort yielded nothing. He didn't have much of a chance in the first place. He was a helluva guy. I wish I had his audacity. The worst of it was he called attention to himself. They were now aware of him.

ROY SHINTANI AND Tamio Tanemitsu, the last leaders of the NMEG in Vancouver, knew they were being pursued after Jimmy was taken. They kept on the run, evading the Mounties any way they could. From the Patricia Hotel, they moved to the New World Hotel. They then went to a rooming house near Princess Street, before finding shelter in the house of a friend. More than once I was with them on the run.

"Tamio, you and Dan take the lane!" Roy ordered, when a NMEG member told them an inu had given them up. The Mounties were on the way. "I'll lead them away."

"Are you kidding? C'mon, we'll all go together."

"No, we'd have a better chance if we separate."

"We're in this together," Tanemitsu said as he pulled at Roy's arm.

"Okay, okay, let go! Listen, we'll break into the old Showa Club. I heard there're lots of secret passageways to avoid the cops."

"Where?" I asked.

"I don't know, but it's better than waiting here. We're sitting ducks!"

Finally they ended up staying at the home of Taniguchi Fuyuko, a Tanemitsu family friend, on Davie Street. Her husband had been sent to a road gang a few months before. She wasn't so much dedicated to the cause as she felt gratitude for what the NMEG was trying to do. More importantly, she hated the keto. Her daughter's white boyfriend had jilted her for being "dirty skinned."

At nine o'clock on a bright and sunny morning in late April, Taneguchi-san answered a knock at the door. She stood with a bouquet of garden flowers in hand before a tall, handsome hakujin in an expensive grey suit who tipped his fedora in a friendly gesture. He introduced himself as "Inspector Gill of the RCMP."

"They're here!" She shouted out a warning in Japanese.

A rustle of panic came from deep within the house. Roy and Tanemitsu made a mad scramble for the back door, abandoning their breakfasts of bacon and eggs and misoshiru, knocking kitchen chairs aside while grabbing their coats. The screen door slammed to the shouts of "Hold it right there!" and "We gotcha! You can't escape. Give it up." The two young Nisei ran right into the arms of three constables waiting for them just outside.

I inspected the scene of the kidnapping afterward and talked to Taniguchi-san. I soon learned that the Mounties had taken the two NMEG men to the immigration building where they would stay until arrangements could be made to send them to POW Camp 101 at Angler, Ontario. Jimmy and Kawai had been transferred back east before. Those who ratted on them would not be known until everyone gathered again in the concentration camp.

The attention of evacuees going to interior towns is drawn to the fact that when families are placed in these towns, they are required to buy their food at their own expense.

While housing is provided, each family or group of families will board itself by the purchase of supplies — from the local stores in the towns. They will be dependent upon the income which they receive from husbands' wages and children's allowances, or other independent income.

— *The New Canadian, May 2, 1942*

22.

Late April – Early May 1942

I was increasingly alone, standing in the middle of all the chaos. My writing was useless. I wrote a few insufficient lines, but the paper would soon disappear as our own with the commission taking over. I turned my thoughts to physical action, but how far was I willing to go was the question.

I ran into my old pal Dicky Mitsubayashi. I hadn't seen him since the days just after Pearl Harbor. He miraculously appeared at an NMEG meeting in Vancouver. I saw my chance to catch up, especially with news of his parents.

I must admit I hadn't thought of him much during all the madness. I knew his old man had been taken into custody, of course, and hoped he was okay, but I had my own problems. His family's strength would see them through, I thought.

When I finally came face-to-face with Dicky, an odd sense of guilt came over me. He looked the same, except a resentment burned in him, like the deep fire of a blast furnace. The furrows in his broad forehead seemed well defined, as if carved by worry.

"Hey, Dicky!" I said as friendly as I could before the meeting. "What d'you know, what d'you say?"

"That's 'Dick,'" he retorted dismissively.

"Huh?"

"Call me 'Dick,' not 'Dicky.'"

"Yeah, sure. So what's doing?"

"I'm joining the Yamato Boys, Etsu Kaga's gang. They make sense to me."

"Hey, I know those guys. They might be more than you can handle."

"Look, the government kidnapped my dad. They stole my education. And now they want to exile the rest of us, destroy what we got right here," he growled.

"Listen, I got friends who're working to set things right, to get back everything. To get what's owed us," I declared, half-believing it.

His face turned ashen. "My mom's sick. She's having nightmares every night. At least Kaga knows what's what. Not like the oyabun Morii and that boss of yours at the *The New Canadian*. Cooperation, my ass."

Before Dick and I could continue our reunion, the chairman called the NMEG meeting to order. If Dick truly was a Yamato Boy, I wondered why he wasn't using his Japanese first name to be in tune with the spirit of the group. Did he even have one? I suddenly realized I really didn't know my old schoolmate anymore.

Word spread soon thereafter that Kaga called a meeting of all the Yamatodamashii members and interested parties. About seventy men showed up outside the Patricia Hotel on East Hastings; the gathering quickly started blocking the road. I was impressed, but most weren't members; they were just curious and angry. I supposed I shouldn't have been surprised to see Dick in the crowd, but I was.

"So you're here," I commented.

"That's a stupid thing to say."

Before I could explain, Kaga announced from the small land-

ing of the hotel's front steps, "It's time. We must surrender ourselves to the authorities."

The crowd ignited in protest. My mind spun with worry. I feared
the jail cell.

"No, wait. Hear me out!" Kaga said raising his voice. "While I
was incarcerated, I admit to being a little down, but then I realized
this was the best way to serve the Emperor! If we're in jail, we can
inflict more damage than we can now. On the run, we're like little
mosquitoes irritating our enemy from time to time. In jail, we'll all
be together, linked by a common cause like the Buddhists up in Sandon. We'll be able to bide our time for the right moment to strike.
We will be prisoners with honour!" he shouted triumphantly.

The cheer of one united voice rose louder than anyone had
heard in Powell Street since Roy Yamamura last hit a home run.
Kaga had done it again; he convinced everyone, even the curious,
to follow him. They all agreed it was time to make their presence
known outside the NMEG. Their fathers would be avenged!

ON THE "DAY OF VICTORY," as Kaga called it, before joining
everyone at Powell Ground at about three in the afternoon,
Hammerhead was seen at the Tokiwa Yu bathhouse, I ate a thirty-
cent bowl of chicken *donburi* at Tengu's, and Kaga raised a glass of
beer at the Imperial Arms Hotel on Dunlevy. Fifty men milled
around the pitcher's mound and spread out to cover the entire
diamond.

The late April sun was still high in the sky, its warmth a great
comfort after so many overcast days. The trees around the park
were still, as if the wind were holding its breath. Many took in the
moment, some remembering the heroics of the Asahi team on
that very field. It was now their turn. It was the time to reveal the
Yamatodamashii Group to the public.

After much conversation, back slapping, and good wishes, fifteen men led by Kaga and Hammerhead entered five black sedans.
The Hammer grabbed my hand and pulled me inside. Our con-

voy headed slowly along Powell Street and out toward the immigration building. The remaining men followed on foot.

The few Japanese still in the area came out of shops, rooming houses, and homes along the way to line the street as the spontaneous parade passed by. Eyes shone with tears; arms raised to wave white handkerchiefs in an extended farewell; many deciding to join at the last moment. The sun glowed brighter. Even I felt my chest swell with pride. Perhaps maybe my parents saw me and cheered for me.

Others grabbed what they could and ran up to the sedans to pass fruit, *musubi*, buns, clothes, and even a brown fedora through the windows. Cheers rose to greet the Yamatodamashii Group as we waved back as if victory were at hand. It was our proudest moment. Kaga finally saw himself as a soldier in the Emperor's army off to find glory.

Once outside the Powell Street area, we turned right at Burrard Street and headed straight for the railway lands and the immigration building, an evil square block of concrete and barred windows just beyond a cobweb of CPR tracks. The building served as a detention centre for the "most dangerous" of the Japanese Canadians — the Japanese nationals and community leaders — before they were sent off to concentration camps back east in Ontario.

From the hill overlooking the building, Kaga surveyed the rat's nest of tracks below like a *shogun* looking over a battlefield. An uneven path of wooden planks wended its way to the front doors. Behind him, supporters lined up noisily waiting for Kaga to give the signal. With a flourish of his right hand, the fifteen men shook each others' hands and proceeded down the hill to the path. I took up a rear position and followed. We all walked quickly and steadily as if willing to meet fate and history head-on.

"WHAT DO YOU WANT?" an officious-looking captain angrily shouted as he met what must've looked like a bizarre enemy brigade in front of the massive double doors of the building. He was a sour man, his eyes squinting, and his arms folded across his ample chest. He didn't look like someone who tolerated any nonsense.

Kaga stepped forward with growling confidence and demanded, "Take us in! We're giving ourselves up."

"What for?"

"Breaking curfew. Defying the order to leave Vancouver. Littering. Take your pick," he said sarcastically.

Two armed soldiers joined the captain. "That'll be enough of your smart mouth!"

Kaga calmed down. "We've come to give ourselves up," he stated as clearly as he could. "I was arrested for violating curfew and the police didn't realize I was also wanted for not reporting for road camp. All of us here are in a similar situation."

"You're talking about a Vancouver police matter," the captain mistakenly answered, not really listening. "Now clear out of here and take it up with them."

"But we're guilty!"

"Clear out!" the captain repeated as he retreated with his men inside.

Standing in stunned silence, the Yamato Boys stared at the locked doors. Kaga finally turned and spoke to his followers: "All right, sit down. We'll stage a sit-down right here until they take us in. Fujita-san, you brought some musubi, ne?"

"Yeah, my okaasan wanted me to eat right."

"Well, break 'em out. You other fellahs must have good mothers too! Where's the food we got on Powell Street? Looks like we're gonna be here awhile."

A young man approached me and asked, "How long will this take?"

"What's your name, short-stuff?"

"Toshiki Umeda — Tosh, really." He smiled, innocently enough.

"Well Tosh, really, it'll take as long as it takes," I answered. "How old are you?"

"Eighteen."

"I bet you're seventeen."

"Eighteen in a month."

"As old as that? Well, happy birthday to you, *Tosh*." I turned away grinning.

CAMPFIRE SMOKE CLOUDED the air; stray embers floated up and flared out before the upper windows of the prison. The open field of tracks and bare land in front of the immigration building was filled with protesters sitting around the various fires, talking to one another, and enjoying the open-air moment. The original fifteen had been joined by several others in sympathy for the cause.

Eventually, soft voices sang a patriotic song to the Emperor. The stars shone brightly overhead, a gift to the protestors and to other community members who watched the spectacle from abandoned buildings on the hill above.

I thought it odd since here we were out in the open and breaking curfew, yet no one cared: no air raid warden, no police, no military, no Mounties, and no BC Security men.

I envied guys like Tosh. Though he wasn't that much younger than I was, the almost-eighteen-year-old was certain about the cause. He had enough energy and spirit to take on the world. I was not sure I did.

IN THE MORNING, many more supporters came from Powell Street with food and tea. Bullet Gotanda of all people showed up to join the protest.

"What're you doing here?" Hammerhead snarled.

"Wanted to see what was happening," Bullet answered.

"You're with the Cooperators."

"I just came to watch. Can't I do that?" Bullet said sincerely.

Before things got out of hand, Kaga interrupted: "You're welcome, brother. What's in the bag?"

"Manju," he answered. "My contribution to the cause."

We all sat in gentle conversation to keep spirits high and to say goodbye. My okaa showed up. I saw anguish in her face as I told her everything would be okay. She didn't believe me, of course. "Shinobu-*kun*, please come home with me. You'll be safe there," she pleaded.

"I can't Okaasan, there's a principle at stake here," I answered in Japanese.

"Your father is worried about you."

"Ha! I doubt that."

"He is!" she insisted, and continued, "I'm so worried about you. Don't fight *Canada*. There's nothing to win here. Let me go talk to Shoyama-san. He can help."

"No, Mama, you go home. You be safe."

Hammerhead's mother also came to see her son for what she thought was the last time.

"Don't worry, Mama," he began, "I'll be fine. This is something I've got to do. You and sis'll be all right. We'll probably laugh about this years from now."

His okaasan stood before him with damp eyes and a frowning mouth. She looked at him, not fully understanding his English, but perhaps she saw her son's strength. Hammerhead was concerned about her, especially since his otousan was one of the first to be taken. She still didn't know his whereabouts. The night before, she had had a premonition of harm coming to her son. "Ghosts rose by my bed and started screeching at me!" she told her son.

"That don't mean nothing, Mama. Nothing's gonna happen to me," Hammerhead assured.

AND SO IT WAS at about five o'clock that afternoon, the officer, Captain Henderson, and a detachment of armed soldiers emerged from the immigration building to arrest Etsu Kaga and the rest of us for defying curfew and violating orders to evacuate Vancouver.

23.

Once Captain Henderson reported the sit-down, the higher-ups had issued an order to arrest us dissidents. He didn't want to do it, what with all the paperwork I guessed, but he didn't have a choice.

We spent the night in the vast open space of the building's fourth level without dinner (though some managed to sneak in leftovers from the sit-down), and an insufficient number for the blankets to bare canvas cots. A few crudely fashioned tables and chairs stood scattered about the place. The floor was unfinished cement, as cold and as inhospitable as visiting Morii-san for a favour. There were barred windows that opened inwardly on three sides — no curtains, not even black ones — no touches of home.

Even so, spirits were high despite being as uncomfortable as we were. Words of anger erupted every so often when someone complained about the conditions.

I had my doubts as I huddled in a dark corner. Once in a while Hammerhead or Tosh came over to shoot the breeze. No one talked about the situation, but I couldn't help thinking that Kaga had made a tactical error with this strategy. The cold settled in my stomach.

The next morning we ate a breakfast of two slices of bread with a stingy spread of butter, a cup of thin coffee, and one egg, scrambled and thickened with powdered milk. But we were all right.

By late morning a huge number of supporters marched from the hill overlooking the building down to the foot of the rise. Their cheers drew us to the many open windows; we crowded around and jostled each other to see the sea of waving arms. Inspired, we waved back. Every one of the supporters, we liked to think, stared at the solitary and solidly built prison, swelling with pride and shouting encouragement.

The nearby waters of Burrard Inlet remained a calm blue-green. Thick black smoke billowed from the prison chimney. The soot and steam mixed with the overcast skies. Quite suddenly the sun broke through and several beams of light struck the nearby Marine Building and reflected into the confines of the immigration building. The early light appeared dull at first, almost a thin grey, but soon warmly massaged the bare concrete floor.

Besides the eighteen Yamato Boys, there were about sixty-five others, including me, the late-comers, and others already there for various offences. Through an arrangement, relatives came each day to the hill to wait for a signal from their loved ones, usually a piece of clothing, familiar to the visitor, tied to the bars and flapping outside the window. They then knew their relative was okay. Inspired, Hammerhead tied a piece of white cloth to the bars as a symbol of the fight.

One morning a few days after our arrest, when the air was sweet and light, one, then another, and then two more white scarves appeared, held between the bars by prisoners, until what looked like fifteen flicked and snapped in the rising wind, signalling that the cause was still alive and well. The crowd yelled out a ban-zai!, a collective sigh of relief followed.

I refrained from waving a scarf; I never imagined my parents would be out there.

As if on cue, many Issei in the crowd outside shouted out the names of the Yamatodamashii Group members; Nisei waved their own white handkerchiefs. *"Ganbatte!"* everyone shouted in support.

What a glorious time! The voices made their way down the slope of the hill, through the patchwork of railway tracks and thorn bushes, and scaled the soot-caked walls of the immigration building to us, like a river to the sea. Everyone's spirit rose high above the bleak circumstances. The Coast Mountains of North Vancouver presented a bright horizon.

AT THE END of the month, a huge crowd gathered in celebration on the hill. It was the Emperor's birthday, and we started singing "Aikoku Koushinkyoku." The melody drifted outside and floated in the air for a moment before the slight drizzle rained the song on the loyal supporters. Soon everyone joined in. We sounded like a battle of choirs.

There was no sake, fancy food, or decorations, but we made the best of it: sitting, clapping to the beat, and singing at the top of our lungs. Some of the fellahs even danced like it was a festival in Powell Ground. It certainly lightened the mood. The people from the hill waved their arms while we waved pieces of cloth; every inmate now flourished the familiar symbol of defiance and protest.

The singing lasted well into the evening. The voices could be heard for miles around. A few of the supporters remained on the hill unwisely close to curfew. Darkness settled quickly as the tardy scrambled back home or stayed in the building overlooking the hill. No one knew when the law would, or would not, be enforced.

A city in complete darkness: the usually lit-up Hotel Vancouver and the other buildings of the downtown area formed black hulks in the fading sunset before sinking into the night. There were only stars above us prisoners. Each of us Enemy Aliens pinned our hopes on them; they were a distant glimmer of a better way of life in the coming years of expected turmoil, wandering, and shame.

EVERY DAY MORE and more supporters came. I didn't know that so many Japanese were still in town. Their cheers were long and loud. Though the sight of the crowd warmed our hearts inside the prison walls, the boom of distant boats on Burrard Inlet reminded us of what we had lost; the sounds dragged the day into sadness.

The campaign of defiance continued until one day in early May when it was announced that Colonel William Strickland had taken over command of the facility. Strickland, a career army officer, was assigned to restore order. No one knew him, but the guards let it slip that he was a "hard ass."

Kaga rallied his troops by explaining that the actions of the Yamatodamashii Group must have made the BC Security Commission realize they were serious. The immigration building was now a potential powder keg, possibly inspiring others to take up arms and rebel. "It's working!" he cheered, and then said something odd: "Morii-san would be proud."

Strickland, a man of icy conviction, stood an intimidating six-feet tall, with scars on his neck — from some untold battle many wagered. When he arrived in a chauffeur-driven black sedan, I could tell even from a distance he was determined to do his duty efficiently and quickly.

His first order was to close all the windows in the prisoners' area and to keep them closed, with nails if necessary — a low blow since the dirty glass and bars already shut out much of the city life and salty brine of the ocean. "How could they do that?" I asked Kaga, who remained mum on the subject. What could he say? All the men were outraged. Hammerhead kept pounding his fists against the wall — so much so that he eventually bloodied his fists badly. He might've even broken a few bones in his hands. I tried to get him released but to no avail. Strickland just didn't give a damn. There was no sympathy for the troublemakers, even if one stood pathetically with makeshift bandages wrapped around his hands.

As a result of Hammerhead's rash action, the colonel then decreed that we were to stand at attention in a line two feet away from the windows until we tired. This would discourage the waving of white scarves to those waiting on the hill. Guards checked to see that the orders were followed daily and to stop anyone from waving a scarf.

Kaga then requested through Private Sutherland, a sympathetic guard, a meeting with the Security Commission to negotiate the new conditions. Hammerhead even had the nerve to set a deadline. Many thought that as prisoners we were hardly in a position to negotiate, but no one knew the leaders like I did.

Naturally Etsu Kaga became the chief negotiator, a position he relished. We waited two hours for a Security official to show up. It was a hellish wait. I really wondered how a guy like Hammerhead kept his cool.

"They ain't coming," Dick Mitsubayashi concluded, his patience grown thin.

Tosh started pacing. "I shouldn't have done this. I miss my okaa." The teenager yearned for the comforts of home. I couldn't blame him.

Some, like Kaga, began to ramble on philosophically. "We are Japanese. We've got to prove it to the military and, more importantly, to our people in Powell Street, in BC and beyond. Our very actions..."

One hour and fifteen minutes past the deadline, Colonel Strickland unlocked the door and entered the large holding room with two armed guards. Even with the peak of his military cap lowered over his eyes, he looked angry and made sure all of us knew it. "Look here, you little bastards!" he hollered. "I hear you're going above my head, but it isn't going to work."

"Now see here!" complained Kaga as he stood up to the colonel.

"Shut up!" Strickland countered as his ham fist struck Kaga's cheek. The guards automatically raised their rifles. Stunned, and with no chance to use his judo skills, Kaga fell backwards to the ground hard, and a couple of the Yamato Boys rushed to pull him out of harm's way.

"There's no use in waiting for the Security Commission to come hear your whining," the colonel continued. "I'm in charge here, and you'll do as I say. You savvy? And don't go to Private Sutherland again," he warned. "He's gone."

It was true: the one sympathetic guard was reassigned to Tashme, where Jimmy Isojima's family was interned. I later heard the soldier had tried arguing with his superiors to hear the prisoners out, a fatal mistake.

The colonel then tipped his hat, almost in a sarcastic gesture, and left the room, the door slamming shut behind him.

THE NEXT DAY, with the sunlight beating against the dirty windows, we lined up in a row, as ordered, and stared at the closed windows two feet away. Two privates were on guard near the locked exit. The room was strangely silent. The authorities had made no effort to improve the conditions since we were taken into custody. The cots were still bare, the number of blankets inadequate. Hammerhead's white cloth tied to a detached broom handle stood as a flag in the corner. Slowly one man and then another, began complaining about the absurdity of the situation.

"My otousan is out there. He has a right to know I'm all right!"

"How could they let my sixty-five-year-old mother rattle around the house alone and going nuts with worry?"

One of the guards yelled for everyone to shut up, but it was a useless command. Both guards stood frozen in place, unwilling to do anything, perhaps afraid to do anything.

Angry voices continued to rise louder and louder until someone lunged for one of the windows, pulling and opening it to the rush of fresh air. Catching the spirit of anarchy, Hammerhead grabbed at a window and struggled to open it because of his crudely bandaged hands. Frustrated, he grabbed a convenient chair and in a sweep of his arms smashed the glass.

The signal had been given. The immigration building riot had begun.

The two guards immediately escaped through the door, locking it. The prisoners battered their bodies against the door until it gave and crashed open. Many grabbed fire hoses, unwound them, and turned them on. Water gushed into the staircase as wild and thundering *kiai* filled the building. Dick led the others in hurling benches, cots, and tables, smashing them against the walls and windows. All the frustration, anger over his dad, and the shame he and his family suffered must've finally detonated. His flushed face burned with rebellion.

The rest of the men, fuelled by adrenaline, grabbed at the bars and pried them free, the plaster crumbling. Tosh quickly grabbed Hammerhead's flag and joined Kaga, who led a group through the

smashed-in door after the water had been turned off. I followed.
Just as we made the top of the stairs, a volley of gunshots rang out
from below. Kaga and Tosh fell back as everyone retreated into the
holding room. I tasted blood; I had bit my lip hard. Filled with hor-
ror, Tosh grabbed at Kaga, whose shirt was splattered in a chaos of
red blotches. But Kaga was not hurt; he had not been shot. Just as
Tosh was about to ask who had been, someone picked up the fallen
flag and led a second wave through the door to the stairs. More
bullets rang out and ricocheted off walls and ceiling, hitting no
one. Again, the men retreated.

Gas plumes suddenly appeared with the fizzing sound of tear
gas canisters.

Everyone huddled inside the room. Kaga called for wet blankets to be held up to their faces to stop the effects of the gas. But
then more smoke canisters came through the broken windows and
ignited inside. Cries, screams, and coughing followed. I and several
other men doubled over from the fumes. "Poison!" Tosh called
out. "It's poison gas."

I MADE IT over to a broken window to get some air. Outside a
platoon of soldiers surrounded the building, their bayonets shining
in the noonday sun. The whizz of tear gas canisters going off
continued.

And then silence. No one moved. At some point, someone man
aged to wave the white flag outside one of the windows. The crowd
below cheered. The soldiers automatically clicked their weapons
ready, but the cheering continued until the voices were choked off
abruptly. A couple more smoke bombs flew inside and went off. The
flag was immediately withdrawn. It was at that moment someone
at the window threw out a white scarf; it fell in a graceful dance on
the breeze to the train tracks below. It looked like an act of surrender. I saw a battlefield of wounded and suffering soldiers before me,
rubbing the sting out of their eyes and writhing in pain. We were all
together, but each alone in his misery.

Tosh sat, sobbing into his crossed arms.

"You okay?" I asked.

"I didn't sign up for this." He looked up. "I want my okaa."

"None of us did." I put my arm around him. "Don't worry now. It'll be all right. Your okaa will be happy you're all right."

Kaga stood and searched the room for the worst off. He first found Dick Mitsubayashi cradling his banged-up arm, and called for assistance. He continued until he came upon a still body. He kneeled down and raised the man's head to hold. It was Hammerhead, shot during the mêlée, in shock and bleeding badly. Others came over to help, to offer comfort.

The riot was over; the day was lost.

Funeral services will be held at the Armstrong Funeral Home Thursday afternoon, May 10, at 2 o'clock, for Hideo Matsumiya, 21, who succumbed to a fatal illness May 3. He was found dead in a rooming house at 391 Powell Street.

— The New Canadian, May 6, 1942

24.

Soldiers quickly came into the holding area and took the wounded out on stretchers. The rest of us licked our wounds and surveyed the damage. None of us could believe it got so out of hand so rapidly. At about ten o'clock in the evening, two more soldiers with rifles entered and called out, "Dan Sugura? Is there a Dan Sugura here?"

"Yeah, I'm Dan Sugiura," I corrected.

"You work for *The New Canadian*?"

"Yeah...so?"

"Come with us."

They pointed their weapons at me. As mystified as I was, and as filled with dread as I was, I had no choice but to comply.

As it turned out, they took me to Tommy Shoyama who was waiting near the front entrance. I was dumbfounded.

"Tommy? What're you doing?"

"Getting you out of here."

"What? No wait..." And that was that. The next thing I knew I was sitting in his office at the *NC*. Packed boxes were everywhere in preparation for the move. Irene and Frank were nowhere to be seen; I assumed they were either asleep in bed or no longer in town.

"I told you to keep away," Tommy scolded, his glasses clouded with weather and worry. "You've forgotten your family."

"How'd you know...how'd you get me out?"

"Your mother came to me and asked...no, begged me, to help."

"You can't come swooping in and forcing me out!"

"You wanna be behind bars?"

"You don't understand. There's a story —"

"Don't give me that line again. You don't want a story."

"Okay. Okay, I don't want a story. I wanna do something about this...this raping of our rights."

"Watch your language."

"Tommy, you've got to let me do something. I'm going to go with them," I declared, pointing in the general direction of the immigration building. "You can't stop me."

"You want to do something? Meet me here tomorrow morning at 9:00."

"What for?"

"I want to show you what you can do," he said. "Don't try to get back into the immigration building. The authorities know who you are."

I WAS THERE bright and early the following morning. Tommy was too, his eyes filled with concern and compassion. I was burning with rage; my face glowed red.

We walked to the pier on Burrard Inlet. A Union Steamship liner was moored to the dock as passengers readied themselves to board. Crew members were attending to the suitcases, boxes, and trunks piled up on the platform.

"What're we doing here?" I asked obstinately.

Tommy said to look closer.

And there they were: Watanabe Kaga, his wife Akiko, and their twin children, Emiko and Chiemi.

"The boat is headed for Squamish. From there they'll go to Lillooet, a self-supporting camp."

"How? Watanabe claimed poverty."

"That's what I want you to find out. That's what you can do to help our people."

"For what? *The New Canadian* is gonna be taken out of our hands."

"Not forever. I've been told we can regain control once we're in Kaslo."

"When?"

"October, maybe November."

I must admit, my curiosity was tweaked. My resentment subsided; I could forgive, but not forget. That day the clouds were low over Burrard Inlet as their steamer sailed through Second Narrows leaving behind the jagged city skyline. The ocean was black, the sky grey with flecks of blue, green, and perhaps yellow. The rising fog was thick.

I made some enquiries. Reverend Tsuji speculated that Watanabe had turned *inu* in order to gain a place in the East Lillooet camp. But specifics were not to be had. I actually wanted a face-to-face with Watanabe to look into his eyes. I long suspected he was involved in some kind of deceit. Cynicism settled in the bottom of my soul like water seepage in a mineshaft.

When I approached Tommy about East Lillooet, he advised, "I think you should first go see Kunio at Christina Lake." Kunio Shimizu had escaped the clutches of Morii's machinations through his fiancée Marion and her family. They somehow managed to get him to their self-supporting camp. Deals like that it seemed were being made all over the place. Neither Tommy nor I held any enmity toward him. Anything for love.

I knew this was a delaying tactic. The whole thing was to prevent me from joining the Yamato Boys. I appreciated Tommy's concern, but I was my own man. He had to realize that. I said nothing in return; I just stared until he agreed to East Lillooet, skipping Christina Lake altogether.

Tommy spoke to the Security Commission about a travel pass. I made one other request: a pass to Tashme. I decided to see Gladys and her family first, and then find Jimmy and the Yamato Boys back east. I, of course, didn't reveal my whole plan. Tommy shrugged and made no comment. He added the destination to the request.

BEFORE I LEFT for parts unknown, I attended a Morii rally. I guessed, given the number of supporters that came to the immigration building, I shouldn't have been surprised to see a sizable crowd of Issei with more than a few Nisei. I knew the commission had dissolved the Liaison Committee. This was perhaps the reason why.

The Oyabun continued to give speeches preaching cooperation, but now he was seen as a Government lackey. No one except the weak and desperate listened to him. He still claimed to have the welfare of the Japanese at heart. More importantly, he stuck to his guns by saying the pride of the divine Emperor was at stake, something fewer and fewer Issei cared about. It was all lies; he was hastening the dismantling for his own purposes.

"I know I said that just the men would be removed and not the families, but I promise you, I will bring everyone back together soon," Morii told a large crowd. His voice quivered as he spoke, squeezing out all the sincerity he could muster to the people before him. "I've made a new deal with the commission, and I have the guarantee of Austin Taylor himself."

No one believed him. Some former Morii supporters suggested that the Oyabun himself had come up with the strategy to flush out the nationals in Hastings Park. Isamu Otagaki, the informer, could never have come up with a plan like that all on his own. He was no bright flame in a chouchin at *Obon*. And then there was the corruption in the Liaison Committee.

Several community voices rose up against Morii and his "committee" as a result. The end of his appointment was not enough. It was clear that Ottawa had no intention of reuniting Japanese-Canadian families in a month, or ever. The bitter taste of deception must have coated Morii's throat.

Panic began to spread throughout Powell Street and out in the camps. Talk was that a new law was coming to ban each and every Japanese Canadian from returning to the coast, even after the war. There was even a hint of deportation, citizen or not. Morii had no way of stopping this; in fact, he may have been helping the ban.

Damn the Emperor, damn Japan, and damn Powell Street: he was taking care of Number One.

At the Japanese Hall rally, I saw an unexpected change in Morii's character when confronted with the open hostility of *his* constituency. The Oyabun no longer spoke of cooperation with the Government; instead, he seemed to be apologizing of all things.

Tommy and I watched the gangster from the back of the room. Irene soon joined us. I was so happy to see she was still in town. I tried to say something, but she naturally called me an idiot and pointed to the Oyabun. I just smiled.

Morii, with his eyes squeezed shut, chose his words carefully. His short, compact body tightened with the tension of the moment. The audience shifted uncomfortably in their chairs as he spoke, their discontent festering in the mounting heat of the hall. A few Nisei leaned against the cool green plaster of the back wall to show their defiance, but they refrained from jeering.

Too bad Jimmy wasn't there. He was long gone by that point, picked up by the Mounties and sent away. He would've been quite transformed seeing the Oyabun's downfall. Once arrested, perhaps at the indirect order of the gangland boss, he had thrown himself into a tornado of self-doubt and bewilderment from which he would never quite recover. Seeing Morii in such a vulnerable position might have saved him from all that.

"The guy's all wet," said Lucky Nagami, son of the Powell Street baker and confectioner.

"Yeah, he's washed up," agreed Blackie Nagai, grinning at his pun.

Tommy and I remained silent as we listened to Irene's translation of the Oyabun's Japanese carefully.

"I've been lied to. The Security Commission guaranteed that all the families would be reunited in Vancouver. But they won't keep their word. You know I lost my position. When they no longer needed me, they got rid of me. Don't you see? I was trying to keep everyone together... trying to bring everyone back... but that's not what they wanted. I...I...I wasn't working fast enough to get everyone out. I didn't want that. They wanted that and so got rid of me. I am not responsible. I have always had your welfare in mind."

A chorus of boos from the audience rose up like an ocean wave. "Stop lying to us!"

"Damare!" he commanded. "The Emperor will come for —"

"Shut it, you goddamned Mikado lover!" yelled a Nisei from the back.

The dissent grew steadily and quickly into a storm of English and Japanese. "My mother got dysentery in the Pool because of you!" declared someone from the middle of the crowd. "Inu ... inu ... inu ..." the mob chanted.

"You knew all along that we'd never see our families again! How much blood money did you get?"

Morii ignored the accusations and continued, now trying to shout above the din. "You have nothing to fear ... you have nothing. ... I have another guarantee. A good one this time from a reliable source who has never betrayed me. I ... you can depend on him. You will be rewarded for your suffering...after we win the war —"

Someone closeby threw a bottle at the podium and caught the Oyabun's left cheek. He recoiled, covering up his face with both hands, wobbled, and ducked under the podium, but he quickly stood up in an effort to recover. His face bloodied, he cried out in a pitiful voice, "Please ... please ..." His bloodstained hand reached into the air in a useless bid to win back his people.

Individuals began shuffling out, shouting their rejection of, and disdain for, the slumping Oyabun. Even his henchmen were powerless as more and more people headed for the exit. Minor shoving took place; Suzuki and Moriyama quickly moved to block the exit but were shoved aside by the crowd. Morii gamely stood atop a nearby chair while calling out in desperation.

25.

Though I savoured Morii's downfall, it was all getting to be too much for me. I found myself crying in moments when I was home from the Patricia. The house was empty, my mother busy *donburo* in the store packing things up, putting things away. I didn't know where Dad was.

Then the day came when my parents had to move out. Okaasan descended into a deep sadness, so much so she could cry no more. Otousan remained stoic, though his vow to stay no matter what came to nothing. He went through the motions of leaving, not really acknowledging the reality. A military truck arrived and Dad and I loaded it. The amount of luggage and boxes seemed small considering the imposed limit of three hundred pounds of possessions per family were contained inside.

I could see the worry and skepticism on my mother's face. I tried to reassure her, but the words never came. Not until the train station.

On the platform, the pile of suitcases and wooden boxes lay at their feet. I uselessly straightened them, a pathetic gesture.

"Leave them alone," Okaa commanded. "I hate packing... reminds me of leaving Japan." Mom quietly held a handkerchief to her face.

"I'll be at Kaslo with *The New Canadian* gang," I said to her. "I was told you're going to Lemon Creek. You won't be so far away. I'll get a pass and visit you from time to time."

I also promised to look for my brother Herb and his family. I heard he was ordered to leave his home in Cumberland shortly after people were moved out of Hastings Park. Thank the Buddha, he and family were spared the Pool; don't know why, just lucky I guessed. Maybe they would all be close together. I must admit I fancifully imagined I'd marry Gladys one day, and we'd all be together with Jimmy and his family; his and my parents would be busy taking care of the grandkids while forgetting this ordeal.

I stared at Otousan, who refused to make eye contact. I sighed, said goodbye to my distressed Okaasan and left. As I walked toward the exit, the train whistle blasted. I took one last look, and there was my father crying on Mom's shoulder, her arms half-wrapped around him like a blanket against the cold. He had suddenly realized it was all true. He had lost everything.

It's over a month now since you left. Didn't we give you a grand send-off? Half of Japtown was down at the station. There was shouting and laughing and waving of handkerchiefs. Somebody's gramophone was playing "Blues in the Night." The pretty Nisei girls were out in full force...

It's sunny today on Powell Street. The sun is warm and comfortable. To think that only a few days ago it was so cold, and I was pouring down curses on Vancouver weather...

The baseball season has started at Powell Grounds. Crowds of fans flock to every game as if they didn't know the Asahis aren't playing anymore. The Wurlitzer from Sisters' Coffee Shop wails its Japanese popular songs defiantly across the grounds...

Some evenings I wander down to Ernie's to drown my sorrows in a bottle of Coke. Then some silly dope would start playing the Wurlitzer like mad as if to get the most out of his last days at Ernie's...

It won't be long now. With a glad heart, I shall shake off the dust of Vancouver.

— *The New Canadian, May 20, 1942*

26.

As I strolled along Powell Street after leaving the train station, I grew despondent over the consequences of our identity, our sin. The Japanese houses were resolutely silent, some boarded up, others with windows gaping open, delinquents having smashed them for kicks. Stores stood empty, their signs in *kanji* defaced, painted over, or torn away. The once proud Buddhist church stood with broken windows, bashed-in doors and walls scarred with graffiti. The language school, Uchiboro's Dress Shoppe, Union Fish, Ernie's Café, Uchida Bookstore: all waited for rot to set in.

My father's breakdown devastated me. I wanted to run back, to hold him in my arms, rub his back, and tell him it was all right. But all I could do was walk away, abandoning my parents while swelling with regret and shame.

I suppressed my guilt and wrote in my latest notebook:

the Powell Street
buildings
    cried seas and
  oceans as compassion

sank within the muted Kuroshio

I noticed I now had quite a pile of books, but I couldn't take them all with me back east. *Nimotsu naru.* Maybe Tommy...no, Irene, could take them to Kaslo.

I quickly moved into the Patricia Hotel before the Mountie vultures came. I then packed for my travels to Lillooet, Tashme, and Kaslo.

SELF-SUPPORTING SETTLEMENTS had sprung up all across British Columbia in obscure places with names like Christina Lake, Minto, Bridge River, Magna Bay, and Taylor Lake. Hisaoka got his wish; everyone wondered if the great man could live with it.

Among the self-supporting camps, East Lillooet was a special case. Though the town of Lillooet was sizable, the locals weren't all that friendly to the Japanese Canadians. The only welcome was a handful of Canadians on the train platform. Every man had a leather-satchel face that scowled at the new settlers with suspicion and hate. A few carried rifles.

The good Canadians of Lillooet, it seemed, didn't like the idea of hundreds of Japanese coming to their part of the world. So they had voted and decided to put the Enemy Aliens across the bridge over the Fraser River in a wide area of dead land east of town that they named "East Lillooet."

I arrived on a bright, crisp day in early June; the mountains shone in sharp relief with a topping of snow and the mass of blue sky above. I could smell the fresh-cut pine in the air. How could anything be wrong?

Most of the three hundred or so self-supporters lived in organized rows of tents in an open field. Too few tarpaper shacks had been completed and occupied; others remained skeletal frames with rough exposed floors vulnerable to the elements. The privileged inhabitants' clothes were threadbare, unable to stop the cold winds. I was welcomed, but offered little except my own tent. Confusion bubbled in my head. *This can't be the cushy life.*

After settling in, I walked throughout the encampment, noticing a faint fetid smell lingering in the air. It acted like some perverse guide to Dante's circles of hell. After conversing with many along the way, I found out what the story was. The townsfolk, as a comic torment, decided to locate East Lillooet adjacent to their garbage dump. The rotting food, junk, and accompanying rodents were the perfect backdrop for the Enemy Aliens.

I later learned the first group of Japanese Canadians, which came from Vancouver in early April, had it the worst. They found nothing but sagebrush and dirt. The cold wind reminded everyone of killer winters past and to come. They had to buy tents and pitch them in the dark. They also had to buy food and supplies, which included a few kerosene lanterns. Predictably, they quickly ran out of money.

Shigeishi-san, a devout Christian woman frosted with age, told me about those early days. During the first night, the evacuees huddled in the one large tent they had bought together from a local man. He overcharged of course. They shivered under barely adequate blankets when they heard a mysterious rustling outside. The sound of horses snorting and moving about frightened everyone to distraction. She swore it was the Four Horsemen of the Apocalypse. Finally, after angry and curious voices were heard, she stuck her head through the opening of the tent only to fall back, screaming loudly.

Some of the men then slipped through the opening and saw the unearthly sight of eight or ten men on horseback in the moonlight: Indians attracted by the white canvas and bright kerosene lamps. Shigeishi-san peeked again out of curiosity. She never knew what the "savages" wanted because they rode off, probably scared by her guttural cry.

Yasuura Koji, the Issei Kikajinkai representative, supervised the building of the makeshift houses. As a result, a sea of tents and a few hastily built cabins rose in the forlorn field. The Wickwire Lumber Company was more than happy to overcharge for materials: $150 to $200 per house, depending on the size desired. Early every morning, volunteers from the camp carried water in buckets and cans from down the hill to the Fraser River about half a mile away. The town proper had plumbing of course, but no provisions were made for East Lillooet. After some time, a committee negotiated with the townsfolk for drinking water to come in barrels on trucks. It was difficult to negotiate because the townsfolk would only meet on the bridge at a time of their choosing — sometimes early in the morning, sometimes late at night, sometimes both.

Most of the Japanese had brought clothing and four days worth of food from Vancouver, but no one knew how long this internment was going to last. There was nothing "temporary" about this measure. So rationing had to be put into place. Fruits and vegetables were not easily had; no one knew how to grow them. The internees were businessmen, professionals, and well-to-do people, not farmers.

By June, food was becoming a real concern. Though a small makeshift market flourished on the town side of the bridge, the East Lillooetians quickly ran out of money paying the exorbitant prices. The market was taken down and the Japanese Canadians took to scouring the surrounding land for anything to eat. Someone found a patch of *warabi*, enough for all in the settlement, but every last plant was soon picked. Others were lucky enough to catch small animals, though many had to be taught how to prepare the carcasses and cook them. The women cut into the beasts, exclaiming, *"Iyarashii."* But it was fresh meat. Weeds, shoots, bitter dandelions, wild mushrooms, tender inner bark, and leaves, all went into thin soups (any remaining *dashi* was meted out niggardly). No one was concerned about how safe something was to eat. They counted themselves lucky; only one rather sickly man died of suspected mushroom poisoning.

Rice was *the* precious commodity. Some women had their children scrounge every nook and cranny for stray grains of rice carelessly dropped in the early days. They soon did without rice, but it hurt not being able to dig into a heaping bowl of the staple.

It was hardest on the kids. Families took to eating only twice a day to preserve rations. Some mothers forced their sons and daughters to take a noon-day nap so they wouldn't have to hear the whimpering and interminable chorus of "I wanna go home... please mama, take me home..." That's when I noticed how skinny the children were. Everywhere I went, children with haunted eyes devastated me. I wished I could conjure up a mountain range of rice and banquet tables of *ogochisou* for them.

During my exploration, I casually asked where I could find the Watanabes. Shigeishi-san directed me to a small newly-built shack at the end of the main drag, a wide dirt road down the middle of the camp. The building seemed sturdy enough, though the walls were obviously thin; the snowcapped mountains in the background were spectacular, with no other cabins obstructing the entirely supernatural view. Shigeishi-san then sent me off saying, "Go with God."

27.

Watanabe-no okusan stood out in front of her crudely built cabin, with its disjointed corners and untrimmed roof, hanging wet, limp laundry. I barely recognized her from her photo on her husband's desk back in Steveston. She was pleasingly plump then. Now she seemed haggard; her face was drawn, her youth evaporating. Most of the inhabitants looked as she did, but there seemed to be an extra burden on her. Most remarkable was the fact that it hadn't been that long since she arrived.

"Watanabe-san? Gomen nasai, ne. I am Sugiura Shinobu and I'm visiting from Vancouver . . . I mean Kaslo."

"Hai," she said in a cheery voice. With the prospect of company, her eyes beamed, and without a hint of suspicion, a smile graced her face.

We bowed and exchanged pleasantries. I then asked if I could see her husband.

"Oh, he's not here at the moment. Probably at some meeting."

I then explained I wanted to learn what brought them to East Lillooet. For *The New Canadian* I revealed. I knew I had caught her off-guard, and she immediately grimaced. I assured her it was mostly for my own interest, for posterity, since the paper wasn't in our control for the time being. I didn't tell her I wanted to confirm what kind of deal her husband had made with the Security Commission.

She relaxed and invited me to sit outside in the sun. The weather-beaten chair, salvaged no doubt from the local dump, creaked at the joints, but held. At least the garbage heap was good for something. The accompanying weather-peeled small table was just the right height for our tea. She served the *ocha* in a Japanese pot and cups, which maintained some of their colour and grace. Sitting with me, she was remarkably chatty. I guessed she was starved for company. Still, I perceived a reservoir of secrets within her that I would never tap. I had to fill in the gaps.

I learned that the Watanabes and four other families boarded a CPR train after the two-hour boat ride to Squamish from Vancouver, a town at the northern tip of Howe Sound, and headed for Lillooet. The wilderness closed in on the tracks as the train wound its way through rock, forest, and rivers until the small town came into view.

Her first impressions of Lillooet were somewhat lyrical. "It was so beautiful. I loved the smoke climbing up the mountains. It was just like being home in Japan."

But grim reality soon intruded when they got off the train. The Watanabes were met by BC Security men in grey overcoats who pushed them into "stagecoaches" (cars with their roofs torn away) for a short ride to their new home in East Lillooet. Just outside town, they crossed a wooden bridge over the Fraser River. It must've seemed like some kind of border between civilization and the land of *Yomi*. The driver warned them not to cross the bridge back to town without a pass, on penalty of death.

She placed her hand over her mouth as she said in Japanese to her husband, "The gaijin would sooner shoot you than ask questions."

"There isn't much law out here," I observed.

Skeletal cabins, the bare lumber wet and shining brightly, greeted the Watanabes. With no cabin available, they were escorted to an oversized tent. When she saw them, she gasped. She couldn't believe her eyes. Promises had been made; none kept, apparently.

The Security man told her they were there on their own dime, as it were. I can only imagine the effect on Watanabe.

THE SHADOWS GREW long and the wind picked up as evening drew closer. The tea was cold, but she warmed the pot with tepid water from inside her cabin.

"Etsuo's eyes were red and crazy," she spoke with all sincerity, "and he was shaking all the time. I was afraid because he was truly afraid."

The sun was low in the cradle of two mountains when Okusan noticed that we had been talking a good long time.

"Goodness, how long have we been sitting here? The tea is cold again," she said while palming the pot. "I've kept you long enough talking such nonsense."

"No, no," I protested. "I've been enjoying your company."

"You must have other things to do and I have cooking — " she said with concern.

"One more thing, Okusan, if you don't mind. Please."

"Yes?"

"When did you get this cabin?"

"Oh, a few weeks after we arrived. We were lucky, I guess. There was a push to get the cabins built."

"Not everyone is in yet," I remarked.

"True . . . true," she said wistfully.

"Where are the children, by the way?"

"Oh, off somewhere," she said almost as an aside.

"And how are they?"

She sighed. "When hunger came round like a wolf, I had to talk to my husband. I told him we can't go on like this. Emiko was getting to be skin and bones. Lucky for Chiemi, she's stronger. But they both can't last much longer."

Watanabe-no okusan bent over and sobbed before me without hesitation, without embarrassment. She had been crushed by the prospect of starvation. The lament floated on the steady breezes that swirled in and about the tents and cabins, like a water current.

I LEFT WATANABE-NO OKUSAN to her sorrow. Tears too filled my soul as I walked away. Like all Japanese Canadians, she held in so much. But for some reason, she let most of it out for me, a complete stranger. Maybe it was because I *was* a complete stranger, and not a resident of East Lillooet. The Evacuation helped. Only such extraordinary circumstances could have effected such a reaction.

My stomach hurt with intense sympathy and I asked myself what I was doing. It wasn't my goal in life to make middle-aged women cry. I should be sitting in Ernie's with Dicky or Jimmy talking about girls or school or work over a soda. Not this. Not this torment.

As I walked about the camp, I came across two girls, both in their late teens, gazing into the distance. When I approached them I had the feeling they were sisters.

"Hi!" I said. "Are you the Watanabe girls?"

One twisted around and scowled: "Who wants to know?"

The other quickly interrupted, "I'm sorry. My sister is too rude for words."

I must admit I was taken aback, but not so much by her impudence. There was something else about her that both attracted and repelled me. "That's . . . that's okay."

"I'm Chiemi," answered the first abruptly; she turned back to the view.

"Yes, we're Watanabes. I'm Emi."

"I was talking to your mother —"

"Oh! You're the new one in town. Word gets around fast, you know," Emi explained.

Okusan was right. Emi looked frail, but was as charming as could be. Despite the hardness of her gaze, her soft eyes, nose, and cheeks conspired to make her pretty. Chiemi was indeed stronger, her body athletic, but she was gruff and unfriendly. Yet there was *something*. I didn't know what at first, but then, when she faced me, I saw that her eyes were misaligned. One was sloped off-kilter.

"I'm . . . I'm . . . only here temporarily," I stammered.

"So are we," Chiemi said sarcastically.

"I mean, I'll be leaving soon. For Tashme. I've got a pass."

Emi almost whimpered. "I wish we could go with you."

Chiemi softened. "Are you coming back? I mean, Mom likes company, is all."

"Yes," Emi added. "Come back and have dinner at our house.. . I mean, we could all spend more time talking."

I really didn't want to leave — their friendly, coy ways tickled me, but I just had to leave the camp and strained to give them credible reasons. I made assumptions: there was little food, and I was taking up space in the assigned tent. I also would become a burden on the meagre water supply. (I didn't say this but my own food supply, brought from Vancouver, was running low.) They bought it and bid me farewell. I left the girls, promising that I'd contact the Red Cross on the settlement's behalf.

I sacrificed my face-to-face with Watanabe Etsuo for another reason, one that had implications for my future. I had to see Gladys.

My plan to visit Tashme was uppermost in my thoughts. I wanted to tell Gladys how I felt. I needed something to live for. The memory of her touch still warmed my skin. Maybe she would laugh at me but I had to go for broke.

28.

Tashme was the least isolated of the internment camps. It was only fourteen miles southeast of Hope, a small town that offered a few distractions, and about 100 miles east of Vancouver. I thought of Gladys's joke: "Hope is just down the road." Surrounded by the Cascade Range, Tashme sat on the AB Trites farm, leased by the Government for $500 a month. When the first internees arrived in the spring of 1942, workers had built 350 cabins. In neat rows, they looked like grave markers. The large barn that was already on the property was divided into thirty-eight apartment units, each housing eight people. It became known as the "Apartments." The camp name was a "tribute" to three of the Security Commission's top dogs: TAylor, SHirras, and MEad.

The place wasn't so bad according to the inhabitants. The only overseers were a couple of government administrators and Private Will Sutherland, who'd been sent there as punishment after his interference at the Vancouver immigration building. I had never met him in Vancouver so I checked in with him first. He was an affable enough guy. Handsome as hakujin go, but he tried a bit too hard to be a friend, instead of being a guard.

As I trudged through the spring mud, I noted the beauty of the mountains partially hidden by mist and the imposing barn in front of me. I heard birds chirping. I stopped to gaze at the roll of the land gently sloping toward the forest depths.

"Hey stranger," a lilting voice said from behind me.

The hairs on the back of my neck stood up, and a tingle shot through my spine. "Gladys!" I said as I turned. Her hair had grown longer than I remembered it. Her face, that glorious and soft-featured face, was as open as ever. Her body had been sculpted with the curves of womanhood. She laughed at my outburst.

"What're you doing here? I thought you were up in Kaslo with the paper."

"Yeah...yeah." That damned nervous stammer. "I got a pass. I'm...I'm due, that is, I'm on my way...on my way back to Vancouver from Lillooet to help move *The New Canadian* and..." My voice petered out. I was prattling on.

"Same old Danny. Tashme is a little out of your way, isn't it?"

"Yeah, I thought I'd drop by to see how you are...I mean, you and your parents."

She laughed again but I didn't mind.

"I want to be able to tell Jimmy you're all right."

"You're seeing Jimmy?" she said anxiously.

"Yeah, I'm gonna go to Ontario after Vancouver. Jimmy's a priority."

She crooked her elbow in mine and pulled me toward her family's cabin. "You have to have supper with us. Mom'll be so happy to see you. Oh, I'm so happy you came!"

"You are?"

"Of course, silly."

IT WAS LIKE old times: the same simple delicious meal of fish and rice. No garlic, but shoyu for flavour. Where Okusan got the fish and shoyu was anyone's guess. She served some *tsukemono* saved from Steveston. And of course ocha.

Okusan asked all kinds of questions about Jimmy. I told her what I knew of him after they had left Vancouver, but I could say nothing about his time in Ontario. She seemed disappointed, but she drew strength from my promise to see her son and pass along any message and gifts she cared to give.

They conveyed what I said to their otousan and he grunted acknowledgement. I wasn't so sure he fully grasped who I was and what connection I had to his son. At least, I could see that the mountain air agreed with him. He was now walking, in his way, all around the camp.

After the dishes were done, Okusan put her husband to bed and sat with him until she was too tired to stay up. Gladys stayed with me by the potbelly stove. The heat reached out, touching her cheeks before massaging skin, limbs, the heart, and the soul. The fine lines around her eyes radiated out to her slightly parted lips. We talked quietly.

"Danny, you were so shy back in Steveston."

"What do you mean?"

"You never talked much to me. You're not my brother, you know."

"Well, I'm so much older..." I wanted to dispute her claim since I remember talking quite a bit the evening after the boat round-up. But I thought better of it.

She laughed. "You're not that much older."

"I am so, five or six years!" I sounded like I was ten.

Gladys suddenly pressed two fingers to my lips to shush me, and I thrilled to her touch. I realized that in moments like that all my concerns were irrelevant. She then swivelled and put on a coquettish smile. "I wanted you to talk to me. Lots."

"You did? Why didn't you say something?"

"Girls don't do that. I can only imagine what you would've thought of me."

I didn't respond, but I did smile. We stayed in communal silence after that and well into the night.

Sometime between sundown and moonrise, we stood outside the cabin face to face. I gazed into her darkening face and raised my hands to hold her in place, as if she would disappear if I didn't. I then moved to kiss her. For a split second I thought I felt resistance, but then she relaxed into my arms; her hair was as warm as a summer's day; her kiss was like a soft rain.

I self-consciously touched my chin and I confessed, "I ain't no great catch, Gladys. No Cary Grant..."

198 • THE THREE PLEASURES

"Sh-h-h," she said, and closed her eyes as we kissed again. "You ain't so bad," she concluded as she beamed in the night air.

Starlight etched across our brows and I saw my future unfold.

IN THE MORNING we were exhausted, having stayed up all night, but we were lifted far above ourselves, or at least I was. The whole thing might've seemed capricious, but that was what love was for us. I finally found the one, ironically, in Steveston, a "hick" town. Was I really that stupid?

The camp was good, Gladys told me over breakfast, until Morii's men arrived. The Security Commission, as a favour to Morii for ferreting out some of the nationals in the community, provided provisions for his men — his thugs really. The gang members inherited Tashme, or "Kojima Village" as it became known among Japanese Canadians.

Sensei Kojima, the judo master turned village boss, set himself up as leader soon after he arrived. He had his boys bully everyone into voting him camp leader. He then built a still somewhere in the woods — very much a Black Dragon tactic. Late at night, they drank and gambled in one of the cabins. Who was there to stop them? One lone soldier? Curfew had been lifted for the camps, so many of the Issei found themselves joining in out of boredom or a sense of loyalty. Soon the Kojima men hired or forced many of the young women into "service" to bring in "customers," just like Showa Club days.

"Oh, Danny, it was awful. You remember Onizuka Kazuo?"

"No, who's he?"

"You know, the man stabbed during the boat round-up."

"Yes . . . yes I do know him," I said, my stomach gurgling in the memory.

Onizuka had just been reunited with his family in Tashme after six months up at the Three Valley Gap road camp. It disturbed him to no end to find that his teenage daughter, Haruko, was forced to work as a waitress. His wife, Chisato, had been powerless. Both feared the worst for her.

In a violent rage, Onizuka and his friend Izumi Masumi, the decorated WWI vet, stormed over to Kojima's cabin one night and broke through the door. "He and Izumi-san grabbed his daughter and made for the door. But Rikimatsu stopped him," Gladys said.

"Rikimatsu? He's here?" I asked.

"He knew it was Onizuka right away," Gladys continued. "But instead of punishing him, Rik-san said he could go with his daughter if he said why he was stabbed."

"All Onizuka said was to ask Morii-san. Ask him why he sent the money to Steveston. Remember that?"

"That's all he said?" I asked. "And he got away with it."

"Yes, that is until..." A few days later, Chisato found her husband beaten and lying on the ground behind the Apartments. Cross-legged next to him was his friend Izumi, in shock and cradling his broken arm. She immediately went for help. Kojima and his gang had their revenge for their impudence.

Gladys explained, "Before Onizuka left for the hospital in Kamloops, he told his wife his stabbing was a case of mistaken identity. The Oyabun had thought he owed him money. He was wrong."

So the money to help the fishermen was sent out of guilt. Who would've thought Morii was capable? "How's Onizuka doing?"

"Don't know, haven't heard a thing."

I was furious. It was bad enough in Vancouver, but now here too. There was no way to escape the Black Dragon. Then Gladys told me something that disturbed me even more.

Shortly after arriving in camp in April, the Isojima family was surprised to find they enjoyed life in the mountains. The fresh air seemed to help Otousan. He could hobble around the camp on his own, and soon discovered where he could buy some bootleg whiskey. He was caught drunk now and again. His wife, too, enjoyed the stability that had returned to their lives. Jimmy was missing and they were living in a shack, but life had become routine. As for Gladys, she mixed with the other teenagers in camp, but soon found them lacking.

"All they want to do is dance and have parties. They talk about boys all the time."

I smiled to myself.

"But Danny, it's gonna be 1943 soon enough. This war can't last forever."

Then Private Will Sutherland started paying attention to her.

Everyone in Tashme knew he wasn't happy. Sutherland had been done in by us at the immigration building. His military career was essentially over. On top of that, the solitary soldier resented being in an isolated camp with only a hick town down the road. He had an eye for the ladies, and was frequently seen "talking up the girls," despite their being Japanese teenagers. His flirtations caused much dismay for the parents. The girls, for their part, enjoyed the attention.

"The girls say he likes me," Gladys said. "I don't believe it, but he does spend a lot of time with me."

"I oughta have a talk with him. Tell him what's what."

Gladys smiled at me as she wrapped her arms around my neck. "You're sweet."

"No, I'm serious. Maybe I should stay."

"I can handle him. If I walk around with my father, he wouldn't dare do anything."

Made sense, I supposed.

"Besides, you have to find Jimmy for us. You promised."

I knew there was something I didn't like about that soldier. Though he was sympathetic at the immigration building, he was one of those fast-talking mugs who found life easy, even if they got into trouble. He probably advocated for the Yamato Boys for some personal advantage. These guys were smooth and charming in a greasy kind of way. A deep sense of anger, and then fear, swelled in me.

Against my better judgement, I agreed to leave to find Jimmy. I gathered some bottles of tsukemono, spare clothes, and a few letters for Jimmy from Okusan before hitting the road. I also took with me Gladys's love.

My mind was set: once I returned to Vancouver, I was determined to tell Tommy I would go to Ontario. Nothing could stop me.

AS I WALKED down the road to Hope, it started to rain. Then an odd sensation came over me. The silver rain, like bits of starlight in the drizzle, turned into syllables, consonants, and then words. They joined together and then conspired to turn into a poetic premonition. My knees buckled. I committed the poem to memory until I could write it in the notebook I had brought with me.

I wheeled around to see Gladys as she stood vulnerable, and perhaps regretful, waving goodbye in the gathering darkness of the forest. She was the poetry of cold, crisp air and distant, unknown seas.

> *walking*
>   *by the sea,*
> *the wild waves*
>   *sing chords*
> *dark   of sorrow and shame.*

> *her seaweed hair*
>   *drifted with the*
> *currents of water and wind*

> *as her weathereyes closed to the clouds on the horizon.*

How time flies. It's been five weeks now since that day you, Dad, and little sisters walked out of that yellow house and into a large, waiting bus.

I didn't wait to see the bus pull out, did I, Mom? Gosh, somehow I couldn't. I walked down the bridge and ran up the steps into your bedroom. I looked around and the realization that for a long time I wouldn't see you in that room left me with a hollow, dull, sinking feeling.

Today, for the first time since you left, I took a hurried trip there to my beloved home country. You know it's supposed to be a forbidden area for persons of Japanese race, so I had to have a permit to go there . . .

The only place there's any fishing now is over at the towhead on the "Jap Bar." I think the name should be changed to "Finn Bar" now.

— The New Canadian, June 20, 1942

29.

"**D**anny, I'm sorry to tell you this, but your friend, Nishizaki . . ." Tommy spoke in his calm, reassuring voice, full of warmth and sympathy. "Hammerhead? What happened?"

"He's dead," he said with finality.

"C'mon Tommy, don't joke about a thing like that."

"I'm sorry, Danny, but it's true. He succumbed to his wounds a few days ago."

Disbelief turned to shock. My body felt like it was caving in. Pain ate away from my insides. I looked at Tommy and saw truth staring back at me.

We stood in *The New Canadian* office in Vancouver within a canyon of boxes. Frank's scrawl marked them for Kaslo, an obscure town in the middle of the Selkirk Mountains, some five hundred miles away. He and I were the only ones from the *NC* left in town.

I needed Irene's strength, Frank's wildness, and Kunio's steady intelligence, but they weren't to be had.

"How? How?" I asked uselessly as I reached out for a chair.

When I sat down, Tommy continued. "I have an interview with Colonel Strickland. I want him to explain why your friend's death was judged to have been of 'natural causes.'"

"Natural causes? That's nothing but…nothing but bull roar!" I could feel emotion and tears welling up inside me. "They can't be serious."

"Would you like to come?" he asked.

OUTSIDE THE COLONEL'S office, located down an echoing hallway just to the right of the front doors of the immigration building, Tommy adjusted his glasses fastidiously as we waited to be summoned. The place — with its grey walls, dull floors, acrid smoky smell, and cold air collecting in its corners — had the chill of eternity about it. I was reliving my past.

I was nervous, and I couldn't see Tommy being calm either, like it was a walk down Powell Street on a Saturday afternoon. At 1:45 in the afternoon, we were let into a sunny room by a rigid uniformed soldier. The light flooded in through a large floor-to-ceiling window, its expanse of glass protected by steel mesh. I squinted in the brilliance and I felt my way toward a chair. I could sense the presence of the colonel who remained a hulking silhouette behind a plain wooden desk. No one said anything for what seemed like forever.

Finally, Strickland cleared his throat. "You're Tommy Shoyama?" he asked, his pronunciation fairly accurate.

"Yes, I am."

"And your friend?"

"An associate of the paper," Tommy said simply.

"Good," the colonel said abruptly. "I've asked you here to clear up any misunderstandings about the goings-on here. You know about the riot, of course." He paused, waiting for our acknowledgement. "Well, I can't say that I blame them. Their requests were not out of line. If I were in their shoes, I might've done the same thing. I just want your people to know that I was acting on orders. I tried to reason with my superiors. Even asked them to back down and let the men stand by the windows. Who's gonna get hurt by that? But I had my orders."

He couldn't blame us?

"What will happen to the men now, Colonel?" Tommy asked quickly.

"Well, I can't let this go. Too much damage done. I sent them off to Ontario — a place called Petawawa. It's a detention centre."

"Isn't it a prison camp?"

"Now hold on," he said, raising his hand. "No one's calling it a 'prison camp.'"

I was fuming with anger. Tommy warned me not to say anything, and I fought the urge for his sake more than mine.

The colonel was holding something back; I could sense it. He wasn't coming clean with us. Maybe he was afraid of what it might mean to his career if the shooting came to light.

"Colonel, just one last question. Can you tell me about the gunfire?" I asked.

"No," he said, and we were summarily dismissed.

THE DAY AFTER, seagulls cried overhead. Boats moaned in the distance under an overcast sky. The wind came up from the ocean, carrying the crisp smell of brine and seaweed, and coaxed us to forget our troubles and remember the better days long past. I was going to miss my home.

Tommy, as usual, was in his office jotting notes into a book. Maybe he realized we were living through significant events and he needed to record everything. Just like me.

"Tommy? Sorry to bother you, but I've got something to say."

He stopped writing and looked up at me. "Sure, Danny, fire away."

"I'm leaving."

"What are you saying?"

"For Petawawa."

"No you're not. You can't just waltz into that...that concentration camp."

"I'll tell them I'm a reporter."

"That won't work," he sighed. "Listen, you're needed here...I mean I need you up in Kaslo. Irene and Frank are already up there waiting for us."

"No, you listen. I gotta go. I was part of that riot for a reason; I have to do something. I can't just twiddle my thumbs on the paper. I don't know if it'll ever come back once it's gone."

"It will. I have assurances."

"What are you, Morii?"

"Shut up. Don't you dare insult me!" Tommy barked.

My eyes grew wide. That was the closest I had heard Tommy swear. It was clear I had hit a nerve, and I was sorry for that, but he couldn't thwart me again. "You had no right to pull me outta the immigration building! I was right where I wanted to be."

"What are you saying?"

"I was fighting back!" I yelled. "You're a coward, Tommy. You do nothing but sit in here working at a defunct, useless newspaper! Cooperation has brought us nothing...nothing but heartache and suffering. You're nothing but an Uncle Tom! I'm going, with or without your blessing."

He just stared at me for a while, then he closed his eyes. I immediately regretted my words, but... He continued to sit in silence as I walked out the door and, I thought, out of *The New Canadian* for good.

30.

If ever there was a time of doubt in my life, it was on that train in late June as it rumbled through the BC mountains to the still Prairies and Ontario's landscape of rock and forests. I wondered if I was doing the right thing. I had no plan other than to just show up at the camp and hope they'd take me inside. Maybe Tommy knew best; I should've gone to Kaslo to stay wrapped in *The New Canadian* like a baby's blanket. I could've brought Gladys there. As I stared at the wilderness outside the train window, I realized I had never been so alone.

And what had I said to Tommy? A coward, an Uncle Tom? Who did I think I was? He was the bravest, most principled man I knew. Despite my insolence he had seen me off at the train station, appearing seemingly out of nowhere, like some kind of spirit. I hadn't asked him; in fact, I hadn't seen him since the blowup. On the platform, I avoided talking to him out of embarrassment. And he said nothing to me. He just gave me a thick envelope, turned on his heels, and walked away. I stood dumbfounded. I opened it on the train. Inside were a travel pass, a letter of introduction and, in effect, a get-out-of-jail letter signed by Austin Taylor himself of all things.

With every passing minute I felt a gnawing hollowness within my stomach, like an army of ants carving out a colony. How did Tommy do it? Not only the package of documents but all the other times: he had gotten me out of the immigration building; he had known about Morii and Steveston; and, most of all, he had known about Hammerhead's death before anyone. Was he an inu cooperating with the authorities for favours? No, he didn't have a deceitful bone in his body. But he was clever, clever like a fox, and got things done, mysteriously. There was always a touch of the supernatural about him. Maybe he was a *kitsune*, a changling, a trickster, who did things to benefit me… the fox was also fickle; if he wanted, he could bring bad fortune into my life.

Distracted from thoughts I couldn't resolve by the monotony of the clacking tracks, I pulled out the *bento* that I had made for myself. I hesitated opening it because the smell of the *takuwan* would attract unwanted attention. It was bad enough I carried Isojima-san's bright-yellow bottled *denbatsuke* in my suitcase. I just hoped it wouldn't break open accidentally creating a stink in the Pullman car. Hakujin hate the smell of something they think is rotten.

In the end, I thought better of it and put the cardboard bento box away. Better to be hungry than have soldiers throw me off the train.

The kitsune entered my mind again, and I saw my mother bedside. When she was young and strong, she told me the many Japanese fairytales about the trickster fox. I delighted in the tales and her comforting love. I now regretted how I treated both her and Tommy. I bowed my head and surprised myself by crying, softly and full of shame and grief.

I ARRIVED IN Petawawa a little over a week before July 1st, Dominion Day. I wasn't in the mood to celebrate Canada's birthday. A few months ago, I would've stood up and sang "The Maple Leaf Forever" with the best of them. But now I had no home, no country, no future, all due to my cursed face. All I could look forward to was rejoining my friends.

I managed to hitch a ride with some friendly soldiers going to the camp. They must've thought I was Chinese. I guess they couldn't imagine an Enemy Alien wanting to go to a prison built for him. Who they thought I was, I would never know, but the bucktoothed countryboy tested me. "You ever heard of the Yankees?" he asked.

I answered immediately, "You mean the team with the Sultan of Swat, Lou Gehrig, and Joltin' Joe DiMaggio?"

They let me ride in the back.

The Petawawa Prisoner of War Camp sat at the end of a winding dirt road hidden by thick patches of white birch trees and wiry underbrush on the shores of Centre Lake, well outside its namesake town. Even under a brilliant sun, the camp was dark, grim, the light only exposing the skeletal bones of the prison: three layers of barbed wire ten feet high, with watchtowers at each corner, surrounded the camp and separated the inmates from the peaceful waters not one-hundred-and-fifty feet away. There was no hope of escape.

The camp was made up of several army tents and ten wooden huts housing five-hundred German and Italian prisoners of war, and some three-hundred Japanese, about half of whom were Nisei. A jagged doubleline of barbed wire, like a surgeon's stitches across the stomach, segregated the Japanese from the Germans and Italians.

I was a fool to think I wouldn't be noticed in the back of the truck. Two over-muscled guards rousted me out, and I stood before them.

"What're you doing in this truck?" one soldier asked.

"I'm here as a reporter for *The New Canadian*," I said, deliberately lying.

"What's that?"

"Never heard of it," said the other.

"A newspaper, a Japanese-Canadian newspaper based in Vancouver."

"Japanese?" the bumpkin driver blurted. "We were carrying a Jap?"

Fortunately, the guards ignored the outburst as I pulled out my travel papers, but not the Taylor letter.

As they read the documents, I explained that I wanted to interview the Japanese internees for my readers. Most if not all of the men have family back in BC who would like to know how they are. I played the reporter bit to the hilt, though I never intended to send another story back to Vancouver or Kaslo. I had said goodbye to the *NC*.

They agreed to let me in, but first, I had to report to the camp commandant.

ONE OF THE guards escorted me inside until a familiar figure rushed up to us. His familiar voice made me feel instantly warm inside. It was young Tosh. He looked a little thinner, especially in the face, than I remembered. "Danny, what're you doing here?"

I looked back at the guard who nodded his okay, and I continued to answer my friend. "I thought I'd rejoin you guys," I said as I exhaled a heavy sigh.

"How'd you get here? How'd you get into the camp? How —?"

"Stop with the third degree! I'll tell you everything in a bit. For now, let me say I came in on that supply truck back there," I said and pointed behind me.

In the next little while, most of the Yamato Boys and the immigration building gang joined us out of curiosity. No Etsu Kaga, but I figured I would see him eventually. There was a lot of back-slapping and good-natured ribbing.

"You should've seen young Tosh there," someone guffawed. "He was crying like a baby the first day we got here!"

"I was not."

"It's okay, Tosh," I reassured. "I'm sure everyone felt the same way."

No one mentioned Hammer. Too painful a subject, I reckoned, but I did wonder if they knew. I was too busy in Vancouver to mourn because I just had to get out of town, but I thought about him constantly.

Then a looming, intimidating figure backlit by the sun approached. It was Bullet Gotanda. I avoided eye contact.

"Hey, I know you. Have we met before?" Bullet asked.

"Yeah, probably on Powell Street."

He was dimwitted, with a memory like a colander. He hadn't recognized Kaga in front of the immigration building as the one who kicked his girlfriend in the head all those years ago — something I would remember.

He accepted my answer, but eyed me suspiciously as others welcomed me. In the middle of all the laughter, a figure from the past shouldered his way through the growing crowd.

"Danny-kun!" Reverend Mitsubayashi said in his comforting voice. His eyes beamed as he continued: "So nice to see you again. You look fit."

"Sensei. I never imagined you'd be here."

"I'm the camp minister," he revealed.

"Your family okay? Where's Dicky? He is here, isn't he?"

"No. He's in a hospital in Revelstoke."

Dick's arm had become progressively worse as the train lumbered through the mountains. Takashi Kawai described how Dick's face had grown pale; his body feverish. Finally he'd collapsed to the floor. The Yamato Boys and guards immediately came to his aid. His arm was bleeding and oozing pus. The smell filled the entire train car. The officer on duty had ordered him off the train to be taken care of in the nearest hospital.

After hearing the story, I didn't say a thing, and cast my eyes downward; deep down I hoped he wouldn't be the second fatality of the riot.

The next to greet me was the camp leader, Tanaka Tokikazu. Standing tall with a receding white hairline, round metal glasses, and tightly set mouth, he was a highly respected Issei even before the war, maybe because he attended universities in both Japan and America before coming to Canada to teach. He climbed the academic ladder until he became the superintendant of all the Japanese language schools. During his career, he had mastered the rare abilities (for an Issei) of reading, writing, and speaking English.

Tanaka still had the temperament of the superintendent he was before the war. He gave off a kind of confidence that demanded obedience. His hands were large and strong, a workman's hands, which for some reason inspired trust. Although his eyes had a lazy curve to them, his gaze behind the glasses always said there was a wise mind fully engaged.

I warmed to him immediately. Responsible for all inmates and for carrying out all the edicts of the camp commandant, Tanaka-san could easily have been labelled an inu, but was not because of the trust he inspired.

Tanaka-san, on many occasions, had approached the comman-dant through the camp sergeant-major on behalf of the men on matters of general welfare. He had developed the reputation of being *urusai* in a good way.

After spending a good long time with the camp leader and the others, my escort guard grunted and I headed straight for the camp commandant's office building on the other side of the camp grounds, just outside the barbed wire enclosure. Accompanied by the guard and Tanaka-san, we went inside and met Lieutenant Colonel Howard Sheffield standing in front of his desk as if he had been waiting for me. I noted the smell of the place — cigar smoke and floor wax. Made for a potent aroma combined with the picture of the King on the wall and the Union Jack standing behind his desk.

Sheffield appeared like all the other popinjays in the military, a no-nonsense officer with moustache, dimpled chin, and broad shoulders. His uniform was sharply pressed, precisely clean, his well-oiled revolver shiny and handy. He was another in a long line of soldiers who obeyed his politician superiors in Ottawa without question.

The remarkable thing was he didn't have me searched. Tommy's letter must've paved the way for my immunity. So I managed to keep a couple of notebooks and pencils and the Isojima's takuwan. The rest of my notebooks were in my room at the Patricia Hotel.

"Welcome to the Petawawa Prisoner of War Camp," he opened. "I received word about you from Vancouver so you were expected."

Tommy, I thought. Maybe he was a kitsune. I presented the colonel with my travel papers, except the Taylor letter.

"You a reporter, eh," he said with a touch of irritation in his voice. "You won't get a story here."

I said nothing.

"I told the men and now I'll tell you," he continued. "In a little while, maybe in the next couple of days, all of the men will be afforded the opportunity to leave here of their own volition. There will be an interview process for those who apply; after which, those deemed not to pose a menace to society will be allowed to go anywhere the law allows. In the meantime, while you're here, you'll be treated like any other prisoner. You will obey all the rules of the camp. You will be dealt with severely if you do not. No exceptions." The commandant's booming voice resonated in the clear, crisp Northern Ontario air, stifling the distant loons' loud and plaintive call.

I was soon installed in the Japanese area, which had many tents a fair distance away from the five cabins made of wooden planks and tarpaper roofs. Four were living quarters where I was destined to live; the fifth was the mess hall. I suppose I received preferential treatment for my reporter status. After being assigned to Hut Nine with the Yamato Boys, I was escorted by the guard and the camp leader to the Quartermaster's Hut and issued a uniform, made of rough, blue-denim material. "Hey, what's this red circle on the back?" I asked. "It looks like the hinomaru!"

"It's a target," Tanaka-san said quietly.

Life quickly became a very boring routine. Everyone in camp woke up at precisely 6:00 a.m. when it was still dark outside, and ate breakfast at six-thirty. At roll call, right after breakfast, we stood in a straight line shivering in the frosty air, stamping our feet and exhaling clouds of warm steam. We must've looked like comical penguins, flapping about as we did. The sun barely broke the horizon, giving off a brilliant, if splintered and brittle, light. Despite the promise of summer in the air, temperatures still dropped close to freezing at night and took forever to recover during the day.

The Yamato Boys were no longer the rebellious force ready to die for the Emperor. But they were angry, and angrier still with each passing day. Once in a while, someone would realize he was in the middle of nowhere, and start to panic. "I gotta get outta here! They can't keep me, I'm a Canadian."

"Steady, boy, steady," Reverend Mitsubayashi would advise, his eyes crunched with concern.

"No, you don't understand. I don't belong here. Maybe you *Japs* do, but I'm not like you. There's been some mistake," he would ironically proclaim in Japanese. Only a good slap to the face by the reverend would bring him to his senses.

There was little to do in the small and cramped huts. In my hut, piles of unpacked clothes languished on the worn wooden floors between rows of rickety bunk beds. The only odd feature was an abandoned collection of pots and pans scattered here and there like inanimate frogs. No one mentioned them, not even in idle speculation. On the walls, some of the men had managed to put up a photograph or two of loved ones. Tosh's older sister, in a flow-ered summer dress, sun hat, and flat shoes, her legs bare as she leaned against a log on a beach in Stanley Park, became the pinup girl for Hut Nine. All the attention the photo received upset him, but he was proud of her enough not to take it down.

"*Oi*, Umeda!" called out Bullet Gotanda. "Can I borrow your sister's picture?"

"What for?" he asked casually.

"I just want to borrow it for awhile," Bullet answered with his hand out.

"I said what for?" Tosh asked again, a little more insistent.

"I'm just going for a walk and I wanna show the guys. I'll bring it back no problem."

"What guys?"

"Um…by the latrines…I…"

"Don't do it," a chorus of voices went up.

At first Tosh didn't understand, but then caught on. "Kusotare!" he cursed, and took the photograph off the wall. "Iyarashii!"

"Come on!" Bullet's smile irritated, more than charmed.

"Hey, they put stuff in the food to put you off that kind of thing!" someone called out.

"It don't work on me!" Bullet claimed.

Everyone guffawed and the incident passed. Most of the men had sweethearts back home, in another life. In a confessional mood, Tosh, as young and inexperienced as he was, revealed something of his life up in the Okanagan Valley before his family moved to Vancouver.

"Shoot, Saturday night dances were the place to be. The whole town showed up. And there was Judy, Judy Evans, a gorgeous blonde just my size, with a farmer's daughter's good looks. Man, I had a yen for her right away. The band played "String of Pearls" and I asked her to dance. When she said yes, I was in seventh heaven.

"We didn't say much, but I felt an urge and I knew she felt it too. I leaned in and kissed her lightly, you know what I mean? She even closed her eyes! I didn't see those guys coming at me. I just heard Judy scream when I crumpled under a knuckle sandwich to the kidneys. They dragged me outside into the dark and kicked me on the ground until they had had enough.

"The beating was worth it," he admitted.

The perfume that surrounded her never left him, he claimed. The curls of her blond hair probably tickled him in his sleep.

In the end, no one could blame an oaf like Bullet.

By lunch at eleven thirty, the temperature would finally be on the rise, reaching, some days, a high of eighty degrees Fahrenheit, forcing everyone to discard their coats, jackets, and even shirts to stand in their undershirts. The sun at its height seemed like a cruel overseer tormenting his slaves.

A few men even went barechested for the afternoon sumo matches and baseball games. A kind of baseball league formed among the huts, bats and balls supplied by the administration — no gloves however. It was out on the makeshift field I first saw Etsu Kaga.

Tosh told me he had been in solitary for a punch-up with one of the guards. Still the same old Kaga, fighting the good fight. But there was something different about him, not just physically, though he was considerably thinner, his cheeks hollowed, his eyes bulging and trembling. His still muscular body was supported by spindly legs. He didn't seem to recognize me; he certainly didn't say a word to me. I wanted to talk to him about Hammerhead, but I could see in his eyes the image of our friend's wounded body cradled in his arms. I left him alone.

Hut Nine's baseball team was headed by Kaga. Well, he was a natural-born leader, but he wasn't a coach. He instead led by example. Being built close to the ground, he snagged grounder after grounder as the nimble short stop. Teammates called him "Sawamura-san" after the teenage phenom who had struck out Gehringer, Ruth, Foxx, and Gehrig in succession. Although not a pitcher, some said Kaga displayed the same athletic skill and *gaman* as that gifted Japanese ballplayer back in 1934.

The showman in him came out when the crowd encouraged him with a banzai or two. Kaga dove and tumbled to the delight of onlookers. His antics brought to mind the mighty Asahi teams of old. He could've been one of them, for sure. He had missed his calling.

The only problem with Petawawa was the camp grounds; home runs were common in that small area. Fortunately the guards, entertained by Kaga's antics and the team's prowess in general, were tolerant enough to retrieve balls hit beyond the fence.

Afternoon roll call was at 4:00, after which supper was served in the mess hall, a simple cabin with benches and tables and an open kitchen from where meals of stew or fish with potatoes and a hot vegetable were ladled onto metal plates by bored-looking military cooks. No rice or shoyu.

Evenings were filled with conversation, cigarette smoking, or gardening in the setting sun. Some men grew tomatoes, cucumbers, or potatoes in a patch of ground by the fence to maintain their farming skills, to add to their diet, and to relieve the boredom. They even gave some vegetables to other inmates.

No one was allowed outside after nightfall, and everyone was in his bunk by seven thirty. Guards came in at ten o'clock to count heads, often stubbing toes in the dark despite their flashlights. They must have been angry or embarrassed at the laughter that came from inside the huts after they left.

After the bunk inspection, the men would begin conversing. "Boy, that Mariko is sure good-looking!" an anonymous voice in Hut Nine might say.

"Hey, what's that?" Tosh said, his head jerking up. "Who's that talking?"

"How did an ugly guy like you get such a looker in your family?"

"Oh, a wiseguy, eh?"

"Can I borrow her picture? I need to go to the latrine."

"Damare!" Tosh could almost see the smile shining in the darkness.

"Cut it out, you guys!" Bullet said. "It's a simple favour. Give the guy a break."

A burst of laughter would ring out in the flickering shadows. The sweep of guard-tower searchlights soon stifled the joviality.

"I hear Sheffield's gonna call for applicants to leave this dump soon," someone else offered.

Kaga suddenly rolled off his bunk to stand tall with his bare legs far apart and his eyes glaring into the darkness. "Yeah, that's right. And I hope none of you is thinking of applying. We've got to stick together in our cause. We're here to reunite all of our families."

Everyone was taken aback, surprised to hear him talk in the first place, and then to learn he still clung to his ideals.

"But if we're let out, we can go where our families are!" someone yelled.

"Is that so?" A stray beam caught Kaga's eyes from outside and they flickered with determination. He became the old fire-breathing namaiki again. "What about all the others separated from their fathers and brothers? What about them, eh? And aren't you forgetting about all the soldiers of our homeland shedding their blood overseas? What about our duty to them and His Majesty?"

"You remember what happened at the immigration building and tell me you're gonna apply to get out of here. Remember what they did to us, our families, our people! Hammerhead...Hammer ..." Kaga choked on his words. Tears glistened in the faint light. "Remember what they did to him. We must continue to use our citizenships to demand our rights, to cause as much trouble for the enemy as possible. Remember, we are prisoners with honour! Don't let Hammerhead die in vain!"

Voices barked out a loud banzai.

31.

The next day, the camp commandant began his interviews. Instead of asking for volunteers to apply, he decided to interview everyone one by one in order to find those suitable for release. Etsu Kaga was one of the first summoned to Sheffield's office.

I watched from a dirty window as Kaga walked with two guards to the commandant's office. So Kaga knew about Hammerhead. I assumed everyone else did as well. I did wonder how they would react if they heard he had died of "natural causes." I said nothing, no need to add fuel to the fire.

Kaga came back from the interview after forty-five minutes. He looked shaken, his skin a shade of pale that rivalled a winter's day, but he kept a brave face. Tosh leapt to his feet and rushed to him. He believed, or wanted to believe, his leader was victorious. Kaga addressed everyone in Hut Nine. "I stood before the *bokenasu* Sheffield in his office. He tossed an envelope across his desk at me like he was Bogart. I caught it right away, recognizing it as the one I wrote yesterday.

"'Your letter didn't make it out,' he said to me.

"'*Eigo wakarimasen*,' I said to him.

"Told me he knew I understood. I'm a *knee-sai* from Skeena. *Knee-sai!* — would ya get a load of the mug!

"So he got up and smiled at me. He said, 'You were a troublemaker in Vancouver.'

"'I gave myself up,' I said back to him. 'I voluntarily went into the immigration building.'

"'Whatever the case may be, you're here now.' The bakatare

TERRY WATADA • 219

then snatched the letter out of my hands. Said I would be here for the duration. He then stuffed the letter into his pocket before sitting down. 'You're unsuitable for release,' he told me!

"'I didn't ask to be released,' I told him. And with that he dismissed me.

"I then asked about my letter. He just touched his fingertips together and told me he was sending it to Ottawa. I shrugged my shoulders like I didn't care, and all of you know I don't. But the hint's not lost on me. He's telling me I'm being watched."

Kaga may have won the day but, late at night, I saw that he lay awake, staring at the ceiling. From time to time, he tossed and turned, never sleeping. I thought I saw the shadows reaching out for him like long arms. It was just my imagination but he looked afraid.

THE NEXT DAY, someone informed the hut that a few Nisei had decided to take the Government's offer to leave camp.

"*Chikushou!*" Kaga roared. "We've got to stick together."

"But if they want to go...they must have family —" Reverend Mitsubayashi began to offer.

"Anybody know who they are?" he said, cutting off debate.

No one in the hut said a word until a meek voice spoke up: "I think Doctor Hori knows."

The Security Commission declared Dr. Chikao Hori from Kaslo "trouble" and sent him to Petawawa.

"What? Who said that?"

Isamu Otagaki, the informer, raised his bony hand; his face appeared sheepish and downcast. "I heard there was a meeting in Hut Eleven last week. A bunch was talking to Doctor Hori." He looked as guilty as Judas after he took the thirty pieces of silver. "Who it was, and what they spoke about, I don't know."

"Ah, don't listen to him. He's an inu, a well-known inu!"

"Yeah, and the beatings he's gonna get should cure him of that right quick," Bullet threatened in English, knowing Otagaki was placed in Hut Nine because every other hut and tent had refused him. After Hastings Park, the dog transferred from one camp to another: first Sandon, where the Buddhists spurned him; then to Tashme. He figured he'd be safer in Kojima Village, a stronghold of Morii gang members; he thought he had the Oyabun's blessing in the first place. Unfortunately, the inhabitants there didn't tolerate him any more than any other camp. After many threats and beatings, overseen by the yojimbo Rikimatsu Kintaro, Otagaki begged Private Sutherland to send him back east. Sutherland granted the request, mostly to cover his own behind in case the dog complained, was hospitalized, or killed. The young private was in enough trouble as it was.

"Never mind," Kaga interrupted. "I just hope for everyone's sake here no one talked to that kuso Hori."

We soon learned that ten Nisei from Hut Ten had talked to the good doctor about leaving. The young ringleaders had secretly asked him for advice. Kaga then decided to talk to Dr. Hori himself.

AT ABOUT 1:30 A.M. on the morning of July 1st, the searchlights made their usual sweep of the grounds; it was a moonless night, and all was quiet in the huts except for the deep snoring. I slept fitfully as a result, waking up every so often.

Unexpectedly, loud shouting, wood splintering, and a peppering of popping sounds broke the silence. More panicked cries, indistinct orders, and warning shouts followed. Then firecracker explosions in the air were heard. There were sharp pings off hard surfaces and the sound of kicked-up dirt as everyone woke up. I came to a seated position.

"Hey, you hear that?" I asked.

Angry voices in the room coughed, "Who the hell is making all that noise?"

"It's too Goddamned early for Dominion Day," someone swore groggily.

Another volley of explosions went off, but this time, someone cried near the window, "Holy shit, those aren't fireworks...from the towers! Hit the deck!"

I rolled and dove to the floor just as bullets splintered the walls and strafed my bunk while other bullets ricocheted off refugee pots, pans, and skillets. Reverend Mitsubayashi covered his head with his arms as he huddled in a corner.

The door to Hut Nine burst open and Tosh Umeda dove flat to the floor. "They're trying to kill us!" he screamed as he wriggled to safety.

"Who's shooting?" Reverend Mitsubayashi shouted.

"The guards...the guards," Tosh spat out, gasping for air.

"Why?"

"Where's Kaga-san? Where is he?"

The questions remained unanswered as the noise and confusion grew and grew until at last everything stopped...a few minutes later.

Discontent spread like wildfire throughout the four Japanese huts. In Hut Nine everyone grumbled about the gunplay. "We are rats in a cage... What've they done to Kaga-san? Tosh, what happened to him? I don't know, I don't know. Ah, leave the kid alone. Can't you see he's all shook up?" No one slept.

AT SUNRISE, THREE guards and their lieutenant stood as usual in front of our huts waiting for the prisoners to assemble for roll call. They acted as if nothing had happened. Like everyone else, I remained very quiet, I didn't even dare move. Tosh crouched by a window and said in a low voice, "They're waiting for us."

Word via an anonymous brave messenger had come from Hut Eight a few hours before dawn. "Tanaka-san orders everyone not to line up for morning roll call," he whispered at an open window. Reverend Mitsubayashi had wondered if that was such a good idea, though he was just as angry and perplexed.

When no one came out of the huts, one by one the guards broke rank and turned to one another as if asking what to do. The lieutenant ran to the administration office outside the perimeter.

As prisoner representative, Tanaka demanded later that morning to see the camp commandant with five other representatives for an explanation of the army's actions. When Sheffield responded, saying he would talk to Tanaka in the interest of "clearing the air," but only to him, the inmates, including the Yamato Boys, began a hunger strike.

I slid between my bed and the wall, going over in my head what had happened just a few hours before. I felt myself tearing up, my hands shaking. I placed my palms over my eyes, but I still heard the gunshots. The war surrounded me, consumed me; the war then defined me. *Tommy was right, I wasn't cut out for this. Who was I kidding? Would I be joining Hammerhead?*

"I can't go with no food," Bullet complained.

"Aw," Reverend Mitsubayashi laughed. Despite being deeply worried about the situation, he tried to lighten the mood. "Do you good. Get rid of that belly!"

"Come on fellahs," Tosh encouraged. "Let's get serious here. The anniversary of our Emperor's victory in China is approaching! Take strength from that."

"How do you know that?" Bullet said with a sneer.

"I read."

THE BARRACKS WERE filled with make-busy activity. Some of the men settled into their bunks. Others resumed an old card game. Tosh paced the floor. I thought for sure he would've broken down. He was a better man than I. Others read books. All in an effort to take their minds off the smell of bacon and baked beans wafting in from the mess hall, an unusual meal specially prepared to torment us protestors, no doubt.

"Where'd them bastards get bacon?" Bullet came to his feet. "You guys don't understand, I got to eat."

"We all do!"

"Not like me," the oaf said with a pout. "I think I'm addicted."

"Baka. You addicted to saltpeter?"

"I told you that stuff don't do nothing for me."

"Will you stop talking!" someone demanded. "The gut and the groin, that's all you ever think about!"

Bullet sheepishly lowered his head and fell silent under a barrage of laughter.

"They're playing with our heads. Don't you see that?" advised the good reverend.

By evening, the commandant gave in and allowed the select committee to meet with him.

IN THE SHADOWS of Sheffield's office, the six reps, including Reverend Mitsubayashi and me, gathered and stood solemnly, allowing Tanaka to speak. I had recovered enough to participate. The reverend thought I'd be an asset since I was a reporter.

"Shots were fired into our sleeping quarters," Tanaka began. "Is this not against regulations?"

Sheffield sat erect in his chair, clasped his hands together, and without taking a breath said, "It's not against the rules. The guards are fully trained to respond to all emergencies."

"What emergency? There was no emergency," Roy Nishijima, a phlegmatic man from Tanaka's hut, shouted.

Ignoring the outburst, the commandant continued: "In last night's incident, the internees were solely responsible because they went outside of their huts after lights-out, and didn't respond to orders."

Tanaka betrayed his surprise.

"Ah, so you didn't know this?" Sheffield smiled.

"Surely what your guards did was an overreaction?" Tanaka responded slowly, almost sarcastically. "If what you say is true, then the men must take some of the responsibility, but the guards don't have the right to fire right into our sleeping quarters."

"Shooting into quarters is wrong!" repeated Roy emotionally. "Isn't that right?"

"No one was hurt," replied Sheffield.

"That's beside the point!" Roy said, nearly shouting again.

"Easy Roy-san…we're all reasonable men here," Reverend Mitsubayashi said in his soothing way. "We'd like to talk to the Spanish consul general about this incident."

"I can't allow that," Sheffield finally said.

"Why not? Most of us are Canadian-born citizens. The rest are naturalized. Are we not allowed our citizenship rights and our human rights?"

"It's true you were interned as POWs," Sheffield conceded, as if anticipating a counter-argument, "but you are as you say Canadian-born or naturalized citizens, and as such are not entitled to speak to the Spanish consul."

"That's absurd," Tanaka concluded.

"How so? Spain represents Japan's interests. You are considered to be British subjects —Canadians, as you said so yourselves."

"But you said we're POWs."

"You are and you aren't. It's complicated. I'm just following regulations."

My brain reeled. I said nothing; I just observed so I could write it all in my notebook later.

Seeing no alternatives, Tanaka sighed. "I see. It's a matter of hats, and we will always have the wrong one on when we ask for something." He shrugged before adding, "We have no choice but to continue not to answer roll call."

"So be it, but all rights and privileges will be cancelled immediately. No more mail, canteen access, gardening, or movies, you understand?"

"If that's the price we pay …" With that we shuffled out to report to the rest of the camp.

"I think we understand each other," Tanaka whispered to Roy, the good reverend, and me. The others smiled in a self-satisfied way. I fell into a gloomy mood fearing the worst.

32.

Sometime during the third day of the protest, an ominous military vehicle arrived at POW Camp 33 Petawawa. Out stepped an impressive looking officer of high rank. Lieutenant Colonel Sheffield saluted him sharply, and the two marched into the administration building leaving everyone to guess who he was and what would happen next.

Major-General Harrison MacPartland was altogether a different officer: more no-nonsense than the lieutenant-colonel if that were possible, and he had no fear of open confrontation. In fact, he thrived on it. Shortly after his arrival, the major-general appeared in the open and, by himself, headed straight for Tanaka Tokikazu's hut. What a sight he was in his sharply-cut hat, tailored uniform, and riding crop. The men took an instant dislike to the man.

"All right, you lay abouts, what's all this about?" he barked from the doorway of the hut. He spoke loudly enough for everyone to hear.

Tanaka-san, perhaps a bit intimidated, shuffled forward, smoothing his hair with his hands. "And whom might you be?"

"Who-mmm? Who-mmm?" MacPartland mockingly laughed.

"Who the hell do you think you are?" Roy Nishijima cursed.

"Yeah!" I added. As soon as the strike was called, Tanaka-san had asked that I be there in his hut as a reporter, anticipating a confrontation with the military brass.

Tanaka-san pulled him back. "Take it easy Roy-san. Let the man speak."

The tin soldier dismissed the irritating fly. "I am Major-General Harrison MacPartland of Petawawa Military Headquarters. And who the devil are you?"

"Tanaka Tokikazu, camp leader," he said as he bowed deeply.

"Right. I'm here today to clear up this roll call situation. I've been thoroughly briefed and I understand why you're not obeying orders. I assure you, the shooting incident will be investigated, but will be treated as a separate issue. POWs must obey wartime rules and regulations, as must the military respect your rights. But know this, anyone who contravenes these regulations faces lifetime imprisonment or death by firing squad."

The words weighed heavily. I could see that Roy couldn't believe what the major-general was saying. "But we're not POWs! Your colonel said so himself."

MacPartland ignored him. Not allowing the facts to get in the way, he continued, "Now, I don't want to take things that far, but if you don't answer roll call, I will be forced to take action. It is now 8:45," he said tipping his eyes to his wristwatch. "You have five minutes to get out there and form for roll call. If you do not comply, I will be forced to take action and you, Mr. *Tan-aka*, will bear the consequences." The major-general then snapped his heels, turned away, and headed across the compound.

As Tanaka mulled over the major-general's ominous words, a few inmates stared from the open doorway in disbelief. What "action" was this bokenasu about to take? I and several others could see the tin soldier marching stiffly to the front gate. On the other side of the fence, a dozen fully-armed soldiers stood aiming their rifles straight at our huts. The major-general stood erect at the gate, his arm crooked to count the seconds away. "Four minutes!" he shouted, his voice ringing in every corner of the compound. They were ready to shoot on command.

Prisoner panic erupted. Tosh swung around and shouted, "Oh my god they mean it." "They can't do it." "We're Canadians." "Doesn't that mean anything?" Some scrambled to find a convenient cooking pot or pan for protection. Others closed their eyes to recite the *nembutsu*. One or two called to rush the guards.

At three minutes, Tanaka-san rose to his feet, gathered himself together, and walked through the door. "Enough is enough," he shouted outside.

TANAKA TOKIKAZU, WITH head held high, walked right across no man's land to the major-general. He was the beacon of reason in a world gone crazy. The sun, just beginning to get hot, cast a raw light on the drama. We held our collective breath from inside our hut as the major-general, ignoring Tanaka, called out, "Two minutes!"

No one said a word, horrified at what was taking place. Reverend Mitsubayashi murmured the nembutsu to himself.

"One minute, thirty seconds."

Finally, at the one-minute mark, Tanaka reached the fence, bowed, and beckoned for the major-general to approach him. Mac-Partland stopped the countdown. A short conference later, both men nodded in agreement. Tanaka then raised his arm to signal all the men out of their huts onto the grounds.

A few didn't trust what was going on. "They're gonna shoot us! Right out in the open like we we're animals brought to the slaughter!" Tosh exclaimed. Those too scared to act, like the inu Otagaki, stayed back under their bunks. Reverend Mitsubayashi came out into the sunlight first. The grim expression on his face told everyone he wasn't afraid of dying. I soon followed. I looked around to see members of all four huts emerging and walking forward to meet their fate. Each man looked at the others half expecting never to see one another again. The air crackled with tension. A slow, sad wind sent the chill of death through each body.

"Major-General MacPartland has agreed to dismiss the armed squad so that we can explain what's going on to the Issei, the immigrants, here," Tanaka informed us in English so the guards wouldn't fire mistakenly. "I told him they can't understand a word he says, and they need to know."

Tosh stepped forward, angry like a wet dog. "Haven't you forgotten something here? Kaga-san? They probably killed him like they killed Hammerhead," he claimed in Japanese. As he continued he felt his voice rise in intensity. "If Kaga-san were here, he'd say we should finish what we started and, if we have to, die. Die like Japanese!"

"Tosh's right," someone in the crowd agreed. "Today is the

anniversary of Japan's attack against the Chinese tyrants! Our deaths will commemorate the Emperor's heroic undertaking! Let's rush the guards!" Grumbling quickly merged into one voice of protest.

"Stop this baka talk!" Tanaka and Reverend Mitsubayashi commanded in unison. "There will be no more talk of dying for the cause," Tanaka-san said. "MacPartland will stand by his word to investigate the Dominion Day shooting if we answer roll call this morning."

"No! He's a liar. They all are!"

"He's also letting us conduct our own investigation," Tanaka added.

"What good will that do?"

"Listen, all of you," Tanaka said, before switching to Japanese, "the major-general looks like a man of his word. We've made our point; let's cooperate and see what they do next. If they don't follow through, we then have more than enough reason to retaliate."

A general hum rose; the majority agreed. And just then the crisis was over.

DURING THE MORNING roll call, I stood with the men of Hut Nine and listened to the names. The captain of the guard mispronounced every one clearly, floating every misshapened syllable in the air. He finished the list and was about to dismiss the formation when Tosh shouted in anger, "How about Etsu Kaga's name?"

Everyone froze in anticipation as the question reverberated beyond the barbed wire, causing birds to take flight and wolves to howl. The captain and his officers seemed startled. One guard raised his rifle to the ready.

The captain drew to attention and spoke slowly, "I'm not at liberty to say."

THE ONLY CASUALTY of the "Battle of Petawawa" was discovered a few days later. It wasn't Kaga. Reverend Mitsubayashi came across

Isamu "Sam" Otagaki in a heap in a remote corner of the camp, with many wounds and bones broken, including his jaw. The man who tried to save his own skin ever since Pearl could not be saved from a severe stoning. Several rocks, some stained with blood, lay nearby. No one took responsibility, though many had wanted to kill the man ever since the day the inu walked into Petawawa.

The rocks themselves deepened the mystery. They were normally found on the rocky shores of Centre Lake. How they got inside the camp was anybody's guess. And no one knew who had done the deed. Some suspected Bullet Gotanda, but the behemoth's whereabouts were accounted for several times over. Bullet was, however, overheard to say cryptically, "I buried the dog in potter's field." He never said anything more about the incident afterwards.

The authorities took the badly injuried Otagaki away, never to be seen again. We presumed he had died. In the end, he was a man to be pitied. He sold his soul, after all, the night Dicky and I spied him on Powell Street kowtowing to the Mounties. It seemed every Japanese Canadian paid for his sins in the end.

A dog will always die a dog's death.

33.

The causes of the July 1st incident remained a mystery in the months that followed. Kaga's whereabouts was part and parcel of the mystery. Was he being interrogated somewhere in a secret dark cell? Tosh put forward the improbable possibility that he had escaped. "He can do anything," he stated. It killed us not knowing.

The official position about the shooting was brief like any issued by the Government. The following was in the only issue of *The New Canadian*, to come to Petawawa, written by some Security Commission lackey:

> *A disturbance occurred on the night of June 30 - July 1, 1942. Hearing rumours that ten men were to be released, a group "knocked Dr. Hori about" and searched his belongings to find the names of the ten men. These men were then "threatened and badly handled," and the guards entered the compound firing warning shots to break up the disturbance.*

Still, I was happy to see the paper; feeling its pages reminded me of the gang I left behind in Vancouver. God, I missed them, Tommy especially.

A COMMITTEE OF inmates, headed by Tanaka Tokikazu and including Reverend Mitsubayashi, Roy Nishijima, and me, formed about a month after to investigate the matter. Our findings were a little more illuminating, but inconclusive. Tosh Umeda gave the most credible testimony:

"That loudmouth Hori... sorry, Doctor Hori... he was the cause of it all. The inu in Hut Ten, you know Takeda, Miki, and that Ogawa fellah, they wanted out and they were talking to Hori. He said it was okay, saying there was a 'serious manpower shortage in BC,' as if that mattered to us. Once we heard about it, a few of us, led by Kaga-san, paid a visit to Hut Eleven to talk some sense into the doctor. No fisticuffs intended. The sight of us should've frightened him into keeping quiet. We cornered him all alone.

"Kaga asked him why he was working against us.

"'I'm doing nothing,' he answered, shaking in his boots.

"I told him we got to stick together.

"He said, and I quote: 'You want us to renounce our God-given rights as Canadian citizens and be Japanese? You're crazy.'

"'What are you, Christian?' Kaga yelled. 'Look where that's led us.'

"I could see the red in Kaga-san's cheeks, his arms trembling as he grabbed Hori by the front of his shirt. 'Stop talking treason,' he said.

"'Why, you gonna kill me? You're in a prisoner-of-war camp, you bakatare! You'll be facing the hangman's noose within a week.'

"Bullet Gotanda picked up a chair and smashed it against a wall. The door burst open at that moment and three or four Hut Ten Nisei came to the rescue. Fists, arms, and legs were flying everywhere. I didn't recognize anybody, but they were most definitely from Hut Ten. But with too many bodies in too small a space, I and everyone else started to panic just as the searchlights swung onto the hut. That was our signal to go. We bolted outside. The cold air fogged my breath, making me feel so out in the open. Then came the first gunshots. I think they were a warning, but I took it as my cue to scramble. I headed for the door to Hut Nine, feeling the gun sights on us. Sand kicked up all around. I tasted dirt. Bullets whizzed by me, the machine gun fire ringing in my ear. I felt death at my shoulder. In what seemed like forever, I made it to the door and flung myself through it. I was safe, or so I thought.

"The gunfire continued and I heard the bullets coming through the walls and pingponging off pots and pans. I thought I was a dead man. I thought we were all dead men. But then in a matter of seconds it was over.

"Why did the guards open fire? And why not warning shots? They just shot straight at us like they wanted to kill us. Sure there was a commotion, but why didn't they investigate first, send in guards, instead of firing at us? And what happened to Kaga-san? He was in front of us when he ordered us out, but then I lost sight of him in the confusion. Once I made it to safety, I realized he was nowhere to be found. Not even a body on the ground."

PERHAPS THE MOST interesting testimony came from the "loudmouth," Dr. Chikao Hori, a slight yet elegant man. He had been investigated in Kaslo and judged to be an "Incorrigible Japanese," despite being a Nisei. He was then imprisoned in Petawawa. His Japanese education was his downfall.

He had been highly respected for the good work he had done in the Steveston area as a family doctor. Consequently, he was elected adviser to the Nisei while in Petawawa. Being a wise man with an old soul, he had that strange glow about him, like he was someone who knew exactly what to do in any given situation.

Dr. Hori was rather strong in his denial of any responsibility for the incident when he came to address the committee — rather eloquently I might add:

"I've supported the Nisei Mass Evacuation Group's activities wholeheartedly from the very start, but I don't agree with the likes of the Yamatodamashii Group. They're troublemakers at best, traitors at worst. When I met with some of the men of Hut Ten, I had no idea that the camp commandant had selected men for release to the sugar beet farms in Alberta.

"I never requested an interview with the camp commandant for these men. Some of the Yamato Boys, I hear, accuse me of actually arranging release applications for these men. That's nothing but a lie. What I'm saying is that these Yamato Boys attacked me without any proof or evidence. To me, it was clearly a mistake, and so I took the beating without resisting. They call themselves true Japanese who follow the Yamato spirit, but they have chosen to turn their backs on bushidou and attack me in a cowardly and shameful way.

"These Nisei who approached me are worried about their families and their futures. They are desperate to get out. In front of them was a golden opportunity to do so. Even if I were to advise them not to leave, I believe they would have done so anyway."

AMONG THE MANY questions about the incident, the reason the guard tower opened fire on the huts in the first place nagged at everyone within the camp. If there had been an all out riot or a mass escape attempt, it might've been justified, but a few men in what amounted to a schoolyard fight? At the most, they could've fired warning shots. Why not investigate peaceably? When they opened fire, it was clear these were no warning shots. Maybe panic, perhaps. And where was Etsu Kaga? Tosh kept insisting that he walked through the barbed-wire fence and disappeared. Roy Nishijima thought he saw guards take him away just after the shooting, but it was too dark to tell actually. We kept asking, but no one answered.

The entire incident was destined to be a footnote in history, for word soon came that Camp Petawawa was to be closed with all inmates moved to Angler, a POW camp north of Lake Superior.

34.

About a month after the "Battle of Petawawa," as we came to call it, the Government decided to move all the prisoners to other facilities. We needed to be separated out and segregated; Petawawa was like a Balkan powder keg, more space was needed, I assumed. We weren't told anything. Just pull up stakes and leave, was said. I don't know where the Italians and Germans went, but the Japanese Canadians were all hustled to the far western reaches of Ontario.

Angler POW Camp 101 sat just north of Marathon, Ontario, a small town riding the sloped back of the great mythical wolf, Lake Superior. The smell of dead fish hung heavily in the air the day we arrived. That smell was a constant companion. The nearby jagged beaches were hidden from view by forests and low-lying rocky hills. The Angler outpost was far more isolated than Petawawa with Ottawa nearby, even if no Japanese Canadian could visit it. Angler stood on a sandy flat with three rows of barbed wire, ten feet high, defining its perimeter. Six machine-gun towers were strategically placed for maximum surveillance.

Each of the camp's five wood-frame H-shaped structures, covered with tarpaper, consisted of two large dorms joined together by a smaller middle area. Each dorm was not partitioned, and large enough to house eighty bunks. The middle contained the showers, washroom, and laundry facilities. Complex One held the kitchen, dining rooms, library, barber shop, shoe and clothing repair shop, a small newspaper room, and a classroom or two.

We stood in formation before the camp commandant. Lieutenant Colonel Herbert Parker was quite upfront with us about an escape that had taken place. He wanted to make the camp rules and restrictions clear, and to explain why no prisoner was allowed to possess a can of any kind.

THE YEAR BEFORE Pearl, the German officers and a U-boat crew occupying Hut 5B, right next to the barbed-wire fence, had effected an escape. They had laboriously dug a tunnel from under the floorboards using only tobacco and juice cans. After about a month, they managed to dig five feet down and 150 feet out, well beyond the fence and into the bush.

On the night of April 18, 1941, two days before Hitler's birthday, twenty men made their bid for freedom. The escape was soon discovered at bed check. Sirens sounded, searchlights flickered, and dogs released. The bush came alive with flashlight beams, yelping dogs, cries of panic, and warning commands. Shots rang out.

When the mist and smoke cleared, two German officers were dead, and another wounded. Two others actually made it as far as Moose Jaw. Once outside the perimeter, they had covered their scent with black pepper. They sneaked into Marathon, stole Purvis Johnson's row boat, and followed Lake Superior's northern shore line. In the end, they were captured in Saskatchewan trying to arrange passage to Japan of all places.

Parker was small, slight in build, and possessed a high-pitched voice — kind of funny actually, but no one laughed. The "Little Napoleon," as he was soon dubbed, read out a series of standing orders. Pretty standard stuff, except he emphasized the last one: "POWs who offer resistance to orders, incite or engage in riotous conduct, will be severely dealt with, by force of arms if necessary. Offenders in this respect will receive the most extreme punishment possible."

He bragged he was not going to have another successful escape blotting his "stellar service record." He obviously knew about the "Battle of Petawawa."

The Yamato Boys and Tanaka-san were assigned to Hut 5B. I

looked around and noticed Rev. Mitsubayashi was not among us. I asked Tosh.

"Sorry, Danny, but he didn't come with us. He decided to go west to help the other sensei. Maybe he wanted to find his son." As a minister, he was needed in BC and so was easily granted leave.

The Petawawa Men, as we became known, were quite comfortable in our new surroundings, despite the strict regulations. After all, such formalities had been a regular feature of Petawawa. The Yamatodamashii Group still existed, but they decided not to broadcast it. Guys like Tosh and Bullet maintained their passion for the cause, maybe out of anger over what had happened in Petawawa, or maybe out of innocence or immaturity.

I was content to be known as a "Petawawa Man," in light of my friendship with so many of them, though I did have many moments of doubt. Maybe I should get back to Kaslo to help Tommy and the gang re-establish *The New Canadian*, once the Security Commission relinquished control. They must be there by now, I reasoned. I wondered if Tommy would have me. Most of all I missed Gladys. I surprised myself with intermittent crying jags I couldn't control. Maybe I was my mother's son.

The days then dragged into weeks as routine settled in. I speculated with Tosh about what was going on in the Pacific War. No one had heard a radio broadcast in a turtle's age. No one had read a paper, not even the *NC* other than the one about the July 1st incident. And no one ever talked about Etsu Kaga, his whereabouts, or his fate. I, of course, was worried. I didn't want to lose another friend to this damned war; however, there was nothing to say he was dead, and there was nothing I or anyone could do to find him.

One day, Bullet Gotanda started acting oddly.

"What the hell are you doing?" I demanded, as I watched the hulking Nisei stomping on the floorboards with his heavy boots.

"Just looking."

"Looking? Looking for what?"

"Nothing."

"Aw, c'mon Bullet." Tosh clued in in a split second. "They would've filled in that tunnel by now."

"You never know. You just never know," he said, stamping his feet until roll call that evening.

But then Bullet turned his attention to me. "Hey, why weren't you with us in Petawawa?" the oaf growled.

"I was there," I insisted.

"Not from the beginning. Hey, you was the one taken out of the immigration building! What were you doing? Betraying us, I bet. You was pretty cozy with dem soldiers. You're just like Otagaki, and you should join him in potter's field."

I denied everything, saying I had a perfectly good explanation, but knowing I would reveal nothing to anybody, especially to a Neanderthal like Bullet Gotanda. I didn't want to cause resentment. A need for self-preservation came over me, as my body tingled with fear. The lout didn't say anything more, but then he confronted me between huts a few days later and let his fists to do his talking. A punch to my jaw sent me reeling, followed by more blows to my stomach. It was like the downtown streets before Pearl all over again. No old ladies to save me this time. I buckled and fell to the ground. Before Bullet delivered the *coup de grâce* with a rock he magically produced I heard a familiar voice.

"Cut it out! Leave him alone!"

Bullet stopped, dropped his weapon, and bolted after being discovered.

"Jimmy? Jimmy, is that really you?" I slurred through the pain. Though Jimmy was one of the principal reasons I had made the journey, my old pal had completely slipped my mind. No one in camp had mentioned him.

"Sure is," he said, helping me up. He looked a little worse for wear, but he was a sight for sore eyes, literally, with his broad smile, beaming face, and that head of hair. "Geez, you really took a beating."

"Aw, maybe I deserved it."

He fell silent.

"How long you been here?" I asked after recovering somewhat. "Anybody else come with you?"

"You know Mr. Tanemitsu and Mr. Shintani... aw ..."

"Who Jimmy, who?"

"Mr. Kawai."

"Yeah, that's right. We were close like a murder of crows in Vancouver," I said smiling. "What happened? How'd you end up here?" If it wasn't for the barbed-wire fences, I might think we were back home. All we needed was a table at Ernie's.

"Betrayed. An inu gave us up."

"Yeah, I knew that," I said. "So many were. Where is everyone? Can I see them?"

"Yes, but they've changed. This place does that to you."

"What do you mean?"

Jimmy then talked about the radical element in Angler. Their natonalist spirit rivalled that of the Yamato Boys, maybe even surpassed it. Originally, the leaders of the NMEG and other namaiki destined for Ontario were identified by the JCCL as ganbariya to mock them. Once together in Angler, these men liked the idea of being rebellious and stubborn, so they embraced the name, ganbariya, as their own.

AT THE BREAK of every dawn, all the Japanese prisoners were required to gather in front of the huts until the sergeant-major bellowed the command, "Six paces forward march!" We formed into a military line, came to attention and saluted the captain of the guard.

The Ganbariya too had their own daily observances. After the morning roll call, the camp leader, Takashi Kawai, conducted a ceremony where the men, including Tamio Tanemitsu and Roy Shintani, bowed deeply while facing the rising sun. The gathered then cheered: "All together now: *Gyohai! Saikeirei! Banzai!*"

Jimmy went on to tell me that since Takashi Kawai arrived in Angler, he had been stirring up the men to get the Government to recognize the NMEG and to negotiate the Evacuation in family units, as he had done back in Vancouver. He first looked for an ally in Uchiboro Shigeichi since he had been such a firebrand in Vancouver, but the man was now broken, his future collapsed. The man's eldest son had been killed by a troubled young man with a dinner knife in Bay Farm, an internment camp near Slocan. The incident had been random, the troubled man, yet another affected by the internment, no doubt, was deemed not responsible for his actions and taken away to a prison for the criminally insane in Ontario. Uchiboro rarely appeared and, when he did, he spoke to no one, shuffling along as if he had aged thirty years overnight.

Undeterred, Kawai shifted steadily toward the harsher, more nationalistic stance of the Ganbariya or Perseverance Group. Perhaps it was because he had been betrayed by one of our own. Maybe the Mounties had done something to him during their interrogation after his capture in Vancouver. But what had really happened was anybody's guess.

The Yamato Boys' presence in Angler, though none crowed about it, only served to strengthen Kawai's new belief. He saw them as like-minded allies in a common cause. Though he actively recruited them, only the gullible, like Tosh and Bullet, fell for his line. He was deeply disappointed and blamed Tanaka-san for every-one's reluctance to join him. "He will pay," he was heard to say ominously. Kawai began to see himself as the lone leader true to the ideals born in the dark days at the beginning of the war.

A greying Tanaka Tokikazu was more than a little shocked at the sight of these men expressing homage and a pledge of loyalty to the Emperor. He beseeched them to stop. "You must put an end to this. We had enough trouble in Petawawa with that kind of thing. Don't you know we're being watched very closely all the time?"

The Ganbariya thought him an old man whose nerves were shot from the rumoured goings-on during the Battle of Petawawa. It's funny what gossip can do to you. They ignored him as a result.

I decided to write their version of what happened in my note-book to show the extent and effect of gossip:

They dragged Tanaka kicking and screaming into the middle of the compound. He was held up by two guards. The little shit from Ottawa then ordered the camp commandant to take out his revolver and hold it against Tanaka-san's temple. "You have five minutes to line up and answer roll call," he announced.

Tanaka said nothing but everyone could see what was about to happen. His lips were trembling, his hands shaking. Sweat beads appeared on his forehead.

"They're bluffing."

"Four minutes!"

"No, they're not." The men didn't know what to do. No one could look at the other in case the idiot fired prematurely.

"Three minutes! Ready your weapon." The bastard cocked the trigger and the men became agitated.

"Two minutes and counting."

The men decided what to do and fell silent. The hut door yawned open at the one minute mark. Tanaka fainted dead away.

35.

A week after my arrival in Angler, a remarkable thing happened. Under armed guard, Dick Mitsubayashi walked into the camp, to my great relief. Everyone wanted to celebrate since he hadn't been seen since Revelstoke. He was thin, especially in the face, and had an unsteady walk. He appeared empty somehow, wizened beyond his years. Then I saw it: his right arm was missing. We all stood back and stared, not saying a word.

His wound had developed gangrene. The infection had set in during his transportation, and by the time he was settled in the Interior hospital, it was too late. The doctors decided to amputate.

After stopping by the commandant's office, he was escorted to Hut 5A. Tosh was the first to greet him.

"Mitsubayashi-san, what happened?" he blurted out. An obvious and embarrassing question, but Tosh was still a teenager despite his hard experiences.

Dick would have none of it; he pushed past him and found an empty bunk. He lay in resolute silence. Tosh approached him as a mourner does a loved one at a funeral, but was led away quickly. Everyone shuffled to the corners with eyes averted and left Dick alone.

Once word got to him, Tanaka-san came by to commiserate and fill in Dick. Still, there was no reaction. Dick simply stared into space as if nothing existed, as if nothing was important. But then Tanaka-san told him about Reverend Mitsubayashi.

"My otousan?" Dick asked, suddenly coming to life.

"Yes, he was needed back in BC."

Dick sat up, his rage revived. He glared with liquid intensity at the lost chance.

I didn't know what to say. A chill came over me at the sight of his amputation. Tears seeped into my being, like rain water through a leaky Vancouver roof. I finally approached my old friend sitting alone on his bunk.

"Hey, Dicky, what'd you know, what'd you say?" I knew how stupid that sounded as I said it, but I thought perhaps I could conjure some sense of our past. None was to be had.

Rubbing his upper arm, Dick seemed ashamed of the emptiness and turned away. My pal had changed; his decrepit state gave his complexion a ghost-like translucence, made all the more poignant by his flaccid, impotent right sleeve. I normally would've turned away as well and quietly made a hangdog exit, but I forced words to come forward. "I'm sorry, Dick. Would you like to talk about it?"

Dick then did something unexpected. He slowly bent over on his bunk and started to cry. Sorrow streamed out onto his pillow as he convulsed with emotion. My vanity told me he felt he could let go with me. I rubbed his back with my hand to soothe and comfort him. My father came to mind. "It's okay Dicky. It's okay," I repeated, saying what I should've said to Otousan.

When he calmed down, he called the doctor who'd amputated his arm a "butcher," since Dick had no say in the matter. But his anger wasn't only because of his arm. There was a seething pain in him, as if acid burned his insides. Sadness swelled within me; the Government did this to him, to me, and to all of us. Something was amputated from all our bodies.

I knew my chum's story would not end well.

36.

Angler received a great deal of news despite being so far away from the events taking place in British Columbia. War news came intermittently over the camp PA system. Community news came not so much from censored letters or newspapers (the *NC* no longer existed for these men), but from new inmates and Buddhist ministers visiting the camp. It didn't matter that the information was unreliable, dated, or based on gossip. For Jimmy Isojima, any news was welcome, though I had nothing up to date.

Soon after our "reunion," Jimmy and I sat in his hut facing each other at a table, relaxing as old friends and wishing we had some beer. I presented him with the tsukemono from his mother. The twin bottles gleamed golden yellow on the table, not so much because they reflected light, but because of what they stood for: home. He took one and opened it, and the smell of a Japanese summer filled the room. He picked some of the fermented *daikon* out with his fingers and tasted it.

"Ma-a-a, *tokubetsu-na*. Does that ever taste good!" he elated. He immediately broke out the *hashi* and plates and the two of us shared a memory.

Jimmy ate like a hungry man to fill his soul, drained empty by missing family, home, and familiar surroundings. Too bad we didn't have any rice. That would've made things perfect.

After a long silence, he asked, "How's my folks?"

"They're good. They send their best." I sounded like everything was normal. "Your dad's walking better, and Gladys..."

"What about Gladys? Is she all right?"

"Oh yeah, oh yeah, she's fine," I said reassuringly. "I...I mean, we..."

"You got a yen for her, don't you?" he said.

"What? No...I mean, yeah," I confessed and lowered my head in embarrassment.

"What are your intentions?" he asked, mocking me. "I'm her oniisan, you know. I have a right to ask." He then laughed as he reached over to pat my shoulder. "Don't worry, I ain't gonna bite you. It'll be great having you as a brother-in-law."

I relaxed and we shared a few minutes of happiness.

Before I left for afternoon roll call and dinner, I did express my concerns about my girl. "The guard there, Private Sutherland, he's trying...well, he's trying to make time with Gladys. He's...making her feel really uncomfortable."

"A soldier? Can't be. He wouldn't do nothing, would he? He's a military man for crying out loud!"

"Take it easy. Gladys doesn't think so. They *are* in the middle of an internment camp."

"Yeah," he said, though worry lines etched his forehead.

"Listen, Jimmy, I got a get-out-of-jail card, so after a little while I'll go back and take care of Gladys and your parents."

"A get...what?"

"I'm here on a voluntary basis, and I got a letter that says I can leave anytime I want. Tommy arranged it for me. That's the power of the press," I said, grinning. "I can't believe the military would cross me up."

After a considerable pause, Jimmy revealed, "I saw Watanabe Etsuo standing in the shadows the day I was arrested."

That explained much. I had thought his wife was hiding something from me when I saw her in Lillooet.

"Didn't you hear me? I said Watanabe gave me up!"

"Yeah," I acknowledged. "I'm not so surprised. We suspected something was rotten about that guy."

I then told my pal about the conditions of the East Lillooet camp: a field of sagebrush and dirt, and not much else. The self-supporting families were condemned to lives of fruitless work; old, worn tents or jerry-built living quarters; and little food. Poverty and starvation were their constant tormentors, death their only release. The Security Commission had crossed up Watanabe and the other families.

All Jimmy could say was, *"Bachigaatatta."*

REVEREND MITSUBAYASHI APPEARED in camp shortly after Jimmy and I caught up with each other. The good minister had heard his son was in Angler and so wanted to see him. He asked permission of the Security Commission. It was granted for reasons of compassion, and so he travelled all the way from Raymond, Alberta. His spirit affected all of us; a sense of hope rose in the camp.

We left father and son alone in the hut, but we couldn't help but see and hear them through the open windows and thin walls. Both of them were overcome at the sight of each other. "Papa...Papa," Dicky cried as he raised his empty shirt sleeve, "look what they've done to me. I'm sorry Papa...I'm sorry." The reverend wrapped his arms around his son.

Dick had been in steady decline since his arrival. He was sickly and rarely left his bunk. His mouth sagged open, as if he lacked the strength to keep it shut. At night he constantly groaned in his sleep, the noise steadily rising in volume until he screamed out in pain — a nightmare slicing into him.

Bullet, the idiot, wanted to beat him unconscious, but many of us stood in his way. I ached for a good night's sleep too, but understood what my old classmate was going through, although I didn't know what he was sorry about. No one did.

After the moment of bedside sorrow passed, Reverend Mitsubayashi quietly told his son that he was there to bring him back to his family in southern Alberta. "The war is over for us. Okaasan wants you home," he said in Japanese. "Your sister misses you too."

"No!" Dick screamed and pushed away. "You've been bought off too! Don't lie to me...I'm your son. I'm staying to fight."

We were so startled by the outburst that many of us moved away from the window a good distance, but I stayed.

Dick became so agitated that his father had to call in guards to force his son from his bed and into the waiting truck.

That was the last time I saw Dicky. Because of his weakened state, he died in Raymond about a month later.

37.

By September I had been with the Yamato Boys, the remnants of the NMEG, and the Ganbariya for months. The Battle of Petawawa, Dicky's suffering health, and Hammerhead's death played havoc in my mind. And where was Kaga? Was he in a deep, black prison cell or was he dead?

My crying jags continued. I'd be fine until a wave of emotion came over me, like Hokusai's blue tsunami, the artist's most famous woodblock print with a great wave about to engulf men in boats depicted, and I would lose control, unable to stop for several minutes. I was nervous all the time. I heard shooting when there was none. I heard screams in the night. I tried to imagine the void of death. I often became so frightened I rolled out of my bed and fell to the floor. I sometimes ran the length of the floor, but would stop at the door when I saw bullets ripping through the wood and tearing me to pieces. Only then would my panic subside.

Jimmy's friendship helped a great deal. He at least kept me somewhat grounded. But most of all I missed Gladys. I imagined her soft voice telling me everything was all right. I breathed in her perfume; I caressed her smooth arms; I kissed her soft lips. I hadn't heard from her since I last saw her. It was time to go.

I made an appointment with Lieutenant-Colonel Parker. Then I saw Jimmy.

"I'm gonna go, Jimmy," I said. "Back to BC."

"You using that get-out-of-jail card?"

"Letter, but yeah. Is there anything you want to give or say to your mom and dad?"

"I got nothing to give, but tell 'em I'm okay. Tell 'em I miss them, and only wish to be together in Steveston again."

"Sure, sure."

"You not talking to Glady?" he said with a slight smile on his lips.

"Yeah...yeah," I said embarrassingly.

He laughed and slapped me on the shoulder. "I'm sure she'll be happy to see you! Give her a kiss for me."

"Ah, cut it out," I said.

"On the cheek, you idiot!"

LIEUTENANT-COLONEL PARKER examined the letter carefully; he held it up to the light looking for anything fake about it, no doubt. Satisfied of its authenticity, he put it down on his desk and lifted his gaze. "So you're leaving."

"Yes, sir."

"Says here, you wanna go back to Vancouver."

"Yes, sir."

"Don't you know there's no one left there...all of your kind, that is. The Evacuation is complete. There's nothing to go back to."

I hadn't known of course, but deep down I suppose I knew the exile should've been completed by now. I did have a hollow sensation growing in my stomach, but couldn't start crying in front of this ketsunoana. I held my ground as best as I could.

The colonel continued: "I can authorize you to go to Kaslo. That's where your paper is now. Your people are probably expecting you."

I thanked him, accepted the travel pass, and left to pack and say goodbye.

JIMMY WAS GOOD with me going as were Tanaka-san and many others. Bullet was standoffish and glared at me while tossing a rock up and down. The message was not lost. It was hard saying goodbye to Tosh.

"You're leaving?" he said with an astonished look.

"Yeah, it's time to go."

"But Kaga is still missing. We got to find him. And what about the cause? We gotta keep fighting."

"Sure, Tosh, but I can do more back with the newspaper. It'll soon be Nisei-controlled again." I didn't want to tell him the real reason I wanted to go had to do with Gladys.

"Well, if that's what you want," he said in a resigned way.

"I gotta go Tosh. Please forgive me," I said with finality. "Listen, I'll see you again. Trust me."

And with that I left the poor boy, mourning and shivering as if I had just died, and the rest of Angler.

THE TRAIN RIDE back to BC was so much quicker than the trip out to Ontario had been. Funny how that is. The stubby trees of Ontario led to the flat prairies, which disappeared into the foothills of Alberta, and the train became absorbed by the surrounding mountains. I was home again, and all I needed now was Gladys.

38.

Lieutenant-Colonel Parker had told the truth. By the fall of 1942, the dismantling of the community and exile of Japanese Canadians on the West Coast were complete. All land and business deeds had been turned over to the Custodian. All institutions were halted; some were re-established in the Interior and beyond, but most weren't. Every Japanese-Canadian man, woman, and child had to make a choice: to cooperate, to protest, or to negotiate. Most cooperated. Only the namaiki tried to reason with, or fought against, the powers that be. A few resorted to selling out their own to make the path easier, but once in camp they would ponder their ill-advised decision.

MOUNTAIN AIR: IT is one of the great pleasures of life. Kaslo was good for all of us. Tommy had a spring in his step, a gleam in his eyes, and a touch of hope in his voice. Irene, too, was much better. The Pool incident became a memory marooned in the backwaters of time. Frank was Frank, owing to his youth. I was aware of absent friends and family, but I quickly realized how much I missed *The New Canadian* or rather *The New Canadian* staff. They were family to me. I only saw one issue while in Ontario.

But I was rather busy for such a luxury. The last days in Vancouver, the Battle of Petawawa, and the strange endgame that was Angler were filled with betrayal, violence, and even murder. I was glad to be away from it all, and closer to my Gladys in Tashme.

The new office in Kaslo, complete with adjoining apartments, was above an assayer's office with a view of the "downtown" area, comprised of only one street. The building, a two-storey wooden structure, was typical of the area. Though weather-beaten, it looked solid enough.

We were the only Japanese allowed in town. Dr. Chikao Hori had been residing in town for the townsmen's convenience until he was taken away to Petawawa. The locals, at first, wanted us in a large field just outside of town where all the other internees lived. The camp of crude wooden shacks was populated by just under a thousand inhabitants and was surrounded by mountains covered in thick forests. Tommy had successfully argued that the internment camp didn't have the facilities necessary to put together editions of the paper. And since the paper was government-sponsored with rent money, salaries, and publication and distribution costs, the NC added to Kaslo's economy.

Irene and Frank greeted me like a long-lost relative. Maybe I was the Prodigal Son. Tommy may have thought so, but didn't say anything. I could tell Tommy was still mad at me. I wanted to apologize, but he resisted eye contact, and I hesitated to bring up our clash.

When we all went to a celebratory dinner at Wong Kee's in town, Tommy declined and told us to go without him. No one objected; we didn't want to hear an embarrassing explanation. We soon carried on as if nothing had happened.

So Irene, Frank, and I enjoyed a sumptuous Chinese meal of chow mein (light on the mein and heavy with bean sprouts), sweet and sour pork, and a vegetable dish at the paper's expense. We also ordered rice; it was Chinese but the first I had in seemingly forever.

"So how was it back east?" Irene asked.

"Oh, it was good. Learned a lot. Glad I went. Glad I left." I knew my staccato answers weren't satisfying, but I didn't feel like opening up.

"I heard there was a shooting," Frank ventured.

"Yeah. I read the Government's article about it in the NC," I said.

"Oh, that was weak and just bureaucratic speak," Irene insisted. "What really happened?"

"Well..." Fortunately I was saved by the waiter bringing heavy plates of glistening food.

At the end of the evening, Irene presented me with my notebooks, all tied up with a red ribbon. I thanked her profusely, and held them like they were bricks of gold.

Quietly Frank then asked, "You heard about your friend... what was his name?"

"Which friend?" I asked, dreading the answer.

"Nishizaki," Irene informed.

"Hammerhead? What about him?" I said, feigning ignorance.

"They said he died of 'natural causes.' Can you believe that?" Frank said.

I remained mum on the subject, the pain being too much to bear.

I APPROACHED TOMMY about a week later. He sat at his desk as usual. It was as if he never left the New World Hotel on Powell Street. The first edition of the paper was due to come out in November, and he had to get his ducks in order, pronto.

"Tommy? I wonder if I could talk to you."

He looked up as he had always done, and I felt like a student visiting the principal.

"Tommy?" I repeated nervously. "I'd like to ask for your help getting a travel pass to Tashme. Can you do that for me?"

"I suppose so. Why, what's in Tashme?" I hesitated, and he turned away as if anticipating some kind of embarrassment.

"The Isojima family, I'd like to tell them about their brother in Angler. I mean son."

"Brother? Is there someone else you want to see?"

"Yeah, his sister," I finally revealed. "She's really swell and..."

He held up his hand to stop me. "I'll do what I can, but can you do me a favour on your way."

"Sure."

"Drop in on Lillooet. I hear there are some strange doings up there."

"Like what?"

"Can't say exactly what. That's what I want you to find out."

CONSTABLE MACGREGOR, THE only army officer assigned to Kaslo, was a fairly big man with large, red cheeks, and brighter hair. He really had nothing against us, and so was quite accommodating about issuing me a travel pass to Lillooet only. Tommy said he would send me a second pass to Tashme once he completed the paperwork.

I was suspicious, but let it go. Was this some kind of revenge? Tommy was a man of quiet dignity; he would never entertain such thoughts. I took him at his word. In the back of my mind, I wondered if the trickster in him was coming out.

39.

I thought what Tommy thought was "strange doings" in East
Lillooet was the disappearance of an old man named Takahashi
Minoru. "Crazy old man," offered MacGregor before I left
Kaslo. "Lit off like he was being chased by the devil himself. No
one could've stopped him." But I couldn't be sure.

Before I left, I placed my notebooks, save a couple, in a large
box and buried it in the backyard of the assayer's building. No
telling when I would be back.

THINGS HAD IMPROVED in East Lillooet. The summer temperatures had peaked and subsided, and the crops the inhabitants
planted had grown well despite the cool nights. They had become
farmers with lighter hearts about the future. The harvest was
abundant. Everyone was preparing for the winter as they shared
what they had; hunger was at last kept at bay. Tomatoes from the
Nakatsus, plenty of *nasubi* from the Tanabes, and Old Man
Nakashima managed to find a field of *matsutake* somewhere. He
never revealed the location of his secret patch, but kept everyone
supplied with the nearly sacred mushroom. People ate well, and
even better when the Red Cross provided food supplies like flour,
canned meat, and a meagre amount of sugar. There was still no
rice but the "evacuees" made due with potatoes. It seems the publicity of starving internees did not sit well with the Security
Commission particularly in light of Takahashi-san's disappearance
and presumed death.

The settlement was taking shape. By autumn, more and more

wooden buildings went up to replace the tents. The school was finished and a church had taken root. Hide Shimizu, the only accredited Japanese-Canadian educator in BC, came to train senior highschoolers in the camp to be teachers, and Reverend Tsuji made sure East Lillooet was a regular stop on his rounds. Sato-san of the Steveston Fishermen's Association lent the church a Buddhist scroll written by the Abbot Rennyo himself. It was the only remnant of the old days. A parishioner observed, "I thought all Japanese stuff was burned up. Shows what I know."

As I walked between the long row of cabins and tents, I soon spied a familiar man. It was Kego, the stranded fisherman the Isojimas billeted during the Steveston boat round-up. He was a sight for sore eyes; he looked as rumpled as ever — as unshaven and as slightly bent over as the last time I saw him. He lived in a newly built shack at the edge of the woods. He kind of recognized me. "Hey, you that boy back in...in..."

"Yeah, Steveston. I was with you at the Isojima house."

"Yeah...yeah," he said slowly, solidifying his memory. "Liked that family. Say, what happened to them?"

"You speak English?"

"Course I do, what did ya think?"

"I don't know, I just remember you talking nothing but Japanese."

"Yeah, fooled you too, huh?" He chuckled as he rubbed his whiskered chin.

"Evacuated, like everyone else. Tashme."

"Come again?"

"The Isojimas," I explained. "Like you asked."

"Oh, yeah." He paused to think. "What you doing here?"

"I could ask you the same question. How can you afford this place?"

"Ach, they don't care about the money no more. They let anybody come who wants to. So I came to see what was going on. It's better now, but maybe I'm a bit sorry I did," he said. "Now what's your excuse?"

"Why are you sorry?"

"Oh, things I seen," he said sadly.

"Some reporting for *The New Canadian*," I said avoiding his statement.

"What?"

"My excuse . . . for being here."

"Oh. Oh, reporting, eh?"

"Hey, I was here earlier this year. I didn't see you then."

"I been kicking around lots of camps. Just got here at the beginning of summer."

"Really?" I said with a smile. "Maybe you could fill me in about the goings-on around here. I heard things."

Kego confirmed that Hisaoka Bunjiro, his wife, and their ten-year-old son had arrived in East Lillooet. Apparently someone had spoiled Hisaoka's name in Christina Lake, his camp of choice. When I heard that, I assumed Kunio Shimizu had led the drive to discredit Hisaoka.

"Hisaoka looked like a mess," Kego said. Still, Kego claimed Hisaoka maintained his determined outlook and stoic attitude.

I imagined he'd been moved by the sea of ramshackle shacks and tents, their canvas billowing in the rising wind. I recalled how the encampment looked like a military siege had settled in for a long bleak campaign.

"Guess he didn't expect it. Nobody told him about East Lillooet," Kego said scratching his balding head. "A small crowd gathered round him when he showed up. That crowd grew fast. Everyone had something to say."

Everyone's money was gone by the summer; many wore rags; some looked no better than a "Chinatown bum," Kego said. Some of the elders died of worry. "I gotta say though," Kego began, "no one blamed Hisaoka, accused him, or mauled him where he stood. That made things worse, I suppose. At least when someone's mad at you, you could find the strength to defend yourself. But with everybody quiet, he got weak right before all of our eyes. He must've thought it was all his fault. The next day I sees him head-ing straight for the bridge, you know the one that leads to town. 'Hisaoka-san, don't cross the bridge!' I says. 'They'll kill 'ya for sure.' Then the damnest thing happened: the man turned to me and gave a wave, as if to say whether he lived or died made no difference.

"For some reason, I followed him to the BC Security office set up in a town church. Don't know why, but a couple of boys from the camp joined me and we surrounded him, willing to take a bullet. As brave or stupid as we was, each of us got the shakes waiting to be shot, but no one did. Nothing but nothing was gonna stop him that day. I mean I could feel dem rifles on us from the townsfolk's houses as we moved past the bridge headed for town," he repeated. "Some ketojin came out once we reached the main street. I was a-scared; I could see they hated us with their beady eyes following our every step, but I had forgotten what living in town was like. There was a movie house, a hotel, diners, and grocery stores. Made me realize how bad we had it. Hisaoka looked as calm as the sky above, but I could feel the cold sweat on my brow as we moved along. Strange that no one yelled at us, not even calling us Japs. We made it safe and sound to the building and waited for him outside. He was a brave man for sure.

"Hisaoka-san came out after a bit, and we went back to East Lillooet."

I imagined the wait must've been excruciating.

KEGO THEN SAID Hisaoka called a meeting. There he announced he was to blame for the conditions of the place. He was so ashamed of himself, he decided to go alone voluntarily to Angler. His family would stay behind. It would take awhile, but he was determined to atone for his sins.

"Then a strange thing happened," Kego said. "Watanabe Etsuo, you know him?"

I nodded.

"The man walks up to Hisaoka and claims he should be the one to go to Angler. Can you beat that? Well, no one knew what he was talking about, especially Hisaoka, so everyone ignored him, even though Watanabe kept saying it was his fault."

Hisaoka left a week later in the custody of two RCMP officers.

In his soiled pinstriped suit and rumpled hat, Hisaoka-san had gripped tightly a small valise, appearing small, defeated, resigned to his fate. Hisaoka Bunjiro, his wife and little son, Haruo, waited with sullen faces, all tears having been shed throughout the night. His boy hadn't slept a wink in case his father left without saying goodbye. As per Hisaoka's wish, only the camp leaders, including Watanabe, were there to see him off, though Kego was hiding nearby.

The two tall Mounties waited as Hisaoka breathed deeply and then bowed slightly to his family, who returned their own bows. He turned to Watanabe and bowed again.

With that, he solemnly walked to the car and soon departed East Lillooet.

As if on cue, a lone wolf had howled from the nearby woods. Kego swore it was Takahashi, the mad man who had run into the forest never to be seen again.

Kego then heard Watanabe muttering to himself. He kept repeating over and over, loud enough for all to hear, "*Warukatta . . . warukatta.*"

From that day forward, no one talked to the Watanabe family. It was as if Watanbe had admitted to betraying Hisaoka, even without proof. He became a pariah.

"You shoulda seen them," Kego said. "It was a sad day."

The Watanabe family took on a sadness like some kind of heavy coat.

40.

"I was wrong. I was wrong."

After hearing Kego's story, I had to see Watanabe or, failing that, Watanabe-no okusan. I knew of Watanabe's treachery, he was the reason Jimmy got caught, but I wondered about Hisaoka's role in all this. Watanabe paid the price to get into a self-supporting camp with his family intact: shame, suspicion, and maybe hatred from all who knew him.

I left Kego and ventured forth to see Watanabe's wife. I found her as I did in the spring hanging laundry, but in a new cabin. The blue sky behind her provided an idyllic background.

Though she seemed nervous, she was happy to see me. She made tea and set the outside table. I noticed the teapot now had a hairline crack. I palmed a cup in my hand and informed her I had heard of strange occurrences in camp. I wondered if she knew of any.

She sighed and proceeded to tell me what had come to pass since I last saw her, beginning with Hisaoka's departure. "After the stagecoach faded from view, everyone went home. Etsuo walked slowly. It was a bright day, but his gloomy mood couldn't be broken."

"Speaking of your husband, may I see him?" I asked.

Okusan's face collapsed before me. She broke into a sustained cry.

I turned away, not knowing where to look or what to do. She abruptly stood up, rattling the table.

"Sorry... I am sorry," she blubbered, and ran clumsily into her cabin.

I was stunned. What had I done?

"He's dead," Kego said simply.

"He's dead? How?"

"Suicide."

"Why didn't you tell me before I made a fool of myself?"

"You didn't ask, young fellah."

Kego's cabin was sparsely furnished: a straw bed, an old table and chairs, not much else. A kerosene lamp. Certainly no food in the place.

"Okay, tell me about Watanabe."

AFTER HISAOKA DEPARTED, Watanabe became an empty vessel. His eyes froze in a vacant stare. At times he shook involuntarily. It was as if guilt had eaten his body away like a cancer. Kego told me everyone knew he worked with Hisaoka to get into a self-supporting camp, but it was more than a simple deal. Some whispered about Watanabe betraying Japanese nationals, but no one could offer proof. I knew Jimmy was the proof, but said nothing.

Things got a little dicey for the Watanabe family from then on. They moved into another shack a fair distance from the edge of the main drag. It was a small, long-abandoned miner's shelter, with only one room to house four beds, and a small cooking area. Oku-san and the girls scrounged for furniture in the nearby garbage dump.

"Wouldn't want that place myself," Kego claimed. "It's a bit of a hike to get fresh water, and for the kids to go to school. My guess is that Watanabe-san wanted to be away from everyone."

The word was Watanabe-no okusan wanted it that way too, since their arguments grew in volume and frequency. They had become an embarrassment to the community and themselves. Family life became one of strife.

Their battles over doing the right thing were constant. Watanabe claimed he "did his duty for Canada." She must have wondered how he could live with himself giving up so many of their friends.

"You heard her say that?" I asked incredulously.

"Well, something close to that. They weren't whispering to each other. Everybody heard and we guessed," he said winking.

In the weeks that followed, Watanabe's ravings and mutterings continued on a daily basis. His wife fell more and more into herself. The Watanabe daughters always went outside to stay clear of their arguing parents. Watanabe was tired all the time, moping in and outside of the cabin for days. Then, in a burst of energy, he ran around the camp yelling out crazy things: "Warukatta! Burning corpses. Everywhere burning corpses! Warukatta!" He was more than a concern to his family; the camp residents saw madness in his eyes.

"The kids...well, they ain't kids no more," Kego continued. "You gotta feel sorry for them, but they got good heads on their shoulders."

"So tell me about the suicide," I asked Kego in a somber voice.

"Well, one night things came to a head. Yelling or screaming from the cabin. Dishes smashed and the kids ran outside."

"You saw all this?"

"Woke me up. I ran to the cabin to see if I could help." With one hinged leg, Kego pushed back from the table; he pulled out a rolled cigarette and lit it, the curls of smoke suspended in the air.

I loved the smell of cigarettes; it reminded me of Vancouver days. I had given them up after I left. No money to buy them anyway. Didn't realize how much I missed the habit until that moment. His coughing brought me out of my reverie and he resumed his story.

It was a beautiful, clear night with the stars and full moon pouring light upon the cold late-summer landscape. I could see light in my mind's eye streaming down the mountain slopes in a bright and consistent starfall. Kego claimed that Watanabe had hit his wife and she had fallen to the floor, sending a teapot flying. Watanabe's glasses had come flying off with the effort.

"That's what I seen on the floor when I went inside: furniture smashed or turned over, a pot and glasses. I was told Watanabe had grabbed a rope and ran out into the forest. He had no coat and screamed as he ran. I yelled to stop him, but he had too much of a head start. Crazy bugger running off like that."

Okusan had come to the doorway and called for him to return. Though the moonlight was strong, Kego and others did not dare to follow into the dark, cold woods. Cabin lanterns lit up windows as more and more neighbours came out of their homes to investigate.

"He must've been running blind with the darkness and no glasses and all." The next morning, Kego and some other men formed a search party and combed the nearby woods.

"Hard to find. I thought tracking him would've been easy, but the strange part was that Watanabe's trail petered out."

His tracks simply disappeared in the middle of the woods, causing the search party to look straight up, but there was nothing but swaying trees. Watanabe was gone without a trace.

"I was out there three days when I finally found him hanging from a tree."

Kego found him on the edge of a clearing about four miles from East Lillooet. Watanabe was dead, and only speculation remained.

"Damn'dest thing I ever did see," Kego said, scratching his head. "It was sure quiet up there in the mountains. If it wasn't for his body swinging up there, I could've had a nice sit-down. Funny thing too, there was a pack of critters circling under him. Wolves. I thought they wanted to pull him down for dinner, but as I got closer, I realized they didn't want food: they were guarding him! The lead wolf snarled at me as I come closer.

"Then I heard my name, 'Kego! Kego!' It was the rest of the fellahs. Good thing too, because I couldn't've handled them wild devils all by myself. As soon as they showed, the wolves disappeared.

"No one believed me, of course, even with all the tracks around, but maybe the fellahs knew something spooky was going on, because besides the disappearing footprints, when we cut the body down, there was no mark on him. No rope burns, no bruises, no cuts — nothing. Perfect, like he had gone to sleep. He was even smiling. And the strangest thing of all, after three days, you'd think he'd be stiff as a board out in the open like that. But no, nothing. Fresh as a daisy, he was," Kego explained. "After we found him, the lay minister in-camp, Nakamura Kenichi, said a few words and the nembutsu. We cremated him right then and there, under the tree. Seemed the right thing to do somehow."

For weeks afterward, some in East Lillooet swore they heard the faint but sure sound of howling.

41.

To add insult to injury, a few weeks later, Watanabe-no okusan received word that her cousin had died.

"What happened?" I asked Kego.

"She died in a fire. In Minto. She was in the cabin next to Morii. Morii got out in time, but she didn't. I heard she didn't even try."

Minto? "What started the fire?"

"Don't rightly know, though some say a *hinotama* hit the roof and started it."

I then remembered Okusan's cousin, Miyamoto Yoshiko, a woman of scandal thought to have killed her daughter and husband over some gigolo.

After arriving in Minto, apparently the Oyabun made arrangements to drag a cabin from a nearby mining site for his paramour. Miyamoto-san never left that cabin, preferring to stay inside, out of sight. Passersby, however, swore they heard her crying steadily.

"Funny thing, though, Okusan wasn't all that hysterical over her cousin's death like you might expect. I heard her say something like, 'So it's come to an end...' Not sure what she meant by that exactly, but she was sure down in the dumps with the news and of course her husband."

It was my turn to sit back and have a hand-rolled cigarette. One of Kego's. It was the first I had in months. I drew on it deeply and tasted the acrid flavour. A nice sensation swelled in my brain. I blew out a stream of smoke. It plumed and dissipated. I felt good as the tension slipped away.

"How's Watanabe-no okusan these days?"

"Don't rightly know, but I did see her sitting near the woods,"
Kego said. "For hours at a time. Didn't seem to bother her none."

"And her daughters?"

"I heard one of them talking to her once."

I bet Emiko was the one to approach her.

What you doing, Okaasan? the daughter had asked.

Nothing child. Listening mostly, just listening.

To what?

The quiet of the dark trees.

Do you hear anything?

A crying woman, Okusan replied.

I was later inspired to speculate in writing:

*Trees and shadows undulated in front of her like the sea. Akiko
strained to listen, and sure enough, she heard a woman's lament. She
stood and moved forward, wondering who it was. Inching ever closer
to the rim of the woods, she turned her head to her good ear. Unexpectedly, quietly, she whispered, "Yoshiko-sama?"*

the wind
            howls
    like a wolf; moaning

like grief itself.

42.

I stayed in East Lillooet for a few more weeks waiting for Tommy's promised travel pass to Tashme. I didn't bother Okusan or her daughters. I figured they wanted to be left alone. Kego generously offered me his floor, which was made comfortable with extra straw and blankets.

A letter, very official looking, finally arrived. It was not what I expected. It was a pass to Kaslo, not Tashme. An accompanying note from Tommy said I was needed back at the paper.

Needed? Is this another delaying tactic? He promised me . . . he promised. I was angry and frustrated. He must've known how important Gladys was to me.

I had no choice; I went back to Kaslo.

Black Dragon Operates Within B.C.
News-Herald
September 26, 1942

When Tommy spread open in front of me the green pages of the *News-Herald*, borrowed or stolen from Kaslo's RCMP office, I couldn't believe my eyes. They had done it! Back in May, thirty-six representatives of hakujin organizations and Japanese organizations not belonging to the *Nihon Jinkai*, Morii's businessmen's association, had sent a brief to Ottawa alleging that Morii Etsuji was the leader of Canada's Black Dragon Society, a criminal organization with a fierce loyalty to the Emperor and close ties to the *Sokokukai*, the Fatherland Society, a sister organization to the Dragons. The Oyabun, in this capacity, supposedly encouraged espionage activities in British Columbia on Japan's behalf.

Everyone in the office was overjoyed: Morii's downfall was complete. At the language school, I had at first been shocked seeing the Oyabun's face covered in blood but soon drew pleasure from it. I did not like my reaction, but I couldn't help myself.

But then there was Tommy. I was filled with resentment at Tommy's broken promise to me. I had conjured up many scenarios on my way back to Kaslo. I saw myself yelling at the top of my voice about the injustice, about Tommy's selfishness, about his deceit. I expected my editor to be contrite and full of shame. But I was wrong; I was needed after all.

Tommy, as usual, didn't let his emotions show, but I'm sure he was more than pleased. The way he read out the *News-Herald* article with such gusto made even Irene smile. It had been a long time between victories. Frank tossed loose paper in the air as he let out a celebratory whoopee! He actually danced a jig — according to his Scottish roots — he claimed with a wide grin.

Even though the Japanese Liaison Committee no longer existed, these were serious charges — serious enough for a BC daily newspaper to question why the RCMP hadn't looked into Morii's criminal and political activities, and why the BC Security Commission had picked such a pro-Japan man to help in the removal of the Japanese from the Coast.

A judicial inquiry was set to open in Vancouver in early October. Judge J.C.A. Cameron, a big cheese with a face heavy with age and wisdom, would preside. He was from back east with connections high up in the government. It seemed the allegations caught everyone's attention.

This was all sweet news to us. We at *The New Canadian* saw the larger implications of this inquiry. If Morii was found guilty and placed on trial for his crimes, maybe, just maybe, Japanese Canadians in general would be exonerated and the Government would be forced to send us back to Powell Street, Steveston, and the Coast.

In the last ten months since Pearl, I had grown harder, my callow youth gone the way of a Morii promise. I noticed in a mirror my face was darker, thinner, and sharper at the edges. Cynicism took hold of my soul. With the Morii news, I could afford a smidgen of hope.

Tommy Shoyama never said, "I told you so," but it was there in his smirk, in the spring in his step, as he worked to make the new office operational. The British sense of fair play was something he believed in.

He somehow managed to obtain special dispensation from the BC Security Commission for Irene, himself, and me to go back to Vancouver. Tommy performed his magic, again. Frank stayed in Kaslo to hold down the fort; he didn't complain since he couldn't see what fun there would be in sitting in a "stuffy ol' courtroom." Still the teenager, I supposed.

But before we left, Irene took me aside and talked to me seriously. "Danny-boy, I want to tell you something."

"Okay, shoot."

"Well, I'm not sure how to tell you this," she confessed.

"When has that stopped you before?" I said with a smile.

"Your mother's dead."

That stopped me in my tracks. I stood motionless, not even to seek a chair.

"Tommy told me to tell you you've got to make a choice: go with us, or go to Lemon Creek to take care of your father and your mother's affairs."

The Government's letter of exile had been her death sentence. It was only a matter of time before Okaa had worried herself into an early grave over the store. She felt it was gone forever, and now so was she.

I surprised myself by feeling nothing at the news; all the recent tragic deaths inured me to such a loss, I supposed. I wondered if Otousan held her in his arms until the end. Seemed out of character. Initially I couldn't imagine it, but then again seeing them on the train platform taught me to expect the unexpected.

So Irene glared at me with impatience and said, "So which will it be, Vancouver or Lemon Creek?"

After a long pause, I said, "Vancouver."

THE DARK, RICH wood of the courtroom made it seem like a grand palace. In addition to the wood flooring, wood panels ran up the walls to a thirty-foot-high tin ceiling with Victorian designs carved into the soft metal. Two overhead fans swirled, pushing the unusual heat to and fro, offering no comfort. None of us in the upper gallery were used to such finery, and we stared in wonderment. Especially Irene, whose mouth was wide open until Tommy closed it as he usually did. His reward was a punch to the arm and a shush from a court official nearby.

Judge J.C.A. Cameron, a portly gentleman with wispy hair atop his balding head, fleshy jowls, and wise eyes, slumped in his chair behind the bench observing the proceedings with a weary, but attentive, gaze. A thin, shiny film of sweat on his forehead was clearly visible, but he remained still in his uncomfortable black robe. The all male, Canadian audience shifted; many felt the prickly beginnings of a heat rash. No one had told the janitor to shut the furnace off that day.

Morii Etsuji, sitting with an interpreter and RCMP officers, examined his manicured fingernails. At first glance he looked bored, with only a trace of a grimace showing below his stubby "Hitleresque" moustache. Though clothed in his customary black suit, too small even for his short body, and bow tie tight about his neck, he was not sweating. From time to time he felt for the slight, but visible, scar on his cheek; other than that, he calmly waited for the inquiry to begin.

Tommy, cleaning his round wire glasses, said there was something about Morii that seemed different, a clue perhaps to his true state of mind. It was the Oyabun's own eyes, twitching every so often, and the mouth, the lips trembling slightly in unguarded moments. Could it be? Did he have regret in his heart? Or was Morii just plain scared?

First to rise was Senator John Wallace de Beque Farris, counsel for the *News-Herald*, in bow tie and three-piece suit. The paper was a real Jap hater, and so saw an opportunity to skewer the enemy. So they had sponsored the good senator to prosecute the criminal and the Government at the same time. For us, John Wallace de Beque Farris was welcome; maybe he could exonerate us by default.

Both Irene and I were surprised how tall the man was. Despite his more than six-foot height, he stood comfortably, his arms crossed over his thickening middle as he gazed over his gold-rimmed glasses toward the bench. Even more impressive was his name. It sounded like it came right out of a William Faulkner novel. His voice was anything but Southern when he addressed the court, but it was booming and clear, like a Dixie orator.

"Your Honour," he began moderately, "I am here before this august body, not with any anger in my heart, but with a desire for justice. To expose a rot within a community whose cooperation in these dark days we have come to admire. We must question the decisions of the BC Security Commission in bringing to power an obvious enemy of the people. We will bring to light the corruption within the Royal Canadian Mounted Police in its dealings with this man, Mr. E. Morry."

A lump in my throat grew as I came to realize he understood us. *We are Canadians willing to cooperate, but not willing to tolerate injustice. Morii must be found guilty.*

"Let me begin with some background. The Black Dragon Society is a fascist organization in Japan. It is loyal to the Mikado and operates as a criminal organization preying on the weakest elements of Japanese society. Their purpose is to make money on one level and, more importantly, to bring the people in line with the Imperial government. Its roots are in the *Ya-zoo-ka* crime syndicate. They in fact may be one in the same," Farris said. "The Black Dragons have been operating in Canada, in British Columbia, and in Vancouver in particular since the arrival of one man. And that man is in this courtroom today.

"Heed my words, your Honour, Mr. E. Morry is of such base moral character, he has exploited and brutalized his own people in any position he has held. I intend to prove him to be of such disloyal, dishonest, and vicious character that this inquiry will see no other alternative but to recommend incarceration in a federal prison for him and his nefarious cronies."

I could've listened to Farris all day. His Ottawa Valley inflection was music to my ears as his conviction rose and fell with emotion. Yes sir, the good senator was a man to reckon with. He was a reason I could be proud to be a Canadian. I wondered if Morii knew it.

The first witness was an important one: Inspector Benjamin Gill. Now here was a man of low "base moral character." Irene was particularly anxious to hear his testimony ever since the Hastings Park concert debacle. Tommy had to quiet her down several times since she kept calling him "bastard" under her breath. The people around us gave her more than a few disapproving looks.

"Inspector Gill," began the senator after the preliminaries had taken place, "you've known Mr. Morry for years now, isn't that right?"

Before speaking, the RCMP inspector pinched the crease in his gabardine slacks. "Yes, since 1921, when I enlisted his aid in uncovering an immigration fraud ring."

"Oh, and what was the result of that investigation?"

"We were very successful, arresting 213 illegal Japanese immigrants. We deported about 160 of them. Mr. Morry's information was key to the arrests."

"And why did Mr. Morry have such *key* information?"

"He's a community leader."

"A community leader?" The senator raised a finger to emphasize the point to his audience. "Is it not true, Inspector, that Mr. Morry is more than a community leader? In fact, he is a gang leader, and that it was he who was the real focus of your investigation?"

"Of course not," Gill answered, twisting away and clearing his throat uncomfortably.

The senator got him dead to rights. I felt the swell of anticipation in my chest, the tingle of victory at my fingertips. Vindication was about to be had.

"Isn't it true that he extorted as much as $4,000 per illegal immigrant for naturalization papers and fishing licenses? Did he not know exactly who was and who was not an illegal?"

"I can't comment on that."

He hadn't denied the accusation. My fists started squeezing. I knew Morii was a crook, but not to this degree.

Addressing the hushed crowd in the courtroom, the senator suddenly faced the Mountie. "Why didn't you arrest him, Inspector?"

Taken aback, Gill barely blurted out, "Arrest him for what?"

"For his collusion in an immigration scheme that included bribery, kidnapping, and conspiracy to violate Canadian immigration laws."

Gill shifted his gaze; the courtroom buzzed with anticipation.

"At the very least, you must've been anxious to ferret out the corruption amongst officials with Mr. Morry's testimony."

Gill squirmed. *You got him, you got him. Give it to him: the coup de grâce.*

The senator then took a different tact. "What do you know about boxes of chocolate?"

The inspector stiffened with the question. I too was confused, and more than a little curious.

Archibald Locke, the nervous and bug-eyed attorney for the BC Security Commission, leaped to his feet. "Objection, your Honour. The question is irrelevant to the issue at hand."

"Overruled," the judge said calmly. "I'm interested in where this is leading."

The senator nodded and then continued: "Boxes of chocolates, Inspector. I believe you know the significance of such boxes in connection with Mr. Morry...no? Maybe I should enlighten you. 'Boxes of chocolates' is a euphemism for a bribe. The money came in, well, chocolate boxes. But you knew that, didn't you Inspector?"

Bristling in the implications floating about the courtroom, Inspector Gill took the time to collect himself. "I'm sorry but I cannot comment on such matters. The dossier on Mr. Morry is sealed and cannot be opened in the interests of national security," he recited while staring at two fellow officers sitting in the front row.

National security? The depth of the corruption was starting to make me dizzy.

Discontent rumbled through the courtroom, causing Judge Cameron to strike his gavel to call for order. Senator Farris objected to the witness and demanded he be compelled to answer. After some thought, the judge called Archibald Locke and the senator into chambers. Oddly enough, Inspector Gill's two colleagues rose to their feet and followed. The judge glared at them, but then shrugged and allowed them into the office.

Ten minutes later, they all emerged to take their seats again before Judge Cameron announced his decision. "The dossier on Mr. Morry is indeed sealed and will not be produced or referred to in the interests of the public good," said the judge as he peered over his glasses.

I stood bolt upright and, nearly choking on the ruling, cleared my throat noisily as the courtroom grumbled in protest. "He got to them. Morii actually got to them," I groaned.

Tommy bowed his head as if mourning. Irene said nothing, her mouth locked tight. She wasn't going to cry about the loophole Morii had just jumped through; that would be admitting defeat. It was too early for that.

The Oyabun sat unmoved, didn't even smile, though his attorney tried to acknowledge the victory by nodding several times.

THE INQUIRY PROCEEDED downhill from there. Several witnesses in a row could neither offer, nor confirm, any evidence against Morii. The Nisei from the camps the senator called were simply too afraid to testify, with the exception of Sad Maikawa, who reiterated how the Oyabun had sent him to a camp with his family intact. To him, Morii was a saint.

The final two witnesses were the prosecution's key ones: Assistant Commissioner Mead of the BC Security Commission and Morii Etsuji himself.

Assistant Commissioner Mead, a graying man with blemished

skin and a no-nonsense disposition, took the stand first. He appeared nervous, fiddling with his thick glasses constantly.

"Assistant Commissioner Mead, are you familiar with this photograph?" Senator Farris produced a dull, black-and-white photo from his file.

"Yes."

"What does it depict?"

"Mr. Morry and a Japanese dignitary taken before the war."

"Who is that dignitary?"

"I'm not sure."

"You're not sure," Farris said almost as if mocking the overweight yet comfortable Assistant Commissioner. "Is it not a Mr. Su-mee-da, the National Director of the Fatherland Society during a visit from Japan?"

"Yes, come to think of it, I believe it is," said Mead, clearing his throat.

"And isn't it a well-known fact that the Fatherland Society is connected to the Black Dragon Society?" Without missing a beat, the senator continued. "Can't you concede or even assume then that Mr. Morry, *because* of the photograph and his alleged criminal activities here in Vancouver, must be a member of the Black Dragon Society, a criminal and right-wing political organization based in Japan?"

"That photograph proves nothing," Mead asserted, suddenly coming to life. "Mr. Morry is a leader of his community and therefore has every right to play host to all kinds of dignitaries. He played host to the Crown Prince in the 1920s. Is he a member of the Japanese Imperial family then?"

The courtroom broke into laughter, then quickly subsided with the sound of the gavel.

The senator soon found his second wind. "He may be a leader, sir, but not of his community, but of the Black Dragon Society in Canada."

"Senator, please," the judge said. "Enough of the grandstanding. Get to the point."

"Speaking of the 1920s, Mr. Mead, did you not know that this fine upstanding leader as you describe him was once tried for murder?"

"Yes, back in 1921."

"Ah, at the same time as Inspector Gill's investigation into —" he said, pointing to the trio of Mounties sitting in the audience.

Judge Cameron raised his hand as a warning.

The senator returned to his original thoughts. "So you knew that this man was a possible member of a criminal organization and had committed murder."

"He was not convicted as a murderer," the commissioner interjected.

"No, you're right there, only of manslaughter. With a year's probation as punishment, I might add. And why was that?"

"No witnesses."

"No witnesses? Now isn't that strange, since the police did have someone willing to testify at the time?"

Mead let out a sigh as he fell back into his chair. "I have no knowledge of that."

"Records show that the police, and then the RCMP, interrogated Morry and the key witness at the time and shortly thereafter the witness, a Mr. Hi-ran-o, disappeared. Coincidence?" On that note, the senator turned his back on the witness. "So here is a probable gang leader," he continued, raising his voice as he addressed the court audience, "a suspected murderer who may have hindered justice, and a man you knew to be openly supportive of Japanese imperialism in China."

"Your Honour?" Locke objected.

"Sustained. Get to the point, Senator."

"The point is with these connections and the manslaughter conviction, how could you in all good conscience appoint him to such a lofty and important position, chairman of the Japanese Liaison Committee?"

In a slow burn, Mead answered, "Yes, he was convicted...of manslaughter...and placed on probation, which he duly served. This is all meaningless."

"All right, let's forget that a seventeen-year-old boy died at his hands."

"Senator," the judge warned.

"Commissioner Mead, didn't you take into account Mr. Morry's anti-British, subversive speeches?"

"His speeches were not subversive in any way!" Mead stated emphatically. "Your witnesses were mistaken. If they had been anti-British, then there would have been cause for alarm, but for the most part they were... they were given merely in the spirit of charity."

"Charity, Commissioner Mead?"

"Yes, to raise funds to buy wool blankets and canned goods for the soldiers."

"Japanese soldiers."

"Yes, Japanese soldiers. They were our allies before Pearl Harbor," Mead said, obviously irritated with the senator's tenacity.

"What has become of the money since Pearl Harbor?" Farris asked without missing a beat. "Put into a fund for the families with fathers in the road camps?"

"I assume so, just as your own witnesses said."

"Are you sure?"

"I know for instance that when the fishermen were hauled off their boats after Pearl Harbor, housing was inadequate, and so Mr. Morry donated money to feed and clothe them in Steveston. Maybe that came from the fund."

The senator stretched his girth before speaking again. "Is there any document that records the amount and recipients of these donations?" He stared accusingly. "There isn't any, is there, Commissioner?"

Ignoring the interrogator, Mead was determined to have his say. "We secured cooperation from the Morry gang... er... group because we couldn't get such cooperation from the second-generation Japanese. Those hotheads! It's their fault! Their campaign of vilification has brought us to this needless inquiry. When true Christian Canadians like us go out of our way to do something good for these people, they never appreciate it."

Judge Cameron jumped on him immediately. "You will keep a civil tone about you, sir, or I will hold you in contempt," he warned with shaking jowls.

A chastised Mead continued, "Look, I personally have nothing against these Japanese in Canada. I mean they are a law-abiding people, and I didn't want any harm coming to them by some fanatics in our province. I was saddled with the task of moving the community out and off the Coast. Don't you see that I needed calm and cooperation from the Japanese during the uprooting? I felt that Morry could do the job without incident," Mead said sincerely. "He was the best man for the job."

"Then why did the commission dismiss him? I mean if he was 'the best man'?"

"Well, he was...he was..."

"Of no use to you anymore?" the senator completed.

"He had finished his job."

"I need some air," I said to Irene, and excused myself.

UPON MY RETURN, the Oyabun took the stand. Accompanied by his interpreter, the always lugubrious Kawasaki Kazuo, Morii-san moved slowly. He seemed frail, small, exposed as he was to the scrutiny of the law. Once in the chair, he looked up and glowered at us in the gallery as if to accuse us of betraying him. Irene was so affected she moved to the back wall. Tommy sat riveted in anticipation. The Oyabun was about to be brought down, and there was nothing the one-time saint could do to avoid it. There were no longer any payoffs to be made, no one to bully, and no one to turn to for protection.

"State your name," began the Senator.

"Oyabun, the court humbly asks for your name," Kawasaki asked in Japanese.

"Morii Etsuji," Morii answered in Japanese. "I am grateful for this chance to address a public forum." We knew the Oyabun could speak English; however he requested an interpreter to translate the subtleties of his testimony, which he wasn't capable of expressing in English. Tommy opined Morii asked for Kawasaki for the exact opposite reason: to deflect the hard and possibly embarrassing questions. Wouldn't be the first time.

"Mr. Morry, please tell the court what the Black Dragon Society is," Farris pressed.

"I have no idea."

"I'm afraid he knows nothing," Kawasaki replied with an ingratiating smile.

"That's a lie," Irene mumbled loud enough for those nearby to hear.

"Oh, come now, Mr. Morry, surely you are a good Japanese," the senator continued incredulously. "You've claimed such in your speeches."

The Oyabun sat immobile, unflinching.

"Surely you know of the Black Dragon Society — a fanatical group in Japan loyal to the Emperor with honour above anything else. They are the new *sam-yur-eye*, are they not? Do your duty to the Emperor and then die!" He stopped for a dramatic pause. "There is honour amongst thieves!"

A flutter of laughter, followed by the gavel, floated through the court.

"Only," the senator continued, "in this day and age, they extort money, kill for political gain, and are involved in gambling, illegal alcohol, and prostitution."

"Senator," the judge interrupted, "how do you know all this?"

"Dr. Frederick Anderson, your Honour. He is professor of Oriental History at the University of British Columbia."

Judge Cameron seemed impressed and nodded his approval.

"So, Mr. Morry, putting aside your connection to the Black Dragon Society for now, I have to ask: as one who has professed loyalty to the Mikado and who values honour above all else, are you asking this inquiry to believe that you have no knowledge of the society?"

Kawasaki slowly and perhaps nervously translated the questions and the answers.

Morii said nothing for a pregnant minute before stating in a calm, emotionless voice: "I am a Japanese community leader whose sole purpose during the early days of the Evacuation was to help those of my people in need."

"I'm glad you brought that up, Mr. Morry." The Senator pounced: "The precepts of the Black Dragons are to revere the Emperor, love and respect the nation, and to defend the people's rights. Help the poor and innocent Japanese as much as possible. Is this not right?"

"I am a Japanese community leader whose sole purpose during the early days of the Evacuation was to help those in need."

"We've heard a lot today about a fund used ostensibly to help those in need during the Evacuation. Does it exist?" the senator continued. "It would seem to fall within the Black Dragon credo."

"Yes, there is a fund," Kawasaki translated.

The senator reared back, relieved that the truth was about to be exposed. "How much is there in it?"

"Not much now but we raised about $5000 altogether."

"About $5,000 since before the war," Kawasaki interpreted, "but there isn't much left."

"Where did it go?"

Morii barely shifted in his chair. "All gone to help the mothers of families whose fathers were taken away."

"To the mothers and children of those in the road camps," Kawasaki translated.

"Names?" snapped the senator.

"Oh, I don't know, there were too many to remember."

"He doesn't remember."

"No records, Mr. Morry?"

"Why would I keep records? I'm a generous and concerned man giving freely out of a great sense of duty and charity."

"No, Senator, none were kept."

"How did you raise the money?"

"And how was the money raised? Through pamphlets, donations in church, perhaps?" Kawasaki asked Morii.

"I just asked," the Oyabun answered succinctly in Japanese.

"You just asked? Didn't you 'ask' by using your judo gang members to intimidate, bully, and beat your victims into giving money? Extortion, in other words, Mr. Morry?"

"No," he said tersely.

"Are you not still sending supplies to the Japanese military machine through this 'charitable' fund? Are you speaking at rallies to incite the community against the Canadian government? Are you supporting espionage activities here in Canada? "

"No."

Kawasaki explained quickly, "He didn't do any of those things."

"Did you pocket the money yourself?"

"Senator Farris," the judge interceded, "is this leading to anything substantive?"

"Your Honour, I understand Mr. Morry's reticence in answering my direct questions. The Black Dragons promote dissent in other countries by acting as provocateurs and then..." Farris stopped suddenly seeing the incredulity in the judge's face.

"Senator," interrupted the judge, "it is not illegal to give money to Mr. Morry for charitable purposes and the Security Commission did give him the latitude of basing Evacuation decisions on individual situations. Can you not pursue a line of questioning that indicates illegal activity? I mean that's why we're all here."

"Mr. Morry," Farris sighed and started again: "How did you convince the RCMP to place selected evacuees lower on their lists? Bribes, perhaps? Did you get the money from the evacuees?"

"Objection," interjected Locke, the Security Commission's lawyer. "The senator has yet to establish Mr. Morry's widespread practice of deferment for profit."

"Sustained."

"Mr. Morry, what is your connection with the RCMP?"

"I'm sorry, Senator, but that question cannot be asked as I have ruled previously," Judge Cameron stated.

"Are you involved in racketeering?"

"Senator," warned the judge.

"Well, then, what is your connection to the Black Dragon Society? Tell it to us straight. Are you or are you not a member? No? Then how about the Fatherland Society?"

"No."

"But you were known to have distributed copies of the magazine *Show-ko-ku* which means 'Fatherland.' In one particular issue, you are listed as president of the Vancouver branch of the *Show-ko-ku* Society," the senator stated.

"They flatter me. Must be a misprint," Morii retorted in Japanese.

"A misprint? You've been seen in the company of prominent members of the Fatherland Society. We have the photograph of you and Su-mee-da, the national director of the organization in Japan. And given your reputation with others of your own community, the so-called 'help' you give to the poor and innocent, and the connections I have just shown, is it not possible that you are a member, if not leader, of the Black Dragon and Fatherland Societies here in British Columbia?"

The judge interrupted at this crucial juncture. "What is your point in all this, Senator?"

"Military intelligence now suspects Japan, through the Black Dragon and Fatherland Societies, to have spies in British Columbia, perhaps preparing the ground for a fifth column. Your Honour, they actually changed the governments of Korea, China, and Japan through subterfuge. That's why I must...we must get to the bottom of Mr. Morry's activities right here in Vancouver!"

The revelations were astounding. Is this what really went on in BC? Are there agents in the internment camps? My eyes grew wider with every accusation.

"Are you a spy, Mr. Morry?" The senator glared at the man in the chair. "What is the nature of your relationship with the RCMP?"

"Senator!" said the judge as his gavel came down.

"Your Honour, can't you see the implications here?" Farris pleaded. "This man is clearly a key member of a criminal organization that's known to dabble...nay, is immersed in espionage.

They meddle in other countries. Corruption, violence and assassination follow. Don't you fear what these creatures will do in Canada? Do you want our great country to be annexed by Japan ...like Korea? Do you want our prime minister or other key members of parliament cut down where they stand? Think about the Governor General!"

"Get a hold of yourself, Senator."

"Your Honour, I implore you to open the file on Mr. Morry! Let me have access so we may know the truth once and for all."

"Stay on point! Don't engage in fanciful speculation. I cannot and will not undo my ruling," Cameron answered. "Now proceed."

Collecting himself, Farris continued after some time. "Mr. Morry, the question stands, are you a spy?"

Morii sighed, ignored the question, and proceeded to mount his own defence through the squirming Kawasaki.

"I do things for my people, the Japanese in Canada. They must be reminded they are Japanese first. So I provide things that do just that. You and all Canada-jin do not understand all that I do, I do for them. My work for the Security Commission was...how shall I put it? Philanthropic. My goal was to protect my fellow Japanese in Canada, to keep them together as a community, as a people. That was why I agreed to be part of this Japanese Liaison Committee. I thought I could negotiate the reconstitution of Japanese families. I had a guarantee...I can't help that the Security Commission didn't agree with ..." He stopped at that point, realizing perhaps he was about to reveal too much. He instructed Kawasaki not to interpret the last part. "If my people hate me for my good intentions, then so be it."

"I can't stand this!" I shouted in the uproar that followed the Oyabun's judiciously translated statement. Key sentences were left out. I stormed right past Irene and out of the gallery into the foyer.

I tasted bile at the back of my throat. It was obvious that Morii would get off. Though the accusations were stunning, the case was too weak against him without that RCMP dossier. There were no direct connections between him and the Black Dragons or the Sokokukai despite everyone knowing there were. Why the senator

brought in Maikawa, I would never know. The one Morii supporter, and he had to pick him. Perhaps he was the only one the
senator could find who would talk. And the evidence! It was all
based on rumour and hearsay, though the intelligence on the Black
Dragon Society was compelling and rang true. My stomach ached
with the prospect that Morii wouldn't answer for his crimes.

Both Tommy and Irene soon joined me outside the courtroom,
their faces as grim as my soul.

"Did you hear that interpreter? That inu misinterpreted the
questions! Left out all the key words in the answers," complained
Irene as we stood accompanied by a couple of Mounties outside
the courthouse.

"The Mounties not only get their man, they get their man off!"
I quipped. The guards stood unperturbed.

"Do you think he was a spy?" I asked. "Are there spies in the
camps?"

"We'll never know. Not without that RCMP dossier, and that'll
never see the light of day." Tommy breathed deeply before
continuing: "All his finagling paid off in the end. I just wish I knew
the other deal he had."

"What other deal?" Irene asked.

"I don't know. It was just something the Oyabun said in the
Japanese Hall."

"About what?"

"About someone else besides the Security Commission giving
him a guarantee."

A thought flashed in my mind. "Wait a minute, could it have
been Matsuoka?"

"Who?"

"Matsuoka Yosuke!" I exclaimed, the name coming into my
brain out of nowhere. "The diplomat's son was Morii's protector
when they first came over from Japan. He's a big man in the Japanese government now," I explained. "You know Morii's deal with
the consul general fell through. Who else could he turn to after
the Security Commission?"

284 · THE THREE PLEASURES

Matsuoka added another note of intrigue to the Oyabun's machinations. "Could be," Tommy agreed and fell silent. "At least," he continued after a time, "the Evacuation and internment were looked at in the mainstream press and in a court of law. But Morii, I'm afraid, will get away scot-free."

"I can't stand this! Come on Tommy…we gotta do something …we gotta…" I shouted in frustration. "I'm sick of Morii, Matsuoka, Gill, the inu and their twisted ways!"

THE INQUIRY PROVED to be a double-edged sword as Tommy later found out after reading Judge Cameron's ninety-eight-page report repudiating the charges against Morii, the RCMP, and the BC Security Commission. While putting together *The New Canadian* in Kaslo, Tommy gathered us together to convey the highlights and discuss the implications. "The judicial system," he concluded, "has in effect exonerated and supported the methods used by the government agencies in evacuating and interning the Japanese in British Columbia. I suppose we should've expected that, but the ruling makes Morii, no matter his intentions, the worst enemy we ever could have had."

I knew it was over; our banishment was complete. It didn't matter if there were spies in the camps. Everything was gone, including our self-respect, our faith in what was once our country, our futures. All the festivals, customs, traditions, religion, music, art, sports, food, businesses, institutions, and personalities of our community had been crushed into the ground. Morii's exoneration underlined the Government's efforts.

While in Vancouver, we didn't have the heart to go to Powell Street. I imagined the shadows of where we all walked, of where we loved. Where once there was so much life, now only dead souls roamed the streets. It was a ghost town and the haunting had begun.

The Mounties wouldn't have let us go, anyway. We were still Enemy Aliens.

43.

Tommy was right of course. Once it was clear all of Morii's good intentions had blown up in his face, the Oyabun did all he could for himself, and was paid well for his conniving. A true member of the Black Dragon Society might once have committed ritual suicide. In the end, however, the Oyabun was not doing his duty for the Emperor, but was in it for himself.

Tommy tried to rally the troops. There was a newspaper to resurrect. He kept reminding us it was our duty to keep the Japanese-Canadian community together through the paper, once we regained control from the Security Commission, maybe in November. Collectively we would soldier on, and be a vital link.

At least that was the party line. In truth, I didn't think we were that "vital." I mean I was just working up puff pieces about various pick-up baseball or hockey games within the camps. Maybe I was the sports editor I had initially thought I would be. Oh, there were letters from Nisei trying to get in touch with other Nisei. There were announcements and reports about concerts, parties, and social clubs, but nothing of real substance. We put them all on file to be published later.

I wanted to write the raw truth, especially about the Government doing everything for racist reasons and not "for our protection" or as "temporary measures," but couldn't. I could see the BC politicians sitting back, hands folded on their fat stomachs, grinning with satisfaction. I hated that none of my "real" pieces ever got printed. I felt so useless; the NC was not for me.

DURING OUR DAY-TO-DAY, Irene told me about Morii's departure from Vancouver while I was in Angler during the summer of '42.

Morii, his wife Misao, his two strongmen Moriyama and Suzuki, and a mysterious woman with her head covered and her face hidden rode away in a couple of sedans driven by Mountie constables, and accompanied by Gill himself, Irene's nemesis. They headed to Minto City, an abandoned mining town in the Interior. Rumour had it the place had indoor plumbing, electric lighting and heating, and furniture.

"It figures," Irene said. "Just who do you have to kill to get a sweet deal like that?"

At the Inquiry, she and the rest of us found out. This was Morii's payoff. His "guarantee" that he had mentioned in public was for himself, not his constituents. Because he had delivered the Japanese without much trouble for the Government, Morii, under the protection of the Security Commission, was to sit out the war in ideal conditions. Matsuoka Yosuke had nothing to do with anything. Still, I was sure the Oyabun would keep that ace up his sleeve.

Word had it that Minto, one of Hisaoka Bunjiro's self-supporting camps, was given to Morii as his own to do with as he wished. The authorities even allowed him to pick and choose the inhabitants. His thugs, Moriyama and Suzuki, were deposited in Tashme on the way to Minto.

Then there was the mystery woman. Irene guessed she was Miyamoto Yoshiko, the woman who had killed her daughter and stuffed the body into her furnace. Then she killed her husband, all for some gigolo. Back in 1940, Morii had saved her. Everyone knew, and yet no one knew, officially. When she revealed her face in an unguarded moment as she walked to the caravan of black sedans on that summer's day, Irene saw her heavy cosmetics, the lips full and wet, the nape of the neck pale and gleaming.

Miyamoto-san paid a heavy price to escape the gallows. For his bribery of the police, the Oyabun had taken her house, her business, and her soul.

As for Morii himself, he was stoic, but Irene had noticed a hint of defeat in his sagging face, in his indifference at exposing his scar, and in his slow, awkward gait. He completely ignored the small Japanese-Canadian crowd to see him off as if, as Irene had observed, a large part of him had died during that last meeting in the Japanese Hall a few short weeks before.

I told Irene that Miyamoto Yoshiko had died in a fire in Minto a week or two after arriving; my guess, it was a suicide. I didn't reveal that she was Watanabe-no okusan's cousin. Irene sighed and said, "She got her wish."

I REALIZED IN the end, the Oyabun had created a whirlpool of deceit, corruption, betrayal, oppression, and violence that made the entire Japanese-Canadian community suffer the shame of separation and exile, the humiliation of being labelled "Enemy Alien," and oblivion. I had to do something for my own peace of mind.

There was only one chance left for me: Gladys. Then, and only then, could I turn my gaze to the future with hope in my heart. Maybe it was "just down the road."

With this issue The New Canadian *resumes publication from new offices in Kaslo, BC, where new headquarters have now been established at the plant of the* Kaslo Kootenaian.

Returning to its former weekly basis, each issue will have eight expanded pages, each of which will contain some fifteen inches more reading material than formerly. Four pages of the paper will appear in the English language, the other four in the Japanese language.

Subscription rates will continue as formerly, 40 cents per month, or $2.00 for six months paid in advance.

— *The New Canadian, November 30, 1942*

44.

I t wasn't all pitchforks and tears in Kaslo. There were some good times. Christmas was only really celebrated by Japanese Christians, but with the New Year of 1943 approaching, Kaslo's Japanese population turned to preparing the *osechiry-ouri*. It would be the first observance of the holiday since January 1941. Sure it was freezing cold outside with snow piled high, but it was time to forget the Custodian, the exile, the camp conditions, the smashed dreams, the callous brutality, and all the troubles for a little while.

It helped that Morii Etsuji, of all people, sent a hundred pounds of rice as a gift. The Oyabun had apparently turned a new leaf, becoming religious and deciding to make amends after the threat of jail and the taste of hell fire. He had even built a small Shinto shrine in Minto. Curious, since he was a Buddhist. Maybe he felt a little guilty about Miyamoto-san.

At the paper and in Kaslo, there was some resentment, because it was common knowledge that Minto was the Oyabun's payoff for his "work" for the Japanese Liaison Committee, but no one refused the much-coveted rice. Everyone salivated at the sight of the small mountain-sized prize. Many hoped deep inside that it was a sign of good things to come.

In the Kaslo camp's newly built Buddhist church hall, the women gathered early New Year's morning to begin cooking and preparing the celebratory dishes. Soga-*no obasan* made *onigiri* with a homemade *umeboshi* embedded within each and wrapped with *shiso*. For those who ate the sour tsukemono, it meant good health. Nakashima-san's matsutake mushrooms were a hit as always — very tender, even if they had to be revived in water. People also brought along preserved fresh-water fish from their abundant summer and fall catches. Irene and some of the Fujinkai women joined in with cookies they had made with flour and sugar from the Red Cross.

I was just happy to be out of the office and away from all the bad news.

There was no church service, though Tsuji Sensei visited for a short time and said a few words. "It's hard to feel gratitude for our present state, but we are true Buddhists, and must find things to be grateful for. The Security Commission has provided lumber to build more facilities. You have some running water thanks to Tasaka-san's ingenuity. Your children are getting an education because of Shimizu Hide-san. I understand the harvest was plentiful and the government is providing, so none of you will starve. We are all blessed with a wonderful meal today and I personally want to thank all the families who contributed. Let us join together in gratitude to the Buddha for all that we have."

AFTER OSHOUGATSU, AN order-in-council allowed the Office of the Custodian of Enemy Alien Property to sell off all Japanese-Canadian property held in custody without the owners' consent. Letters from all over the interior of BC came into the Kaslo office telling of miniscule payments for their homes, farms, and fishing boats.

I thought of Jimmy immediately. I knew his family still owed on the $50,000 cost of their boat. What was the most he got? About $100 I wagered. Another injustice done because the Government could.

Internees also started being released from the camps, but they had to move east of the Rockies. To where? Who knew? A city like Toronto was closed to them. City Halls of many major cities barred the Japanese Canadians from moving there. A rumour quickly spread that those who wanted to move to the Coast were denied and judged disloyal. They would eventually lose their Canadian citizenship and move to Japan. As a result, many stayed put, though the Japanese Canadian Committee for Democracy and the Co-operative Committee on Japanese Canadians, mainly white Christian groups, assisted with resettlement.

Irene, Tommy, and I, sometimes even Frank, wrote editorials about the inequitable treatment, but we were shot down by the Security Commission every time. So much for regained control.

TOMMY WAS OBVIOUSLY still mad at me. He hardly said anything to me; Irene was often his mouthpiece. I understood. I had said some pretty cruel things. It didn't help that he was so generous with me.

So it was typical that when I walked into the Kaslo office one day in late January, he kept his head down, but held up a piece of paper. My travel pass to Tashme. Not for right away, but for March. Though I was anxious to get on with my life, I decided I could wait.

All I could say was, "Thank you."

As I left the office that day, I heard a meek voice say in return, "Goodbye. See you in another lifetime."

All I could do was bide my time by working for the paper until March.

THE TRAIN RIDE to Hope was made less tedious with dreams of Gladys, my sweet girl with the slightly protruding abdomen and lanky limbs of her tomboy body smoothing into the soft curves of womanhood. The promise of our future together had made me forget the Evacuation for a time.

It was March and winter had started to loosen its grip. There was still snow on the ground, but the warmer temperatures promised better days ahead. *Spring is the time for love,* I thought.

A strange fog rolled in as I walked along the dirt road from Hope to Tashme. It wasn't thick, but it seeped out of every corridor of the surrounding forest and clung to everything, even me. Hell was murky.

Once I reached the camp, I could see fairly well. The place seemed abandoned, but I knew that couldn't be. So I began my search anticipating the sight of Gladys emerging from the cool, moist gauze that had settled.

Around the corner of the Apartments, the imposing central building, I breathed a sigh of relief. In the distance a steady plume of black smoke rose into the air mixing with the grey mist. I detected the distinctive smell of incense. *The Buddha is near.* A crowd milled below the smoke, with some people clearly standing in *gasshou*. It was a funeral, a cremation. I heard the distinctive drone of chanting; the religious echoes and spiritual landscape chilled me.

As I approached, I saw and heard the crackling pyre. I saw Kojima and his minions; I saw a Mountie and a Security Commission representative in their grey overcoats and fedoras. I saw evacuees I had met before. The crowd respectfully listened to the chanting Reverend Tsuji as he performed the funeral rite. Then I saw Isojima-no okusan standing in front. Her head hung in sorrow as she muttered the nembutsu. Her posture spoke of a feebleness that had beset her body. I guessed almost instantly that her husband had died. But where was Gladys?

Someone greeted me quietly before informing me the funeral was indeed for Isojima-san. It was Moriyama, Morii's henchman, of all people. He gently pulled me away from the crowd to tell me of the horrid details of the man's death. He had been found dead, lying totally naked in a nearby field. He had first drunk as much alcohol as he could, as if to muster enough courage, before he took a blunt butter knife, and with an astonishing amount of strength stabbed the right side of his abdomen with great effort. After about a three-inch deep cut, he must have gone into shock and fallen to the ground, exuding an enormous amount of blood. Like so many others, he had lost everything, and so, I assumed, the burden of history crushed him to give up the only thing left him: his life.

Exquisite pain leads to the pleasure of oblivion.

I felt completely astonished, reviled, and sick to my stomach. "Where's Gladys?" I asked, quickly searching the assemblage.

"Gladys?" said Moriyama.

"Yeah, Isojima's daughter," I said.

"Oh, so you don't know."

45.

Moriyama remained mum about Gladys. His broad face was ashen and took on a pained look; I suspected the worst news. He escorted me to Reverend Kenryu Tsuji's cabin just before the end of the cremation.

After the henchman, Moriyama, deposited me at Reverend Tsuji's cabin, I sat in the semi-dark cabin impatiently waiting. Reverend Tsuji had been in Kaslo to celebrate Oshougatsu. He was pressed for time then since he had to make his regular rounds. After visiting New Denver, Sandon, and Slocan, he came to Tashme. He entered his cabin calmly as if expecting me and settled into a compassionate pose. I was deeply afraid of what he was going to say.

"Has something happened to Gladys, Sensei? Is she all right?"

"Danny, I know your parents, good Buddhists. I was sorry to hear about your mother. I don't believe she suffered. Take comfort in knowing she is in the Pure Land."

"Yes, yes, yes, thank you, but what about Gladys?"

"This is difficult to say . . . She, Gladys, is also in the Pure Land."

"What are you saying?"

"She has died."

His words hit me like pots falling off a shelf. My stomach filled with saltwater and I could taste death at the back of my mouth. I didn't believe a word of it, and ran out of his cabin through the funeral crowd calling out Gladys' name over and over until I came face to face with Isojima-no okusan. Her hands were clasped in front of her; her hair was a mess of hanging grey; her face collapsed and full of sorrow. And then I knew, Gladys was dead.

I looked numbly beyond Okusan and saw two grave markers:

one for Isojima-san, and one for Gladys — my sweet, young, innocent Gladys. The ground beneath me opened.

I was floating in the ocean's depths. The vastness of the water overwhelmed, yet I could see myself from a distance — a curled sea creature, like a seahorse or shrimp, within a void of black and grey. I traced the gradations of grey below me leading to a dark profundity. My lungs suddenly strained for air and I realized I was the figure drowning. I looked up and saw the surface shimmering beneath a crystalline blue sky. I swam for it, but couldn't move, floundering in place. I was caught between the struggle to survive and the easy surrender to death. I was curiously buoyed above the vastness of the ocean by a current, the Kuroshio, and swept along to the land of comforting oblivion; I succumbed, gulping for air and finding only a vacuum of water crushing my body. I viewed the boundless ocean depths and felt profoundly alone.

WHEN I REGAINED consciousness in the middle of night, I was in a bed. Hovering over me was Tsuji Sensei with a worried look. I felt a cold compress on my forehead. I was beset by feverish thoughts. In my sleep, I was told, I had from moment to moment broken into fits of madness with cold sweat rising on my skin and uncontrollable shaking. Frustration settled within as events swirled inside, not giving me any peace.

"Sensei," I asked in a groggy voice, "tell me what happened... to Gladys."

"Maybe later, Daniel."

With a surge of energy and anger, I sat up and grabbed the reverend by the front of his shirt. "Tell me, Sensei, I need to know!"

WHAT HAD STARTED as a mere flirtation the previous year had grown into a full-blown obsession for Private Will Sutherland. The soldier finally approached Kojima Sensei to help him get Gladys alone — to "keep everyone away from us so I could talk, just talk, to her," Sutherland allegedly said. It cost him $50 and a favour or two, but two of Kojima's thugs brought a terrified Gladys after school to a clearing in the woods near the camp. They left her standing there shaking in front of the soldier, more infuriated than frightened.

"We heard her screams from the camp grounds. We found her lying on the ground severely injured," Reverend Tsuji told me. "She was in the bed you are in now. In a semi-conscious state, she told me all."

Gladys had screamed at Sutherland and soon began hitting him. But then he grabbed her and attacked her viciously, striking blow after blow against her body. She struggled and squirmed against him. Given his strength and size, he soon subdued her and had his way with her. He left her for dead.

After being accused much later by the reverend, Sutherland simply said, "I'm a white man and you bloody Japs are all the same! When someone like me, a true Christian Canadian, goes out of his way to do something good for you people, you never appreciate it."

"I informed the Security Commission, and they sent two RCMP officers to investigate. They took Sutherland away for questioning," Reverend Tsuji said. "While I waited, Gladys died of her injuries."

He looked for my reaction, but I did nothing.

"You should know, she called out your name several times... until she couldn't anymore."

That brought me around. "Where is Sutherland, in jail?" I asked.

"No, I'm afraid not."

THE OFFICIAL REPORT stated that "Gladys Ijima [sic] died as a result of rape by unknown parties." Private Will Sutherland was questioned as the last person to see her alive. He was "thoroughly" interrogated and then dismissed. Transferred, but a free man.

AFTER A FEW DAYS, I mustered all the strength I could and finally left Reverend Tsuji's bed, seeking him out. "Sensei...I'm...I'm... I'm going to be staying here. Maybe help Isojima-no okusan if she'll let me. But I'm worried about Jimmy," I said. "He's back in Angler. Has he been notified? I know I should be with him, but I just don't have the strength to make that journey."

The young minister smiled with compassion — the same compassion he exhibited when he helped with the Hastings Park concert, which felt like a hundred years ago. His eyes beamed with understanding. "I'm sure someone has told him. Or will."

"That's just it, Sensei. He shouldn't hear it from some hakujin official. That would be too cold. I'm not sure how he would react —"

"I won't be able to get back there before the official notice comes down from the Security Commission."

"Yes, but at least coming from you, it'll be easier...no, not easier...you know what I mean." It just seemed better if the minister, with his good heart and comforting presence, delivered the bad news.

He agreed, and said he would report to me after.

46.

In a moment of clarity some weeks later, I thought about Ruby Kojima, Tommy's former girlfriend. I decided to seek her out; she and her father were still in Tashme. She was a voice from the old Vancouver days. Maybe I could find some solace in talking with her.

Kojima Sensei's hold was broken after Gladys' death. He was seen as complicit in bringing about the tragedy, though he himself was not arrested. The commission did station a troop of Mounties in Tashme. In quick order they smashed the alcohol stills, ended the gambling dens, and transferred the worst of the thugs out of the camp. Rikimatsu was sent to Angler. Consequently a peaceful gloom settled over the camp.

The Kojimas lived about as far away from the Apartments as you could get without leaving town. I met with Ruby during a rather warm May day on her porch, encircled by a white picket fence. The "shack" was done up with curtained windows and front and side gardens. If not for the fact that there was a war on and Tashme was an internment camp, I would have said they were spending a summer vacation at the cottage. Such were the perks the camp boss enjoyed. The place was called "Kojima Village" by the Japanese inhabitants, after all.

"Hello," I said tentatively. "I'm . . . I'm —"

"Yes?" she greeted. "Young man, are you all right?"

I must've been shaking. I felt the sweat on my brow. *What's wrong with me?*

"Here, sit here," she said, pointing to a porch chair.

Ruby served tea and senbei. The rare rice crackers were

another testament to her father's prominence. She was bright and beautiful. I could see, with her perfumed hair in cascading locks, her delicate manicured nails, and her well-appointed clothing, why Tommy fell for her. Truth was, I was surprised how stylish she was in the wilderness. Charming, well mannered, and eloquent, she sat with perfect posture as she conversed with me after I had calmed down. She knew who I was after a time, and guessed why I had approached her.

"That poor, poor girl," she lamented. "I didn't know her, but I and the whole camp felt the loss. We all knew who was to blame, but couldn't do anything about it. Then what happened to her father, quite a terrible way to go. I lit incense every day for weeks."

I didn't know how to bring up her own father's responsibility, but in the end I didn't need to be so coy. She was quite open about the subject. I breathed deeply as I knew it was the time for honesty.

"I approached my father," she confessed. "I had a sinking feeling about everything. One day, I found him sitting in the sun, wondering I suppose at the absurdity of the peaceful landscape of trees and mountains in the wake of what had happened. He looked worn out and perhaps guilt-ridden."

Kojima Sensei was warm to his daughter until she brought up Gladys. He denied even knowing her. He became incensed, stood up, and castigated Ruby for accusing "your own father." Of what, neither Kojima nor Ruby said.

"What happened after that?" I asked after a pause.

"He stormed away from the cabin to where I don't know. It was at that moment that I knew all the rumours, all the accusations, were true. All the gatherings of those strange men in our cabin and back in our Vancouver home, all the gossip Mother and I endured.

"But there is good in him. I saw how much he brooded over that girl. Her death really touched him deeply. He could not have foreseen her fate and not have looked out for her. I believe that perhaps it is the beginning of the end of his own life."

With that dire prediction, our conversation came to an abrupt end. She would not admit to any connections to Morii or any wrong-doing in Tashme. That would've been disloyal to family; that wouldn't have been Japanese. I took my leave, but as I stood she asked me one last question. "Have you seen Tommy? How is he?"

"I saw him a while ago in Kaslo. He's fine. Much more relaxed than he's ever been."

"Will you be seeing him soon? You know we were friends back in the glad days."

The "glad days": such an odd thing to say. I nodded and lied, "I don't know, but I suspect I'll see him sometime. Should I give him your regards?"

"Yes, please."

As I walked away, however, she called to me. "No, don't say anything to Tommy. Can you do that?"

I waved my assurances.

The sale [of property and fishing boats] conducted by the Custodian of Japanese property revealed that on June 19, a total of $2,006,015 had been realized. The balance of $1,809,307 came from the sale of real and personal property, and of this $811,225 was applied to sales of land for use under the Veterans Land Act.

— *The New Canadian, July 1, 1944*

47.

I ended up staying in Tashme for another year. Despite my soul being scrapped raw, Jimmy and the others in Angler lurked in the back of my mind. I hoped that with Kaga gone and the Ganbariya muted by Tanaka Tokikazu and others, the cause was dead. But Jimmy was another case. There was no way of telling how the tragic fate of his family had affected him. I waited for Reverend Tsuji to return with news.

The expression *kicking a man when he's down* held great significance for us during the summer of 1944. The Government stepped up its program to expunge our future in Canada. They began to assess which Japanese Canadians were "loyal," later to be dispersed throughout the country, and which were "disloyal," to be "repatriated" to Japan once hostilities ended.

Reverend Tsuji finally returned to Tashme in early July. Sitting in the glow of his presence, I patiently listened to his news, not wishing to jump the gun on Jimmy. He reported that, as I expected, with the moderating influence of Tanaka Tokikazu in Angler, the general tension in the camp had subsided. As time wore on through the fall and into the winter of 1943, more and more Nisei and younger Issei were being released through the work-release program, which was designed to lower the cost of internment and to solve employment shortages in BC and Alberta. The program may have begun with the interviews prior to Dominion Day, 1942, in Petawawa. The few who stayed loyal to the cause, however dead it was, remained under the influence of Takashi Kawai and Jimmy Isojima.

Something had snapped in Jimmy. He had not taken the news of his sister and father's deaths well, and had begun hitting the walls of his hut with his fists until they bled profusely. He was subdued by inmates and guards before being taken away. After leaving the camp infirmary on his own steam, he looked and acted normal enough — right as rain, according to Reverend Tsuji — but one day out of the blue he stopped addressing everyone by "Mr." and started saying even stranger things about his family to the Ganbariya members and even the guards.

The minister claimed, "Once he gets back with his parents and Gladys, everything'll be fine. He thinks they'll go back to Steveston. He'll marry a woman named Hedy and Gladys will find someone, maybe even Tommy Shoyama.

"He then mentioned you. He knows you're sweet on her."

His ravings verged on pure lunacy. "Jimmy believes they'll all live together in the old house. Take care of their father by getting the boat back."

Reverend Tsuji could see that Jimmy had lost his mind. No one doubted it, but still no one said anything, feeling this was Jimmy's way of dealing with loss. So the good minister did not report him.

When given the opportunity to leave by the commandant for compassionate reasons, Jimmy had said he didn't understand the offer and soon joined the Ganbariya. "Not till we've won," he supposedly said. *Won what?* I wondered.

In Angler, the Government finally decided to let men who were judged loyal to Canada to leave the prison camp in order to return to their families as part of the work-release program. Their promise to reunite everyone was finally coming true. With every departing group, however, a small group of Ganbariya, led by Jimmy and Takashi Kawai and including Roy Shintani, Tamio Tanemitsu, Bullet Gotanda, and Tosh Umeda, met the free men at the front gate, jeering and even spitting at them.

Reverend Tsuji kept his distance, watching them for any sign of violence. "Traitors! Collaborators!" the minister remembered the Ganbariya shouting. "You're going to help Canada's war effort, you bastards! We'll hunt you down and then you'll see. You'll see." Such sentiments ran like a cold, black current beneath the calm surface of the rapidly emptying camp.

A series of National Film Board motion pictures will make their interior town premiere in Tashme, July 3 and 6, with afternoon and evening performances in "A" Building.

The films, some of which are in natural color, depict scenes of eastern Canada, including where large numbers of relocees have settled...

The films will be shown later in Greenwood, July 18; Kaslo, July 12; Sandon, July 14; Lemon Creek, July 15.

— The New Canadian, July 1, 1944

48.

By the summer of 1944, the BC Security Commission increased pressure on Nisei to leave their respective camps. The rumoured threat to disenfranchise and repatriate the "disloyal" to Japan after the war was confirmed among the Japanese Canadians in the various camps. That time may have been close since the news in the *NC* told of the enemy Japan close to defeat.

But I couldn't be bothered, because I ached for Gladys. I could sense her presence at times and I'd reach for her thinking I'd be happy again, but then she would evaporate like summer rainwater. I dreamed of her every night: her face pale, her body sheathed in light. She had no legs, no feet, as far as I could see. She floated out of the wilderness toward me, her aura expanding and enveloping me, but I felt no warmth, no comfort. And then she slowly dissolved into the night. She didn't say anything, yet I always awoke thinking she had said something. Something I couldn't remember, maybe about her fate, maybe about the Pure Land. All I ever knew

304 • THE THREE PLEASURES

was that because of her silence, the woods surrounding me seemed to tighten its grip and I was suffocating in its chokehold.

After one particularly restless night of nightmares, I suddenly remembered Watanabe's death. His body had been immaculate, untouched by decay or the wolves circling beneath to protect him. I thought at the time it was a figment of Kego's imagination. But maybe it was true; perhaps Gladys lay in a pristine state somewhere deep in the wild, the wolves watching over her too. I hadn't been there when she died; I wasn't at the cremation. I only went on what people had told me. Perhaps she was safe, away from pain, away from this petty world full of suffering. Maybe that was what she was trying to tell me.

This war, this damn war, it had stolen time from us, our time together. I had to leave her, abandoning her to sick vanity. If only I had stayed. If only I could've protected her. If only...

I became lost. I remained in Tashme. Angler was impossible. Kaslo was out of the question. I had to be near her. Gladys was now everywhere: in the rustling trees, between the sad, ramshackle cabins, down the road to the far horizon. She was woven into the chaotic filigree of vines, branches, and underbrush that surrounded me. I sat *seiza* in front of her grave marker for hours every day.

Watanabe entered my mind again. The winds within the forest reminded me of his wife saying she'd heard a crying woman; did I hear crying as well? I often stood on the edge of the woods and whispered Gladys's name.

One night, a hinotama flew across the midnight sky.

deep seashadow wet Gladys,
    softliquid Gladys.
            I am so
lonely...
Gladys. a firescar
    across
            the

starry, starry bluewater
night

[the stone of a firedrake]

I watched Isojima-no okusan from afar. I had no stomach to talk to her, to try and connect with her, even though we might've helped each other. She often did housework for her missing family. I heard she changed and smoothed the sheets on the beds every day, though there was no longer a need to make all three. I saw her streaming tears when she strung the family's clothes on the line. She forced her eyes away whenever children, loud and playful, enjoyed themselves in a nearby field. She spoke to no one and no one approached her. Not even the Buddha could relieve her sadness; He had abandoned her. I and everyone else in camp left her alone with her grieving.

AT SOME POINT in September, I knew I had to leave. I approached Reverend Tsuji.
  "Sensei, how long are you staying here?"
  "Oh, Danny, I have to move on this week, in fact."
  "Where are you going?"
  "New Denver, Sandon, my usual rounds."
  "Are you going to Angler?"
  "As a matter of fact, I'll be there next spring."
  "Could I go with you?"
  "Oh, I don't know. Don't think the RCMP will issue two passes."
  "Can you help me?"
  He smiled and said, "I'll try."

AND SO IT WAS that by the spring of 1945, I received a travel pass to Angler. Sensei had come through for me. It came through just in time; the Government threat had materialized into something real. Three orders-in-council in January had empowered the Government to take the disloyal and strip them of their citizenship and deport them at the end of the war. Even the loyal were forced to make a choice: give up citizenship and move to Japan or move east of the Rockies never to return to the Coast. Many in the camps signed repatriation forms. I pitied the Nisei women who were forced by their fathers to go to Japan, a place they had never been. I heard Ruby was to go with her father, but I did not confirm the rumour. Couldn't blame the old man. What was left for him in Canada? But I feared for Ruby.

I boarded the train and made the trip back east once again. After a day, monotony and then boredom set in. The train was like a moving mausoleum. I could hardly breathe, the air was so thick with dust; with the shades mostly drawn, it was dark and frosty inside; and no one spoke. Thankfully the other passengers kept to themselves, not even interested in the passing panorama.

One man did lean over to ask where I was going. Must've thought I was Chinese. "Back east" was all I could say. The truth, but hardly the whole truth.

All I could do was close my eyes and whisper Gladys's name over and over.

49.

shivered at the sight of the POW camp. It was the same, barbed wire, cabins, and all. The guards hardly blinked when I presented them the Mountie pass and Tommy's original letter identifying me; they let me in with no questions. And again they didn't search me. The power of the press.

The first person I ran into at Angler was Tosh. He looked different somehow. He had been exercising and put on muscle. "Preparing for the end fight," he informed me. I let that go. He then caught me up on prison events.

HISAOKA BUNJIRO HAD caused quite a stir in Angler back in the late summer of 1943. It had taken nearly a year to arrange his transfer from the immigration building in Vancouver. He had been incarcerated there after Lillooet as a "precaution," given his new status as an "incorrigible." According to Tosh, when Hisaoka had entered the camp accompanied by several guards, he looked feeble, sporting a salt and pepper beard and squinting eyes. The lines cracked in his face spoke of many sleepless nights and a torment deep inside. He had lost a lot of weight; he was a pencil-line of his former self. Still, he marched onto the grounds with dignity, stumbling now and then, but his back was straight and his shoulders thrown back.

Though he avoided everyone in the days that followed, Hisaoka settled quickly into his new life, tending his patch of garden allowed him by his fellow prisoners of Hut 2A. Gossip swirled around him like the dark winds in the nearby woods. No one knew why he was there and everybody wanted to know. But he wasn't saying a thing.

I, of course, knew about Watanabe's suicide in Lillooet, but I wasn't going to get ahead of Tosh's story.

When Jimmy first saw Hisaoka, he became particularly nasty. Called him an inu and threatened to spit in his face. After all, he assumed Hisaoka had had it all cushy with his Security Commission deal. Tanaka-san took Jimmy aside until they could find out the full story.

Everyone found Hisaoka's presence in camp very odd. Eventually Jimmy's curiosity got the better of him and he, with Tosh following, walked straight up to Hisaoka while he was tending his garden. Hisaoka stopped hoeing and rested his foot on the blade. He remembered Jimmy from when he worked with Watanabe Etsuo.

I could hear Jimmy boldly asking, "What're you doing here?"

"Same as you," Hisaoka would've answered.

Then Jimmy brought up his deal with the Security Commission, accusing him of buying his way into a camp with his family.

"I'm here *because* of Lillooet," he sighed.

As the story unfolded, Jimmy changed his mind about the man. Though he resisted it, a grudging respect for Hisaoka grew within him, and later among the other imprisoned men after Jimmy repeated the story about the situation in Lillooet. Jimmy was particularly affected by Hisaoka leaving his family behind. "There's one more thing…" Jimmy had said in the end. He wanted to know what happened to Watanabe.

Hisaoka went back to his hoeing and said, "Last time I saw him was on the day I left. Watanabe was happily getting along in life with his wife and two kids."

THE OFFICIAL LETTER about Otousan and Gladys came to Angler through channels that took a great deal of time. When it arrived in the camp leader's hands in the late fall of '44, Tokikazu Tanaka hesitated to tell Jimmy, even though he knew it was his duty. Fortunately Reverend Tsuji arrived, and finally told Jimmy in his quiet way. After Jimmy's first outburst resulting in a self-inflicted injury, stay in the hospital, and period of delusion upon release, Jimmy faced the reality of his family's destruction. He told Reverend Tsuji it was a lie, just like every other lie he had heard from the BC Security Commission, the politicians, and the military command. He wouldn't even consider the possibility.

Jimmy held on to his belief. "It's a lie!" he had barked at Tosh and anyone who approached him.

Everyone, especially the minister, understood. Reverend Tsuji took his time before offering his condolences.

Tosh continued with his story. A few days later out of desperation, Reverend Tsuji, accompanied by Tanaka the camp leader, sought Uchiboro Shigeichi's help. Tanaka-san was just as troubled by Jimmy's state of mind as Reverend Tsuji, and could not think of anyone better than Uchiboro-san to console the young man. Jimmy respected him above all others.

The founding member of the NMEG occupied a single room in a remote part of Angler. Uchiboro was given such a privilege because he was one of the first to arrive, and he was an important captive for the Security Commission. The old man stumbled about the room as if any movement was a burden. He had heard of the tragedy.

Tanaka-san asked him to talk to Jimmy.

"This Idou has brought out the best and the worst in us," Hisaoka said philosophically. He shook his head slowly as he looked at a picture of his family.

Both the camp leader and the minister sought to bring the subject back to the matter at hand. Tanaka informed Hisaoka that Jimmy made no sense. He was telling everyone he'd never marry, never have children.

Uchiboro-san said, "He should think of the future...our children are the future." He then waved the two men away.

They left Hisaoka sitting on his bed, staring at the photograph of his family, and sobbing.

THERE DIDN'T SEEM to be anything anyone could do. So they left Jimmy alone. Then, a few days later, everything came crashing down and ripped Jimmy apart like a tsunami — Watanabe; his father; his sweet sister; his long lost girl, Hedy, all gone. Jimmy's impulse, similar to the first time, was to tear at his eyes, the official letter crumpled to the ground. Blood trickled down his cheeks. He took to wandering the encampment like King Lear on the moors. "Damn the Emperor...damn the Buddha...there is no God," Jimmy screamed as he walked. Reverend Tsuji, Tosh, and others took him to the infirmary before he could do further harm to himself.

After weeks of recovery in the camp infirmary, Jimmy got it into his head to travel west to Tashme. Once there, he swore he'd exact revenge on the soldier for what he did, claiming it was the way of bushidou. Reverend Tsuji hadn't the heart to tell him Private Sutherland had been transferred to an undisclosed post.

Tosh saw the frustration build in his friend as Jimmy realized that no one was going to release him. He snarled at any administrator who approached him to offer sympathy. He cursed every soldier in camp. He spat at and pushed away anyone who tried to help. Finally, in a frantic rage, he climbed the nearest barbed-wire fence. Guards drew their rifles and waited for the order to shoot, until Reverend Tsuji interceded and begged them not to.

50.

He appeared like a ghost dragging his feet out of the heat shimmer of a hot and humid day in Angler. His hair was long and matted. His face was pale with sweat dripping off his straggly beard. His small body struggled hard against the exertion, his movement hobbled by the handcuffs and chains around his legs. The haunted look of his eyes and his thin body came into sharp focus. Etsu Kaga had returned to us.

Kaga was escorted directly to the commandant's office where he spent a good half day. At first, everyone guessed he was going through "the talk." But he was in there too long for that. The men guessed he must be going through some administrative rigmarole. No one knew for sure, but all eyes were glued to the front door of the hut the entire time Kaga was in there.

When he finally came out, the warm wind made him shiver as if touched by death. Kaga stumbled as he walked, saved from an embarrassing fall by one of the guards. They placed him in Hut 5B where the Yamato Boys dwelled along with a few other Nisei and Issei.

Kaga sat on the edge of his bunk, his elbows on his knees, his hands balling up a piece of torn and soiled white cloth he had pulled from his pocket. It was a rag, the last of the flag Hammerhead had made during the immigration building riot. Kaga's eyes, dry and veined like desert riverbeds, stared out, empty of their former passion. His back curved as if still carrying an immense weight. His hair had turned mostly white. He was only twenty-eight, but he looked like eighty.

The crowd in the compound stared in disbelief but stood back as the guards escorted Kaga to our hut.

The first man to approach him inside the hut was Tanaka Tokikazu. "Kaga-san, it's good to see you again...to know you're alive." The camp leader searched for the proper words, but it was useless. "Do you want to see Reverend Tsuji? He's just come back from his rounds of the BC camps."

Tosh Umeda shouldered his way through the crowd and kneeled before his mentor. "Kaga-san! Kaga-san, where've you been? What did they do to you? Were you in Petawawa? I...no one saw you. I told everyone you escaped. Walked right through the barbed-wire —"

With a sudden burst of energy, Takashi Kawai came out of nowhere pushing his way through and said, "Cut out that kind of talk. He's all right. Can't you see, can't you all see, he's come back to us to carry on the fight. The cause is still alive!"

Reverend Tsuji had to say something. "Please, leave the man alone. Can't you see he's not in any condition —"

A flicker of recognition appeared in Kaga's eyes. "Cause...?" he eked out.

"Yes! See," Roy Shintani said to the uneasy minister.

"You remember?" Tosh added. Everyone thundered agreement.

"Stop it," Tanaka objected.

"Damare! He remembers the cause." Tosh's eyes were bright with joy as he continued excitedly, "It's so good to see you, Kaga-san. The cause can go on now that you've come back."

Kaga slowly, painfully, rose to his feet. He looked beyond the occupants of Hut 5B. "The cause...the cause...the cause is dead." The crumpled piece of white cloth rolled from his hand onto the floor below.

NO ONE KNEW what had happened to Kaga since the Battle of Petawawa. Some speculated that he was put into solitary confinement, probably somewhere other than Petawawa, and interrogated until now. There was no way to know for sure; Kaga, certainly, was-n't talking. In the shower, I saw old bruises and injuries on Kaga's body. When I asked about them, he just walked away in silence. Was he tortured? We would never know.

Kaga seemed to get better, keeping to himself, mostly, but walk-ing around the camp. One day after about a month, he spontaneously vomited in the middle of the compound. He curled over and didn't stop until he coughed up blood. He fell to the ground; his body con-tinued to convulse. Tosh panicked and called for help. The guards came and dragged Kaga-san away. "Escape Kaga-san! Escape Kaga-san!" Tosh called out to him. I tried to calm Tosh down by talking sense. I assured him Kaga was going to the infirmary, maybe an out-side hospital. Tosh began to cry as if in mourning. We didn't know Kaga's fate until the day we left Angler.

A survey indicates that more than half of the 23,867 Japanese in Canada want to be repatriated to their homeland when the war is over, the Vancouver Province reported July 18.

The survey has been completed among the 15,144 Japanese in British Columbia and 8,676 want to be repatriated. They have signed applications to be taken away, when the war is over.

— *The New Canadian, August 8, 1945*

51.

August 6, 1945, the day the sun went nova over Hiroshima. When the Yamato Boys and the remaining men of Angler first received word through the days-old issue of the *Province* distributed by the commandant about this new monstrous weapon, no one could believe it. One bomb killed thousands in a flash? We stared at one another in quiet shock, not comprehending the enormity of the situation, the creation of a new world reality.

Tosh was the first to ask, "Is this . . . ? It can't be."

"Don't be stupid," Takashi Kawai said. "It's a lie like everything else. You can't believe they got a bomb that has that much power."

"Maybe it was a coordinated aerial attack," Tosh offered.

Bullet agreed. "Yeah, dem guys is lying. It's business as usual."

"I don't know, it sounded pretty convincing," I said.

"They're all liars," was the consensus.

Over the camp's PA system less than a week later, the commandant announced the end of the war. The radio recording of the Emperor speaking to the Japanese population confirmed it. Again, no one in Hut 5B believed it.

Kawai stuck to his guns. "That was an actor."

"Do you really think so?" Tosh asked.

"Of course. The Emperor never speaks in public. Never will. You were executed even if you looked at him whenever he paraded through the street."

True, the voice sounded weak to me, very uncharacteristic of a god, certainly not what was expected. Even over the speaker system, I could imagine a man defeated by his responsibilities, his beliefs, his burden, as if hollowed out by the war dead and mass destruction of his cities. Reverend Tsuji worried that all the Yamato Boys could do was to hang on to the belief that everything conspired to defeat them. So the war-ending bomb became the "Lie of Hiroshima," and the "Emperor" was an actor.

ON APRIL 29, 1946, the Emperor's birthday, the last of the Japanese were officially set free from Angler. They were each given fifteen dollars in government stake money. In light rain, a cluster of men stood with Reverend Tsuji at the gaping gate, gazing at the barbed wire now powerless to keep them inside. The guards themselves milled around them offering a handshake, a smile, and a wish of good luck. The minister thanked the guards on behalf of the men, who accepted all with slight smiles, blaming the rain for dampening their gratitude.

Once outside, the free men threw their ragged uniforms, the red hinomaru faded to a washed-out rust, into a pile to be burned. They turned one last time to look back at the camp where Takashi Kawai and the rest of us bowed to the weak sun rising in the east. Our cry of Banzai! rose high and loud. As the last of the Ganbariya, we were determined to stay in Angler until the Government admitted to perpetrating the lie of Hiroshima and gave us compensation for the ill-treatment we and all the Japanese in Canada had suffered. And we did, until the Government transferred us to a military base in Moose Jaw, Saskatchewan.

Reverend Tsuji kept his opinions close to his chest. He assumed this would all be over in less than a month when everyone accepted the fact that Japan had lost the war. I knew better. I decided to stay with the Yamato Boys and the Ganbariya, even if Moose Jaw became the site of our last stand.

I thought about my buried notebooks in Kaslo. They were lost to me now, perhaps to be discovered decades later by some archaeologist who would resurrect our story. Curious relics of an unknown past.

Those already released called us bakatare for continuing the lost cause. Walking toward the trucks that would take us to the CPR station, we passed the potter's field gravestones, some carved with a fancy cross and angels, others a simple stone, which marked those who were fated to stay in Angler forever. The Nazis Herbert Loeffelmeier, Alfred Miethling, and Walter Uenk. The Japanese inmates who died of "natural causes": Kanesashi Kisao, Shirakawa Masanao, and Etsu Kaga.

In British Columbia, action has been started on behalf of two persons of Japanese ancestry to seek a judicial order that this government is powerless to repatriate any Japanese Canadians even if they have signed forms requesting repatriation.

It is indicated that the Japanese will press a claim that those who signed these forms did so under duress.

— The New Canadian, August 8, 1945

EPILOGUE
Fall 1946

To live is to love,
To love is to grieve.

Two hundred days. Two hundred days from February 24, 1942, when Government edicts put into motion our expulsion; that's all it took to dismantle the Japanese Canadian community. To do so they assaulted us, tore us apart, and tossed us to the winds. Every place I knew, everyone I knew, everyone I loved: gone. The West Coast lay barren of our presence, every trace expunged.

A simple stroke of the pen and we were removed to small, obscure, godforsaken ghost towns in the Interior. We became splintered, fragmented, and separated into smaller groups and individuals, connected, however loosely, through the pages of *The New Canadian* and the gossip among the internees who managed to get a travel pass. Our stories became broken sentences and no one could repair them. And if that weren't enough, the government made sure we couldn't return to our homes on The Coast. We were condemned to wander the country like the lost tribes of Israel. Some committed suicide by wandering into the wilderness, dying of exposure; most struggled in alien communities, their names, places, history, stories, music, and dances obliterated. No one told our children of our shame.

I foolishly thought a hero would rise up against our tormentors. But no; the Three Pleasures: Morii Etsuji, Watanabe Etsuo, and Etsu Kaga — Tommy, Kunio Shimizu, Irene, Jimmy, the NMEG, Hisoaka, Tanaka, and so many others all failed in their attempt as redeemers. In the end there was the total loss of everything.

I no longer had the taste of salt on the lips, the smell of brine tickling the nostrils, the faint sting of the Kuroshio flowing in, around, and through my body. The current had brought my parents to Canada, provided a living for some like Jimmy, and comforted all with its familiar warmth. Our ocean home was gone.

I no longer knew the friendship of Dicky Mitsubayashi, Hammerhead, and Frank. I no longer found comfort in family, whether with my father and debilitated mother, the Isojima and Mitsubayshi households, or *The New Canadian* gang. Time long gone. Desperate to find meaning, I joined the remnants of the Yamato Boys on that rumbling train to Moose Jaw, a dried-out place in the middle of the country. Maybe it was my last trip across this alien country. I found comfort in knowing Jimmy would be there, having recovered from his wounds. He was waiting for us. I recalled what Dick once said to me: "I got no choice." We had no choice.

I grieved my mother, Isojima-no Otousan, Dicky, Hammer, Kaga, even Watanabe and Otagaki. My mind floated back to that funeral in Powell Street before the Evacuation.

"Matsumiya was lucky to die now."
"Why?"
"He won't have to go through what's coming."

Maybe he was lucky not to have to wander the country and see what became of all of us.

But then there was Gladys. With her, we could've dwelled in each other's love and gained strength. There would have been so many years ahead of us to hear the rain as we slept in the comfort and safety of marriage; to laugh at the antics of yancha children; to enjoy the holiday dinners and the gardens of home; and for me to see the sea breezes play with her hair; to feel the small of her back; to touch the moon reflected in her eyes.

I could no longer taste Gladys' lips, the soft curve of her kiss gone forever with a single act of obscenity. At night, I wondered if she dreamed. And if so, of what? Did she walk along Moncton Street, wet and salt-whipped, to see boats pulling out to sea? Did she stroll along Powell Street, stopping to embrace me with love and care? Such strange thoughts remained a mystery in my life.

> *the maddening*
>   *presence of the eternal past:*
> *it*
>   *cannot be changed   it will not*
> *be changed yet*
>   *every-*
>   *thing is changed.*

The mysterious dreams of the dead: *Shikataganai.*

GLOSSARY OF TERMS:

aho, ahotare	foolish, stupid
Aikoku Koushinkyoku	"The Patriotic March" or "The Nationalism March"; a popular patriotic song of the early Showa era
baachan	grandmother(colloquial)
bachigaatatta	punishment, retribution
baka, bakatare, bakayaro	a fool, an idiot; or, as an expression: "You idiot!"
Banzai!	A celebratory cheer, "Hurrah!"
bento	lunch box
biiru	beer
bokenasu	Japanese-Canadian expression: stupid people (noun)
bousan	a monk; colloquialism for minister or lay minister
bocchan	term of affection for a young boy
bon dance	short for Obon dance. See Obon
bushidou	the way of the samurai
Bussei	Young Buddhist Association; short for Bukkyo seinenkai
butsudana	household Buddhist altar
-chan	form of address to children or a younger loved one
char shiu	Chinese barbecue pork
cheongsam	a body-hugging one-piece Chinese dress for women
Chikushou	a curse: "God damn it!"
chouchin	paper lantern
daikon	Japanese radish
Damare	(vulgarism) "Shut up!"
dashi	soup stock
denbatsuke	renowned pickled daikon (radish) from New Denver BC
desu	auxiliary: That is so.
dojo	exercise hall
donburi	bowl of rice with meat and vegetables on top
donburo	Japanese Canadian term for "down below"
Eigo wakarimasen	"I do not understand English."
Fujinkai	Buddhist Women's Club

Gaijin, gaikokujinnon	non-Japanese; a foreigner, an alien, usually referred to Caucasians; used by some Japanese to refer to Nisei, and even Issei
gaman	perseverance
ganbariya	those who persevere
Ganbatte	"Keep at it!"
gasshou	pressing hands together in reverent respect
gomen nasai	"Excuse me"
Gyohai! Saikeirei! Banzai!	patriotic chant: Devotion! Homage! 10,000 years!
hachimaki	stylized headband, usually with a hinomaru emblazoned on it
Hai	"Yes" or "Okay"
hakujin	white person
Hanamatsuri	the Buddha's birthday festival
hara kiri (or hara-kiri)	most often refers to a form of seppuku (or ritual suicide), often miswritten as "harikari"
hashi	chopsticks
Heimin Shimbun	*The Commoner Newspaper*
high-kara	expression: highfalutin, snooty
hinomaru	the symbol of the red sun; Japanese flag
hinotama	falling star; or fireballs containing the souls of the dead
hondo	main temple hall
Idou	Japanese Canadian term for the "Evacuation"; "The Move"
inaka	rural
inu	dog
Issei	first (immigrant) generation of Japanese Canadians
iyarashii	distasteful, unpleasant, disgusting
-jin	a suffix attached to a country name to denote nationality
-ka	participle; added to a word, it becomes a question
kanji	Chinese ideograms adopted by the Japanese
kawaisou	pitiful
-ken	prefecture
keto, keto-jin	(pejorative) a white person; (literally) hairy human
ketsunoana	(vulgarism) asshole
kiai	battle cry
Kika Nisei, Kika	Nisei who studied in Japan and then came back to Canada
Kikajinkai	nickname for the Naturalized Japanese Canadian Association "self-supporters" citizens group
Kimigayo	Japanese national anthem
kisha	steam train

kitsune	fox, a mythical creature in Japanese fairytales, a trickster, a changling
kokeshi	wooden doll
kome	rice
-kun	a form of address to boys
kuromame	black beans
Kuroshio	the Black Current or Japan Current of the Pacific Ocean
kuso, kusotare	(vulgarism) You shit! You son of a bitch!
kyabin	a cabin
manju	sweet rice cake
Maru	title of an ocean going ship (similar to H.M.S. or U.S.S.)
matsutake	a type of mushroom highly valued by Japanese
meiwaku-kakeru	an inconvenience causing trouble
Mikado	an archaic name for the Emperor of Japan
miso, misoshiru	fermented bean paste, bean paste soup
Minshu	labour union newspaper in BC, known as the *Daily People*
Mountain Police	colloquialism for Mounted Police, i.e. the RCMP
musubi	rice ball; (expression) "breaking *musubi*": "breaking bread"
-na	indicates emphasis
namaiki	troublemaker, impertinent
Namu Amida Butsu	a Buddhist expression: "I rely on the Buddha of Infinite Light and Life."
naniyo, nani, nanja	(expression) What?
nasubi	eggplant
ne	(expression) You see. You know. Isn't it?
Nembutsu	an expression of gratitude to the Buddha (recitation of Namu Amida Butsu)
Nikkei	Japanese living outside of Japan; Nikkei-jin
Nihongo	Japanese language
Nihongo hanase	"Speak Japanese"
Nihon Jinkai	Japanese business association
Nihonjin	Japanese person
nimotsu naru	become a burden
Nippon	Japan
Nisei	first generation of Japanese Canadians born in Canada, considered to be second generation Japanese Canadian
- no okusan	the wife of
nonki	careless, mischevious
obasan, oba	an older lady, an old hag
Obon	summer Buddhist festival: the Festival of the Dead

ocha	green tea
ochazuke	rice in tea
ogochisou	feast
Ohaiyo gozaimasu	"Greetings"
Oi!	"Hey!"
oishii desu	it's delicious
ojisan	elderly man
okaasan, okaa, kaachan	mother
okusan	wife
onara	vulgarism: fart
oneesan	elder sister
onigiri	rice ball
oniisan	elder brother
oningyo	doll
osechiryouri	New Year's delicacies
oshiri	buttocks, ass, bum
Oshougatsu	New Year's Day
otousan	father
oyabun	boss, according to Japanese hierarchical conventions, an oyabun is akin to a foster father; the Oyabun: "Boss"
raku raku	comfortable, easy
Rennyo	Eighth Abbot of the Shin Buddhist sect (1415 – 1499)
sake	rice wine
-san	honorific: Mr., Mrs., Miss.
Sansei	third generation Japanese Canadian
seinenkai	political club
seiza	sitting calmly to meditate
senbei	rice crackers (usually stored for company)
sensei	teacher, master
shikataganai	(expression) "It can't be helped" or "I have no choice"
shiishii	urinate
shiso	beefsteak plant
shogun	general
shouji	paper screens
shousei	invitation
shoyu	soy sauce
Showa	referring to the Showa era of Japanese history (1926 – 1989)

soba	buckwheat noodles
Sokokukai	The Fatherland Society
sumo	Japanese wrestling
Taihen shitsurei itashimashita	(formal expression) "Please excuse this discourtesy"
Tairiku Nippo	*The Continental Times of Japan*
takuwan	pickled daikon radish
tatami	straw floor mat
tempura	deep fried vegetables and seafood in batter
tengu	legendary evil creature
Tenno Heika, Tenno	the Emperor
tokubetsu	special, exceptional
tsukemono	pickled vegetables
tsunami	tidal wave
umeboshi	pickled plum
urusai	annoying, loud
warabi	bracken fronds; their fiddlehead greens can be eaten
warukatta	it was bad; it was my fault
yakuza	Japan's organized crime syndicate
Yamatodamashii	the spirit of ancient Japan
yancha	mischievious
Yobiyosejidai	Era of emigration; yobiyoseru: to call
yojimbo	bodyguard
Yoroshiku	"Pleased to meet you"
Yomi	realm of the dead; hell

NAMING CONVENTIONS

Issei names follow the Japanese convention of last name first.
Nisei names follow the western convention of first name first.

Japanese-Canadian newspaper excerpts are all taken from *The New Canadian* and are all unattributed. They are in the public domain. Attributed excerpts are fictitious.

AUTHOR'S NOTE

I wish to thank the following people for their support, advice and friendship in the writing of this book: Tane Akamatsu, Ian Cockfield, Brian Kaufman, the staff at Anvil, and Ken Noma. A special note of gratitude to Jim Wong-Chu who was with me at the beginning but could not be at the end. I will miss his strength, commitment, and the wonderful dinners we had together.

ABOUT THE AUTHOR

Terry Watada is the author of the novel, *The Blood of Foxes*, a collection of short fiction, *Daruma Days*, four books of poetry, two children's books, the nonfiction title *Bukkyo Tozen: A History of Jodo Shinshu Buddhism in Canada 1905 – 1995*, and two manga style comic books. Terry is also a musician and recording artist. Mr. Watada lives in Toronto.